Ellen Hart
Presents

MALICE DOMESTIC 15:
MYSTERY MOST
THEATRICAL

MALICE DOMESTIC ANTHOLOGY SERIES

Ellen Hart Presents

MALICE DOMESTIC 15: MYSTERY MOST THEATRICAL

An Anthology

Edited by
Verena Rose, Shawn Reilly Simmons
and Rita Owen

Published by Wildside Press LLC
www.wildsidepress.com

ACKNOWLEDGEMENTS

The editors would like to thank John Betancourt at Wildside Press for his constant and unwavering support to Malice Domestic and these editors.

The editors would also like to express their special thanks to the selection committee—P. J. Coldren, Carla Coupe, and Maureen Jennings. As a result of their hard work and dedication to excellence, we present for your reading enjoyment *Malice Domestic 15: Mystery Most Theatrical.*

TABLE OF CONTENTS

All stories are original to this Anthology

continued

PREFACE

ELLEN HART PRESENTS

Apple pie and ice cream. A hot summer day and a cold beer. A wintry evening and a cozy fire. I think we can all agree that some things are simply meant to go together. Continuing with that theme, what could be more delicious than a mix of mystery and the theater?

The backstage lore of an ancient craft; theatrically poisonous gossip; a small, glittering world filled with masters of disguise strutting on and off the stage; big egos throwing tantrums, flinging tiaras, and a singular ghost light shining from the darkness of an empty stage—these are some of the elements that compel us to settle into the magic and keep on reading.

It's always fascinated me that writers go through much the same process in developing a character as an actor does. To inhabit a persona, to understand an individual's inner life, plan their actions, and make them believable, a writer, like an actor, asks questions. What does this person look like? Sound like? How do they dress? Move? Most important of all are the questions that get at world-view and intent. What does this character want out of life? What does she want in the story, *why* does she want it, and why does she want it *now*? Both the writer and the actor have to dive deep to find those answers. Sandford Meisner, the great acting teacher, once said, "Acting is doing things truthfully under imaginary circumstances." I think that's a powerful statement, as well as an ambitious undertaking, for both an actor and a writer.

One of the main characters in my Jane Lawless mystery series is a theater director—a woman aptly named Cordelia Thorn. This vivid, outrageous, sometimes egotistical, always larger-than-life persona has fought to wrestle the limelight away from my main character since the first novel appeared on bookstore shelves. In my fourth mystery, I used Cordelia's personal history as a backdrop.

A Small Sacrifice begins with a flashback. We're introduced to two acting students, both in their final year of drama school at the University of Minnesota. Each man, filled with youthful, testosterone-fueled bravado, boasts that he has more acting talent than the other. Since they have no real way to prove such a thing on stage, they decide to take their superior abilities out into the real world. They each devise a crime they will commit, trusting their skills to carry them through without being caught. (I pilfered the general idea from an article I'd once read in *People* magazine.)

One of the young men in question ends up being arrested and sent to jail, while the other stumbles over the woman of his dreams while committing his crime, which is never discovered. The mystery then moves to the present, to a theater in a small town in rural Wisconsin, where these two men, along with their theater department pals, have gathered—not for a reunion, but for something much darker and more difficult. Cordelia Thorn is one of the pals. By the end of the novel, theatrics have taken a backseat to a more poignant, nuanced truth about life, sacrifice, and the depth of the love these friends still feel for each other.

We all have our favorite theater mysteries. Those written by Dame Ngaio Marsh come to my mind, as do several by Simon Brett, Reginald Hill, and Anne Perry. We love the humor and the fun. We're drawn to the settings and the personalities. And that's why I ask you to consider the volume of short stories you're holding in your hand. As you read, I guarantee you'll find these stories are all part of that same long and hallowed tradition. After all, the theater is where we sit in the dark and watch people in the light teach us about what it is to be human. Theater mysteries are where we go to be both enlightened *and* entertained.

And thereby, as Shakespeare once said, hangs the tale.

Ellen Hart

MYSTERY MOST THEATRICAL

THE ROCK STAR
By Frances Aylor

*Past and present collide in a fiery community theater
fundraiser when a dedicated insurance agent relives
the thrill of his rock band youth.*

He practiced hitting the high notes in the shower, where the
swirling steam caressed his vocal cords and the loud whoosh of
water gave him privacy to belt out his warbling falsetto, without his
teenage children complaining that he was "pitchy." They had
picked up that criticism from one of those television talent shows
where amateur singers waited, with wide eyes and nervously
clenched fists, for the judges to decide if they were on their way to
stardom.

Buck Wheeler wasn't looking for stardom. At least, not now.
Back in his early twenties, his band had crisscrossed through the
South, playing small towns and clubs, wherever they could corral
together enough fans for a road trip that was tantalizingly close to
breakeven. He'd pranced in tight pants in front of a microphone,
guitar firmly in hand, standing center stage with his drummer and
keyboard player as they grinned at their adoring audience.

Their band was good. Everyone said so. Buck still had the
newspaper clipping that proclaimed them "the best new rock band
of our age," a treasured bit of hyperbole that was carefully framed
to protect it from wrinkling, yellowed just a bit after being proudly
displayed for years on his bookshelf before he finally shoved it to
the back of a drawer. The band was good. Just not good enough.
Not good enough to justify the expense of months on the road. Not
good enough to support a wife and new baby.

After the baby was born, he and Margie returned to the county
of Foreman where he had grown up, to the job his dad had held for
him in the family business. Buck surprised himself by slipping
easily into the role of insurance salesman, content to protect
people's homes, cars, and businesses against the everyday
accidents and misfortunes that threatened to derail their
comfortable lives. He joined community organizations, donated
generously to various worthy causes, coached Little League
baseball, and was elected to the county Board of Supervisors on a
platform of protecting traditional values and the rural way of life.

Older residents of Foreman County still remembered him as the long-haired high school heartthrob whose penetrating high notes once caused tears to run down the cheeks of quivering teenage girls. When local thespians scheduled a summer musical, they pressed him to take the lead part.

At first, he turned them down. He was too old, he said. Too out of shape, with a softening belly and prominent love handles. And his voice tended to squeak out on the high notes. But they insisted. It was for a good cause—a fundraiser to support the 18th century building that began life as a colonial tavern and was now home to a popular dinner theater.

The tavern had been an important gathering spot in its early years, a welcome destination for men who traveled as far as their horses could take them in a day, in search of a warm meal and a spot to spend the night, even if they had to double or triple up on straw-stuffed mattresses. Local legend said that George Washington and the Marquis de Lafayette had plotted battle strategy there during the American Revolution.

Unfortunately, modern roads and fast cars had made the tavern obsolete. Abandoned by its owners, it perched unsteadily for years by the side of the highway and was scheduled for demolition when it was discovered about fifteen years ago by a group of New York actors. They found the warren of tiny rooms and uneven floors charming, and could see beyond the rotten beams, crumbling plaster and leaking roof, envisioning the tavern as the perfect home for a dinner theater. They bought the ramshackle place and began renovations.

The old tavern sucked up money as it was grudgingly transformed to meet modern codes. The more obvious improvements of new paint and plaster, of getting rid of mold and patching the roof, were not enough. The guts of the building needed an overhaul. The antiquated electrical system had to be updated. New air conditioning was needed to make muggy summer nights endurable. Each time the owners felt they finally had finished the updates, a new problem surfaced. Fundraisers became a way of life for the theater managers.

Buck's insurance agency provided coverage for the building, which made it difficult for him to ignore the continued pleas to participate in the fundraiser. Buck Wheeler was a big deal in the community, they said. A lifelong resident. A member of the Board of Supervisors. A former rock star. His name on the marquee would guarantee a sellout crowd.

Back at home, Buck pulled the old newspaper clipping about his band from the back of his sock drawer. A bittersweet rush of fond memories reminded him of the heady days of his youth, when anything seemed possible. And he said yes.

Now, on opening night, Buck peeked through the stage curtains at the sold-out crowd. The theater was in the basement level of the tavern, with the floor steeply pitched so the owners could cram in as many bodies as the fire marshal would allow. There were a lot of familiar faces in the audience. His wife Margie sat in the front row, along with his children Rollie and Kate, who looked bored as they scrolled through their cell phone feeds. Drew Hughes, who owned the local dry cleaner, and Chuckie Dreyfus, who had recently opened his second barbecue restaurant, sat midway back with their wives. Patty Lewiston, the reporter for the county paper, perched at the end of the second row, talking to those around her, no doubt gathering background for her upcoming review.

And then he spotted Alton Humphrey, trying to blend in with the crowd. Alton was an out-of-state developer who had been pressuring some of the locals to sell their land. He wanted to assemble enough acreage to build a mixed-use development of commercial buildings and high-density residential units.

Buck knew his constituents didn't want that. There was already too much development in the county, sprawling subdivisions of endless streets and fancy cul-de-sacs. His people wanted wide open spaces, with horses grazing in pastures by the side of the road and geese flocking to scattered lakes. Long-term residents weren't happy with the influx of commuters whose SUVs caused traffic jams on Foreman's twisted two-lane roads and whose children overwhelmed the local schools.

Alton wanted to bring even more congestion to the county. He and Buck had already had several contentious meetings. Alton said the development would bring more jobs and lower-cost housing. Buck told him it would bring too many people, too much traffic, and too much crime. Buck was sure that most of the supervisors would never support Alton's rezoning request.

The weak link in Buck's crusade was Emmet Ralston, who sat beside Alton as they waited for the musical to start. Emmet had lived in Foreman only five years but had already made a name for himself in county circles, being voted to the Board of Supervisors at the last election. He lived in an enormous brick two-story Colonial in a large-lot subdivision and drove one of those gas-guzzling SUVs that clogged Foreman's narrow roads during morning commutes.

Emmet wanted to bring more growth to the county. He didn't care about horse farms or flocking geese. He thought Alton's proposed development was a great idea, something that would bring in convenient shopping, more jobs, and a broader tax base. If some of the scenic parts of the county had to be sacrificed for wider roads and easier city commutes, well, that was the price of progress.

Sallie Minnows sat a few rows in front of the two men. Buck knew that Humphrey had been pressuring Sallie to sell her land. She was a lifelong resident of Foreman whose husband had been killed in a farming accident years ago. Sallie had raised two children all by herself, hiring seasonal workers to help her manage the hundred acres that had been in her husband's family for generations, selling corn and tomatoes to local groceries and produce stands.

Buck had met with the feisty, freckled grandmother to encourage her not to sell. He told her that the supervisors would never support the rezoning, that he personally was spearheading the effort to keep the county rural. "I know this is what your husband would want," he told her as they walked through towering rows of corn, "to keep this land intact for you to pass on to your children."

"Not sure the children are interested," she said, pulling her long white braid in front of her shoulder. "You know my daughter's in California, doing some commercials, hoping to make it as an actress. And my son is in Florida, running a charter fishing boat business down in the Keys. I hardly see 'em. They didn't even come here last Christmas."

"They're young yet," Buck told her. "Someday they'll want to come back to their homeplace. And we're going to help you save it for them."

She scratched her sunburned nose. "It's tough to make a living as a farmer. Remember that drought last year? About wiped out my tomato crop. Alton says if I sell, I'll have plenty of money and time for fun. I could travel. Take one of those around-the-world cruises." She sighed. "I'm getting too old to manage all this. I can still drive a tractor, but there's lot of things I'm not so good at anymore."

Buck shook his head. "Alton's one of those guys who always thinks they know more about what our county wants than the people who have lived here for years. You know our folks don't want change. Foreman is a magical place. We want to keep it that way."

"Maybe." She spotted a fat groundhog perched on his hind legs, stretching up to rip ears of corn from the sturdy stalks. Intent on his thievery, he didn't notice Sallie until she was right beside him. She landed a well-placed kick that sent the animal flying high over the rippling corn tassels. "Get out of here, you devil," she shouted. He landed with a soft thud in a distant furrow.

"Sallie, that was amazing. Never knew you could run that fast." Buck laughed. "A kicker couldn't have shot a football through the goalposts any slicker than that." He peered through the crowded rows. "Guess he's buzzard bait now."

"Naw, I caught him wrong. Kicked him in the butt. Probably only knocked him out for a bit. You gotta kick 'em in the head if you want to kill 'em. I learned that the hard way when I got attacked a couple of years back by a rabid dog."

"You killed a rabid dog? By kicking him?"

"Steel-toed boots," she said, digging her heel into the soft earth, pointing her toe toward the sky. "A woman on her own has to protect herself, any way she can."

She wore those same steel-toed boots for tonight's musical, Buck noted. In fact, she wore them everywhere—out in the fields, through tick-infested woods, to the grocery store, to church. Buck had never seen her with any other type of footwear.

Buck sidled away from the stage curtain as the band members moved out front and began to tune their instruments. He lined up with the other singers for the opening number, nervously straightening his costume and tugging at the clump of dark brown hair stuck to his bald head. He felt ridiculous wearing a wig, but the director insisted, and Margie said it made him look incredibly sexy, so he gave in. He just hoped the audience didn't laugh too loud when they saw it.

The curtain opened as the band started the first number, a rousing medley of rock songs. Buck pranced out onto the tiny stage. As expected, the audience started laughing as soon as they spotted him and his fellow actors in their elaborate makeup and free-flowing hair. But they soon got into the spirit of the performance, clapping their hands and stomping their feet in time to the music.

By the third song, Buck's nervousness had disappeared. He was at one with the music, transformed into the performer he had always wanted to be. Suddenly he wasn't a middle-aged insurance agent explaining the dry details of a high-deductible policy. He wasn't a chubby, bald dad who fought daily with his two prickly teenagers.

He was a rock star, part of the best band of his age, sharing his amazing talent with adoring fans. His skin tingled. Blood coursed wildly through his veins. He put more energy into his dance, snapping his fingers, shaking his shoulders, pointing from the floor to the ceiling. He grabbed the microphone, threw back his head and hit several measures of falsetto notes with ease.

Suddenly his mic went dead.

Nothing to worry about. Equipment malfunctions happened. The important thing was to keep going, keep the audience involved until the sound guys could get out there and fix the problem. He kept singing, projecting from his diaphragm so his words bounced against the back walls.

He noticed that the people in the first few rows were standing, pointing toward the backstage curtains where gray smoke curled out, drifting along the edge of the stage, wrapping around the ankles of the band members. For a moment he thought it was just special effects, dry ice brought in to add drama to their performance. But the band stopped playing and jumped to their feet just as someone shouted, "Fire!"

Then the lights went out.

People screamed as darkness wrapped around them, fumbling their way along the rows of seats toward the narrow aisles, growing more frantic as the smoke thickened. A few flipped on their cell phone lights, but folks still tripped on the steep steps that led up to the exits, falling as those behind them kept pushing forward. Couples tried to stay together, holding hands as they funneled toward the doors, yelling out for their loved ones as colliding bodies forced them apart.

Someone slammed against Buck. He dropped to his knees as desperate actors scrambled over him. Behind him, orange flames ripped through the heavy stage curtains. The intense heat melted his wig tape. The curly brown hair slid off his head. He was no longer a rock star.

But he was still an insurance guy. His job was about keeping people safe. Making sure they were protected against the hazards of life. Against dangerous storms that sent falling trees crashing against their roofs. Against speeding cars that hydroplaned on icy highways. Against fire.

His first thought was for his family. He was relieved to see them near the top of the stairs, close to the exit. Then, fighting his survival instincts, Buck headed toward the backstage dressing area, to make sure everyone else had gotten out. He called out, coughing as the smoke filled his lungs, "Anyone back here?"

"Help," a voice called. "I'm trapped."

Buck pushed through the flames. Darlene Hestor stood at the entrance to her dressing room, paralyzed with fear. Buck grabbed her by the hand and pulled her to the stage. She screamed as the fire scorched her ankles. "Is anyone else back there?" he asked.

"Judy. I think she's in the bathroom."

As Darlene headed for the exit, Buck made his way down the

hall and pushed open the bathroom door. "Judy, you in here?" he called as he moved from stall to stall. "Judy? Hello? Anybody here?"

The only answer was the crackle of flames. Buck turned back toward the stage, staggering through the thick smoke. He stumbled into some equipment. The drums, maybe? The keyboard stand? Confused, he whirled around, desperate for fresh air. If he kept the flames at his back, he should be able to reach the exit. But the side curtains were now burning, and flames surrounded him. Which way was out?

Dizzy, disoriented, Buck fell flat and army-crawled on his stomach across the stage, all elbows and knees, dodging the flames. A heavy object crashed down beside him. A ceiling beam? The lighting boom? He veered to the side as he pushed his hands out, desperately feeling his way. And then he hit empty space, and he knew he had reached the edge of the stage. He rolled down to the floor and headed for the gap between the smoldering seats. He could do this, work his way up the aisle, get to the exit. He was safe now. All he had to do was stay calm and stay low.

He screamed as something smacked his head. He threw his hands up in a futile attempt to protect himself. What was that? Did the chairs collapse? Part of the wall? The pain was so intense that he froze in place, unable to move. And then it hit him again.

***

Outside, sirens punctured the country stillness as firetrucks raced to the scene. Jagged streaks of flames danced along the roof. Firemen in helmets and yellow jackets jumped from their trucks, positioning ladders to reach the smoking upper floors even as the intense heat caused glass to pop out of the windows.

Alton Humphrey and Emmet Ralston stood near the theater exit, grabbing people's hands as they emerged from the dense smoke, leading them to safety. Theater patrons wandered through the parking lot, calling out for friends and loved ones lost in the desperate rush from disaster. Margie, who had been sitting on the front row, was one of the last to escape. She clutched her children close, watching the actors race out the door, some in the middle of costume changes, dressing robes wrapped around their underwear. Darlene Hestor ran out, wig askew, one false eyelash hanging low like an escaping centipede.

"Where's Buck?" Margie called out, grabbing her arm. "Did you see him?"

"He saved my life," Darlene said. "Pulled me out of the fire. And he went back in for Judy."

Firefighters donned masks and air tanks to enter the basement theater, threading fire hoses into the narrow aisles. Silver streams of water jabbed through the thick smoke. A fireman carried Sallie Minnows out, her head lolled back, blood spattered down her dress. Her white braid, now gray from smoke, dangled toward the ground. He handed her off to the rescue squad folks, who strapped an oxygen mask over her face, loaded her into their ambulance and took off, siren screaming, for the nearest hospital.

Margie rushed toward the theater entrance and tried to push her way in. "You can't go in there," the fireman said.

"My husband's still inside," Margie said.

"We'll look for him, ma'am. But it's solid flames in there now. You can't go in."

Multiple hoses and sheets of water were no match for the dried-out timbers of the centuries-old tavern. Television crews were on site now, filming dramatic shots of the burning roof as it collapsed. Police worked the crowd to figure out if anyone was still inside. By the time the fire was finally extinguished, even the untrained eye could see that the building was a total loss.

Miraculously, there was only one casualty. Buck Wheeler.

Darlene Hestor repeated her story multiple times to television cameras. Each time she told it, she added a few new details. By the time the story was picked up on morning news shows across the nation, Darlene explained that Buck had broken through a locked door to rescue her. He had thrown a heavy coat over her to extinguish the flames that singed her flouncy costume. And he had tossed her across his shoulders to carry her through the fire. Then he had gone back into the flames to search for Judy, who as it turned out, wasn't in the bathroom after all. She had taken off at the first signs of smoke and was one of the first to escape the flames.

There was no doubt about it. Buck Wheeler was a hero.

Sheriff Gibson and his forensics team searched through the rubble. They determined that the fire started from a short in the HVAC system, which caused sparks to filter down on sheetrock and paint cans stacked in a back room while contractors worked on the renovation. At first, they thought Buck Wheeler died from smoke inhalation, but a closer look showed his head had been smashed in, his jaw shattered. Ceiling debris was scattered around him, but nothing that matched the size and shape of the blunt object that had caused his death. They quickly decided that Buck Wheeler had been murdered.

Alton Humphrey was the logical suspect. Everyone knew he and Buck had been at each other's throats over the rezoning for the proposed development. Sheriff Gibson brought him in for questioning, wanted to lock him up, but Alton quickly called in a high-powered lawyer who got him released. As the investigation progressed, the sheriff realized there was no evidence tying Alton to the murder. No fingerprints. No DNA or trace evidence on Buck. No murder weapon.

Emmet Ralston was also questioned. He and Buck had argued over the future growth of the county. Emmet had openly expressed his frustration that Buck stood in the way of good jobs and a stronger tax base for Foreman County.

But again, there was no evidence. And residents remembered that Alton and Emmet had stood at the exit of the theater, helping others escape the crippling smoke. Surely a murderer wouldn't have hung around to do that. Without a murder weapon, without any solid evidence, neither could be tied to the crime.

At least they had the decency to stay away from Buck's funeral. It was held in the old Baptist church that Buck had attended since childhood. Locals mingled with out-of-towners who had heard Buck's story and wanted to honor him. Tents were set up on the lawn to handle the overflow crowd, with speakers broadcasting the poignant tributes given by Buck's many friends.

Church ladies fussed for days to cook enough fried chicken, ham biscuits, and casseroles to feed the hungry crowd. They laid out rows of cakes and endless pies, including Buck's favorite, pecan.

The county paper reprinted that old article about Buck's rock band being "the best of our age." Margie dug out recordings of Buck's early songs to play at the funeral. The tunes were picked up by DJs across the country. Two of them stayed on the top-ten charts for the next month.

The local bank set up college funds for Buck's children, and donations poured in from around the world.

The tavern was too damaged to be rebuilt. But with the insurance money, community donations, and a six-figure contribution from Alton Humphrey, plans quickly progressed for the new Buck Wheeler Community Center to be erected in its place. The tasteful brick building would house a theater, meeting rooms, and office space.

Buck became a national hero. The rock-star insurance guy. More famous now than he'd ever been when his band was touring the South.

Alton Humphrey went ahead with his development project, easily gaining approval from the Board of Supervisors now that Buck was no longer there to lead the opposition.

***

Sallie Minnows watched the lights of St. Lucia fade away as the cruise ship sailed to its next port.

She was using this cruise as an opportunity to reinvent herself. She had cut off her long braid and dyed her hair a soft brown. Spent some serious hours in the spa trying to undo all those years of damage squinting at the sun. Shopped in the cruise boutiques for new outfits to wear to fancy dinners and shore excursions.

One thing she couldn't give up was her steel-toed boots. They weren't the best for travel. In the airport, she'd had to tug at them while bracing herself on the edge of the conveyor belt, so she could put them in that plastic bin and then walk through the metal detector in her sock feet. And they weren't the easiest things to put back on, either. She couldn't do it standing up. She had to find a bench to sit on, angling her foot to push her toes as far down as she could, then jamming her heel into the boot.

But they made her feel safe. After all, a woman on her own had to be able to protect herself, any way she could. Nobody would mess with her when she was wearing those steel-toed boots.

She felt bad about Buck Wheeler. But he'd been wrong when he said the folks in Foreman didn't want change. She was tired of being land-rich and cash-poor, of getting up before dawn to finish her chores before the scorching sun made it too hot to stay outside. She'd done her part, kept the farm going for years after her husband died, raised her children. It was time for something new.

She glanced down at her boots again. They were old. The heels worn and scuffed. At least the bloody stain at the toe had finally darkened to brownish burgundy. She'd tried everything she could think of to get that stain out. Dish soap. Saddle soap. Baking soda. Even bleach. Nothing worked.

They did look a little ratty. Maybe she should get a new pair. Something a little more fashionable. After all, she wasn't a poor old farm woman anymore. Now that she had sold the homestead to Alton Humphrey, she could buy anything she wanted.

PERFECTLY AWRY
By Anne Louise Bannon

While putting on a new play in a storefront theater in Los Angeles, Daria Barnes finds herself faced with more than just the usual financial and artistic challenges.

Work in the theater for any length of time and you are going to see some seriously crazy stuff. All those hyper-creative, emotional people? It just goes with the territory.

Take Bobby Mossman, for example. Those of us who worked with him thought his fascination with staging the Perfect Crime was a little weird. Nobody, but nobody, thought he'd actually do it. I mean, he didn't give off any of those scary vibes, like he didn't care about hurting people. If anything, it seemed like an intellectual exercise to him.

We were mounting our show in a cracker box theater on the unfashionable end of Melrose Avenue in Los Angeles. I came into the office that afternoon, seriously annoyed. Bobby pulled a pack of cigarettes from the back of the rusty file cabinet. He was tall and slender, with long, thinning blond hair and sparkling blue eyes.

"Bobby, I just went to get the gels Jill asked for and the card was declined," I told him. Gels are colored plastic sheets that go over stage lights.

"I'll take care of it, Daria," he said.

The rumble of the actors rehearsing on the stage suddenly burst into a roar.

"Lee, if you don't learn your lines, I swear, I'm going to shoot you!" Tom screamed.

Tom Cimelli, our director, had also written the play about a soldier suffering from PTSD and holding bar patrons hostage. Lee was Lee Harmon, Bobby's partner in life. Tom was workshopping the play with visions of Broadway. Bobby's job was to raise the money to put it on so that Lee could keep acting. My job was to spend as little of the money Bobby raised as possible.

"Careful what you wish for," Bobby said with an odd snigger. "Now, all I have to do—"

"Bobby, we don't have time for the Perfect Crime right now," I said, glaring at him.

"I'm not playing," he said.

He was certainly in one of his moods. I deeply hoped that didn't mean he and Lee were fighting again. I looked him over. He usually wore his hair loose, but that morning he'd brushed it into a ponytail. He'd shaved off the usual stubble on his chin, too.

Bobby coughed, then shook a cigarette from the pack. Instead of putting the pack back in the file cabinet, he put it in the pocket of his light blue dress shirt. He had on dark gray dress slacks, too. He looked like he was about to go fundraising, and with two weeks to go before opening, that meant only one thing. We were almost out of money.

"We need those gels," I told Bobby. "If Jill doesn't warm up the lighting, the stage is going to look like a morgue."

"I'll take care of it," Bobby said again. He held up his cigarette. "I'm going for a smoke."

There was no point in antagonizing him, so I didn't follow him out to the alley behind the theater. But something was up. Usually when money ran short, Bobby told me about it and came up with a donation from one of his sources. I was also pretty darned sure we weren't out of money. I'd checked the account the day before. I decided I'd better check again.

The office computer took its time booting, so I didn't really pay attention to the bang I heard, loud as it was. Given the skanky neighborhood we were in on the eastern edge of Hollywood, I heard all kinds of bangs. Could have been a firecracker. Could have been a car backfiring. Could have been a gunshot. I hoped it wasn't a gunshot. A homeless person had been killed nearby the week before by a random shot.

Out of the corner of my eye I saw Jill Levy, our lone tech person, running past the office to the front of the house.

Our theater, like many in L.A., was in a small storefront. Yes, there is a pretty vibrant theater scene here. After all, we have bazillions of actors. They have to do something besides wait tables while they try for their big break. The smart ones do plays to keep their skills sharp. That's how I got into producing plays, which I discovered I liked a lot more than acting. I mean, I still go out on auditions and have a decent rep for learning my lines, hitting my mark, and showing up on time. But what I love doing is putting on plays. Even depressing scripts like Tom's. I didn't mind working for Bobby, either. He could be moody, but mostly he was decent and he was amazingly good at raising money.

I debated going after Jill, but then noticed I couldn't get into the company bank account on the computer. I tried again. It said my sign-in was no longer valid. I called the bank.

"Sorry, but that account's been closed," said the person on the other end of the line.

"I'm a signatory on that account. I didn't authorize that," I said, really working hard to keep from yelling at the poor woman.

"Daria Barnes?" she asked.

"Yes, that's me. I even gave you my social security number a minute ago."

I heard computer keys clicking on the other end. "It appears Mr. Mossman withdrew the money and closed the account this morning."

"What? Did he transfer it to another account?"

"No. He withdrew cash."

I hung up.

"I am going to kill him!" I screamed.

What stopped me was the laughter from the doorway. The man doing the laughing was of average height, but built like a cement mixer, with broad shoulders and a square face. His hair was deep, dark black. He was wearing a dark suit with the slight sheen of polyester.

I turned on the new arrival.

"Who are you?" I demanded.

"Berto Esparza," he said, flipping open an ID case. "I'm a private investigator working for the law firm of Graham, Shipkey, Shipkey, and Rubin. I'm looking for Bobby Mossman."

"I think he's around here someplace." I got up and worked my way around the beat-up desk in the tiny room. "If he's lucky, you'll find him before I do."

"He's the one you're going to kill?" His dark eyes flashed merrily.

"Well, not in so many words," I said, suddenly swallowing. "I mean, it's just an expression."

"What did he do?"

I brushed back my curly dishwater-blonde hair. "He withdrew all the money in the company account and closed it. It was half our budget. I've still got programs and tickets to pay for, plus another ad. And rent's coming due on this armpit of a space."

Berto shook his head. "You may want to start looking for another one. Or some more money. I'm here to serve papers on Mr. Mossman."

"He's being sued? For what?"

"Can't say."

"Probably some sort of fraud," I snorted.

Berto's eyes gleamed and he grinned knowingly.

My jaw dropped. "Holy crud, he *is* doing a Bialystock."

"Huh?"

"*The Producers*." I stumbled over the words.

"Film by Mel Brooks, 1967, starring Zero Mostel and Gene Wilder." Berto grinned.

I had to admit I was impressed that he got the older version of Mel Brooks' story about a producer who raises more from investors than he spends and makes a profit when the show closes.

"Most people would be thinking Nathan Lane and Matthew Broderick." That was the newer, musical version. I shook my head to clear it. "I was wondering if Bobby wasn't getting nice little old ladies to cough up." I looked at Berto. "But that's not fraud, is it? They weren't investors. They were donors. Besides, every penny we had went to the show."

"That you know of," said Berto. "Mr. Mossman is probably just this side of legal. Kind of hard to prove criminal intent when your victim gives you the money willingly to put on a play and that's what you do with it. That's why I'm also trying to find out if there was any other funny business going on. Which given what I heard coming in, I'd say there was."

"With a hey nonny-nonny," I said, getting angry again. "He stole half our budget."

I pushed past Berto to go outside just in time to hear screaming from the back of the theater. The stage area was a largely unfurnished section surrounded by black curtains. Stage right, behind the curtains, was the only offstage area in the theater. The prop table was squeezed up against the back wall of the tiny alcove under a window we had to keep open because it was summer and the AC was on the fritz again. An open door led to the alley.

Jean Frisch, our leading lady, was in the doorway screaming in full-on terror as she looked outside. Berto gently pulled Jean back onto the stage. Tom, Lee, and Dev Lippman, one of the other actors, looked at us with puzzled faces. Berto already had his cell phone out and was calling the police as he hurried out to the alley.

"There's a body out there," Jean sobbed. "With a big, ugly, bloody spot on the back of his head."

"Maybe somebody just hit him," Tom said, heading for the door. "We should be out there taking care of him."

Tom was stopped by Berto's return. One look at Berto's face and Tom gasped and turned pale.

"Maybe we could do some first aid," Dev said.

Berto shook his head. "I'm a former cop. I know a stiff when I see one. Everybody needs to stay right here."

I gulped. "Do you know whose body it is?"

"Somebody with a blue shirt on and dark gray slacks," Berto said, obviously watching all of us.

"Bobby," I whispered, swallowed, gasped, then looked at Berto. "Bobby Mossman was wearing a blue dress shirt and dark gray slacks today."

Lee's wail rose above everyone else's and he sank onto a bar stool on stage.

"I need everyone to stay in this room," Berto said. He looked at the alley as if he needed to be out there, as well.

Shaking, Jill wandered in from the sidewalk outside the storefront.

"What's going on?" she asked, her voice panicky. She was a short woman, with spiky dark hair.

"There's a body in the alley," Jean said, crying and tossing her long brown hair out of her perfectly shaped face. "We think it's Bobby."

"Noooooooo!" Jill wailed. "I was just playing with it!"

"Playing with what?" I asked.

But Jill was too hysterical to answer. She sank into a seat in the first row and hugged herself as she sobbed.

Berto waved me over to the offstage area. "Can you keep everyone here in the theater?"

"Can't you?" I asked, my voice starting to tremble.

He looked back at the alley. "I've got to secure the scene. You, on the other hand, look like you've got it together."

"I suppose," I whispered. I sure didn't feel like I had it together. But compared to everyone else, I must have looked like an oasis of calm.

Lee's sobs were the loudest, even as he began hyperventilating. I'd have questioned it, but Lee was simply not that good an actor. Tom sat on one of the other bar stools doing deep breathing exercises with his eyes closed. Dev sniffled and paced relentlessly while Jean kept mechanically patting Lee on the back.

"Whoa. What's this?" Berto squatted over something on the black-painted cement floor next to the prop table.

It was the little snub-nose revolver we were using for the big scene when Lee's character pretends to commit suicide. It had fallen off the prop table. Berto looked up at the open window, then pulled a small flashlight out of his inside jacket pocket and trained it on the small revolver.

"*Muy interesante*," he muttered to himself.

I laughed weakly as he looked at the window again.

"That's not the murder weapon," I said. "Can't be."

"Why not?"

"It's not a real gun. It's a prop gun. And the whole point of the scene is that it's not actually loaded."

"Looks pretty real to me," Berto said. He moved the light around to the side of the grip. "See that? It's the gun's serial number. Why would there be a serial number on a fake gun?"

"But… But… nobody's stupid enough to—" I stopped.

I know I can be pretty hard on actors. Most of them are decent and reasonably intelligent human beings. But there are a few… how do I put this kindly? They would, in the name of "Being Real," be stupid enough to use a real gun as a prop. The problem was I didn't think we had any of that kind of idiot in our cast.

Suddenly Jill's hysteria meant something. I went back to the stage area and found Jill still sobbing in the first row of the fifty seats that made up the audience area. I sat down next to her and put my arms around her shoulders.

"Jill," I said softly. "I heard a gunshot earlier."

She nodded.

"What happened?"

"It was a real gun," she whispered. "I had no idea. Bobby just gave it to me. Said it would look great under the lights. I knew he was right. But I didn't know it was real. I truly didn't."

"So, you were playing with it today," I said.

"I was aiming out the window and it went off," Jill gulped. "It scared me to death. I ran out to the front. I was praying to God I hadn't hit anything. Anyone."

Jean screeched. "You mean he's been pointing a real gun at me all this time?"

"Apparently so," I said, patting Jill's arm, then getting up.

Jean screamed and collapsed into my arms. I could hear sirens in the distance.

Tom opened his eyes. "Is there a reason you don't use real guns?"

Tom was an Iraq war vet, so maybe you could give him a pass. I wasn't ready to.

"Yeah," I said, patting Jill and getting up. "Like what happened."

"But it wasn't loaded."

I glared at Tom. "Apparently, it was."

He had the decency to go pale again and pick up his deep breathing with even more focus. I slid Jean into a seat next to Jill.

"We don't know that it was the weapon," Berto pointed out, coming out onto the stage. "We're just guessing at this point."

"I don't care," I yelled. "Why the hell was there a loaded gun on my set? That's what I want to know."

Everyone assembled stopped crying and looked at me blankly, except Jill, who shrunk even further into herself. I suppose it was a bit much to expect a real answer. I took a deep breath.

"Who here knew Bobby was about to bolt?" I asked.

Everyone except Berto erupted into confused chatter.

"I did," said Dev, loudly. He was a sandy-haired man with a deep, soft voice. The others stilled. "Well, I didn't really know. But he asked me to fly away with him to Mexico yesterday."

"Bobby?" cried Lee. He looked like he was about to fall off the stool. Jean went over and held him.

I looked at Lee and shuddered.

"That's the thing," I said. "Jill didn't know the gun was real, and she had no reason to kill Bobby. In fact, the only person here who knew the gun was real also had the least motive to kill Bobby, and that's you, Tom."

"Are you sure?" Berto asked quietly.

"Reasonably sure," I said. The sirens grew louder and I figured I only had a few minutes more before the police arrived and did their thing. "So, if the gun was originally Bobby's, and it turned out to be loaded, then who would the logical victim be?" I looked at Lee. "Don't you press the gun to your temple and pull the trigger at the end of the first act?"

Lee turned white. "It couldn't be."

"As in Bobby's Perfect Crime?" I pressed. "Lee, Bobby was being sued, probably by one of our supporters. He closed the company account this morning and took all the money in cash. I don't know how you two were getting on, but the fact that he asked Dev to go with him to Mexico suggests to me that things were not all that great."

"He was being horrible!" Lee wailed as Jean held him close. "He said he was tired of me. I couldn't do anything right."

I couldn't help but think, if only we could get that kind of emotion out of him during the performance. I looked over at Berto to steady myself.

"Maybe," I said. "In any case, Bobby finally had his Perfect Crime. He takes off to Mexico. You use the gun as scripted. Only it goes off and you're dead."

Both Lee and Jean wailed again.

"More to the point," I continued. "Bobby's just dumped you. There's no reason to believe that you haven't pulled off some overly dramatic suicide because you're not around to tell us that you didn't know the gun was loaded. It's about as close to a perfect crime as you can get. The only thing Bobby didn't take into account was Jill."

"I didn't know it was real!" Jill cried. "How was I supposed to know? I've never even seen a real gun before."

Berto looked skeptical, which I could understand. He actually dealt with real guns on a regular basis. However, I totally got where Jill was coming from. The weight of the gun supposedly should have given it away, but I would have assumed it had been weighted to be more "real."

"Exactly," I continued. "Jill was goofing off with what she had every reason to believe was a prop gun and not the real thing. Call it irony. Call it Karma. But Bobby was hoisted on a petard of his own making."

"And what makes you so sure?" Berto asked.

"It's the only thing that makes sense," I said out of the corner of my mouth.

"*The Thin Man*," Berto said. "1934. William Powell and Myrna Loy."

He was right. I'd unconsciously parroted that line from the end of the movie, which is one of my all-time faves.

The police arrived and did their thing. It took forever. However, the physical evidence supported my theory. Berto teased me later that, thanks to me, he'd lost some extra billable hours, but his bosses at the law firm were pretty impressed with how he'd handled things. I couldn't have cared less that he got the credit for figuring it all out, especially since I couldn't have done it without him telling me what he knew.

Jill eventually recovered. Amazing what good therapy will do. She'll even still work with me, but not on anything with a prop gun. We did eventually get Tom's show up and running. Turned out people had been lining up and taking numbers to sue Bobby. So, just to cover our backsides, we figured we'd better mount it, trauma or not.

Lee found the money to do it, too. He told us he wanted to prove Bobby wrong about the script. So much for that. The show closed after the second night. Like I mentioned earlier, it was a pretty depressing piece of work.

Anyway, that's how Berto and I met. It didn't take that long before we got to be best friends. He is the big brother I never had, and while he does have a younger sister, it's like I've been adopted by his family, too. Berto's kids even call me *Tía*, or Aunt Daria.

Berto does bug me sometimes about working with him. While I do the odd job for him now and then, the work he does as a P.I. makes even the stuff I do in the theater look sane. I'll stick with my kind of crazy, thank you. At least that I get.

THE GHOST IN BALCONY B
By Michele Bazan Reed

*Clarissa is determined to be an actress and perform at
Syracuse's grand new movie palace, the State Theater.
When her plans take an unexpected turn, PI Harry
Jerome is on the job.*

Clarissa always said she was born to be in the theater.

She was a sweet young thing, barely twenty, with curly red hair
and freckles betraying her origins on Tipperary Hill, when I met
her serving drinks over at Art's speakeasy. But she was quick to
tell me she was only doing that to keep body and soul together until
she could fulfill her real destiny—to be an actress.

She even had her stage name picked out, Claire de Vianne. "I
think it makes me sound classy and French," she said with a giggle.

"It sure does," I said. "I understand Claire, but where did you
come up with that last name?"

I got a whiff of her favorite scent—lilacs—and felt a curl brush
my cheek as she bent over to whisper in my ear. "Promise not to
tell anyone? It was on a box of glass sconces being delivered to the
State Theater site. I saw them on the loading dock yesterday on my
way to work." She crowed, "That place is gonna be something
grand! Can you imagine? Glass shades all the way from some
factory in France!"

Art's is over on Jefferson Street, and from the day in 1926
when they started building the grand new State Theater on the
corner of Jefferson and Salina, Clarissa spent even more time
dreaming about the day she'd tread the boards.

"Harry," she said to me one day as she served the free whiskey
Art promised me for life the day I tipped him off to federal
Prohibition agents heading for his joint.

"Yeah, doll," I said, raising my glass and nodding thanks to Art
behind the bar.

"Promise me if I'm an actress, you'll come and see me over at
the State?" She had a sweet little pout and employed it now.

"Darlin', if you play the State, I'll be there in the front row." I
savored a sip of my rye, and then added. "And don't say 'if'. It'll
be when."

She beamed at that as she skipped back to the bar to ferry
another round to a raucous group of flappers and swells smoking

and drinking on the velvet settee. They were in for a scolding. Everybody knew Clarissa hated cigarettes. I grinned when I heard her tell one dapper young man to "Put out that coffin nail!"

Whenever I came in, Clarissa made it a point to recite to me all the facts about the new Oriental-style "movie palace" which would feature both vaudeville acts and first-run moving pictures.

"*The Herald* says the State will have 2,900 seats, all upholstered in red velvet," she told me one day. "And the Wurlitzer organ that plays during the movies? It has 1,400 pipes and can make the sound of hoof beats, a locomotive, even birds in the trees." She looked at Art's ceiling, starry-eyed. "Syracuse is going to have one of the grandest theaters in the whole country, and I'm gonna play it. You mark my words!"

With the building site just down the street, it wasn't long before the big shots behind the project found their way over to the speakeasy. Art was only too happy to have them, along with their fat wallets.

It also wasn't long before those big-city types noticed our little Clarissa.

One of the builders took quite a shine to her, and filled her head with promises of a career on the stage. Who knows, maybe they weren't meant as empty promises. We'll never know, now.

***

No Prohibition-era wedding had as generous a bar as Clarissa and Felix's. Art made sure of that. All the regulars gathered to toast our little beauty and her beau.

Just before the couple left to catch the train to Niagara Falls, Clarissa extracted one last pledge: "Remember your promise, Harry. You've got to come see me act at the State Theater."

***

As I watched the theater construction from the vantage point of my fourth-floor office on Salina Street, I often thought about Clarissa and hoped her dream would come true.

Meanwhile, I kept busy with the missing persons cases, suspicious husbands and wives, and the occasional lost or stolen valuables which were bread and butter for me, Harry Jerome, PI.

In the decade since I'd returned to my hometown as a private detective, I'd revived my reputation as a finder. My old nickname from the force—The Hound—started appearing in headlines for my most high-profile cases and reporters gave them mysterious-sounding names like *The Lady in Black* back in '19 and *The Freelance Accountant* in '24.

Except for quiet moments alone in my digs, I almost forgot about the circumstances under which I'd left the force and Lara left me. Those were the times I headed for Art's for a little bootleg whiskey and some companionship. And of course, the latest news about "our Clarissa," as we regulars still thought of her.

They say she took to visiting the construction site daily while her builder husband went about his business, sitting in the balcony's Section B in a ladylike white dress, watching as the opulent theater rose up around her and dreaming of her moment in the footlights.

***

"Did you hear about Clarissa?" Art asked one day, a concerned look on his face. "Some of the building crew were here last week, and one of the barmaids overheard them gossiping that her new husband isn't quite as attentive as he should be. He's been 'auditioning' some of the hoofers trying out for the vaudeville chorus line, if you get my drift."

"Shame," I said. "She deserves better."

"Well, if what they say is to be believed, she may find it. There's some electrician, name of Oscar, who notices her there in the balcony, day after day. Shall we say, maybe sparks will fly?"

I raised my whiskey in a silent toast that our friend would find the career—and the love—she deserved.

***

One day in '27, I opened *The Herald* and gasped. *Builder's Wife Falls to Her Death* the headline blazed. *Budding Actress Topples from Balcony After Witnessing Stagehand's Demise.*

Clarissa had been in her favorite seat, probably daydreaming about her career and watching workers get the theater ready for its grand opening, when Oscar misconnected two wires, electrocuting himself. Whether she ran to save him, forgetting she was on the balcony, or fainted from shock and toppled over the railing, we'll never know, but she landed in the orchestra seating, breaking her neck.

The wake Art put on for her rivalled that of a mayor or a titan of industry. All the regulars were there, trading stories of our little sweetheart and drowning our sorrows in bathtub gin.

Some of the theater people were there, too, including Clarissa's husband. The bereaved widower had wasted no time finding a new sweetie to squire around.

"That's Vivian," Art said, with a nod toward a brassy blond who was loudly offering her condolences to Felix as she hung on his arm. "They say he found her in the costume shop, where she was working as a seamstress. Used the same line, offering her a chance at stardom."

I finished my whiskey and left, before I did something I'd regret.

***

The theater opened February 18, 1928. Since no one had braved the Salt City's lake effect snow that Saturday morning to seek out The Hound's help, I decided to tackle the snowbanks myself and catch the matinee across the street.

They certainly spared no expense, I thought as I entered the lobby with its red-flocked walls and gilt trim. Up the grand, filigreed staircase, the architect Thomas Lamb, who'd just finished Madison Square Garden in New York City, had created an Oriental fantasyland on the promenade lobby. People ran their fingers through the water of a koi pond with real fish, and gawked at a replica Japanese pagoda fountain.

The house was packed to see the elaborate stage show *Milady's Fans*, followed by the Syracuse opening of William Haines and Joan Crawford in *West Point*. It seemed everyone in the city had paid their two bits to check out the new theater.

As I headed for my orchestra seat to the accompaniment of the organist warming up on the Wurlitzer, I looked up at the magnificent Louis Comfort Tiffany chandelier in the lobby, originally created for Cornelius Vanderbilt's mansion. Must've been a bit of glare from those hundreds of bulbs. My eyes started to water as my gaze drifted to the doorway marked Balcony B.

***

It wasn't long after the grand opening that the rumors started circulating. The new theater, everyone said, was haunted.

People reported seeing a young woman in a white dress sitting in a balcony seat. Some said areas of the building were unusually cold. Others swore they could hear a female voice, softly sobbing.

"I was looking for my seat when I saw a flash of white turning into the doorway for Box 5," one matron told *The Herald.* "But when I got there, I could find no one." She paused for dramatic effect. "That box was completely empty…and cold as the grave."

At first, I dismissed the rumors as mass hysteria or, more likely, a publicity stunt by the management to sell more tickets.

Tongues wagged, of course. In the popular imagination, the ghost became equated with the tragic death of the builder's wife. Some even dubbed the apparition "Clarissa."

It saddened me and angered me in equal measure.

One day at Art's I heard a stranger recounting another "ghost sighting" at the theater. I wanted to slug him, and probably would have, until something he said stopped me in my tracks.

"I was the first one up in Balcony B for Friday's matinee, and suddenly the air smelled like my grandmother's garden," he told the barmaid. "There was no one there, so it couldn't have been some dame's perfume, but I swear I smelled lilacs."

Lilacs. Clarissa's favorite.

I'm not the superstitious type, but I couldn't help but wonder if Clarissa was as determined as ever to be in the theater.

***

My theory about a publicity stunt on the part of the theater management appeared to be wrong. About six months after the grand opening of the movie palace, my phone rang, and the operator announced a call from Jefferson 3-4-7-9.

"Mr. Jerome?" a nervous-sounding voice on the other end of the line said. "This is Sam Keene. I'm the box office manager over at the State. We need your help."

Keene went on to explain that the theater management was getting concerned. The talk of a haunted venue at first seemed like it would draw audiences, so they encouraged it. But now they were beginning to see a fall-off in ticket sales, and wondered if some of the more timid theater-goers were staying away.

"We'd like to hire you to get to the bottom of this thing," Keene said. "Whatever it takes."

"I'll need unfettered access to all areas of the theater—at all times of the day or night," I told him.

"Of course," Keene said. "We've thought about that, and we can provide you with a cover story. You're doing follow-up work for Mr. Lamb, the architect, to make sure everything in the design is working out fine. That way, you'll be able to talk to everybody from management to stagehands to patrons, and you can poke around the seating areas and backstage as well."

I thought about it. I didn't care about the theater's sales numbers, but it might let me explore a bit about the rumors surrounding Clarissa. If I could help save her reputation and put the speculation about her to rest, it would be work well spent.

The theater's generous fee for my services wouldn't hurt, either.

"It's a deal," I said, and rang off.

***

I arrived at the theater the next morning to begin my investigation. Keene met me at the door. He looked as nervous as he'd sounded over the phone. "I hope you understand, Mr. Jerome, we require the utmost discretion. We want to quell rumors, not start them." He raised himself up to his full height, which came to my shoulders, and put on a most officious expression.

I fixed him with an icy stare. "I'm a professional, Mr. Keene, you don't need to lecture me about discretion," I said. "As to whether the rumors will be quashed by what I find, that remains to be seen."

The cover story he provided for me worked well. I was given access to the public spaces, the stage area, even the dressing rooms.

I watched the scene painters go about their business creating the backdrops for live vaudeville acts, and got to visit the booth where the projectionist changed reels for the afternoon cinema. Even the organist let me up in the loft where the Wurlitzer's pipes reverberated during the silent pictures.

They were all polite and explained to me whether their spaces worked for them, and noted problems they were having with the design. Like workmen everywhere, they had plenty of gripes.

They also had plenty of gossip, especially when they thought I wasn't listening.

One day, as I pretended to sketch the rigging that soared eighty feet above the stage, I heard a stagehand named Tom Grady talking to his replacement at shift change. "I don't want to put the heebie-jeebies on you, Frankie, but the oddest thing happened to me last night during the second show," Grady said. "I was working the curtain between acts, and during intermission, I decided to take a cigarette break." He looked over his shoulder to see if anyone was listening. Because of the danger of curtains, scenery, and costumes catching fire and causing a stampede among three-thousand patrons, smoking was strictly forbidden in this area of the theater.

"I barely lit up when I heard a woman behind me scold, 'Put out that coffin nail.' I whipped my head back to see who was bossing me around, but there was no one there." Grady nodded at his companion's shocked expression. "Yeah, that's how I felt. Very, very eerie, it was. Very eerie, indeed."

I thought back to Clarissa chiding that swell over at Art's with the very same words, and had to agree with Grady's assessment.

For my survey of how things in the theater were working, some stagehands told me doors previously open were locked when they returned just moments later. Thespians complained about dresses falling off hangers or makeup jars toppling over. Even the organist said there must be a draft in his loft, because sometimes pages turned on their own.

I was walking down a corridor, wondering just what kind of a report I could write for Keene and how that would help the theater put the ghost stories to rest, when I heard voices raised in a dressing room a few doors down. With the hustle and bustle of act changes, no one noticed me as I positioned myself to hear better.

"Don't you sweet-talk me anymore," a woman's voice said. "I've had it with your promises. You told me you'd give me a career on stage and a ring, and so far I've got neither!" I thought I recognized the voice as belonging to Vivian, the seamstress I'd seen on the arm of Clarissa's husband at the wake.

I heard a man's voice, but he was speaking lower, maybe even whispering, and I couldn't make out what he was saying.

The woman raised her voice louder. "No, I mean it! I'm going to the cops. I found those wire cutters you had hidden in your office, and the bottle of laudanum, too. I bet you put that into the tea you asked me to take up to Clarissa that day. It must have made her dizzy and that's why she fell when she saw Oscar die." Vivian started sobbing hysterically. "How could you? That poor girl never hurt a fly." Suddenly she screamed, "Felix! No!" and I heard a thud.

The door opened then and Clarissa's husband stuck out his head, straightened his jacket, and looked to see if the coast was clear before stepping out.

That's when he saw me. I watched recognition dawn in his eyes as he identified me from the honeymoon send-off over at Art's.

One minute he was staring at me with a look of panic as he realized that I had heard everything. The next he turned and headed for the catacombs of the theater.

I was right on his tail.

The warren of hallways and secret passages connected backstage areas, dressing rooms, and exits. Even the actors and stagehands admitted to getting lost in the maze of dark, narrow passageways. I didn't have a chance.

As a builder, Felix was likely to know his way around, I reminded myself, as I struggled to keep up with his zigzag course. One minute I'd catch sight of his coattails, the next there would be nothing there, only a pair of doors, unmarked, and me, wondering which he had run through.

Suddenly, I smelled it: a faint whiff of lilacs. Clarissa. I followed the scent into one of the doors and down a twisty hallway. I caught another glimpse of Felix's jacket and followed.

Door after door appeared, some to the right, some to the left. I tried a couple and they were locked. One swung open slightly and I stepped in, just in time to see a streak of black ahead as my quarry turned another corner.

I lost track of how many turns I'd made and in which directions. Suddenly I skidded to a halt. The passageway ended and across the hall a swinging door led to a stairway going up. I could hear footsteps pounding up the stairs ahead of me and I followed. The stairway led to the second floor, and as I reached the top, gasping for breath, I could just see Felix entering another door. The lighted sign above it read *Balcony B.*

He tried to hold the balcony door closed, but I put my shoulder to it and heard him stumble backward. As I burst through, I saw him running toward the front of the balcony, a desperate look on his face.

"Give it up, Felix," I said as I advanced. "I heard everything Vivian said. You can't get away with this."

"No one will believe you, Harry," he said, a sneer turning up the corner of his mouth. "You're just a down-on-your-luck gumshoe. I'm somebody. I brought a lotta jobs and money to this one-horse town with my work on this theater." He squared his shoulders and preened a bit. "Anyway, I made sure Vivian won't be doing any more talking. So it's just your word against mine."

"Clarissa was my friend, Felix." I let the words hang in the chill air. "I'll make sure you pay."

With a roar, he lunged for me. His hands reached for my lapels and he almost had me, when suddenly his eyes widened and he started to shake. I realized he was looking over my left shoulder. The unmistakable scent of lilacs filled the air and out of the corner of my eye, I could see a flash of white.

Felix put his hands up, shouting, "No! No! Get away from me," and tried to back up. He stumbled on the balcony stairs when his foot caught on the first row of seats and he started to tip, arms flailing.

"Felix! Grab my arm," I shouted, reaching out to him. But it was too late. With a scream, Felix toppled over the balcony's brass railing.

***

Later that evening, after the police had sent a badly shaken Vivian to the hospital and Felix off to the morgue, they recorded my statement.

An electrician working on the lighting for the evening show had seen it all, and testified that I'd tried to save Felix, clearing me of suspicion.

"Any way to keep this out of the papers?" I asked the cop. "There's nobody left to prosecute, and releasing the story will only harm the theater and bring Clarissa's family even more sorrow."

"It does seem like justice has been served," the detective said, closing his notebook. With a tip of his hat, he set out to clear off a gaggle of reporters just outside the theater door.

Drained, I retrieved my fedora and headed for the exit. Once again I caught a whiff of lilacs. It was probably just the rush of outside air as I pulled open the doors of the theater, but I could have sworn I felt the gentle brush of a curl against my cheek as I stepped out onto Salina Street.

"Bravo, Claire de Vianne," I muttered, as I realized I'd finally kept my promise. I'd been there to witness Clarissa's debut performance at State Theater. Somehow, I didn't think it would be her last.

DRAMA-RAMA FLIP FLOP
By Cindy Brown

Directing kids at the Phoenix's Drama-Rama summer theater camp should be fun. Unless you have to deal with a 12-year-old psychopath.

I love kids.

Really, I do.

Even—especially—theatre kids. Omigod, their energy—I caught two of them literally swinging from a chandelier last week—but when that energy is channeled, they amaze me with their creativity and touch me with their vulnerability and make me laugh hard enough that I snort Diet Coke out my nose. (BTW, do not try this at home. The bubbles sting.)

But try as I might, Henry... well, Henry was hard to love. In fact, at times I wanted to kill the kid. Sure, he was creative and imaginative, but his ideas tended toward the gross and scary, like rat zombies. He was a born leader, but one who would merrily walk his followers into the deep end of the pool (which he nearly did before I stopped him). He was smart and talented and charismatic, but in all the wrong ways, like a twelve-year-old Lex Luthor. Henry was going to grow up to be either a super criminal or a star.

I first met Henry last year, on the opening day of summer theatre camp for Phoenix Parks and Rec. It was my third year running the camp, so I was feeling pretty confident as I walked onto the stage of our school-sized auditorium. "Welcome, theatre geeks!" I said to the assembled middle schoolers. "Are you ready to have an awesome time at Phoenix Drama-Rama?" A few yesses from the kids, most of whom were buzzing with energy. "I can't hear you," I said. "Are you ready to have an awesome—*aah*!" Whatever had landed on my head was gloppy and green and running down my face so I couldn't see—and was that a spider inside it?! "*Aah!*"

The kids laughed as I frantically wiped at my face. "You got slimed!" said a voice from above me. The little demon I'd later come to know as Henry had managed to sneak up to the definitely out-of-bounds catwalk with a Big Gulp cup full of slime. When I learned that he'd made the gooey stuff himself and added a few plastic spiders to it, I was impressed in spite of myself.

That was just the beginning. Besides the slime and the aforementioned aborted pool escapade, during the three weeks of camp, Henry:

- Pretended to barf all over his friend's lunch, using a jar of cooked oatmeal he'd secreted away in his backpack (surprisingly realistic).
- Filled a piñata with SpaghettiOs and blew it up with contraband firecrackers. You can imagine what that looked like.
- Convinced all the kids I was a private investigator (I am, part-time) with the FBI (I am not) who was trying to uncover a kangaroo smuggling ring (kangaroos? How do you smuggle kangaroos?).

And of course, Henry never missed a day of camp, always arrived early, and often stayed a few minutes late. (His parents frequently picked him up at the last minute. I completely understood. If I had to have Henry with me 24/7, one of us wouldn't live long.)

So, I was simultaneously worried and relieved when Henry wasn't at camp on time one morning. "Anyone seen Henry?" I asked. Head shakes all around. When he showed up an hour later, he wore a sling on one arm and a hoodie (even though it was a hundred and ten outside). When asked what had happened, all he'd say was, "You should see the other guy."

And omigod, was he in a mood—frowning and touchy and ten times more annoying than usual, and that's saying a lot. "We should be doing *Blood Eaters*," he must have said a half dozen times while we were working on props. (*Blood Eaters* was Henry's movie script—he was a budding psychopath *and* filmmaker.) "*Snow White and the Seven Aliens* is the stupidest play ever."

"Too bad. And stop that." We were cleaning up after making props, but Henry was careening around like a bumper car, purposefully running into the walls. Yes, literally bouncing off the walls. I stood up, dusted the glitter off my jeans skirt, and clapped my hands. "All right, everyone. Finish cleaning up and get ready. Places for the top of the show in five."

The kids put the last prop materials into the cardboard boxes marked "Drama-Rama!," and then walked, ran, and skipped backstage. Henry followed them, scuffing his feet so that his sneakers squeaked loudly on the wooden floor. "Stupid play."

It hurt that he kept saying that. Yes, I was getting defensive over a twelve-year-old's comments, but *Snow White and the Seven Aliens* was my baby. I wrote it specifically for the class so everyone could have a speaking part, and I thought it was pretty clever. I borrowed the space parody idea from a *Wizard of Oz* production I'd worked on, but put my own spin on the idea: Snow White dressed and acted like a spunky Princess Leia, the Doctor from *Doctor Who* was the woodsman who let her get away, and the prince who found her was...

"Captain Kirk is stupid." Henry stood in the middle of the stage, even though his character didn't appear until the end of the play. "Why do I have to be old Captain Kirk? Can't I at least be Jean-Luc Picard?"

"It works better with the story," I said. "Snow White needs to be woken up by someone who likes to kiss women, and —"

"Jean-Luc Picard likes to kiss women."

"—and old Captain Kirk, as you call him, was that kind of guy," I said. "A ladies' man."

"What's a ladies' man?" asked Amelia, the youngest in the group.

"It's a man who likes to wear ladies' clothes," said Rylan (eleven and big for his age).

"No, that's—"

"That's a transvestite," said Chloe (big eyes and a great singing voice).

"I think we're getting off track here," I said.

"Is a trainsvestite like a trainsexual?" asked Amelia.

"Okay. Time to get back to the pla—"

"Captain Kirk is, I mean, *I'm* a trains-sexual?" Henry had a devilish look in his eye. "Does that mean I get to have sex on a trai—"

"No sex!" I shouted

A couple of the girls got wide-eyed. Nice, Ivy, scaring them like that. "I mean... sex is fine. At least between two consenting adults."

"What about three?" asked Rylan. "Is sex between three consenting adults okay?"

"Um..."

"Ivy, can I see you outside?" Lupe, the summer programs director, must have come in to the room unbeknownst to me. Henry smiled like the devil he was.

"Now," said Lupe.

"Of course," I said, wishing Henry wasn't twelve so I could plot revenge. "Mia," I said to the teen volunteer who acted as my stage manager. "Why don't you play 'Character Bus' with the kids until I get back?"

After a dressing down about inappropriate subject matter

(which I didn't deserve) and an admonition about not allowing kids to undermine my authority (which I did deserve), Lupe sent me back to the auditorium. "It went pretty well," Mia said. "So I let them go to lunch a few minutes early."

Good, I'd have time to chill a little. It was stupid, how much I let Henry get to me. He was just a twelve-year-old kid, for God's sake and I was an adult, a theatre professional. I should be able to—

"Miss Ivy! Miss Ivy!" Chloe ran onto the stage from the left wing, her big eyes wide with fear. "Come quick! Rylan's hurt, real bad!"

I jumped the three feet onto the stage, Mia right behind me. We ran across the stage and followed Chloe to a dressing room backstage. A clump of kids stood near the entrance, staring into the room and blocking the door. "Let us through!" I shouted. Little Amelia turned as I passed, her face streaming with tears.

Oh no. Oh no.

Henry stood in the middle of the small room, shaking, his hands covered in blood. More blood—*lots* of blood—pooled around the prone Rylan's head. "Mia!" My assistant looked like she might be sick. "Call 911 and run to the office, tell them what happened." She turned on her heel and ran.

Oh my God, oh my God. Rylan. He was just a kid.

"I didn't mean to." Henry's voice came out in gulps. "We were just messing around, and then he shoved me, so I shoved him back and he fell and hit his head on the counter… I didn't mean to hurt him." He began to cry, big heaving sobs.

"It's okay," I said to Henry, though it was anything but. "I'm sure he'll be okay."

There was no way this still and bloody boy was okay. Omigod, what was I going to tell his parents?

I crouched down beside Rylan, on the floor sticky with blood. Henry's crying escalated into a wail. Several kids joined him in a hellish chorus. "Quiet!" I yelled. Was Rylan breathing? I couldn't tell. A familiar, sweet smell assaulted my nostrils as I put my face close to his, to see if I could feel his breath or—

Stage blood. The smell I recognized was stage blood. This was all a hoax. Yes, Rylan's eyelids fluttered just a bit. *No.* No way. I was going to kill the little—*wait.*

Ha.

"Omigod, omigod," I said, crumpling into the pool of blood and clawing at my throat. "My inhaler. I can't breathe," I wheezed. I learned to make that noise when I was trying to learn to yodel. It's a long story. "Help. Get my inhal—" I collapsed, eyes closed, still clutching at my throat, wishing I had thought about my shortish skirt before sprawling on the floor.

Silence for a moment. Then a jumble of voices:

"Her inhaler?"

"Oh no!"

"She has asthma?"

"Omigod, did we kill Miss Ivy?"

Footsteps pounded down the hall, probably to search my backpack for the nonexistent inhaler or to get someone from the office. The light behind my eyelids got darker as someone came close, blocking out the overhead light. It was Henry—I could tell by the scent of the Bubble Yum he always chewed. I waited until he was kneeling next to me, then...

"*BOO!*" I sat up, spattering fake gore everywhere.

"*Aah!*" Henry fell back into the pool of blood. Then he laughed. "Perfect!" he shouted. "Cut! Did you get that?" he asked a tall kid I recognized as Henry's older brother. He was standing with the group at the door, using his iPhone as a camera. "Got it," he said.

"Nice job, everyone," Henry said. "Great crying, especially you, Amelia."

"Thank you," she said modestly.

"And Miss Ivy," Henry said, "It wasn't in the script, but you were awesome. I should have known you could act."

Should have known his theatre teacher could act? Little turd.

So that's how me and my bright pink underwear ended up on the big screen at the Phoenix Film Festival Summer Camp. Henry later explained how he and the kids had been planning the, uh, event for weeks, rehearsing the kids' reactions, making their own stage blood, and setting up the scene in the dressing room, which is why Henry was late that morning. "The sling and the hoodie were character development," he said. "You know, so you'd think I was especially troubled that day." Like I said, a super criminal or a star.

And yes, I signed a release so Henry and his brother could use the scene in *Blood Eaters*. After all, it's my job as a theatre teacher to encourage creativity, right?

I still want to kill that kid.

IT'S NOT O.K. CORRAL
By M. E. Browning

The Wild West comes to life at the Stagecoach Guest Ranch, but when reality intrudes and takes center stage, the show becomes anything but make-believe.

Cassidy Bailey had shot eight men during the past two weeks. The first one had been fun; after that, it just got monotonous.

She locked the washroom door behind her and balanced the small leather satchel on the pedestal sink. No sense hurrying. No matter how early she was, when they divvied out the weapons, she always got the pearl-handled revolver with the jammed cylinder. Maybe they figured as the sole woman surrounded by a crew of outlaws, she'd know enough to make her single shot count. So far, they'd been right.

She opened her traveling valise. It was a bit of authenticity she brought to a production that sadly lacked much in the way of realism, but she loved being part of the cast of the frontier show, and the guests of the Stagecoach Guest Ranch lapped it up. But Cassidy was a stickler for details. That's what majoring in history will get you—a lifelong dissatisfaction with anything anachronistic. Combined with her minor in theater, she was doomed.

She swapped her skinny jeans and t-shirt for a corset and flouncy skirt. Every time she leaned over, the boning of the corset caught on her naval ring, but her posture had never been straighter.

Beyond the door, cowboy boots clomped across the oak floorboards of the bunkhouse. The steps slowed as they neared. She hoped they'd continue but knew they wouldn't.

"Get a move on, Nellie. You're slower than molasses in January."

She didn't know which she hated more. That the name they slapped onto her character sounded like a horse, or the stupid Ah-shucks drawl Shane adopted even when there was no one to hear. *This is how we talk round these parts,* he'd say. *Never know when there might be young'uns underfoot.*

She yanked the top of the corset higher. It wasn't the kids that worried her.

"I'd be happy to help the little lady out with her laces."

"Not in this lifetime, Shane." The laces weren't even functional. The corset fastened with a series of tiny hook-and-eyes up the front. More steampunk than frontier.

"I told you to call me Sheriff. And as Sheriff McMasters, I order you to open up in the name of the law."

Law. He acted like the badge he wore gave him the authority to do whatever he wanted. In some ways, that made him an accurate representation of the time. On a wild frontier, more than one lawman freelanced as a gunslinger or outlaw when it suited him.

"Go away. You don't have jurisdiction here." She returned to dressing. The fishnet pantyhose were another cheat. Pantyhose weren't even invented until 1959. Stockings, yes, but pantyhose? It was as if no one even researched the garments saloon girls actually wore.

"When all's said and done, maybe you'll let me buy you a whiskey at the bar. Demonstrate how grateful you are that I didn't kill you when I had the chance."

He spoke in character, but the words made her uneasy. He was one of those guys who had all the attributes of a great cover on an awful book; attractive enough to gain attention, but hiding a deeply flawed character inside. He'd asked her out every day since she joined the cast. Each time she'd said no.

She zigzagged the laces around the hooks of her granny-boots. Double knotted them, yanking the laces tight with more force than necessary.

The only thing left was a drawstring purse. She fastened the empty decorative cloth bag to her belt and stole a glance at her watch. Eleven thirty. An ungodly hour for a college senior on summer break. She dropped the timepiece into the valise and grabbed her garter. The cheap polyester lace scratched against her fingers. A red rosette hid the tiny holster like a wilting afterthought. Hurriedly, she slid it over her boot, snagging the rosette on one of the hooks. She bit back a swear word and set about untangling it.

"You listening to me?" He rapped sharply on the door.

She started and the garter tore free. A red scrap of lace clung to the hook like a droplet of blood.

"You know I have a boyfriend."

He snorted on the other side of the door, so close she checked the keyhole to make sure he couldn't see through it.

"Slim Jenkins is a skinny runt and he certainly isn't the most fearsome gun in the west if he lets a common saloon girl get the drop on him."

He knew nothing about her boyfriend. "It's a show, Shane."

"What you need is a strong man like me to take care of you."

She slammed the valise shut. "I don't recall asking you what I need, but since you seem so interested, let me make one thing perfectly clear." She opened the door so fast he took a step back. "It isn't you."

"I'm sure sorry to hear that." His eyes narrowed. "I suspect you'll be regretting them words 'fore too long."

"I'm going to pretend you didn't just threaten me. Make that mistake again, and you can explain yourself to HR."

"That'll never happen." He touched his fingers to his hat and stomped away.

Frontier Adventure, Modern Luxury

Outside the bunkhouse, the air smelled of pine and horses and Cassidy inhaled huge lungsful in an effort to calm down—or at least as much as the corset allowed. The summer afternoon rains that washed across southwestern Colorado had come and gone. Already the dirt was dry enough to kick up little dust clouds as she weaved her way past Hansen's Mercantile and toward the blacksmith's forge.

She knew better than to let Shane get under her skin, but darned if he didn't do it anyway. You'd think he owned the ranch, instead of being a cast member, apprentice blacksmith, and occasional bellhop. Cassidy had grown up on a real ranch. He wouldn't last a day.

She took another deep breath and slowly spun with her head tilted back. There was nothing like a Colorado sky seen through a screen of branches. Even Shane couldn't spoil this.

Ads for the Stagecoach Guest Ranch promised adventure, and the ranch delivered. Guests were met at the imposing wrought iron gates of the resort by one of the namesake stagecoaches. There, a cowboy took possession of their car, making a corny joke about being a reformed horse thief. An authentically bumpy stagecoach ride through pine trees and aspen groves transported guests through history, and by the time they arrived at the resort—a collection of buildings built to look like a weathered frontier boom town—they'd landed in the 1880s.

Guests checked in at the Grand Hotel, but specialty rooms were also available behind the mercantile, in leather-smelling tack rooms off the stables, on the upper floor of the saloon, and in individual cabins scattered across the property.

Cassidy cut through the bone orchard and wound her way around gravestones that sprouted like crooked teeth from the hard-packed dirt.

A boy wearing an obviously new cowboy hat called out, "Hey, Dad, listen to this one. 'Here lies Lester Moore, Four Slugs from a .44, No Les No more.'" He darted to another one and started to read it aloud.

The headstones were replicas of several found in the real Boothill Cemetery in Tombstone, Arizona. Whether Lester Moore was an actual occupant of the cemetery like the men killed in the O.K. Corral shootout, or if the witty marker was merely a ploy to draw tourists into the cemetery was yet to be established to most historians' satisfaction.

In the distance, a cloud of dust rose. The morning trail ride would be returning to the stables. She'd have to hurry, or she'd be late for the show.

The ranch Cassidy's folks owned was seventy-two acres divided between growing alfalfa and raising cattle, but it had nothing on the resort's four hundred acres snugged up against the San Juan Mountains. Here, guests could pan for gold, shoot a bow, ride horses, or participate in sanitized versions of roping (a set of longhorns protruding from a hay bale), branding (searing the resort logo into souvenir wood trivets), and moving cattle between pastures (a glorified trail ride where real cowboys did all the moving of said cattle).

For something less dusty, there were gifts to buy at the saddlery, mercantile, and blacksmith shops. Hungry folk had their choice of chuckwagon grub, gourmet game, and farm-to-table produce flavored with herbs grown in the sprawling kitchen garden. But by the end of the day, everyone ended up at the saloon.

The entire downtown served as an informal stage. Cowboys and guests rode through town and tied up their horses at various hitching posts. Stagecoaches and wagons rumbled between eras. Inside, the buildings sported frontier chic decor with modern innovations. Guests may claim to want an authentic experience, but no one liked outhouses or spotty Internet service.

A rhythmic metallic clang grew louder as Cassidy reached the entry to the blacksmith's forge. Shane barreled out of the double doors and slammed against her shoulder, knocking her off balance.

"Watch where you're going."

A very unladylike word escaped her lips, but he was already out of earshot. The calm she had worked so hard to create evaporated. Shane was a bully and bullies were dangerous.

She ducked through the door of the stone building. Smitty stood in front of an open forge at the far end of the shop. He served as both prop master and armorer, but now the muscles of his shoulders rippled with each hammer stroke as he worked a glowing piece of iron. A woman wearing her weight in turquoise jewelry leaned against the fence that kept guests from straying too close to the forge.

"You just missed the sheriff," he called out.

If only.

The woman glanced toward Cassidy, but quickly returned her attention to the sweaty blacksmith.

Cassidy entered the employee equipment room and found her Colt House Pistol waiting for her on the workbench. On a ranch, a gun was just another tool. She'd dispatched more than one rattlesnake while checking her family's irrigation ditches. This pistol was different. It was a pretty little thing, manufactured in the 1870s. Elaborate engraving swirled across the brass frame and the handle sported pearl grips. When it worked properly, the cylinder held four .41 caliber rounds and resembled a four-leaf clover—which explained why it was dubbed the Cloverleaf. And with only a one-and-a-half-inch barrel, a user would need the luck of the Irish to hit anything.

Frontier life was hazardous for anyone, but more so for women. As a saloon girl, Cassidy would have carried a single shot derringer—it was the only gun tiny enough to stay tucked in a garter. Twice now, she'd jostled the small 4-shot revolver right out of the holster when she ran across Main Street. It didn't take a rocket scientist to figure out how the cylinder had become jammed. Although for the record, it had happened before she came along.

Still, if there was one thing a person from the west could spot at a hundred paces, it was a toy gun. The history buff in her appreciated the effort the resort made to bring realism to the show.

Theater arts took considerable liberties with range-safety rules, but even blank rounds were dangerous. They didn't have a projectile *per se*, but the firing pin still created an explosion, and depending on proximity, exploding gas could be lethal.

As the armorer, Smitty prepped the guns for the daily shows, but Cassidy always performed a safety check. She'd been handling guns for years. It was habit.

The pistol had been recently polished and not a smudge marred the glinting brass. She drew the hammer back and sighted down the barrel, rotated the cylinder. The bottom of each cartridge lay flush with the edge of the cylinder. Just like they should.

Across the forge, Smitty plunged the red-hot iron in a tub of water and the sizzle of steam hissed like an angry snake. *You'll be regretting them words 'fore too long.*

Cassidy's heart beat high in her throat and she stared at the pistol in her hand for a long moment. She had to face facts. No matter how much she wanted to believe otherwise, Shane was unhinged. And she was squarely in his crosshairs.

She propped her foot on a bench and with a shaking hand, wedged the revolver into her garter holster.

The chapel bell began to toll the noon hour and she scribbled a note to Smitty.

Today's script needed a new ending and it was time to pick a fight.

It's High Noon Somewhere

The tap of Cassidy's granny boots marked her progress along the boardwalk, each step jostling the brass in the cloth purse dangling from her waist. Plenty of other costumed employees worked at the ranch, but with the exception of Shane, the gunslingers had all been plucked from the Echo Valley College theater group and had known each other for years. Smitty had once mentioned that Shane had drifted into town like a tumbleweed, but no one knew much about him. The daily frontier show was a cheesy high noon shootout where good always prevailed, hats were either black or white, and everyone got shot, but no one was ever hurt.

The midday sun beat down on Curly Joe as he sat in front of the Assayer's Office, his chair tipped back on two legs with his black cowboy hat pulled low over his face. Resort guests glanced at him as they paused to look in the window at the chunks of silver ore and gold nuggets on display, but no one disturbed his siesta.

An errant gust slapped the iron Wells Fargo Bank sign and it creaked eerily above the door of the narrow building. On the corner stood a solid adobe building with a barred window high on the wall that overlooked the street. Slim Jenkins, the most fearsome gun in the west, would be inside the cell on the other side of the jail wall, waiting for his cue.

It was as if the whole town was holding its breath. Anxious.

Sheriff McMasters leaned against the opened doorframe and eyed Cassidy as she neared. She felt her face twist with anger and struggled to wipe it clear. He grinned as he placed two fingers along the brim of his cowboy hat in a mocking salute.

Cassidy stepped into the street to give the bay mare tethered to the hitching post an apple. It wasn't in the script and she knew it would provoke him. Frankly, she didn't care. The mare's whiskers tickled her palm as the horse lipped the apple out of her hand. It was oddly reassuring. A moment of normalcy in the minutes before everything changed.

"Don't you have somewhere to be, Nellie?" His voice held an

unexpected menace and she raised herself on her tiptoes to see over the mare's shoulders. He'd taken a step toward her, his face flushed.

You'll be regretting them words 'fore too long.

"Now that you mention it, I'm late for a meeting with the devil." She patted the mare's neck, at once reluctant to leave and anxious to get away. No sense delaying. She'd made her decision.

Tinny piano music lured her across the street, and she stopped in front of the saloon.

Inside, Rusty would be slamming a sarsaparilla while sitting at the Faro table with Six-fingered Sanchez and any number of thirsty guests. He had his back to the wall, and his eye to the street, waiting to see the flounce of her petticoat that set the drama in motion. Already other employees were roping off the street behind her to give the actors their space.

"You're a stinkin' cheat!" Sanchez yelled from inside.

The piano music abruptly stopped, and the swinging doors slammed against the outside wall. Rusty crashed onto the boardwalk at Cassidy's feet, rolled twice, and came up in a crouch. "Ain't no one call me a cheat and live to tell the tale."

Guests plastered their faces to the windows. Strollers gathered closer, eager to watch the drama unfold.

Sanchez barreled onto the boardwalk. The six fingers on his right hand twitched above the handle of his gun. "I'm going to give you one chance to hightail it out of this town." He stared hard at Rusty. "And you best start before I change my mind."

More guests craned out over their balconies to watch the show. Cassidy scooped up Rusty's black hat and stepped between the two men. "That's the bottle courage talking. I'm sure we can settle this peacefully." She smacked the hat against Rusty's chest. "Step back inside. Let me buy you a drink." She turned and smiled at Sanchez. "On the house."

"Ah, Nellie," Sanchez said. "You know I can't refuse you when you smile at me all pretty-like."

Rusty snorted. "Well, if this ain't something. Ol' Six-finger's sweet on a sportin' woman."

Cassidy concentrated on not rolling her eyes. Sporting women worked in bordellos, not saloons. "You hush, Rusty," she said. "You know my heart belongs to the sheriff."

Blech. Whoever wrote this drivel should be tarred and feathered, and had obviously never met the sheriff in question.

Cassidy kept her focus on the two men in front of her, but listened for the creak of leather and scrape of metal behind her.

After all, the three of them were just the distraction while Curly Joe set up.

"Gentlemen." Cassidy put her hand to the side of her face conspiratorially and addressed the crowd. "And I use the term loosely." She faced the men again. "Today things are going to unfold a bit differently. First off, you're going to have to behave yourselves."

Members of the crowd chuckled. Rusty and Sanchez exchanged confused looks.

"There's big changes about to take place," she continued. "And when the unexpected happens, I'm going to need your help."

Sanchez was the first to play along with the new script. "You know I'll do anything for you, Nellie."

Rusty opened his mouth to speak when a gunshot drew everyone's attention to the middle of the street. More people crowded the sidewalk to watch the show.

Curly Joe sat astride the bay mare holding his six-shooter in the air and cranked off another round. A rope stretched between the jail window bars and his saddle horn. With a mighty "Yah!" he spurred the bay forward. The window popped out of the wall and bounced into the dirt.

Slim Jenkins wiggled free from his cell and landed with a resounding thud on the boardwalk, his hat firmly adhered to his head.

Under cover of the commotion, Cassidy leaned close to Rusty's ear and whispered, "Bring the extra horse."

His brows furrowed, but he nodded.

Slim planted his hands on his hips and drew in a dramatic breath of freedom as he surveyed the crowd. "Whoo-ee! About time. I couldn't handle another night in the pokey."

A boy behind Cassidy announced. "He's a bad man. Look at his hat. The sheriff needs to do something!"

As if summoned by the child, Sheriff McMaster appeared in the doorway of the jail, his white Stetson a beacon against the dark interior.

This was Cassidy's cue to run across the street to warn the sheriff—as if the gunshot, window demolition, and Curly Joe's ruckus wasn't enough to alert a lawman that something was awry. It also allowed Cassidy to move the grappling hook and window to safety before more horses entered the story.

"Sheriff McMasters! There's been a jailbreak!" she shouted, just in case anyone in the audience harbored any lingering confusion about what had just happened.

Curly Joe wheeled the mare around and tossed a gun belt to

Slim who slung it around his hips.

Cassidy timed her steps onto the boardwalk to coincide with Slim drawing his gun. Seriously, whoever scripted the production severely underestimated the ability of dance hall girls to sniff out danger and avoid it. She readied herself to be bumped from behind. Last time, her boyfriend had been a bit too enthusiastic and nearly bowled her over.

Sheriff McMasters raised his pistol. "Stop in the name of the law!"

Slim grabbed Cassidy around the waist with his left hand and raised his right arm and pointed his prairie pistol at the sheriff. Tactically speaking, it was a terrible way to try to control a hostage. She'd grown up with four older brothers; she'd been training for something like this her whole life. A hard granny heel to the shin as a distraction, sweep the gun, leverage the barrel, *et violà*. She could strip the gun out of Slim's grasp before he could even say ouch.

But Slim wasn't the problem. Shane was. She summoned her best damsel in distress voice. "Sheriff! Save me!" Even she heard the sarcasm. Good thing she was an historian first and an actress second.

"We don't want no trouble, Law Dog," Curly Joe shouted. "Go back inside, no one gets hurt."

McMasters hunkered behind a water trough. In theory, his pistol was aimed at Slim, but Cassidy knew she was the target. *You'll be regretting them words 'fore too long* she heard, even as he said, "Let her go."

"I don't think we'll do that," Slim said. "Seems to me, she's our ticket out of this here town."

"I'm not going to let anything happen to Nellie."

A bald-faced lie if she'd ever heard one.

He continued, "You boys need to do the clean thing, and lay down your guns. Turn yourselves in."

A thundering of hooves neared. Six-finger Sanchez and Rusty careened around the corner on horseback, each holding the reins of a riderless horse.

The sheriff darted to the doorway of the jail, still pointing his gun toward Slim. "You don't want to be no fugitive from the law, Slim. You get on that horse, I'll hunt you down like the dog you are."

"No offense, Sheriff, but I find your hospitality somewhat lacking."

This was the point in the show when Cassidy was supposed to sidestep with Slim toward the horses. From an impossible angle, the sheriff would save the day by winging Slim. Freed, Nellie would hide behind a wagon. Sanchez and Rusty would enter the fray with much tucking and rolling across the ground, shooting from behind cover until the rest of the blanks were used up in a loud free-for-all that thrilled the guests and left three outlaws on the ground. Just as Slim was about to get the drop on the sheriff, Nellie was supposed to use her one shot to kill Slim before he shot the sheriff.

The horses would inevitably make their way to the flowerbed in front of the mercantile and snack until someone collected them. As a denouement, Nellie was supposed to proclaim the sheriff her hero, express her undying love, blah, blah, blah. The historian in her wanted to weep.

Fortunately, this was not that day.

Instead, Cassidy planted a kiss on Slim's cheek. "There's no use hiding it anymore." She addressed Shane. "Sheriff, I know you think I'm sweet on you. But I'm not. In fact, despite all your pestering, I never was. My heart belongs to Slim Jenkins and everyone knows you've wronged him by locking him up when it was you who rustled them cattle off Teague's Ranch."

"Nellie, what in tarnation is going on? You love me." The sheriff spoke evenly, but his face shone with malice.

"I'm exposing you for the yellow-bellied liar you are." She faced her boyfriend and spoke quietly. "I love you. I need you to trust me on this." She squeezed his hand before projecting for the audience again. "Grab the horses, darling. The sheriff and I have some unfinished business." She leaned over and withdrew the small pistol from her garter. When she came up, she straightened her arm and pointed the gun at Shane's chest.

He blanched. "Now hold on. What's got into you?"

"It's not what's in me you need to worry yourself over." She narrowed the distance between them, but stopped well out of reach.

"I'm sheriff of this town."

She drew back the hammer. "Don't make me ask twice."

"Wait, wait, wait!" He stooped down and placed his gun on the ground. "You're making a big mistake."

"Explain to me how, exactly?"

Shane closed his fist around a handful of dirt and his legs tensed.

Cassidy took the slack out of the trigger. "I wouldn't do that if I were you."

He clenched his fist tighter, then emptied his hand and held them both in the air.

"Get up," she said.

Shane scrambled to his feet. For a second Cassidy thought he was going to try to rush her. Slim must have thought so, too, because he came up beside her. Curly Joe, Rusty, and Sanchez weren't far behind.

"Cattle rustlers don't deserve to wear a badge," she said. "*You* aren't worthy. Take it off."

His jaw clenched, but he unpinned the tin star and threw it in the dust at her feet.

She picked it up with her free hand and cleaned the dirt off against her skirt. "Now you're going to step into that jail and set yourself down in an empty cell. And before you get any bright ideas, it'll be the one without the window."

People in the crowd laughed.

"You ain't no better than them other outlaws," he shouted. "And I'll see to it you swing right next to them 'fore this is out." Tears brightened his eyes. "I loved you, and you done betrayed me." He wagged a finger at her. "I've got a long memory and you'll pay, Nellie. You'll pay."

"Uh-huh." Still, she had to give him props for staying in character.

She looked past Shane. At the end of the block, Smitty signaled her. A sense of relief flooded her body. He'd gotten her note.

"Quit flapping your gums." She jerked her head toward the jail door. "Go on."

Shane didn't budge.

Sanchez stepped his considerable bulk forward. "You heard the lady."

Rusty laughed. "Dude, did you not hear? She just declared her love for Slim, you moron. And to think you caught me counting cards. I'm losing my edge."

Sanchez sniffed. "Never much cared for the sheriff, that's all."

Cassidy motioned with the gun and Shane backed into the jail.

Rusty wrapped up the show. "Ladies and gentlemen, you're witnessing the very first time a saloon girl arrested a lawman." The crowd erupted in applause as Cassidy followed Shane into the building. She lowered the hammer, but didn't dare lower the gun until he was in the cell. Sanchez scooted around her and locked the cell door.

Cassidy placed her hand on Sanchez's thick arm. "Will you give us a minute?"

Shane leaped at the bars, gripping them so tightly his knuckles whitened. "Don't leave me here, Sanchez. She's crazy."

"Geez, what am I going to do, shoot him?" She rolled her eyes. "I'll be out for the autograph session in a couple minutes."

Sanchez headed for the door. "Holler if you need anything."

"Will do."

After he'd left, she stepped closer to the bars. The cloth purse hanging from her belt swayed and the contents jingled in the quiet. She turned the pistol over in her hands. So pretty. Potentially so deadly.

"This is kidnapping, you know." Shane rattled the bars. "I'll have you arrested."

"Not if you meet with an unfortunate accident first." She shrugged. "Of course, I don't know how I'd live with myself if you came to harm." Darned if she didn't hear sarcasm again. She really needed to work on that. "Why'd you do it?"

"I don't know what you're talking about."

"Have it your way." In one smooth move, she raised the pistol, drew the hammer back, and took the slack out of the trigger.

He threw himself onto the metal cot and curled into a ball, wrapping his arms around his head. "Don't shoot! It's loaded. Please." He started to cry. "You didn't even give us a chance. We would have been great together. Please. Don't shoot."

"You're an idiot." She pulled the trigger.

Click.

He flinched, and then looked up in disbelief.

"I wouldn't waste a bullet on you." She shook her purse over the desk and the brass rounds rolled across the surface and clinked as they fell to the floor.

You'll be regretting them words 'fore too long. If he thought he could have gotten away with it, she had no doubt he'd have loaded real bullets in his own gun. Instead, he'd loaded them in hers, and then waited for her to shoot her boyfriend.

"Did you really think I wouldn't do a safety check? Not notice you fixed the cylinder? Shined the darn thing until it was spotless?"

"It's my word against yours, stupid."

Cassidy pulled out the desk chair, and sat. "That's the difference between us. My word means something." She leaned back in the chair and pointed to the surveillance camera in the left corner above the door.

"You ever hear of Kate Warne of the Pinkerton National Detective Agency?" She noted his blank expression and added, "First female detective—eighteen fifty." She crossed her ankles. The granny boots had grown on her. "Or how about Phoebe Couzins, the first woman appointed as a U.S. Marshal? Still nothing? F.M. Miller? She rode alongside her male counterparts as a Deputy Marshal in Texas."

"What's your point, Nellie?"

Smitty escorted two deputies into the jail.

"My name is Cassidy." She smiled at the newcomers. "And I'm here to tell you there's a new sheriff in town."

MARY-ALICE IMAGINES HER LIFE AS A MOVIE
By Karen Cantwell

*Mary-Alice knows agents. She knows "the face" and
"the line." She's seen and heard them often enough.
Maybe this time she'll do something about them.*

OPENING SCENE, EXTERIOR PRISON YARD - DAY

An unforgiving August sun beats down on me as I shuffle in
the gravel yard. Someone, somewhere shouts, "Where's Mary-
Alice? I'll get her for this!" Maybe I should be worried, but I'm
not. I'm wearing orange these days, same as all the ladies around
me. My life since that day in 1986, well, it hasn't been easy, but
what are you gonna do? Keep going, I guess. Keep shuffling along.

DISSOLVE TO FLASHBACK, INTERIOR, AN OFFICE

I'm leaning back in the over-stuffed chair, but nothing about
me is relaxed. No amount of fluff can cushion the blow that feels
inevitable at this point. I consider the knife in my purse and wonder
if I have the nerve to follow through.

His name is Cyril Broadstone and he has small, slimy hands. I
don't know that for a fact because he didn't have the courtesy to
shake mine when I entered, but I figure they're slimy. Like the rest
of him. Like all of them. Talent agents. The mosquitoes of L.A. are
soul-sucking nuisances. But without one, sorry folks, no ticket on
the Tinsel Town Express.

A colossal desk separates us. I don't know a thing about wood
so maybe it's cherry or oak or redwood. The thing is polished to a
high sheen and seems as big as a coffin—that's all I know. He
fidgets mindlessly with a cheap retractable pen while inspecting the
résumé on the back of my headshot. The pen clicks open and shut,
open and shut, open and shut. I scan the framed movie posters on
his walls, all current films: *Back to the Future*, *The Breakfast Club*,
Top Gun, *Pretty in Pink*. Below the *Pretty in Pink* poster is a film
still of James Spader, autographed, *Be real. Jimmy*. I have no idea
if Cyril represents actors in these films or not, but on closer
inspection of the Spader still, I realize Cyril has matched Jimmy's
wardrobe piece for piece and feathered his hair in the same manner.

Finally, the pen is dropped, the headshot is dropped, and he clasps his hands in front of him on the coffin-desk. And, as expected, Cyril gives me *the face*. The problem with *the face* is, it's always followed by *the line*. See, I've been in chairs like this before, in rooms like this before, with postered walls like this before, in front of self-important dogs like this. All before.

The scenario goes as such: after the requisite résumé inspection, agent takes a moment, then puts on *the face*. The lips are pressed thin, the eyes go a little soft around the edges, three concerned wrinkles form on the forehead. It seems *the face* is meant to ease the impending agony.

Once agent has assumed *the face*, he or she delivers *the line*. It's always the same. There must be a manual out there where agents practice and repeat until perfect: "Listen…" (Long pause, sometimes a bit of a sigh thrown in to feign sympathy.) "I'm not going to sugarcoat it for you."

So anyway, Cyril gives me *the face*. I brace myself for *the line*. I picture the knife in my purse. It's sharp. It'll do the job.

He winces. "Mary-Beth. Not the best name. Have you considered changing it?"

Knocked dumb by surprise, but relieved that *the face* wasn't followed by *the line*, I find my voice. "Um, it's Mary-Alice. And I changed it already. I used to be Alice-Mary."

He doesn't get the joke or doesn't care. "What is your goal as an actress? Where do you see yourself?"

I'm growing more comfortable with Cyril. Maybe I don't want to stab his heart to shreds. His demeanor is still condescending, but he's asking me meaningful questions. "Movies or television, but I want to do comedy. Humor is my passion."

"You don't give off a funny vibe," he says.

"My clown suit is at the cleaners."

He doesn't laugh. I don't think he understands humor. Clearly, I'm funny as hell.

He spins his chair around to stare out the window behind him. The arrogance galls me. Forget the knife. I imagine myself vaulting over the desk and shoving him through the window in one swift move. I look down to see his rude-man body sprawled on the sidewalk, broken to pieces from the twelve-story fall. Comediennes from around the world, wrongly accused of funny vibe deficiency, applaud my bravura.

As I stare at the back of his chair, I wonder if I should talk to sell myself better, or keep quiet. I decide selling myself is the better option. That's what this crazy town is about after all—artistic prostitution. I'm about to mention my improv troupe and invite him to our next performance. *We've been well-reviewed*, I'll tell him.

Only he spins back around before the words are out.

"Listen…" he begins.

Crap on a cracker. Here it comes.

"I'm not going to sugarcoat it for you."

The pocket of hope is gone. A lump forms in my throat—that happens when I fight back tears.

He keeps it coming. "You're not attractive enough for film or television. That's just how it is. Maybe, and I'm just saying maybe, the best you're ever going to get are commercials playing some kid's mom."

Whoa. He *really* didn't sugar-coat it. At least the other agents were a little gentler. One told me, "You just don't have the look." Another said, "Honey, you look like every other young woman who walks in my door and I need a look that stands out. Nothing personal." Not Cyril. He hits me hard. Translation: *You're ugly, but not so ugly that you can't play haggard old women beaten down by ground-in stains on their son's white baseball uniforms.*

I want to respond. Surely, I should argue the point, but I can't. The lump is a rock now. A boulder preventing me from defending myself. The words are stuck in my head: *I'm only twenty-one and my mother tells me how beautiful I am every day, and oh by the way, stop trying to look like James Spader, you tiny, pesky mosquito man!*

I came into this meeting feeling very Norma Desmond, and yes, I know Norma kills her man with a gun, but frankly, guns scare me, so hence, the knife. But, as I ponder that knife and my future and the story that will be told about me, another hero comes to mind. Dirty Harry. Norma is desperate. I don't want to be desperate. Harry is smooth.

I want to be smooth.

Cyril stirs uncomfortably in his chair since I haven't said a word. "So, I'm sorry, but—"

"Go ahead," I say, cutting him off.

"What?"

"Go ahead. Do it." I unzip my purse and wrap my fingers around the knife.

FADE OUT

FADE IN FLASHFORWARD, EXTERIOR, PRISON YARD - DAY

I wipe sweat from my brow. This heat is killing me. I'm not sure how much more of this I can stand. Gravel dust makes me cough. Someone, somewhere shouts again, "I said, where's Mary-Alice?"

Of course, it's not just someone, it's Cyril. He likes to visit the shoots on occasion, and when he does, I always set up a good practical joke to get him good. Today I had a stagehand put a rubber finger in his coffee. Poor Cyril. He has no sense of humor even after all of these years.

Bette, the assistant director, tells me to get back to makeup and get my face fixed. We'll do a few more takes on the prison yard set and call it a day. Of the fifty-two commercials that I've made as Gotcha Gabby, for Grime Away laundry detergent, the conditions on this fake prison set have been the worst. I won't complain though. As a recent article in the *Los Angeles Times* reported, I'm worth a cool five million dollars while I continue to "keep people laughing all the way to store shelves."

I get to makeup and a young intern there is excited to clean my chair before I sit. Her hunger for this town is fresh, I can tell. We chat. She's surprised I've been acting in commercials since 1987 and honestly stunned when I say I'll be fifty-five in two days.

"How did you make your way into this business?" she asks me.

"I brought a knife to an interview with my now agent, Cyril Broadstone."

"A knife?" Her eyes are wide. "You're kidding."

"Not kidding."

DISSOLVE TO FLASHBACK CONTINUED, INTERIOR, CYRIL'S OFFICE

"Go ahead. Do it." I unzip my purse and wrap my fingers around the knife. "Sign me. I dare you. I'll do commercials. I'll be the best, smartest, hardest working, most lucrative commercial actress you need me to be."

"You dare me?"

I sense his interest under a veil of disquiet. I press on. "I dare you."

He narrows his gaze, picks up the pen again, clicks it open, clicks it shut. Our eyes are locked. My hand clutches the knife still.

"I sell knives," I say finally. I'm lying. I don't sell knives. But I'm gonna sell this one.

He's hooked. "You mean like door to door?"

"Yeah. A struggling actress has to make money somehow, right? I keep one in my purse—for when I ride the bus at night. Protection." I place the serrated steak knife on the coffin-desk. "If I sell you this knife right now, you represent me."

SLOW FADE OUT

FADE IN, GOTCHA GABBY COMMERCIALS MONTAGE, MARY-ALICE VOICEOVER

Gotcha Gabby was born on the spot that night to help me sell Cyril Broadstone a Gitchi-Gazu kitchen knife. Soon, we all went on to sell millions of boxes and bottles of Grime Away laundry detergent. People recognize me on the street, take smiley selfies with me. They laugh at my thirty-second antics. I'm that crazy old friend that's been welcome in their home for years. I'm funny. I'm happy. I'm safe.

Yet the fact is, I walked into that first meeting with Cyril ready and willing to kill him.

Mark Twain once said, "Everyone is a moon, and has a dark side which he doesn't show to anybody."

What I say is, that everyone has a face, and everyone has a line.

Mark and I, we're speaking the same truth.

Listen… I'm not going to sugarcoat it for you.

FADE TO BLACK

THE GHOST OF HAMNET
By R. M. Chastleton

*Asked to write about a deadly fall at the theater, Ham
Laurence finds himself revisiting a place he had
shunned and questioning the cause of another death.*

"They want me to write about a mystery involving the theater?"
Ham Laurence leaned back into the red leather corner banquette
seat that reminded him of his worn-out Doc Martens. "Hasn't that
trope been done to death, so to speak?"

Ham took a long sip from his gin and tonic, the first in his
evening routine in the dark NoHo bar: consume at least one too
many while sneering at obviously underaged NYU students trying
to hoodwink the bartender (rarely successful) and tourists trying to
order food as though this was a British pub (never successful), as
he made a valiant attempt at a freelance writing career (sometimes
successful). Annabella Finnegan, his part-time girlfriend and a full-
time writer at the *Manhattan Monthly* magazine, sat across the
table from him in his de facto evening office space.

"Seriously, Ham," Annabella said, pushing a thick strand of
curly hair out of her eyes. "My editor has specifically requested
you by name to write an article about that actress who fell to her
death two weeks ago from the roof at the Gotham Theater.
Apparently, she was his niece and no one really knows what
happened. He just wants some answers."

"And to sell more magazines. So, he sent you to convince me to
figure it out. What's the play anyway?" Ham searched the Internet
on his open laptop as Annabella craned her neck to look. "*Field of
Hamlet*? Dear Lord, it's a Shakespearean parody about the New
York Yankees. 'Kill him and they will come.' I'd probably jump
off the roof too after acting in it."

"Don't be such a theater snob. With your background, you'd be
the perfect person to investigate."

"Because I'm a former cop? Or because my father used to run
the Gotham and you think I can still get backstage?"

"You have to admit you bring a provenance to the topic."

Ham took a long drink as Annabella ran her finger along the
rim of her glass of cheap merlot while trying to persuade Ham with
her most enchanting gaze.

"First, if I remember correctly, there was no evidence of homicide or malfeasance. Probably just another unwise selfie attempt." He was impressed that he still could pronounce the word malfeasance after imbibing his generously poured drink. "Second, I haven't been back to the Gotham in over five years when my sisters and I finally escaped our father's downward vortex." Vortex was another complex word. Ham was on a roll. "I swore I'd never go back. And I haven't yet. Not even when he died."

"Your father fell off a balcony there six months ago, didn't he?" she asked. "Come to think of it, their deaths sound strangely similar."

"He was a drunk and it was only a matter of time," he said, looking at the glass in his hand while noting the irony. "Not suspicious or surprising. Maybe only shocking that it hadn't occurred earlier."

"There's more here, something sinister." Annabella leaned across the table. "This actress had just landed a huge role on Broadway. Why end it all now? She didn't even have a trace of alcohol in her blood."

"What was left of her blood," Ham said, having been to enough suicides as a cop to know what the effects of a plunge from the top of a building were to the human body. Though the Gotham Theater was only three stories high, the concrete below was not a forgiving host.

"Fine. Don't do it. But you're not staying at my place when you can't make rent."

"Okay, okay," he capitulated. "I don't have any other pressing assignments. I'll go to a show, ingratiate myself with the cast, see what I can find out. I'll write something. It might be about a murder, it might be a review of a disastrous play."

"Great. I'll let him know."

She gave him a quick kiss and left him to brood.

Ham swirled his glass, now only filled with ice. He had intended to stay sober for the month. Save some money and his liver. He assured himself he wasn't addicted, like his father. He just had an issue with self-control. Impulsively downing multiple drinks a night. Regretting it the next morning. Swearing he would never do it again. Then, when presented with a similar opportunity that evening, repeating the torture. He had the same problem with Cadbury Creme Eggs.

Self-control was his weakness. He intended to work on it.

Cursing his return to the Gotham, he rubbed his day-old stubble and the prematurely graying hair on his head. Ham figured that there would be plenty of tickets still available for the eight o'clock show, as there always had been years ago. His bottomless brown eyes scanned those around him one last time, looking for an excuse to not go. Seeing none, he stashed his computer in his fraying messenger bag and pulled on his faded leather jacket. He gave a wink to the bartender while settling his tab and turned down Bleecker Street toward the Bowery. As much as he dreaded returning to his childhood haunt, he needed that paycheck more. And the *Manhattan Monthly* paid well.

On the way, Ham called an old buddy, Detective Joey Peralta, at the 9th Precinct for any details that hadn't been broadcast in the news. It was good to have connections.

"This is all off the record, understand?" Detective Peralta continued without waiting for a response. "Coroner ruled Sophie Beale's death a suicide. No alcohol in her blood. No cell phone or note on her person. According to the director and another actress, she had been depressed. She wasn't happy with her performance and didn't get a role in an upcoming play. You know how moody these artistic types can be."

"Yes, I do," Ham agreed. "I owe you."

Ham immediately picked up on the discrepancy about Sophie's future on Broadway but understood the need to exaggerate to family about one's professional success.

The Gotham Theater was located in the heart of the East Village just off the Bowery and down the block from the former nightclub CGBG before it became a trendy clothing store. The neighborhood protested its gentrification: brick walls covered in graffiti memorializing Blondie and Basquiat were surrounded by art galleries and million-dollar apartments. The theater, an old Vaudeville relic, continued to showcase experimental and avant-garde productions as well as punk rock concerts.

Ham entered the Gotham, shocked at how familiar it still felt and how nothing had changed. The black walls and exposed industrial pipes were plastered with randomly placed posters and stickers. A threadbare red carpet led into the auditorium. The Clash thumped over the loudspeakers.

At the box office, the ticketing agent recognized him and gave him a fist bump.

"Hey, man, long time no see! You chose a good night to return. This will be the first show since that incident a few weeks ago."

He handed Ham his ticket and playbill. As he glanced at them, Ham noticed that his former college roommate, Nate Berkshire, was the playwright. Hopefully, he'd run into Nate later.

"So tragic. I'm sorry I never got to know her."

"On the bright side, we sold out tonight for the first time ever.

You got the last ticket."

Ham wanted to talk to him more about "that incident," but the dimming of the lights indicated that the play was starting soon.

"Come to our backstage party afterwards. You're practically family. Everyone would love to see you again."

Ham accepted his invitation and, after excusing himself to find his seat, relaxed in his realization that this assignment might be easier than he thought. Mingle at the party, get some free booze, overhear some gossip, and then go home and write it all up. If it was just a suicide as the police concluded, Ham was sure that there was plenty of theatrical drama he could wax poetically about.

The five-act play concluded with the Yankees star attacking Laertes, the Chicago Cubs pitcher, with a poisoned bat in the World Series. Ham rolled his eyes, relieved that the Shakespearean sacrilege was finally over, and waited until the audience filtered out to make his way unimpeded behind the stage.

As he wove through actors dressed as baseball players and crew members clad in black t-shirts and Converse high tops, it struck him that no one was smiling. That's not how he remembered it in the past when there were always thankful celebrations of another job well done.

Sophie Beale's death appeared to be casting a pall over everyone.

Ham always felt at home at the Gotham. His father devoted all of his time to writing and directing plays here. Ham and his two sisters joined him after school, learning all about the stage. The Gotham later served as a refuge after their mother walked out on the family. His father, hit hard, spent the subsequent years drowning himself in alcohol. Ham carried him home more than a few times. When they were old enough, the Laurence siblings exited stage left one by one, vowing never to return to the Gotham—and their father—to avoid reopening old wounds. But here he was doing just that.

"Ham Laurence! It's been forever since I saw you last. At a creative writing workshop at NYU five, six years ago, wasn't it?"

Ham smiled as Nate Berkshire, tall and lanky and dressed in impossibly skinny jeans, an indigo blazer, and matching square glasses, emerged from a gaggle of baseball players and bear-hugged him.

"Congratulations! Interesting concept for a play. I was curious how it was going to be pulled off." Ham struggled to get his words out with a straight face, not wanting to mock it in front of the whole theater company.

Nate eagerly led Ham to a group congregating in the back of

the stage whose nods and smiles eliminated any need for formal introductions. In the center stood a tall, thick man wearing an expensively tailored suit. He looked out of place, like a former professional football player who had bought the team after retirement and was visiting the locker room. "You remember Mason Bryce, our theater manager?"

"The prodigal son returns," Mason said, extending his meaty paw to Ham. While his mouth smiled, his eyes glared in derision. "Mr. Laurence, what are you doing back here?"

"Weren't you just the accountant when I left?"

"I took over after your father died. Being competent and committed leads to success. You should try it," Mason said. "I understand you quit the NYPD after graduating NYU with high honors in English. Delayed teenage angst?"

"You could say that."

"What a waste. But you've always been so melodramatic."

"I'm a freelance writer now, so I'm taking full advantage of my melodramatic angst. Thank you very much."

Attempting to break the tension, the actress who played Gertrude offered them red plastic cups of cheap Prosecco.

"I don't touch the stuff," Mason said, waving her off. "No drugs, no alcohol. I need to stay mentally focused at all times."

Too bad Mason's midsection did not evidence his abstinence, Ham thought as he happily accepted the rejected cup in addition to his own. Ham's attention caught on Miranda Alvarez, the actress who played Ophelia, while toasting the actors surrounding him. As he sipped from one of his cups, his eyes slowly drank in her aggressive sensuality, entranced by her long dark hair and curvaceous body which spilled out of her costume. Miranda cocked her head, relishing his attention.

Self-control. He reminded himself of Annabella to break from her spell. Self-control.

Ham turned to Tony, an old scenic designer standing next to him. "I'm so sorry about Sophie."

"Thank you. She was the biggest star we ever had and brought a lot of acclaim to our productions. She will be missed."

Miranda rolled her eyes.

"How are your sisters?" Tony asked.

"Susannah is acting in noir plays in Copenhagen and Judith is in Hollywood writing scripts."

"I'm glad the theatre has stayed in the family blood since William's passing."

"Excuse me. Your father was William Laurence, Gotham's former artistic director and Shakespearean expert?" Miranda asked

Ham, deducing his pedigree and attempting to regain his attention. "You are Ham and your sisters are Susannah and Judith? Aren't they the names of—"

"Shakespeare's children. Yes, Ham is short for Hamnet. My father thought it would be funny to name us after them. A regular riot, he was. Hamnet *Shakespeare* died at age eleven. But I have survived to at least twenty-seven in spite of myself. So, there you go."

"If you keep hanging around this place, you might not see twenty-eight," the dark bearded musical director interrupted as he walked through the crowd carrying a trumpet. "The life expectancy of our company is dropping precipitously, like the paint chips and ceiling tiles here."

"Oh, please," Miranda said. "I don't know why everyone is so torn up. She wasn't a very good actress. I told her that all of the time including right after her opening night performance. She obviously couldn't handle the truth."

"Show some respect," Tony said. "You've been here, what, four weeks? Yet you act like you run the place."

"I'm not saying anything new. She was turned down for a role on Broadway."

"She told you that?" Ham asked. "I heard she got the part."

"I learned otherwise from some colleagues on Broadway," Mason said. "Ms. Beale wanted to leave the company but couldn't get another job. Sadly, she really wasn't as good as everyone here thought."

"She didn't get along with Mason," Miranda said. "Though he was always looking out for her best interests. If she had been smart, she would've listened to him."

Mason led the actress away, his hand briefly circled quite low around her waist with ease and familiarity. She did not flinch, but leaned into him, looking up with wide, adoring eyes. Ham was relieved to be free from the two and the mood eased considerably among the group. While Ham was certain there was some obvious quid pro quo'ing going on between the pair, Miranda had the most to gain from Sophie's suicide. Not exactly the most reliable or empathetic witness, Miranda had told the same story to the police, so at least she was consistent. It was clear that the others didn't agree with their assessment of Sophie.

Ham and Nate emerged through the curtains onto the empty stage and sat down with their legs dangling over the edge. They toasted together and Ham reverently tipped his plastic cup to the second-floor balcony from where his father had fallen. Red velvet topped the balcony's wooden rail and balustrade with matching curtains framing a sea of red seats. Theaters were not made like this anymore and Ham predicted it wouldn't last much longer with rents skyrocketing. At least his father died in the place he loved the most.

"What were you thinking writing this travesty?" Ham said after a long quaff. "I'm sorry, I know this was a big accomplishment for you. But *Field of Hamlet* is such a departure from your previous existential work."

"I know," Nate said. "Your dad encouraged me to write it to expand my repertoire into Shakespearean parody. If he were around to help finish it, he would've made it better."

"He would've burned it. When did you start working here anyway?"

"Your dad took me in after you left, probably to atone for pushing you away."

"Oh, I don't think he really cared about me, only about drinking himself to death. He couldn't even make it to our college graduation, remember?"

"He seriously regretted that. He gave up booze and joined AA after you stopped talking to him."

Ham stared up at the balcony, sorry that he missed his father's transformation.

"He always sat up there while watching rehearsals," Ham broke the silence. "Claimed it gave him a clearer view of what the audience saw. You said he was sober? He must have relapsed."

"He didn't. I honestly don't understand how it happened. He had a fear of heights. Why would he be leaning over the edge? The police didn't ask me, so I didn't get to tell them he was definitely not drinking that day."

"But he reeked of vodka. The police never conducted a blood-alcohol test since he was a known drunk. Maybe they should have."

While on the force, Ham read the police report. A terrorist attack in Midtown prevented his father's death from being given its proper attention. Bad accident. Open and shut. Move on.

"Now that he's gone, the Gotham has gone downhill. Mason arrogantly runs the theater like a tyrant. His choice of productions has been poor and he barks at all of the actors for not being good enough. There's never been enough money for props or improvements, but it's gotten worse recently. I just overheard him on the phone complaining about super high interest loans coming due. He is always threatening to sell the theater. I don't know how much longer it can go on like this."

"What do you know about Sophie's death?"

"Not much," he said. "She was particularly in his crosshairs, getting criticized for everything. Mason favored Miranda, who overacts most of the time and has a piss poor work ethic, but she fills out her dresses better, I guess. Sophie was the better actress by far."

"What happened just before Sophie fell?"

"After the show, she had a fight with Mason backstage and ran out in a ripped skirt yelling that he was making a big mistake treating her like this. I don't know, maybe he told her she was being replaced. She actually did a great job that night, the perfect Ophelia. Next thing I hear is that, well...." Nate looked at him. "Ham, you need to come back. We could collaborate like old times and save this place."

Nate and Ham stood, looking for someplace to stash their empty cups. A member of the lighting crew pulled Nate aside to ask about how to better direct the spotlight during the final scene.

"The garbage is off stage," a voice boomed out from behind the curtain.

"Why aren't you with everyone else?" Ham asked, peeking through an opening to find a stagehand climbing up a ladder.

"I have work to do," he said. "Too busy for celebrations."

"Sorry about that, you should have help."

"Not enough money in the budget. Do more with less, I'm told. It's the same every night. It's not like anyone notices when I'm around anyway, only when I'm not. Mason chewed me out for missing opening night when my son was born. Maybe it was a good thing I wasn't working. He probably would've made me clean up the mess afterwards."

"Were you here when my—when William Laurence died?"

"Sure was. I heard him arguing with Mason earlier in the day, which was not unusual because no one gets along with Mason."

"They were fighting about what? Do you remember?"

"William warned him to keep his hands to himself or else he was going to the police with some kind of proof. It's no secret Mason flirts with the actresses, and I know he's getting it on with Miranda. Maybe he went a little too far with Sophie."

Ham knew that his father avoided confrontation at all cost. If he did have it out with Mason, it would not be surprising that he started drinking afterwards.

Ham left the stagehand and snuck into one of the back rooms that was lined on either side with wheeled clothing racks jammed with costumes. Ham ran his hand along the fabrics. The costume designer, a woman with purple hair and a nose ring, appeared from behind one of racks.

"There are some good memories here, Kirstie."

"Like that time back between the dresses?"

"You were my first." Ham blushed.

"I could tell." Kirstie briefly returned the smile. "Ham, why are you back?"

"I'm writing a story for the *Manhattan Monthly* about the death of Sophie Beale." Ham felt he could trust Kirstie with the truth. "Do you think she committed suicide?"

"Poor thing." Kirstie's face fell. "She was so unhappy a year ago. Once, when I was fitting her for a dress, a big pink frilly thing, she totally broke down crying."

"Because she had to wear a hideous costume?"

"No, she wouldn't let that stop her from immersing herself in her role. She said that Mason kept trying to force himself on her. I told her that was illegal, and she needed to tell your father. Maybe he'd fire him. I guess he confronted Mason, because it didn't happen again."

"That's surprising Dad would do that."

"You know, your father was a good man."

"How was Sophie on opening night?"

"She was elated. She confided to me that she got a part on Broadway and had signed a contract for a really expensive new apartment. Anyway, she was planning to tell Mason after the show that she was leaving. Later, I heard that the role had been given to someone else. I don't know what could have happened in the meantime, but the news must've devastated her."

"I can't even imagine."

The electricity that had flowed through Ham as an awkward sixteen-year-old making out with the twenty-year-old costume designer shot once again down his spine.

"Wanna go explore behind the dresses again for old times' sake?" Ham smiled, blushing again.

"Sorry, I'd love to, but I'm married now."

"That's okay, I was just kidding anyway," Ham said, backtracking. Annabella would go ballistic if she heard he'd hit on Kirstie.

"Do me a favor?" Kirstie said as she hugged him. "Do Sophie proud in your article. She didn't deserve her fate."

Ham returned backstage and watched as Mason and Miranda moved through the crew. Mason caught Ham staring and shot him a warning glance to stay away: this was his domain now.

Wanting nothing to do with any turf battles, Ham eased down the aisle toward the exit. Near the front doors, he recognized an usher cleaning up. His dark hair was now silver streaked, and his thin, bony hands gripped the top of a seat in the last row as he righted himself. The years had not been kind to him.

"Just getting ready for a tour of some VIPs tomorrow. If I were them, I'd stay away." He leaned in close to Ham. "This place is cursed."

"Cursed?"

"I've seen too much. I was one of the first to find Sophie's body. It was so sad to see her broken like that. She wasn't a diva at all, unlike some others around here. She always talked to me. In fact, just the day before she died, she helped me straighten up the front of the house for another tour by these same executives. I wouldn't be surprised if that shady Mason Bryce was involved."

"Why do you say that?"

"When your father died, God rest his soul, Mason told the police that he had been up there alone during rehearsals. But I saw Mason rushing down the stairs from the balcony after he fell, shoving a book and a bottle of vodka in his briefcase. I just figured they were celebrating their new play. It must have been a wild party, vodka was spilled all over the floor. You know, back in the day your dad could drink anyone under the table."

"Unfortunately, I remember those days too well."

The old man yawned. Ham was growing tired, too.

"It's getting late," Ham said. "I should let you finish so you can get home. Take care of yourself."

Wanting to be alone, Ham ducked into the side staircase and climbed until he reached the roof. He dropped his messenger bag, relieved of the physical but not emotional weight that had been pressing on his shoulders all night. He looked out along the skyline. The East Village was like the crease in an opened book: squat brownstones with glittering skyscrapers surrounding it to the north and south. New York City was in his blood and he couldn't run away from it like his sisters had. But after tonight, he regretted abandoning everyone here. He swore he was going to accurately portray what was going on at the Gotham in his article.

Ham leaned over the side of the building, gazing at where Sophie had landed below. He tried to piece the story together to understand how she became so depressed to believe that jumping was her only option. But things weren't adding up, too many questions were still unanswered.

There was no consensus among the crew about whether Sophie was depressed at all. Did Miranda talk her into committing suicide? Did Mason convince his Broadway connections to give her role to someone else? What were they fighting about after the show? Another attempted assault could have pushed her over the edge.

Interlaced with all of this was his father's death. Mason seemed to have a role in that as well. There was more here than just the tragic destruction of an actress's career after resisting her boss's sexual advances.

Suddenly, it all became perfectly clear. He retrieved his phone from his bag and called Detective Joey Peralta.

"Joey, you need to come to the Gotham Theater. It was murder and I can prove it. Everyone involved is here now. I can't promise that tomorrow, especially if this theater closes after tonight, which I think it will."

The metal stairway door suddenly slammed shut. A figure was illuminated from behind by the surrounding high-rise apartment buildings. Ham instantly recognized him by his rotund shape, though he couldn't see his face or what he was holding behind his back.

"Mason, I had a feeling you'd join me."

"What are you doing nosing around here?" Mason asked.

"Trust me, I didn't want to come back. I am the last person who wanted to dredge up old memories."

"Ah, yes, old memories. I despised it when you and your clan ran amok in the theater."

"Now that my father's out of the way, you seem to be profiting nicely."

"Profit? This hole is losing more than it will ever take in."

"Then why stick around? Waiting to get top dollar when you sell it?"

"It's time to wake up and burst out of your artsy punk bubble. The Gotham's only redeeming value is the land it sits on."

"Or are you using it as your own personal brothel? Did you punish Sophie when she wouldn't agree to your advances?"

"I have no idea what you are talking about. I played no part in Sophie losing her big Broadway role."

Mason continued forward toward Ham.

"That's true. You were not responsible because she never lost it. In fact, you wanted her gone and Broadway would have been the perfect escape. Then she might have stopped blackmailing you, right?"

"What are you talking about?"

"For the past year, you've been paying her off to keep her from telling my father or the police that you tried to rape her. When she discovered right before opening night that real estate developers were coming for a tour, she demanded a large percentage of the proceeds and you couldn't abide that. So, you pushed her off the roof. You told everyone afterwards that she lost the role to make it look like suicide. Tomorrow, the same developers are returning to seal the deal and no one would blame you for wanting to sell after suffering two horrible tragedies."

"Always the melodramatic one. You should have followed your father into the theater. It seems you are already heading down his doomed path."

Mason inched toward Ham, his hands still behind his back.

"You killed my father, too, to stop him from reporting to the police that you were embezzling from the theater, money which you used to pay Sophie off. When there was no money left for an upcoming production, Dad analyzed the books and figured out you had been stealing from the accounts. Moreover, he was preventing you from selling the theater to pay down your debts. You doused him with vodka and then pushed him over the railing, making it look like he was drunk, and you took the accounts ledger back so no one else could discover the truth."

"Try to prove it, punk."

Mason swiftly swung a baseball bat from behind his back at Ham's head, forcing him backwards towards the edge of the roof. Ham's police training kicked in. After ducking away from the attack, he grabbed Mason's arm, forcing him to drop the bat and placing him in a headlock. Ham then tipped him over the side of the building.

"Was this what it was like when you killed him? Did you just push him over or did he put up a struggle? You worthless piece of shit."

Rage surged through Ham's blood, as all of the bottled-up emotions from the past finally erupted. The veins in his temples throbbed under a beet-red flush.

Mason's bulky girth made it difficult for Ham to continue balancing him and their feet began to slip. Mason begged for his life as he struggled to keep from falling.

The metal door slammed open again. Led by Nate, Detective Peralta rushed through the doorway and across the roof, helping to pull Mason back to safety.

"What's going on here?" Detective Peralta shouted as he separated the two.

"Arrest him," Ham said, breathing hard as he picked up the bat and pointed it at Mason. "He murdered Dad and Sophie Beale."

Ham handed the bat to the visibly confused detective and collected his messenger bag after straightening his jacket and hair.

"Nate, I like your idea. Let's take over the Gotham and make it successful. This is my home and I want to make my father proud."

Self-control. Ham was working on it.

WHEN THE WIND IS SOUTHERLY
By Leone Ciporin

Newly-widowed Marian may be along in years, but she's shrewd enough to find answers in a senior production of Hamlet.

I'd so looked forward to seeing *Hamlet*, and now I didn't want to be here. Fred should be sitting next to me, instead of my sweaty neighbor, Sally. Fred and I had loved coming to Sunset Manor's performances, watching the resident thespians prove that age was no barrier to creating art. We'd even imagined ourselves joining the theater group when we moved to Sunset in a few years.

During *Macbeth*, I'd leaned into Fred's chamois shirt, sniffed the bits of grass on his neck, and enjoyed the mischievous glint in his eye. Now, I was rubbing shoulders with Sally's damp housedress, inhaling her odd vinegary odor, and watching her fan herself with the playbook.

"I haven't read *Hamlet* since high school," Sally said. "I didn't even read it in high school, actually."

"You didn't have to come. I'd have been fine by myself."

Sweat pooled in her neck creases as she turned to gawk at me. "Marian, I'm glad to be here! Something different to do. And I'm curious about this Sunset Manor retirement community you talk about."

Curious meant nosy. Even when her husband was alive, Sally poked in everybody's business, but in the two years since his death, she spent all day staring out from her window or porch swing, watching neighborhood comings and goings.

After losing Fred three months ago, I knew how it felt to be alone, so I'd invited her. Not that I needed the company. There were plenty of pleasant people here, robust, smiling people who shared my hair color.

"I didn't realize how nice this place was." Sally glanced around the auditorium, her gaze settling on one of the men, who wasn't nearly as handsome as Fred. "Are you really moving here?"

"I'm thinking about it." I'd already started the paperwork to escape the house where Fred once was, and now was no more.

Sally swiveled to inspect a pigtailed girl leaning on her grandmother's shoulder. "Cute little girl."

"Did I show you my latest photos of Benjy?" The first picture I pulled up showed us from the back. I imagined it from Sally's perspective. A balding man in crisp khakis nestled a hand at his wife's waist, while an intelligent older woman bent a helmet of flyaway hair to a beautiful boy's auburn curls. From behind, we were a perfect family.

Right after that snapshot, I'd told Rollie to stop calling Sunset Manor "assisted living."

Rollie had snorted. "Aunt Marian, please. It's where old people live. Who cares what I call it?" Rollie's shirt bore the crest of a fancy country club. I suspected he visited golf courses just to get the shirts.

In the next picture, I held Benjy as he grinned, one ear poking through woolly curls. Benjy was adorable, as always, but my denim dress made me look like a couch.

"Sweet boy," Sally said as I scrolled to a photo of Benjy with his parents, with Alicia's hand on Benjy's shoulder while Rollie barely touched arms with his son. "Rollie looks like Fred in that picture."

Rollie did have his uncle's large ears and prominent chin, as did Benjy. I loved those ears. But Rollie's thin lips and close-set eyes gave him a sour look, while Benjy's eyes were wide and trusting. Whenever I asked, "Who's the best nana?" he'd wrap his arms around my neck and say, "You are." I might only be his great-aunt, by marriage, but with both his grandmothers dead, I stole the nickname.

The lights dimmed. I turned off my phone and the audience rustled into place.

Sally whispered, "So old people play all the parts?"

I bit my lip. She was barely ten years younger than me. "All the actors live at Sunset."

Stage lights brightened, revealing a cardboard castle and a weathered man in a guard's outfit. He shouted, "Who's there?"

A second guard entered. "Nay, answer me: stand and unfold yourself."

***

Rollie and Alicia's house: "A plentiful lack of wit"

Marian eased a dusty Taurus into the driveway of a Colonial just shy of a cul-de-sac lollipop, and grabbed the roses gathered from her garden. The petals hovered on the cusp of full bloom, and dirt still clung to the stems. The sugary scent tickled Marian's nose as Alicia led her to the dining room where Marian put the roses in a crystal vase, pinching a thorn that attacked the buds of her fingers as it died. She set the vase of defanged roses on the table and rubbed her fingers in satisfaction. Benjy's hands would be safe.

As if he'd heard her thoughts, Benjy thundered across the room in Spider-Man pajamas, squealing at the painful pitch children wield.

"Nana Marian!" He leaped onto Marian, who took the blow with a gasp before wrapping him in a hug. As soon as she released him, Benjy reached for the roses.

Rollie plopped the vase on the sideboard. "Flowers are for girls."

Benjy whimpered. Rollie advanced a step. The whimper jumped an octave.

"Your uncle planted that rosebush." Marian pulled Benjy to her.

"They're in the way. I want to see our guests."

"What are your friends' names?"

"Alicia, put Benjy to bed," Rollie yelled. "They'll be here any minute."

"I'll do it," Marian said, tucking Benjy's tag into his shirt. "We have our bedtime routine."

They trotted upstairs to Benjy's room, where the carpet was spotless and the dresser was dust-free. The one spot of clutter was a bookshelf crammed with Dr. Seuss books, a gold piggy bank, and a variety of plastic trucks and stuffed animals. One brave dolphin had plummeted onto the carpet, lying in the middle of a vacuum mark like a swimmer staying in its lane.

Benjy scooted under the covers. Marian tucked in the sheets and tousled his bunny-soft hair with small curls just like Fred's. She remembered walking up to Fred in the garden store, saying, "Your hair looks like curly parsley." Fred's face crinkled. "That's the best pickup line I've ever gotten." Even after cancer balded him, Marian still thought of Fred with those curls.

After three rounds of "You Are My Sunshine," Benjy reached under his bed, pulled out a yellow truck, and stretched it toward her. "For Spider-Nana."

Marian took the dump truck, its flapping bed blocked by a bulge. "What happened?"

He buried his face in his pillow.

"Benjy, what's wrong?"

The pillow muffled his answer. "Daddy broke it. I was a bad boy."

Marian combed his hair with shaky fingers. "You're not a bad boy. You're the best boy in the world." She lifted him to her. "You're Spider-Boy. And Spider-Nana won't let anything happen to her precious Spider-Boy."

Once Benjy fell asleep, Marian raced to the dining room and confronted Rollie, who was uncorking a Pinot Noir. "You smashed his truck."

Rollie inspected the cork. "He's my son. Don't tell me what to do."

The doorbell rang, and Marian said, "What are your friends' names? You haven't told me anything about them."

Rollie disappeared, reappearing with a stylish couple wearing shades of tan, the woman's turquoise necklace bright against the neutral palette.

"Marian, these are the friends I told you about."

"I like your necklace," Marian said. "I didn't catch your names?"

The pair tossed each other a smile. "Bill and Cindy," the man said.

Rollie shook his head. "My aunt forgets things sometimes."

"I didn't forget. You never told me their names."

Rollie patted her shoulder. "Dear Marian."

After wine and conversation about the warm weather and a new movie, Alicia brought out the food, refusing Marian's offer to help. Alicia's pink tee and white jeans draped her skeletal frame as she trotted back and forth.

When Alicia put down a platter of chicken and mushrooms, Rollie announced, "*Poulet de Normandie*."

"Norman chicken?" Marian said. Rollie scowled. Bill chuckled.

While platters circled the table, Bill reminisced about college. "Rollie took dibs on everything. I got stuck with the bottom drawers and the top bunk."

"Just watching out for number one. But I took care of you, too."

"That econ exam." Rollie and Bill exchanged an amused glance.

Bill lifted his wine glass. "We had fun, didn't we, buddy?"

Rollie released a rare grin. "Those were great days." Alicia's shoulders relaxed and she took her first bite of chicken.

Rollie leaned toward Bill, his eyes crinkling. "I'm about to get a promotion."

"You'll be a big shot, huh? I knew you when." Both men chuckled, the women smiled, and Bill took a large helping of potatoes.

Silverware clinked. Cindy said, "This chicken is delicious. You've outdone yourself, Alicia."

"Thank you." Alicia stared at her food. Beneath the scaffold of her ribs, her waist seemed barely wider than the green bean she pushed around her plate.

"What's its name again?" Bill asked. "Something French."

"*Poulet de Normandie*." Rollie rolled the words around before spitting them out.

"Now that you're a big shot, I guess you have to eat French food." Bill pointed his knife at his plate. "It's good, though."

"Norman's thigh is especially tender," Marian said.

"Pass the green beans?" Cindy said.

As Alicia handed her the platter, a drop of sauce spilled. Alicia wiped it quickly with a napkin as Rollie glared.

Cindy said. "We have spills all the time at our house."

"Not in this house," Rollie said.

"Do you have children?" Marian asked.

"Jeffrey's four, just a few months older than Benjy," Cindy said. "They play together."

"Marian, don't be jealous." Rollie turned to Bill. "She adores Benjy, especially since Uncle Fred died. They never had kids of their own."

"I'm sorry for your loss," Cindy said to Marian.

"Thank you." An unchewed new potato scratched Marian's throat as it went down. "This is my first summer without him." She clasped her hands under the table.

Rollie leaned back. "Since we're on the subject of Benjy, let's talk about the beach house. A developer contacted me about buying it. Bill's a real estate lawyer. He knows how much we could get for that house."

"It's near Ocean City, right?" Bill asked. Though he was skinny, he had a turkey neck, as if all the looseness had gathered in one place.

"Between Dewey Beach and Fenwick Island," Rollie said. "Uncle Fred left it to Marian and me as Benjy's trustees. I think Benjy should've inherited it outright."

"Fred probably wanted us to spend time together," Marian said. She recalled their last dinner here, Fred stumbling into his chair, her hands too slow to cushion the blow, his wince morphing into a smile as he glanced around and whispered, "My family."

Marian stared at her clasped hands. Her only family now slept upstairs.

Bill scraped the last green beans onto his plate. "As his widow, don't you inherit the house, Marian?"

Rollie smirked. "My uncle owned it before he married her."

"We spent every summer there," Marian said.

"We can spend holidays in Europe with the money we'd get." Rollie flourished his fork like a conductor.

"Memories are more precious than money," Marian said. "For

both me and Benjy."

"Three-year-olds don't know the value of money."

"Then he won't care about the developer's money." Marian spooned mushroom sauce on her chicken. "And he's almost four."

***

"Ophelia could use a face lift," Sally murmured.

"Hush." I focused on Polonius, who was telling King Claudius that Ophelia's rejection was the cause of Hamlet's madness:

> POLONIUS: And he, repulsed—a short tale to make—
> Fell into a sadness, then into a fast,
> Thence to a watch, thence into a weakness,
> Thence to a lightness, and, by this declension,
> Into the madness wherein now he raves,
> And all we mourn for.
> KING CLAUDIUS: Do you think 'tis this?
> QUEEN GERTRUDE: It may be, very likely.

I glanced at the seat Fred once filled. Very likely indeed.

***

Marian's house: "For some must watch"

"Marian, I haven't seen you all week."

Sally waddled across the street to Marian's house, the last home before the road petered out at a clump of pines. Built back when "*cul-de-sac*" was a French word, the houses along the road varied. Marian's home had smooth brick and a painted carport, while Sally's yellow siding accented her lawn's dandelions.

Sally crunched first her dandelions and then Marian's smooth grass to reach the garden bed where Marian dug between azaleas.

"You're really attacking that weed."

"You have to pull out the roots or it comes back." Marian twisted her trowel. "He's so patronizing! You wouldn't believe how badly Rollie treats people. Even Benjy."

Sally crouched, her cheek nearly colliding with a rusting azalea bloom. "Rollie's not the warmest man, but I'm sure he loves his son. And he's Fred's nephew. He's grieving, too."

Marian snipped the offending azalea. "The only time Rollie wanted to see Fred was when he needed money." She peeled off oversized gloves with "Fred" sewn on the wristband. "Fred loved him anyway. He saw the best in everyone. Even Rollie."

"Maybe you should, too."

"I'll try, for Benjy's sake." Marian brushed dirt from her jeans. "Would you like some tea? I'll make a fresh batch. I need to check a chicken thigh in the oven anyway."

"Want me to check it for you? I saw Rollie leaving the other day and he mentioned you left a pot on the stove."

"The stove is usually where pots sit when they're cooking. He's only buddying up to you to get at me. Come in."

Marian led her past the entry's row of photographs. Sally glanced at the living room, where a deep couch with floral pillows faced a striped chair with an inviting ottoman. End tables held Shakespeare plays, Eliot poems, and mason jars stuffed with smug hydrangeas.

More hydrangeas decorated the kitchen, where a tile backsplash featured sketches of rosemary, tarragon, and oregano. While Marian loaded a battered teakettle, Sally browsed a baker's rack stuffed with cookbooks, a bowl of seashells, and a prosperous bonsai. She picked up a photograph of a man in a denim shirt, his grinning face all ears and chin.

"Great picture of Fred. Camping trip?"

Marian beamed. "Our last one." The beam faded. "I'd have killed anyone who hurt Fred. But how do you kill cancer?"

Marian lifted the sugar bowl lid. Metal gleamed and she pulled out a silver watch she hadn't seen since Rollie stopped by to discuss the beach house. She rubbed granules from the engraving: "To Marian, with all my love, Fred."

"What's your watch doing in the sugar bowl?" Sally asked. Her expression softened. "How are you feeling, Marian?"

"Fine. I didn't put this watch there. But I know who did."

Sally returned the photo gently to the baker's rack. "I know you miss Fred. You two were incredibly close."

"I can't even mourn properly without being made to look senile. People assume that when you get gray hair, you lose your wits."

***

POLONIUS: [Aside] Though this be madness, yet there is method in 't.
Will you walk out of the air, my lord?
HAMLET: Into my grave.
LORD POLONIUS: Indeed, that is out o' the air.

***

Rollie and Marian's house: "A dull and muddy-mettled rascal"

For Benjy's fourth birthday, Marian brought a green dump truck, which she clasped like a talisman as she rang the bell.

"I told you, you don't have to ring the bell. You're family." Alicia waved chocolate-splattered fingers. "The boys are out back." Her shirt gaped, revealing a bruise along her collarbone.

In the back yard, parents clustered in the shade of the patio while their boys raced across the grass, screaming at odd moments, Benjy's smile wide as he led the pack. Marian's echoing smile faded when she saw an orange dog piñata swaying from the limb of a birch tree.

"Rollie, a dog piñata?"

"Benjy keeps asking for a dog. Now he's got one."

"That's not funny. He'll have to hit it."

"It's about time he manned up. My father taught me early to toughen up." Rollie rubbed a puckered spot on his elbow.

"Your father's gone," Marian said. "You don't have to prove yourself anymore."

Rollie swatted her words aside and slumped away, like a defeated batter.

"Rollie didn't get that promotion, did he?" Marian sighed. "He's still trying to prove himself to his father. I always wondered if something happened with his father, something to do with cigarettes. Something…awful."

Alicia stared at the grass.

Marian continued, "What father tells his son he'll never amount to anything? Fred always said his sister could've done better." She paused. "Some women settle for less than they deserve."

Alicia lifted her head. "Well, they're all gone now. The rest of us just have to make it through each day." She handed Marian a slice of chocolate cake.

Marian eyed the nearly empty cake dish. "What time did the party start?"

Alicia inspected the grass again. "One o'clock."

Marian whirled as Rollie walked up. "You said the party started at two."

He took the last piece of cake, a smile fluttering on his lips.

"Nana Marian!" Benjy barreled into her and clamped his arms around her knees. Marian scratched his head. "Hello, birthday buddy!"

She held up the package, wrapped in a crowd of shiny Spider-Men.

"Gift opening is later." Rollie snatched the present. "Benjy, play with your guests." Rollie tipped back his Orioles cap. "Marian, how about if we host your birthday party next week?"

"I'm too old for birthday parties. Numbers don't matter as much at my age."

"You deserve a party. Besides, it was important to Uncle Fred that we keep in touch." He added, "We'll make it a casual picnic next Saturday. Come early to see Benjy before Jeffrey comes to play. We'll start at four, so be here at three."

"Three o'clock. You're sure this time?" At Rollie's nod, Marian said, "I'll be there. I'm glad Benjy has a play date."

Rollie paused. "The developer upped his offer for the beach house."

"Memories are more important than money. You should know, now that you're a father." She nodded toward Benjy, who was laughing with a smaller boy.

Rollie released a puff of exasperated air. "That house is sitting vacant most of the time. We could at least rent it out, make some money."

"I'm going down later this summer. And you, Alicia, and Benjy will come for a week or two, I hope. But you're right, it's a good idea to rent it out the rest of the time, so it's lived in. And watched over."

Rollie jerked his head back. "Did you actually say I'm right?"

They exchanged a look bordering on a smile before Rollie called the boys to the piñata. His baseball cap slid down, nearly landing on his sunglasses. He tipped it back and handed the bat to Benjy.

"Go ahead, son. You get the first hit."

"Don't wanna!"

"You need to learn to hit. Remember that Orioles game I took you to? Swing like that."

Benjy's face scrunched. The bat slid from his fingers.

Rollie grabbed the bat and gave it to a chunky boy who clenched his jaw and stepped into the swing, sending bits of orange onto the grass. A flurry of blows followed, crumbling the paper dog and releasing a spray of candy chased by all the boys except Benjy, who ran to Marian.

Marian wiped his nose with a pinch of her fingers. "Alicia, you have to do something."

Alicia darted a glance at Rollie, who was cheerleading the candy chase. She spoke in near-perfect imitation of him. "Don't tell me what to do."

***

Sally's elbow jabbed my ribs.

"Ouch! Sally, I'm trying to watch the play."

"It's boring. The prince is crazy."

"Is he really?" I pointed to Hamlet, who was talking with the actors about to perform for the king:

HAMLET: Gentlemen, you are welcome to Elsinore. Your hands,

Come then: the appurtenance of welcome is fashion
And ceremony: let me comply with you in this garb,
Lest my extent to the players, which, I tell you,
Must show fairly outward, should more appear like
Entertainment than yours. You are welcome: but my
uncle-father and aunt-mother are deceived.
GUILDENSTERN: In what, my dear lord?
HAMLET: I am but mad north-north-west: when the wind is
southerly I know a hawk from a handsaw.

I whispered, "See? Hamlet knows what he's doing." Sally paid no attention.

***

Rollie and Alicia's house: "Some quantity of barren spectators"

At three o'clock, Marian trotted up Rollie's sidewalk as the windy warning of a distant storm swayed the lawn's lone sapling. She scratched her head, spiking sweaty strands at odd angles, and rang the bell.

Rollie opened the door. "Marian, we were worried. You're an hour late for your own party."

She checked her silver watch. "I'm right on time. Three o'clock."

Rollie rubbed her back as she stepped inside, his sweaty hand bunching her blouse. "The party started at two." He gestured toward a gathering of onlookers with hoisted wine glasses.

"You said come at three."

"All right, Marian. We're just glad you're safe. No smoking, Joe," he told a man lifting a cigarette.

Rollie rubbed a puckered dot on his elbow before giving Marian a quick kiss on the cheek. "Happy birthday."

She stared at his chin, so like Fred's. "Thank you."

Rollie ushered Marian through the crowd. She plucked dirt off her khaki skirt as they angled past a wreath of women in linen dresses, the yellow linen telling the lavender, "You wouldn't think they could mess up Mozart."

Rollie steered Marian around a cluster of laughing men to the makeshift bar, where a row of bottles faced an army of glasses. Rollie engaged a bottle and glass in a skirmish, and handed Marian a glass of white wine. "Nice watch."

"You've seen it before."

Two middle-aged women ambled up as thunder rumbled in the distance.

"These women are from my office," Rollie said. "This is my Aunt Marian, the birthday girl. Doesn't she look lovely?"

The taller woman took in Marian's denim shirt and flyaway hair with a swift glance. "Wonderful," she said in the tone Sally had recently adopted.

That tone followed Marian like a mist as she nibbled cucumber sandwich triangles and listened to debates about whether the storm would head their way. When she started to slice a piece of Brie, a squat woman in a sundress offered to do it for her. When Marian headed to the powder room, Cindy said, "I'll wait outside."

"I know how to use a bathroom."

As Marian left the powder room, a man approached with a somber expression. "Excuse me, ma'am?" His shirt tented his belly. "Fred and I used to go fishing at Deep Creek Lake. We lost touch a while ago, but he was a decent man and I'm sure sorry he's gone."

Marian smiled and accepted his outstretched hand. "Thank you for remembering him." Their hands clasped for a moment before he shuffled away.

She stared at the hardwood floor, covering her sniffles with a cupped palm. A ceramic cup intruded into view.

"I got you tea." Rollie's voice. "Wartberry or something."

"Whortleberry. I can get my own tea."

"I'm trying to be nice."

Marian took the cup and sipped the watery tea until Rollie walked away. Then she tucked the cup behind an empty glass and headed onto the lawn where Benjy and Jeffrey were crashing trucks. Benjy revved his green truck, holding one blistered thumb in the air. A mark ran, ruler-straight, between the puckered burn and the undamaged skin below.

Marian stomped toward Rollie, who hid behind a fog of men. She veered toward Alicia. "What happened to Benjy's thumb?"

Alicia turned away.

Marian stared at Benjy, ignoring a guffawing man, and a woman spilling wine on her foot. She zoomed a finger over her thumb, and thought about a desperate prince.

She watched Benjy a long time.

Finally, she marched up to Alicia. "You think I'm good with Benjy, don't you?"

Alicia's eyelids flipped up in surprise. "Of course. He loves you very much."

"Don't forget that." Marian turned, hovered her arm, and then swept it wide, knocking a bowl of potato chips onto the patio.

Rollie rushed over. "Marian? Are you all right?" As Rollie simpered, Marian faced the audience with a dazed expression.

She allowed Rollie to lead her to a cushioned chair scraped out from the living room. She let him serve her another cup of weak tea before opening pastel bath soaps, and chirpy birthday cards, some with the wrong age. Nobody here even knew how long she'd been alive.

Marian watched Benjy sprint across the yard, his wooly curls flapping.

***

HAMLET: Madam, how like you this play?

QUEEN GERTRUDE: The lady protests too much, methinks.

HAMLET: O, but she'll keep her word.

KING CLAUDIUS: Have you heard the argument? Is there no offence in 't?

HAMLET: No, no, they do but jest, poison in jest; no offence i' th' world.

***

Marian's house: "This plague for thy dowry"

In July, Rollie petitioned for guardianship. A few days before the August hearing, Alicia brought Benjy to Marian's for a negotiated sleepover.

As Benjy grabbed their hands, Marian faced Alicia over the swing set of their arms. "Remember, you promised to tell the judge I'm a good nana."

Marian swung her arm wide, making Benjy squeal in delight. "I'll let Rollie have guardianship, and that blasted beach house, if you both tell the judge I should still see Benjy. That's our deal."

Alicia nodded. Benjy dangled from their arms, the deep blue of his shirt echoing the bruise on his wrist.

Marian leaned toward Alicia. "Everything will be fine. I promise." She enfolded Benjy in a hug, and whispered, "Doubt truth to be a liar, but never doubt I love." She leaned back. "I love you, sweet boy."

He kissed her, a wet smack that tingled her cheek.

As soon as Alicia left, Benjy ran to the back yard, grabbed his plastic trowel, and headed for a clump of blue-helmeted plants. Marian pulled him back.

"Stay away from those. Let's dig up dandelions."

***

After thunderous applause, the curtain swished shut, and we gathered our things. "What did you think of the play?" I asked.

"It's about a crazy prince who kills his uncle for stealing the throne and a bunch of other people die, too." Sally hauled herself to her feet and caught her breath. "*Game of Thrones* did it better."

"I think you missed the brilliance of Hamlet's plan."

***

Marian's house: "Mistress of her choice"

The day after the guardianship decree, Rollie came for the beach house paperwork. Kneeling amid the monkshood, Marian yelled for him to come to the back yard. Amid tall, happy plants stood a wrought iron table, set with a plump blue and white teapot and matching mugs. In the woods, orange-tipped leaves warned of summer's end.

Rollie tromped to the back yard and stared at the tea set, and Benjy's damaged yellow truck in the center of the table. "Marian, you really are batty."

Marian ripped out a weed, its roots shaking in protest. She took off her gloves. "Sit, Rollie. Have some tea." She filled both large mugs and handed him one.

Rollie perched on a wrought iron chair. "I don't have time for tea parties. Where are the papers?"

Marian slid the sugar bowl toward him, her silver watch glinting in the sun. "First, have some tea. Let's be civilized."

After a tentative sip to test the temperature, Rollie downed the tea in one gulp before slapping his mug on the table. "All right, I've had my damn tea. Now, where are the papers?"

Marian leaned back, her own tea untouched. "You swore that I'm incompetent. You got the court to declare that I don't know what I'm doing."

Rollie flung up his hands. "Having tea parties at your age proves the point, doesn't it?" His hands dropped to his side, as if weighted.

"I agree. It will help immensely. I'll still get to see Benjy."

"What do you mean?" His skin paled under drops of sweat. "What did you do, Marian?"

She tapped a wrought iron swirl on the table. "Such a stupid mistake, using monkshood in the tea—though I like its other name, wolf's-bane, better. The bane of predators. It's poisonous."

"Marian, you didn't."

Marian stroked her chin. "Let's see. First, tingling and numbness, starting with the hands and feet. Excessive sweating, too. The face is pale and there's a tendency to faint—but you're sitting, so no need to worry about that." She crooked one finger into her mug handle. "The mind's unaffected, so we can chat, at least for a while. Death can come quickly."

Rollie's skin was nearly translucent. "You'll never get away with it."

"Of course I will. I'm a grieving old woman who's not

responsible for her actions. You said so yourself. Swore to it. And the court agreed. Fortunately, I'll recover, once I get over Fred's death." She paused. "Yours, too."

Rollie staggered to his feet, toppling his chair, and reached for Marian with claw-fingered hands. Marian tilted away and Rollie tumbled into the wolf's-bane, its blue helmets cradling his head.

As Rollie writhed among the plants, Marian picked up the yellow truck and kissed its injured side.

"For you, Benjy," she whispered. "From Spider-Nana."

RAISING CAIN
By Carla Coupe

The four ladies of Raising Cain have been asked to get the band back together for an awards show at Eazy Acres, but first they'll need a new lead singer—and no more accidents.

"DeeDee! Have you heard the news?" Her long, blond hair swinging over her shoulder, Missy Shepherdson cornered me in the hall outside the Eazy Acres dining room. "Miles is getting the Volunteer of the Year award!"

"Really? I thought Chris had it locked up this year. Again." Everyone else was in the dining room, and a pack of wheeled walkers parked in the wide hallway hemmed me in. I tried to skirt them—it was pizza night, and the chef made a mean deep dish—but Missy blocked me.

"No, it's going to Miles. He and Trish want us to play at the ceremony. We're putting Raising Cain back together! Isn't that wonderful?"

"*Miles* wants us to play? Seriously?" We had loved the idea of all five band members living at Eazy Acres Independent Living for Active Adults. Only now there were four. Guilt settled over my shoulders like one of Missy's shawls. "Have you talked to Beth Ann and Sharon? After our last gig, we decided we'd never play together again. Remember?"

The gathered neckline of Missy's peasant blouse drooped over one bony shoulder, and she pushed it up, her bangles jangling. "Jean's death was tragic, of course, but that was almost two years ago. Things have changed. Miles and I are together, we'll be playing again, just like old times, and—"

"And who will sing lead?" Sometimes you had to hit Missy over the head. "Sharon can't play the drums and sing. God knows she tried. You and I kick ass with harmonies, but we're not lead singers. And Beth Ann can't hold a tune in a bucket."

She shrugged, neckline slipping over both shoulders. "Yeah, but Jean would want us to move on, DeeDee. We'll set up auditions and break in a new lead singer!"

"Missy." I sighed and ran a hand through my short gray curls. "Who wants to front for a bunch of old ladies?"

"Lots of people! Why, Fred and Chris. And Dot and Ernie..." She smiled, that sunny, insanely positive smile she'd used to get her way since the day she was born. "C'mon. One more show, for Jean's sake."

I took off my glasses, rubbed my eyes, and caved. "Okay, okay. As long as Beth Ann and Sharon are cool with it, I'm in."

"Oh, DeeDee!" She grabbed my hand.

I reclaimed my fingers, put my glasses back on, and frowned. "But only to hold auditions. If we don't find anyone who suits, I'm not playing." The smell of pizza wafted from the dining room, and my mouth watered. Why couldn't Missy have cornered me on liver and onions night?

"I knew you'd do it! I'll get the signs up tonight, and Trish says we can hold auditions in the all-purpose room on Friday. Gotta go. My pizza's waiting." She blew me an air kiss and breezed into the dining room.

I stared after her. She'd already cleared this with Trish, our activities coordinator? I'd been friends with Missy for sixty of our seventy years, and I still got played. Did Sharon and Beth Ann know about this? Or was I the only one out of the loop?

Making my way around the walkers, I hurried into the dining room. Follow-up could wait until after dinner. I hated cold pizza.

***

The Eazy Acres all-purpose room smelled faintly of boiled cabbage and old socks, and it reminded me of every school gym we'd ever played in. We set up our gear on the stage, with help from Miles Forneau and Chris Lieber, who kept trying to outdo each other by volunteering for everything. The folks auditioning would sing "Hell Raiser," our first number one hit.

I finished tuning my bass guitar. Across the stage, Missy played ghost chords on her keyboard, her peasant skirt swaying. Miles stood in the wings, lean and silver-haired, smiling at her. Chris was busy behind him, coiling a long orange extension cord. At the front of the stage, battered Fender slung over her shoulder, Beth Ann, in her usual black jeans and white tee-shirt, stared off into space. "Getting her head together," she called it. Whatever works.

Someone's amp started to hum. Hand cupped to one ear, Miles stepped from the wings, followed by Chris. I waved them off, rested my bass in the stand, and checked connections. One of Missy's keyboard plugs was loose, so I reseated it.

"Was there a hum?" Missy frowned and tapped her hearing aid. "Time to get these checked again."

I shrugged. Even when she could hear, Missy let our roadies do all the setup and cabling. Me? I always checked the equipment, even when I pissed off the stage manager and sound guy, or in this case Miles and Chris, our self-appointed stagehands. I had only neglected to do it once, and I'd blame myself for that lapse forever.

Sharon sat behind her drum kit and pulled on her fingerless gloves with the cushioned palms. Red leather, of course, to match her iconic fringed vest and headband. She grabbed her sticks and played a quick tarradiddle. "Okay, let's get started."

When thirteen people signed up to audition—who knew there were so many frustrated rockers living at Eazy Acres?—Trish offered to handle the process. Only nine showed. Fine by me.

"Right." Trish consulted her clipboard. "First one up: Chris Lieber."

Chris had changed into a tie-dyed tee shirt and tight, tight jeans. How could he breathe? It took him a minute and some delicate... personal adjustments to make it to the mic.

Beth Ann nodded her head. "One, two, three, four..." We hit the galloping opening bars cleanly, sounding damned fine for old ladies.

Chris was a good-looking guy but he couldn't scream, even with the jeans helping his falsetto. Cracking like a teenaged boy, he tried to power through but failed miserably. The same was true for the next three singers.

Trish's smile started to look pasted on. Marking the paper on her clipboard, she called, "Dot Larue."

A real firecracker in baby blue polyester double knit and carrying her flowered cane, Dot ditched her ever-present crocheting and crossed to the mic.

Beth Ann counted us in. Dot hit the opening scream right on cue.

She was good, the best so far, hitting all the notes strong and true. Too bad she stood stiffly, clutching her cane, with no gestures and hardly any expression.

We finished to applause. Beth Ann nodded at Dot. "Good job. You sound just like Jean."

"I should." Dot grinned and wiped her damp forehead. "I've always been a huge fan. Played my Raising Cain albums so much I wore them out."

"Where'd you learn to sing?" asked Sharon.

Dot snorted. "From twenty years of session and backup singing, waiting for my break." She winked. "Not to mention a lot of one-night stands with musicians and roadies. I know my way around a studio, in front of the mic as well as with the gear."

Trish tapped her pen on the clipboard. "That was certainly... inspiring, Dot. But we have four more."

The next two singers were okay. And then it was Fred Morales's turn. Fred's a sweetheart but no looker. He's bald and pot-bellied, a dumpling, like me. And yet.... When he grabbed the mic, he not only commanded the stage, he stormed the ramparts and took no prisoners.

And his voice! Husky and so resonant it vibrated deep in my belly…well, a little lower than my belly, truth be told. That brought back memories of life on the road, when the five of us played mattress round-robin with fans and roadies and boyfriends.

We were on fire. Sharon pounded the drums, Beth Ann shredded her axe, Missy attacked her keyboard, and my bass line welled up from the depths. The place shook so hard dust floated down from the acoustic tiles in the drop ceiling.

The final chord echoed for a long moment before Trish and the other singers clapped and whooped. Fred bowed and then turned, applauding us. Missy ran over and hugged him.

Everyone was on their feet. Dot clapped but looked as if she'd developed a bad case of heartburn. I glanced across the stage. Miles and Chris stood in the wings, scowling. Missy grinned at Miles, and his scowl turned into a smile. Chris turned away.

Once the clapping died down, Trish said, "We have one more—"

"I can't top that." Ernie Wells hitched up his cargo pants. "I'll stick to our barbershop quartet."

"Thanks for coming, Ernie." Trish marked the paper on her clipboard and clicked her pen. She turned to us. "Do you gals need time to decide?"

Beth Ann rolled her eyes as she put her Fender on the stand. "C'mon, *gals*. Band huddle."

We followed her through the double doors outside to the patio, like when we'd troop out for a smoke break or for a hit of something illegal. Today, the air was chilly enough that no one was sitting at the tables—on a warm, bright day, the patio teemed with residents basking in the sun like lizards.

Beth Ann propped her butt against a table and crossed her arms over her still-impressive chest. "Well? Any objections to Fred?"

"Not me," said Sharon.

Missy clapped her hands together. "He was wonderful!"

"DeeDee?" Beth Ann tilted her head and raised her eyebrows. "What's your take?"

I took a deep breath. "Fred's fantastic. I mean, really excellent. I just…I feel bad for Dot."

Missy fluttered her hand. "She's such a *fan*. Ugh. And besides, she was a *session* singer."

"And why's that bad?" Sharon snapped. "We need our fans. And some of the best musicians in the world are session players or singers."

"I didn't mean it *that* way." Missy flipped her hair over her shoulder, her trademark gesture back when she would pick which lucky guy to bed that night. "I just meant she doesn't have any stage presence. We might as well prop a mannequin at the mic."

One by one, we nodded in agreement.

"Right," said Beth Ann. "Fred it is."

***

The next week was hectic. We chose three more of our songs to play, in addition to "Raising Cain," our signature tune, always known as Jean's song. Somehow, when Fred sang it, he made it his own.

The big stuff is easy—learning words, making sure you're on the beat—but the devil's in the details. We booked the all-purpose room for two hours a day, after the Kozy Krafters put away their colored paper and wood-burning kits and cleared out. Dot was a founding member of the Kozy Krafters, and she lingered occasionally to watch us practice. I hoped she wasn't rubbing salt in the wound.

It was a pain to have to set up and break down every day, and fortunately Miles and Chris both showed up to help, staying to listen from the wings.

We had the usual glitches and minor catastrophes, broken strings and faulty mics. Once, Fred skidded on a slick spot and almost fell off the stage—something oily had dripped there—and another time he lifted the mic stand, and the base dropped, almost crushing his foot. Miles had set up the stand—maybe he'd forgotten to tighten it? I kept a close eye on things after that—practices were tiring, and it's easy to get careless when you're exhausted.

On Friday afternoon Fred, Miles, and Chris helped us move our gear behind the dusty navy velvet curtains. Musically, everything was coming together. After the three of them headed out, Missy reached into her macramé tote and grabbed a bottle of wine.

"Time for refreshments!" She grinned and pulled out three more bottles. "We've worked hard, and it's time for a little pre-show celebration."

Beth Ann took two of the bottles. "Great idea."

She led the way to the patio, where we liberated some juice glasses from behind the food service hatch. Sharon unfolded the corkscrew on her utility knife and deftly opened the first bottle, dividing it among the four glasses.

I cleared my throat. "To Jean." I raised my glass. "Let's do her memory proud."

Missy, Beth Ann, and Sharon mirrored me. "To Jean."

After we each had a solemn sip—bless Missy for shelling out for a decent vintage—we sat back.

"This is going to be great," Sharon said, after knocking back her glass. Sharon would drink whatever was on offer, although she preferred cheap beer. Not that the rest of us were wine snobs. "Even if we never play again, what a high note to finish on!" She held out her glass for a refill.

I heard it first, since my hearing was the best among us, although that's not saying much: the faint sound of an emergency vehicle. I turned toward the drive. No, it wasn't necessarily coming to Eazy Acres, but ambulances were occasional visitors.

Sure enough, the siren grew louder, and an ambulance appeared, heading down the drive, lights flashing. Missy bounced from her seat, glass in hand, and headed inside. Sharon, Beth Ann, and I stayed put. Missy took her unofficial position as medical busybody very seriously. No one got sick or injured without her knowing all about it.

"Five dollars says it's Carl's pacemaker acting up again," said Sharon.

"I'll put a ten spot down that Marty's cold turned into pneumonia," I countered.

Beth Ann just finished her glass and poured another.

Ten minutes later Missy burst through the doors, eyes wide. "Oh my God," she panted. "Oh my God! This is terrible! Fred was pushed down the stairs and broke his leg!"

"What?"

"How?"

"Shut it!" Beth Ann slammed her hand on the table. We closed our mouths, and she turned to Missy. "What happened?"

"He was taking the stairs and fell. He said someone pushed him!" Missy shook her head, tears welling. "And now the show is ruined!"

"Pushed? Don't be ridiculous," Sharon said with a snort. "He must've tripped and is embarrassed to admit it."

Missy took a shaky breath. "Maybe…. But what about the show?"

I set down my glass. "We can still do it. I'm sure Dot would sing."

"But she looks like a lump on stage!" Missy said.

"So? She sounds good." Sharon turned to me. "It can't hurt to ask."

As we finished our wine, Missy described the cute EMTs and how one reminded her of a boyfriend from '69. Or was it '70? That led her down the well-worn "guys I have slept with" path and on to how perfect she and Miles were together, how handsome he was, how the scent of his aftershave always turned her on.

"Okay," said Beth Ann. "But I remember how often he said Jean was the love of his life."

"Well, she's dead," Missy snapped. "And he loves me. A lot. Honestly."

I helped clean up, but the thought niggled at the back of my mind: Did someone really push Fred? If so, who? And why?

***

Dot beamed when we asked her to take Fred's place. She knew all the songs cold, which made our lives easier.

By Sunday Fred was transferred to a rehab facility down the street. I headed over around lunchtime and walked the chlorine-scented halls to his room.

He was sitting in a recliner, his leg in a soft cast, reading the newspaper. An untouched lunch tray sat on the table—meatloaf, green beans, and red Jell-O. Ugh.

"Good, you haven't eaten." I handed him a paper bag. "I stopped at Steinberg's."

"You're an angel of mercy," he said, opening the bag. "Pastrami on rye!"

"With extra mustard."

He ate a few bites, making noises that could've been used as a soundtrack on a porn film. Mustard dribbled down his chin.

"So, what happened?" I asked as he wiped his chin and came up for air.

Ecstasy was replaced by a scowl. "Damnedest thing. I started down the steps, and the door opened behind me. Then someone punched me in the back. I'm just lucky the break isn't bad, and I've had practice with crutches." He took another bite, and his eyes closed.

"It could've been an accident, I suppose."

His eyes opened, and he glared. "Not a chance. I was definitely pushed."

"And you have no idea who it was?"

He set down his sandwich. "It happened so fast. I took a step, got walloped, and then hit the landing." With a frown, he slowly shook his head. "I thought maybe...."

"Fred?" Missy wafted in on a flutter of gauze. "Oh, hey, DeeDee. Fred, how are you feeling, you poor thing?"

Miles appeared behind her, carrying an enormous bouquet of tulips in a vase. Missy must've raided the flower beds at Eazy Acres again.

Miles set the bouquet on the window ledge. "Sorry about your fall."

As Fred finished his sandwich, Missy fussed—plumping pillows, smoothing blankets, and asking Miles to fetch Fred fresh ice water.

"How's it working out with Dot?" Fred asked.

"She's a good singer," I said.

Missy sighed. "She's okay but nowhere near as good as you. I wish—"

"She'll be great." I frowned at Missy. "You just concentrate on getting better, Fred."

She seemed to get the message. "That's right," she said, taking Fred's hand and patting it. "Put your energy into healing." She leaned over and planted a kiss on his forehead, then straightened. "Miles, let's go."

When they left, Fred let out a gusty sigh. "Boy, she makes me tired."

I nodded. "Yeah." I hesitated for a moment. "Before they came in, you thought of something about your fall. What was it? A sound? Something you saw?"

He shook his head. "No…"

"A smell?"

Fred pressed his lips together and looked at the vase of tulips. "Forget it. It's nothing."

***

Sharon and Beth Ann were already on stage Monday when I arrived. Dot sat in the wings, singing vocal warmups and crocheting something pink and fluffy.

"Hey, DeeDee!" Sharon called, unrolling the carpet she used under her drum kit.

Chris and Miles were moving our amps into place under Beth Ann's direction. They waved before returning to work.

"Hi, all." I took the stairs to the stage and started setting up.

Of course, Missy walked in just as we finished. She has a sixth sense about when the hard work is done.

Then we saw the crutch and her face.

"Missy, what happened?" Beth Ann joined Sharon and me as we hurried off the stage, Miles and Chris hot on our heels.

Missy hobbled over to a chair and collapsed, the crutch falling to the floor. Her ankle sported an elastic wrap. She pushed her hair back, displaying a huge bruise purpling her left cheek.

Miles pulled another chair close, sitting and taking her hand in his. "Sweetheart! Are you okay?"

"Use your eyes, man!" Chris glared at him. "What a ridiculous—"

"Can it, Chris." Beth Ann turned to Missy. "What happened?"

Missy sighed. "I was running late this morning…"

Sharon glanced at me. "Typical," she muttered.

"…and I dashed out of my apartment, tripped, and fell. I hit my face on the door frame and twisted my ankle. Luckily, Helen came by and paged the nurse."

"What'd you trip on?" I asked.

"My doormat was bunched over a couple of plastic door stops." Missy leaned back and closed her eyes.

Miles patted her hand. "Could the cleaners have done it by accident when they vacuumed?"

Chris snorted. Miles glared at him.

"So, Missy," Sharon said quickly, "can you play today, or do you want to sit it out?"

Missy opened her eyes, smiled her Brave Smile—patent pending—and glanced at the stage, where Dot still sat, crocheting. "Of course I can play. Dot needs to practice."

Dot looked up. "Oh, I've had plenty experience winging it. Don't worry about me."

"That's right, you were a *session* musician," Missy said with a sniff. "Not a real—"

"Great!" I said before Missy could continue. "Chris, grab a chair for Missy. And Miles, help her onto the stage. Let's get moving. We've got a show in less than a week."

***

We worked a lot on "Raising Cain." Dot sang it just like Jean had, but honestly, Fred's version sounded better.

I glanced over at Missy, bruised and battered, sitting at the keyboard. It had been two years since Jean had sprained her wrist and banged her knee falling down the stage steps. Miles wanted her to rest, but she insisted she could perform. After he left, she asked if I'd have lunch with her the next day…. Something was bothering her.

We never had lunch, because Jean died that night. An accident, according to the police. But I had always wondered.

Missy pounded out her chords. Was her fall a coincidence? It must be.

I wished I could believe it.

***

The award ceremony started Saturday at seven, so we set up our equipment that afternoon. Sound check was at 6:30. I arrived early, and Eazy Acres' AV guru was already at the sound board at the far end of the room.

As usual, Dot sat in the wings, crocheting. She'd ditched her pantsuit for a cute batik caftan that I would have worn 24/7 fifty years ago.

I walked over to the amps. "Hey, Miles."

Crouched behind them, he looked up. "Hi, DeeDee." He shifted, his body blocking me from seeing whatever he was doing.

"What's going on?" I moved to one side, peering over his shoulder, hit by a wave of his aftershave. Phew.

"I wanted to double check the wiring." He stood with a grunt, holding a power strip. "After Jean's accident, I'm extra cautious about anything to do with electricity."

So was I. The shock Jean got from the faulty mic probably wouldn't have killed someone with a healthy heart, but it was enough to stop hers. The EMTs worked hard to save her, without success. My own equipment had been set up wrong, and by the time I fixed it, there was no time to check everyone else's. The guilt would always dog me.

"What's the problem?" I asked.

He held up the power strip. "I didn't like the look of this, so I replaced it."

I saw what he meant. The old strip had been split open and taped back together again. "We certainly didn't use that one during practice."

"I don't know where it came from." Miles shrugged and started toward the stage door. "I'll get rid of it."

I stared after him. I'd never seen that power strip before. Was he really replacing it with a good one?

Kneeling behind the amps, I checked the new strip myself. It looked okay, but just in case, I found another and switched it out. I dusted off my hands. The knees of my black jeans were covered in bits of Dot's pink fluffy wool. Damned stuff ended up everywhere.

Sharon and Beth Ann arrived together. Finally, Missy bustled in, dripping in lace and velvet, our own version of Stevie Nicks. At least she didn't need the crutch anymore.

Our sound check went without a hitch.

The doors opened on a larger audience than expected, waiting to take their seats. There were so many people they had to set up additional chairs.

Suddenly, Missy let out an ear-piercing squeal. "Fred!"

Wielding his crutches like a pro, Fred made his way through the crowd to the stage. Missy went down to greet him, the rest of us following in her wake.

"We thought you'd still be in rehab," I said.

"I got sprung this morning and couldn't miss your show." Fred grinned and looked around. "Where's Dot? I wanted to wish her luck."

Dot stood on the stage, leaning heavily on her cane.

"Oh! I have an idea!" Missy squealed again. "Since you're here, why don't you sing?"

Fred shook his head. "Oh, I couldn't. Dot—"

"You could both sing," said Sharon.

"C'mon! You'll sound fantastic!" Missy glanced at Dot, still on the stage. "And you'll certainly put on a better show than *some* people."

Miles frowned as Trish bustled up. "Fred! How wonderful to see you! You must join Dot on the stage. It would be a shame to waste all your hard work." She helped him up the steps to the stage, then turned to face the audience.

"All right, everyone!" Trish stepped up to the mic. "Find a seat so we can get started." She paused until the room quieted. "I'd like to welcome you to the Eazy Acres annual awards ceremony."

We waited in the wings as Trish handed out several awards, including Best Door Decoration and Most Original Halloween Costume. She presented Miles with an ornate wooden plaque that could have come from a medieval faire shop. The head of Eazy Acres followed with a blessedly short speech about being a family. Then he and the rest of the award winners took their seats at the front of the audience.

"And now," Trish said, "give a warm welcome to Raising Cain, Eazy Acres' own rock stars, with their guest singer, Dot Larue!"

After the wave of polite applause Dot stepped forward and bowed her head, a smile lighting up her face.

When the applause died, Trish continued, "And as a special treat, a man who won't let his broken leg keep him down, Fred Morales!" She clapped as she headed to the wings.

Shouts and applause filled the room and made our ears ring. Fred bowed and when the applause continued, gestured at Dot to join him at the mic. He nodded at Beth Ann.

She launched into "Hell Raiser."

Fred stepped back and let Dot sing the verses, while he sang with her on the chorus.

Dot was good, but unless you were tone-deaf, Fred sounded so much better. She appeared to know it, too, but grimly continued through the set list, gesturing awkwardly with her cane.

Then it was time for our finale, "Raising Cain." Now Fred's song.

When Missy played the opening chords, Dot looked at Fred, her eyes narrowed. Would she leave? No, she crossed the stage to share my mic. Good. She'd sound great on harmony.

Despite his crutches, Fred gave it his all. He couldn't work the stage, but he still commanded every eye in the room.

We came in at the end of the verse, and Dot gestured, swinging her cane wide. It whacked Fred on the shoulder, sending him staggering forward. He collapsed with a scream as his crutches skidded out from under him. Trish ran over, shouting for the nurse who sat in the audience.

Dot looked down at Fred, a hint of a smile on her lips.

Now I understood. "You did that on purpose."

She glanced at me. "What? Of course not."

"You did. I saw you." It all made sense. I stepped closer, away from the crowd gathering around Fred. "*You* pushed Fred down the stairs, so you could take his place."

"Don't be ridiculous." She backed up a step, stumbling over Sharon's drum kit.

I followed her. "You wanted Fred to blame Miles for being jealous, so you spritzed some of Miles's aftershave into the stairwell."

She gasped, not meeting my gaze. "Why would I—"

"I bet if we searched your apartment, we'd find the bottle. And we'd find your fingerprints on the door stops Missy tripped over."

Her arm jerked, and her cane hit Sharon's kick drum, the boom almost lost in the hubbub of voices behind us. "You're crazy!"

"I'm not the crazy one. You're good with crafting tools, you know band gear. Did you sabotage the power strip, too? Not the one with the tape, but the one Miles replaced it with. Then we would blame him for ruining the show. Or maybe you'd discover the problem and save the day, just like you saved the show when Fred fell and broke his leg."

I spotted a piece of pink fluffy wool on her shoulder. "There were bits of wool behind the amps. Someplace you had no reason to be."

Her eyes narrowed, and her chin set. Before I could move, she lashed out with her cane.

I still held my bass, and the cane banged into the edge of the guitar body, instead of my hip.

She raised her cane again, ready to bring it down on my head. I grabbed for it.

Then Sharon yelled "Watch out!" and tackled Dot.

Dot sprawled on the floor, eyes closed, breathing heavily. Sharon got to her feet, dusting her hands.

"You okay?" she asked me. "I heard her hit my kick drum and could see you were in trouble."

"Thanks." I blew out a breath. "Dot's the one who pushed Fred and sabotaged Missy's door mat. She wanted Miles to look guilty."

"Well, damn. Better call the police." Sharon rested her hands on her hips and stared down at Dot. "Too bad. She sounded great on harmony."

***

Two days later, we were back in the all-purpose room. Nothing had been touched since the awards ceremony.

"So much for our comeback." Sharon began to dismantle her drum kit.

"I don't know." Beth Ann looked thoughtful. "Once Fred's leg heals, he'll be a great front man."

Missy nodded. "At least Dot didn't do any lasting damage. Except to your bass."

"Oh, yeah?" I raised my brows. "She always hated being dismissed as a backup singer. She said she was a fan but admitted killing Jean just so she could take her place and get the recognition she craved."

No one spoke for a long moment.

Sharon shrugged. "Just goes to show. You can have a great voice and still be lousy at raising cain."

DEATH OF ANOTHER HERO
By Susan Daly

A local theater group revives its modern version of
Much Ado About Nothing, *reuniting the author, cast,
and crew from 25 years ago. But old sins have long
shadows, and a Shakespearian destiny is awaiting its
cue.*

"Hero, you're a woman in love. Let the audience hear it." The director's compelling tones resounded through the excellent acoustics of the Cedar Falls Centennial Theatre as I observed the rehearsal from the second row. "Beatrice, show your concern for her. Remember, she's your beloved cousin."

"I got to admit it, Maggie," Andy, sitting next to me, murmured, "that woman is some powerhouse."

I nodded, pleased with how well it was going. As the playwright, I was following closely with my script.

"How did the Summer Festival Committee ever persuade a talent like Beth Richmond to direct our quasquicentennial play?" Trust Andy to know the Latinate word for 125th anniversary, and to use it correctly in a sentence.

"She's from here originally," I reminded him. Though I didn't wonder that he'd forgotten the girl she'd once been.

Back in high school, Beth had gone by the unfortunate name of Bitsy. Overweight. Disastrous complexion. Personality of a tuna noodle casserole. Nothing remotely like the dynamic woman she was today.

Once free of the confining strictures of peer pressure from the popular, perfectly coifed and made-up girls who called the shots, she'd reinvented herself. She'd lost a third of her weight, done something with her hair and skin, and majored in self-actualisation and confidence.

Wonder of wonders, she was now a big-name director, equally in demand in both television and theater.

Here she was back in Cedar Falls for the 1993 Summer Theatre Festival. All silk suit, paisley scarf, and elegant jewellery, producing and directing the remounting of *Further Ado*, our centennial play from twenty-five years ago. She was giving it all the professionalism due an opening production at Stratford.

Beth wasn't the only local talent who'd made it big.

I glanced again toward the double doors at the back of the auditorium. I wasn't looking forward to seeing Gary Mortimer again, but damn it, couldn't the guy just show up on time so I could get the first meeting over with?

I returned my attention to the rehearsal. Beth, bless her, showed remarkable patience working with so many amateurs.

Until... "Where's Claudio?" she demanded.

Everyone looked around helpfully, in case he might be lurking in the wings. But if Gareth Caulfield, *aka* Gary Mortimer, had arrived, he wouldn't have gone unnoticed. Or unheralded.

"Okay," Beth said, "it looks like our star player still hasn't deigned to show up."

Definitely less patience with professionals than amateurs.

"I realise Gareth's a busy man," she went on, "and we're fortunate to have him grace our production." She didn't even hint that she was much more busy and important. "So, until he *can* join us...."

She scanned the theater for non-combatants and hit upon Ralph, sitting near Andy and me. "Ralph! Why don't you come up here and stand in for Gary?"

"Sure. Where do you want me?"

That was Ralph for you. Nice, easygoing guy. Always ready to help out. He'd been our set builder back in our original production, getting us paint and supplies from his dad's hardware store. This time around, he was providing pretty much the same support. Only more so.

"Thanks, Ralph. Over there."

Ralph stood where directed, and the first rehearsal of *Further Ado* got under way again.

***

In Shakespeare's *Much Ado About Nothing*, innocent Hero stands falsely accused by her fiancé. Claudio has been easily persuaded that Hero has cheated on him. On their wedding day, he denounces her before everyone. Nothing *she* says is believed.

Vilified and helpless, she falls into a faint and is taken up for dead.

Hero's cousin Beatrice defends her, and demands of her lover Benedick, "Kill Claudio."

Then, two witnesses step up to say it was all a setup, and the lady was indeed innocent. Claudio is in agonies of remorse over the death of his sweet, maligned Hero.

But lo! Hero is actually alive, still eager to marry the slimeball who doubted her virtue, disbelieved her word, and cruelly rejected her on their wedding day.

All's well—as it so often is in Shakespeare—that ends well. For the men. Claudio gets a virtuous wife. So does Benedick. And Benedick no longer has to kill his friend.

But I've never thought much of that ending. Hero deserved a better fate.

Which is why, twenty-five years ago, I wrote *Further Ado*. In which all truly ends well. Hero marries a man worthy of her, and Claudio retires to a monastery to spend his life in remorse and penitence and prayer.

But I still think I let Claudio off easy. Beatrice had other plans for him.

"O God, that I were a man! I would eat his heart in the market-place."

***

"So, Maggie, how'd the first rehearsal go?" Logie, owner and bartender at the Moose & Loon, handed me my rye on the rocks. I looked over at the table where the rest of the cast were catching up on old times. And where Gary, who'd finally arrived just as we were all heading out for drinks, was holding court as the Famous Star Doing an Incredibly Generous Favor for His Old Home Town.

"Not bad, considering our guest star didn't show up until it was over." I took a long sip of my drink and let its magic flow through my body. "But we've got Beth in charge. She knows what she's doing. And she was the one who got Gary to come home and reprise his old role."

"That's some coup." Logie poured himself a ginger ale and leaned on the bar. "Big TV star like him." He didn't seem to realise that Beth was an even bigger coup. To say nothing of the playwright.

Of course, he'd heard of Gareth Caulfield. Who in Canada over the age of thirty-five hadn't? Twenty-five years ago, Gary Mortimer had left his home town to make a name for himself (albeit a fake one). By a set of lucky circumstances, plus some talent and good looks on his part, he'd landed a supporting role as Constable Trent of the Mounties in the new CBC TV series, *The Scarlet Force*. It caught on big time, and through the following seasons he became the lead player, getting promoted to Sergeant, then Inspector. *The Scarlet Force* was exported to twenty-three countries in sixteen languages, and he became an internationally known figure.

After eight years, the series ended on a high note, with Inspector Trent marrying his long-time girlfriend in an episode that broke all audience records. Syndication followed, and it's been running ever since in even more countries and languages.

Gary could have lived forever quite comfortably on the income. And just as well, because he hadn't had a hit since. For seventeen years he'd been appearing in anything that came his way, mostly guest roles on TV series and minor parts in movies.

Lately, however, there had been rumors *The Scarlet Force* was being revived, and Gary had his sights set on making a comeback as Superintendent—or perhaps Commissioner—Trent.

Meanwhile, Gary was willing and available to return for a reprise of his first acting gig, as Claudio in *Further Ado*. The rest of the world may have moved on without him, but in Cedar Falls he was still the Home Town Boy Who Made Good.

Logie murmured, "Incoming actor," and straightened up to serve the approaching customer.

"Maggie Blue!" There was Gary. Still with his sparkling blue eyes, short blonde curls, and that trademark Inspector Trent modest-but-heroic smile. "I thought I caught of glimpse of you leaving the theater."

I couldn't duck his hearty embrace. "Hello, Gary."

"Don't tell me you're still hanging around this dead-end town after all these years."

Actually, it's a good-sized town, and a lively, prosperous one at that.

"I like it, and my family is here." Dad is the local GP and Mom's a high school teacher. "Since I'm a writer, I can work from just about anywhere. So yeah, I'm still around."

"A writer, eh?" The hint of interest in his voice sounded forced. "Had anything published?"

It wasn't worth my energy filling him in on the plays I'd had put on, the TV scripts produced. Or the Governor General's award for Drama.

"A few poems in literary quarterlies," I said. Which was true.

He made an effort to look impressed. "Good for you." He turned to Logie and ordered a Molson Golden. "What are you drinking, Maggie?"

"I've got mine, thanks." I excused myself to join the gang at the table.

I squeezed in between Andy and Ralph, while Gary returned to his seat across the table. Good. I didn't have to knock myself out being civil to him.

They were reminiscing about the original production, and Andy was filling in Sandy, one of our newcomers (playing Hero) on its history.

"Twenty-five years ago, the high school graduating class of

1968 put on a play to celebrate the town's centennial."

"There was all kinds of stuff going on that year," Ralph added, "and you could get a civic grant for just about anything. Somehow, after a night of underage drinking and throwing crazy ideas around, we put together a grant application as a lark and sent it to the Centennial Committee."

"We pretty much forgot about it until we got an approval," Andy said. "Along with the princely sum of $500. *And* the honor of performing for the grand reopening of the newly refurbished Cedar Falls Centennial Theatre."

"So, then you couldn't *not* do it?" Sandy guessed.

"Well," Ralph said, "we had to actually come up with a play. But Maggie had written this great modern version of *Much Ado About Nothing* for English class."

"We all decided it would be a hoot," I said. "It was our last time together. We were all bound for university or other destinies in the fall."

"I was on my way to my first big break as Constable Trent," Gary pointed out. Did he ever miss an opportunity to bring that up?

Sandy looked over at Beth. "Were you the director then, too, Beth?"

"Mrs. Pike was the director," Ralph said. "Our English teacher. She was having a last hurrah before her retirement."

"I just filled in here and there," Beth told her quietly. She didn't really need anyone to remember her as Bitsy, in her social outcast phase, when she'd had to settle for handling props.

***

After too many drinks and too much reminiscence, we all made moves toward home. I live only a few blocks away, so I said goodnight and headed along the river walk in the fresh spring night.

But Gary wasn't ready yet to let me get away. He caught up with me, though the hotel was in the opposite direction.

"Still single, Maggie? I don't see a ring on your finger."

The age-old tell that a woman is taken or available. "No, Gary, you don't. But—"

"Me, too. At the moment. Say, I seem to recall we had a pretty good thing going back then, didn't we?"

I stopped walking and turned to face him. "Well, you recall wrong, Gary. There was nothing between us back in high school."

"No way! I have a distinct memory of that night after the Spring Dance in our last year...."

Shit. It was worse than I thought.

"Gary—"

"Or maybe you just don't want to remember." His voice held a teasing note. "But I sure do. You were so hot—"

"*Carly*," I stated. "You're thinking of my cousin Carly."

Carly, who twenty-five years ago had been cast as Hero opposite Gary's Claudio.

I could see it sinking in, drop by drop. Memory of Carly. What happened with Carly. How Carly wasn't me. Finally, the realization that, maybe, even for a jerk like him, he'd crossed the line. Mistaking an old girlfriend for someone completely different.

I waited. Let him make the next move.

"Oh…" He assumed a *gosh, silly me* look. "Geez, I'm sorry. What can I say? I'm a jerk. Of *course*… Carly. How could I ever forget her?"

How indeed. But he clearly had. And his next words made it clearer.

"How *is* she, anyway?"

Everything just froze within me. I could barely find a word to choke out. Not even the words I'd been wanting him to hear for twenty-five years.

I just turned and walked away.

***

Twenty-five years ago…

"You're pregnant, aren't you?"

Carly nods, her whole body and soul in a state of misery.

I hold my cousin tight, feeling the sobs shaking her vulnerable little body.

"Oh, Carly, sweetie…just hang on. I'll see you through it. We'll work it out."

She shakes her head. "I can't. He doesn't…he won't even…"

"Okay, okay, it's all right. Who is 'he'? Ralph?"

Ralph's a good guy. Maybe—

She shakes her head again. "It's Gary."

Oh shit.

"He said it's not his. Oh Maggie, there's no one else."

I let her talk.

He said she should have known. She should have stopped him. He thought she was safe. He thought she was on The Pill.

There must be a handbook somewhere, with all these pathetic lines. Things to Say When a Girl Tells You She's Pregnant.

"He said I was trying to trick him into marrying me."

I explode with this one.

"Marrying you! Who'd want to be stuck with that—?"

Carly bursts into fresh tears, and I realize I've gone beyond my supporting role.

"Sorry, sorry. And you love him?"

Shake of head. Nod. "I don't know!" This is a heartfelt wail.

"He won't even help you through it?" Fat chance.

"He's got an audition next week for a television role. This could be his big break. I can't stand in the way of his career, just when it's taking off."

I can't comment on that without exploding, so I move on to the most important matter.

"What do you want to do?"

She doesn't know. She's in no state, I realize, to make any decisions. Not right now.

I hold her tight. I'll be there for her, whatever happens. Whatever she decides.

***

Times being what they were in Canada in 1968—to say nothing of the politics—Carly had zero access to safe, legal abortion. The following year a tight-assed law was passed to "permit" a woman to abort if a panel of three doctors decided her health would be in danger if she gave birth. Big help. That remained in force until 1988 when the abortion law was struck down absolutely.

The standard process then was for a girl to visit a mythical aunt for a few months, conveniently living in another province, then return home and carry on as though nothing had happened.

That, or the illegal practitioner. The fall down the stairs. The knitting-needle.

I had a few friends who'd been there, who knew someone safe. I'd have gone with her and helped her through it.

But it didn't happen that way.

Carly called me the morning of the performance.

She couldn't, *couldn't*, play opposite Gary on the stage. The dress rehearsal had been hell.

I understood. In the play Claudio publicly accuses Hero of infidelity, rejects her at their wedding. Is unmoved when she dies of her humiliation.

Could I go on in her place, she asked?

Absolutely, I assured her. I'd written the damn play. I'd helped her learn her lines, back when she'd been in love with Gary.

I told her to stay home and rest. Not to worry about it. I'd see her the next day.

At the theater, I announced that Carly had come down with a 24-hour flu, and could barely get out of bed, and that I'd fill in for her.

The show went on. It was a huge success, despite the last-minute cast change.

***

The next morning Gary left Cedar Falls to follow his quest for fame.

What I didn't know was that right after talking to me, Carly had caught the bus to Toronto.

Gary had given her $100 to "take care of it." On the condition no one knew. He'd come up with the name of someone in Toronto and washed his hands of it all.

The following day, she came home. She took a cab from the bus station straight to our house because my dad—her uncle—was a doctor. She didn't want to tell him what had happened, but he knew. How could he not?

Dad was beside himself with anger.

By the time we got her to Emerg, it was already too late.

Blood loss. Septicaemia.

"Don't tell anyone who it was." Her voice was barely a thread. "Promise me."

I had to promise her.

She died holding my hand.

Dad and I cried together, over a very large bottle of rye.

"If only she'd told us," he kept saying.

I looked at him. What...?

"I'd have done it myself."

Carly's last words had been to protect the unworthy. I had promised to do what she wanted. I'd had no choice.

But I didn't say I wouldn't avenge her if ever I got the chance.

***

The remount of *Further Ado* was a sell-out on all four nights, and a huge hit, only partly due to the fame of the director, the playwright, and one of the leads.

It was an even handsomer production than before. Ralph's family hardware business had prospered immeasurably since 1968, and so the sets were of impressive quality, professionally executed. As a bonus, Hammersmith Hardware had even underwritten the cost of renting the sumptuous costumes.

After the final curtain calls, after the exhilaration of closing night, after the makeup was removed and the costumes were packed away, the cast and crew and supporters all headed out to the closing night party at the Moose & Loon.

I sat alone in the greenroom, hearing the voices grow fewer and the footsteps fainter, the last door slam. Quiet reigned in the old theater.

I waited.

Footsteps down the hall. Gary's voice, airing his impatience.

"Look, they're expecting me at the party."

"This won't take long," Beth assured him. The door opened and Beth, Gary, and Ralph entered.

Gary didn't look pleased to see me.

"What's this all about?"

"Have a seat, Gary," Ralph said. "We just want to talk with you."

He dropped into an overstuffed chair. We might have been having a family chat in an old-fashioned living room.

"You guys don't get it," he said. "I have an important announcement to make at the party."

"Oh?" I said.

He couldn't resist. "It's happening at last. The return of Inspector Trent. CBC is bringing back *The Scarlet Force*, starting with a two-hour premiere episode. I've just signed the contract for the opening special."

And that, his tone said, *is more important than whatever you guys have to say.*

"Congratulations, Gary," I said. "Have you seen the script?"

"Not yet, but the producer has given me an idea of what's in store, filling in the gaps from where we left off seventeen years ago. Of course, I'm older, more mature. I'll be Superintendent Trent, but still involved with hands-on police work. Lots of action. After all, as the hero, I need to *be* heroic."

Beth nodded. "Of course."

He was getting more enthusiastic now. "I've given them some ideas that will make the series better. A younger love interest, for example."

Ralph glanced at me before saying, "But Gary, Trent is married. He and his childhood sweetheart tied the knot in that big final episode."

Gary didn't seem fazed at this. "I'm going to have them kill her off. After all, Réjeanne would be in her forties now—"

"So would Trent," Beth pointed out.

I'd heard enough. Time to get down to business.

"You know, Gary, I never liked you. You're an obnoxious, egotistical jerk. You don't care who you ride down in your quest for success. And trying to kill off Réjeanne so you can cavort with a woman half your age? You really haven't changed."

"Oh *please*, Maggie. It's just a story. You'd think Réjeanne was a real person."

"Carly was a real person."

"Carly?" This seemed to hit him out of left field. "What's she got to do with anything?"

"You got her pregnant."

"What? And you're bringing that up *now*?" He paused, then added, "*If* it was mine."

"Yeah, you decided it wasn't, since the timing would interfere with your new career as Trent of the Mounties."

Gary shrugged. "I thought she'd deal with it."

"You thought *nothing*. You threw money at the problem and forgot all about her. Even when I said she was too sick to be in the play that night, you didn't ask how she was."

He seemed to rummage around in his beleaguered brain for a memory. "Oh, that. Didn't she have a cold or something?"

"She couldn't bear to be on stage with you, because Claudio decides Hero's been unfaithful and denounces her. I had no idea when I wrote the play that you'd play it so true to life."

"Hey, come on..."

"I also had no idea then that while we were performing the play without her, she was in Toronto having an abortion. Alone."

He still seemed unconvinced of any wrongdoing.

"Well, hey, that's sad, but it was a long time ago. I've moved on."

"You moved on the moment she told you."

"So she got rid of it. Her choice."

I couldn't speak. I could barely breathe.

Ralph stepped in, to keep me from doing him harm.

"Maggie isn't the only one who cared about Carly."

"Huh?" Gary's way with words was unimpressive.

"She and I were good friends. Homework, lunch, library, that sort of thing. But she had no idea I loved her. Then I realised she was in love with you. I hated you then, Gary, but I couldn't change how she felt. I figured I'd eventually outlast you."

"And you've held a grudge against me all this time? Just for *that*? Or is it because all these years later, I've made something of myself, and you're still selling nails and mixing paint at your dad's hardware store?"

Ralph's face remained stony.

"No. Because all these years later I found out what happened to her."

Gary's contemptuous disbelief was all over his face.

"What, that she got herself knocked up?"

Now I had to hold Ralph back, with a hand on his arm, while Gary, on a roll, turned to Beth.

"I suppose *you* were in love with her, too."

Beth remained benign. "No. I barely knew Carly. But I sure remember you, and what you did to me on the night of the play."

"What are you talking about? You weren't even there. You weren't at school with us. I'd have remembered—"

"You remember eff-all! Or maybe you remember Bitsy Richmond? The props manager?"

He made an effort. "Uh, yeah. Okay. But that wasn't *you*. That girl was really—"

"Fat? Yes, I was. That didn't mean I couldn't do a job. Thing is, Props is the worst job in the theater, because no matter how often we lay down the law, there's always some asshole who doesn't put stuff back on the props table when they exit. And you were that asshole. You carried your damned dagger offstage and promptly mislaid it. Then you went ballistic when it wasn't there for the next act."

"Seriously? You're as bad at these two. Spending your life moaning because I misplaced your precious dagger."

"Hardly. What destroyed me was when you lost your shit backstage at intermission, in front of the cast and crew and within hearing range of half the audience. You yelled obscenities at me for *your* mistake, and called me things that made me hate myself."

"Oh, get out. I did not."

"You said—and the words were branded on my soul—'You fat, ugly, stupid lesbo bitch, you can't even do a no-brainer job like keeping track of props without fucking it up.'"

"That's pretty accurate," I said. "I was there. I heard it."

Ralph nodded. "Me, too."

Gary looked around at each of us, then he leaned back in his chair with a look of calm contempt.

"Yeah, all right. I've been a real shit. Who hasn't been at some time or another? But you know something? That's all in the past. Isn't it about time you all moved on?"

"Actually," I said, "we all *have* moved on. All except Carly."

"Well, tell her from me *she* should move on, too. That was twenty-five years ago."

"Carly died, Gary. She bled to death from the botched abortion."

Finally, something sank in. Gary turned several shades of grey. His mouth moved without sound.

The rest of us exchanged conspiratorial looks.

"Any reason we shouldn't just kill him?" Ralph asked.

"I don't see why we should let him live," I said. "All the misery he likes to cause."

"And we can alibi each other," Beth added. "Piece of cake."

"Uh, no…you can't be serious." But Gary's uneasy look said he wasn't so sure of that.

I wanted to keep him in fear for his life much longer, but the others took pity on him.

"It's okay, Gary," Ralph said at last. "We're not planning to kill you."

"Of course not," Beth said. "You didn't *actually* think we would, did you?"

Gary breathed again. He got to his feet with an unconvincing little laugh.

"Nah. I knew you were just giving me a hard time. And maybe I deserved it. Geez...Carly. The poor kid."

"Yeah, killing you would be wrong," Ralph said. "And not nearly satisfying enough."

"Wait...what?"

I stepped in to explain. "Instead, we're going to kill someone near and dear to you. Someone whose death will cause you lifelong loss and regret."

The haunted look returned to his pasty face.

"We're going to kill Inspector Trent."

Now that it was clear he was dealing with lunatics, he gave a cynical laugh, and with a few pithy words he turned and left the room.

"Don't worry," I called after him. "We'll make sure he dies a hero's death."

***

Six months later, the TV movie of *The Scarlet Force* was aired as a prelude to a new generation of Mounties in the series revival. As we'd promised, Inspector Trent had his final moment of glory, rescuing three children and their mother from a crazed gunman. Sadly, he died in the act.

Fans loved it or hated it, but they were all ready to move on to a more diverse Scarlet Force, with modern plotlines. Including a strong storyline for Réjeanne, the grieving widow.

The viewers of Canada had outgrown the brave, noble Inspector Trent.

Which is why, when the producers were developing the new series, they went with an award-winning scriptwriter (me) and a director with solid creds (Beth), and gave us full artistic control. Not only that, they found an enthusiastic sponsor in Hammersmith Hardware, now grown to the second-largest hardware and building supply chain in Canada.

That hero's death bothers me, though.

I'd still have preferred to eat his heart in the marketplace.

THE STARS ARE FIRE
By Phillip DePoy

*Playacting and real life are on a collision course
when the stage manager plans to replace the actress
playing Ophelia with the understudy.*

Years ago, I had a friend called Sammy Two Shoes. We grew up together in the streets, pitched pennies, stole hubcaps, got shot at. The kind of thing that makes you somebody's brother. Sammy was in love with a woman who was in love with the theatre. She was what you call a stage manager, which, far as I could figure, was the person in charge. When the director had gone on to another project and the producer was busy complaining about audience numbers, the stage manager had to keep the whole thing on its feet.

Her name was Phoebe B. Peabody, if you can believe it, and she was a knockout. I met her at Reno Sweeney's one evening early. Reno Sweeney's is gone now. So is Sammy Two Shoes. But I'm getting ahead of myself.

I met Sammy at Reno Sweeney's because Blossom Dearie was playing there and who doesn't love Blossom? I was having a good old fashioned Negroni at the bar when Sammy showed up with Phoebe at his side. She stood about five foot six, white-blond hair, eyes greener than money, dressed in junk shop chic. Sammy was wearing one of his favorite suits, the double-breasted salt and pepper with the lapels too wide for his skinny frame. If you asked me.

Sammy had been keeping his relationship on the sly, mostly because he didn't want his new flame to know his old criminals. But that's where I came in. Phoebe was in trouble, and Sammy knew I could help. Because I was considered something of a buttinsky. At least that's what my Aunt Shayna called it. I called it helping a friend.

Phoebe's trouble was named Emory. Emory was an actor. They were all trouble, according to Phoebe, but Emory more than most. Because Emory wanted Phoebe dead.

"Show him the latest," Sammy said to Phoebe.

Phoebe produced a note and put it on the bar beside my Negroni. It said, "How now? A rat? Dead, for a ducat, dead!"

I looked up from the note. "What's a ducat?"

"It's from *Hamlet*," Sammy told me. "That's the show Phoebe is running."

"It's an all-girl cast," Phoebe added, a little wearily. "The director had a *concept*. It's set in a women's prison."

I finished my drink. "Sounds just terrible. How can I help?"

"Razz this Emory character," Sammy snapped. "Get her to stop leaving Phoebe notes like this."

"What makes you think," I asked Sammy, "that I'd be the sort of person to hassle some poor actor just for leaving a note?"

"Tell him," Sammy said to Phoebe.

"Emory wants to kill me," Phoebe said, "because I'm replacing her in the show. She's always late. She doesn't know her lines. She's missed two performance altogether. And we've only been open for a week! Plus, she also tried to kill Nan."

"Nan is what you call a *understudy*," Sammy told me. "The understudy's taking over, see? And this Emory, she's out for blood."

"The thing is, Nan's understudied *every* role," Phoebe told me. "She's the only substitute we got. I can't have anything happen to her."

I locked eyes with Phoebe. "Isn't it just possible that it's all talk? I mean: theatre, right?"

"Emory went to Nan's apartment last night and fired a gun into the poor kid's door," Phoebe said. "It was lucky Nan was in the bathroom."

"This understudy," I asked, "she knew it was Emory?"

"Emory was screaming, 'I'm Ophelia! Not you!'"

"That's the part this Emory dame's got," Sammy filled in. "Ophelia. She's Hamlet's girlfriend."

Phoebe looked at Sammy with love in her eyes, or something like it. "He's seen the show seven times."

He nodded, staring back. "I think I almost got the hang of it."

I stood up, mostly to get away from the mooning.

"Look," I told them both, "I've had people shoot at my door more than once. It's just a way to blow off steam. You're making too much out of this. But if you want, I'll talk to Emory. Where can I find her?"

"The show starts at eight," Sammy said instantly. "Let's go."

"Now?" I looked over at the stage. "No. I gotta hear Blossom. And there's a rumor that Bob Dorough is gonna sit in."

Anyone could see why it was a tough decision: save an actor or listen to Blossom. On the one hand, they say that actors are almost like real people. On the other hand, what if Bob Dorough was really going to show up?

In the end, Sammy prevailed upon my better instincts by saying, "Come on, man, I'm in love."

Sammy Two Shoes in love was a rare monster, and I couldn't ignore it.

So off to a little theatre I went.

***

The theatre, if you could call it that, was on Cornelia Street, not far from where Caffe Cino used to be. Really just a storefront with folding chairs and coffee can lights. The place was deserted, dark, and depressing.

"I'll show you the dressing room," Phoebe told me.

She took me down a hall to a concrete room that would have made a neat slaughterhouse. The walls were lined with tables, and cheap mirrors were propped up. Every chair had a name Scotch-taped to the back. We stopped at the one that said *Understudy*. There was a dead rat on her hand mirror. Fresh.

"It's too much!" Phoebe complained. "The understudy's scared to come in, audiences *hate* the play, the director's in Pittsburgh, and the actors haven't been paid since the second week of rehearsal. Now I gotta deal with a dead *rat*!"

With that she picked up the poor thing by its tail and marched out of the room.

Sammy appeared in the doorway of the dressing room.

"Is she the coolest thing you ever saw?" he asked me.

"Like a daiquiri," I told him. "So, this rat motif is a thing, then?"

"What's a *motif*?"

"Doesn't matter." I sighed. "When do the actors show up?"

"Any time now," he said.

I went to the chair that said *Ophelia*. It was neat as a pin. Makeup lined up, notepad with a pencil in the spiral, an unopened bottle of water. Evian.

Before I could examine it further, I heard voices coming down the hall. Sammy stepped aside and three younger women stormed in. The stopped when they saw me.

"Oh, good," one said, squinting. "Another stage door Casanova."

"He's here to help," Sammy protested, then lowered his voice. "You know. With Emory."

They froze.

One whispered, "Is she here?"

I shook my head.

They seemed relieved. Each went to her assigned seat and a weird silence settled into the cramped little room. Within five minutes everyone was there and seated at her station. Everyone but Emory.

"You really gonna help us with Emory?" Polonius asked me.

"Do my best," I said.

"Good," she said. "She scares me."

"I'm about to punch her in her face," Claudius mumbled, putting on her wig.

Gertrude shrugged. "I wouldn't mind if she got hit by a cab."

Phoebe stuck her head in and said, "Five minutes. But we're holding for Emory."

"Five minutes?" I asked Hamlet.

"We're supposed to start the show in five," she explained. "But since Emory's not here…"

She trailed off and fussed with her shirt. I resumed my examination of Emory's things. I noticed that the pencil stuck in the spiral pad was one of those mechanical jobs, a little larger than most. A quick glance around told me that nobody else had a pad and pencil.

"Why does Emory have a note pad here?" I asked out loud.

Hamlet answered without turning to face me.

"She makes a big deal of taking notes after every show," she said.

"Notes about what?" I asked.

Hamlet shrugged.

So, I opened the pad. The notes were all printed in capital letters.

> HAMLET LEFT OUT THREE WORDS IN "TO BE OR NOT TO BE" SPEECH.
> GERTRUDE CALLED ME A COW BACKSTAGE.
> POLONIUS STINKS.

They were all like that. Just as I was flipping the page, I heard an angry voice behind me.

"What the hell are you doing?"

I turned to see the kid: red-faced, skinny, dressed in black, eyes wild, hand reaching into her bulky purse.

"Are you Emory?" I began.

But the hand came out of the purse with a can of Mace in it.

I didn't mean to smack her hand. It was instinct. Someone on the street pulls a gun, I don't think about it. My hand just does what it does. And in this case, my hand knocked the Mace into Emory's mirror. The mirror did the only thing it could. It shattered.

Mayhem ensued.

Apparently, actors are a superstitious lot. You can't say "good luck." You can't whistle in a dressing room. You can't say

Macbeth, even though it's the name of a perfectly good play. All of which I learned that night. And a broken mirror was the Titanic, the Hindenburg, and Pearl Harbor rolled into one.

It took Phoebe a full ten minutes to calm everyone down. Emory wanted me in jail.

In the end, it was showtime. That drew everyone away from me and onto the stage.

I watched the whole show. Many of the performers got some of the lines right.

When it was over, the audience, all fifteen of them, left quickly. I was about to do the same when there was a scream from the dressing room.

Phoebe shot out of the booth, flew backstage. I wasn't far behind. Sammy was already there. He'd been watching from the wings.

All of the dressing room lights were on, so it wasn't hard to see the blood coming from Emory's neck. She was face down on the table in front of her. The mechanical pencil from her spiral pad was stuck in her jugular. I knew she was dead before I went to feel for a pulse.

***

By the time the cops showed, Sammy and I were gone. We'd both had uncomfortable experiences with the police. I went back to Reno Sweeney's; walked in just in time to hear Bob Dorough and Blossom sing "Two Sleepy People." I don't know where Sammy went.

Next morning I awoke to the sound of banging on my door. This always makes me nervous, because it can't be good that someone is that agitated before noon. I stumbled to the door in my underwear, .44 in hand, stood to one side, and said, very gently, "Who is it?"

"It's Sammy! You gotta help me. Phoebe's in jail!"

I sighed and opened the door. He flew in, same suit as the night before.

"You might have expected that," I told him. "The cops nabbed the person standing closest to the body. That would have been you and me if we'd stayed there."

"I don't care," Sammy said. "You gotta get her off, because you know she didn't do it."

Now, the cops in my neighborhood were overworked and underpaid and people were always tossing lead their way. I had no idea what it was like to be a cop in the neighborhood of a theatre where an all-woman *Hamlet* would play, but they might not be completely committed to their work. Because it was a lazy thing indeed to arrest the person who called in the crime.

***

The theatre was locked, but that wasn't the problem. The problem was the time of day. Lots of people walking by. No privacy in which to pop the front door open. So I wandered around the building to the back alley. It was less crowded and more disgusting. And the back door wasn't locked.

I heard people talking. Someone said, "Couldn't have happened to a nicer girl."

"Is that Hamlet?" I called out.

Silence.

"It's me, the guy from last night." I made it to the dressing room door.

The room was full. All the actors were packing up their things.

"No show tonight?" I asked, standing in the doorway.

"Cops closed us down," Polonius told me.

"Look, man," Hamlet said. "Did you do this?"

"Close your show?" I smiled. "I'm not a cop."

"Stab Emory with her own pencil," Hamlet snapped. "I mean, you said last night you were going to help with the situation, but this was a little severe, don't you think?"

"Me? Why would I stab an actor? I'm not a theatre critic."

"What are you doing here then?" Gertrude mumbled, brushing the last of her stuff into a large paper shopping bag.

"Phoebe's in jail," I said. "And I don't think she did anything to deserve it."

"So you're here to help get Phoebe out?" Hamlet sounded doubtful.

I nodded.

Skepticism reigned, but at least they didn't ask me to leave.

"I would have thought this would be, like, a crime scene," I ventured.

"When I got here," Hamlet explained, "the police were packing up. Case closed. Crime solved."

But it wasn't. So I spent the next twenty minutes talking with the actors. It wasn't especially interesting and mostly useless. Hamlet hated Emory the worst. The scenes they had together were a nightmare, apparently. Emory made up Ophelia's lines and that made Hamlet look stupid. But everyone in the cast had it out for Emory, so there really wasn't a shortage of suspects. As they all finished packing up and started to filter out, I asked the big question.

"So, who did kill Emory? Because I'm pretty sure it's not the one the police have locked up."

I looked down at Emory's place at the dressing table. It was covered in broken glass from the mirror and dried blood from the actor.

"I heard she had a boyfriend she cheated on," Polonius suggested. "She complained about him a couple of nights."

"It wasn't one of us," Gertrude told me. "Actors only *want* to kill other actors; they don't ever really do it."

"I had a girlfriend in college," Claudius said, "who put cayenne pepper in my face powder once."

"What about this Nan, the understudy?" I asked.

"She wasn't here last night," Hamlet said.

"She was scared of Emory," Gertrude whispered. "Emory shot up her apartment."

"I had a girlfriend once who shot at me," Claudius volunteered.

I looked around the room. My impression was that none of these people could kill anything stronger than a bottle of Chardonnay, but I didn't really know the theatre world.

As soon as everyone was out, I took a good look at Emory's place. Most of her stuff was gone, including the spiral notebook and the pencil, of course, but also most of her makeup and some of the bits of mirror. I was certain that the police had taken everything that mattered, but I thought it was still worth a good close look.

I was staring at all the bits of broken mirror when I had an idea about *when* Emory might have been killed. Her place was the tidiest one of all the actor spots when I'd first seen it. Emory was neat. If she'd had time, she would have cleaned up the bits of mirror. And the thing about Ophelia is, she jumps in a river and drowns a good half-hour before the play's over. Which meant that Emory would have had time to tidy up when she came off, before the curtain calls. Which might have meant she'd been killed during the last couple of scenes of the play, when just about everybody in the whole thing is onstage for the final slaughter scene. The main characters *not* on stage, because they were already dead or gone, were Polonius, Rosencrantz, and Guildenstern. Then there was Nan, the understudy, who could have showed up. I thought I'd start there.

***

Less than an hour later, I knocked on Nan's door. It had five bullet holes in it.

"Who is it?" someone asked.

"I'm sort of a friend of Phoebe's," I told her. "Did you hear about Emory?"

Silence. Maybe she hadn't heard.

Then the lock clicked, and the door cracked. Nan peered out.

"I heard." She stood there.

"Then you heard they arrested Phoebe," I went on.

"Yeah," Nan said, "Phoebe didn't do it."

The door opened all the way.

Nan was a pixie: five-foot-nothing, close-cropped hair, dark blue eyes. She was wearing a tee shirt that said "To be or…line?" and no shoes.

"The police came to see you?" I asked, still standing in the hall.

She shook her head. "Gossip's like lightning in the theatre world."

"May I come in?" I asked.

She thought about it, then stood aside to let me in.

There were posters all over the walls and Mozart on the stereo.

"Your place is smaller than mine," I said.

"If I'd been in this room when Emory came over the other night," Nan told me, "I'd be lying here dead."

"Emory was scary," I agreed.

"How can I help you?" she asked, still standing by the door. "Or, really, how can I help Phoebe? I like her."

"Did you kill Emory?" I asked calmly.

Sometimes a thing like that worked. You catch a person off guard, and their face can tell you everything.

Nan's eyes widened.

"Were you in the theatre last night?" I went on.

"I was at Tap-a-Keg down the block," she assured me. "From around seven until after midnight. They know me there. Ask anybody."

"I'll do that." But I wouldn't. I could see she was telling the truth.

"Jesus," she muttered. "Emory's dead."

"Right," I said. "Can you go through a few things with me?"

"Such as?"

"In the last scene, when Hamlet kills everybody," I began, "Polonius and some other characters aren't on stage because they're dead or gone, right?"

"Those characters aren't on stage, but the actors are. They fill out the court. Everyone's onstage for the last scene."

"So, nobody would be in the dressing room?"

She bit her lower lip. "Well, nobody's *supposed* to be. But most of the time Emory didn't come back on. She told me that her performance had made too strong an impression, and she'd be recognized if she came back on stage. She said it would spoil the show."

"But nobody else?"

"No. Everybody else is onstage. Is that important?"

"If Emory was killed during the last scene," I said, "then we have a dozen witnesses who can clear Phoebe. She was in the booth. And there's no way to get from the booth to the dressing room without everybody seeing."

"Because the booth is right there at the back of the audience," she agreed.

"Doesn't tell me who killed Emory," I said, "but it does tell me that *Phoebe* didn't do it, and that's all I care about."

It seemed clear to me that I'd have to talk with the other cast members to see what had been up with Emory the night she died. If it was true that she often didn't appear in the last scene, the actors, and maybe other people, would know that she might be in the dressing room during that scene. It would be the ideal time for someone to slip in, ice her, and be back on stage.

So, I went to talk to Hamlet.

***

Hamlet's address was Central Park West. Apparently, Hamlet's parents were loaded. They weren't home, but Hamlet was, along with some sort of little dog that yapped and snapped.

Hamlet was hung over.

"I can't believe they closed the show," she muttered. "When am I gonna get another chance to play Hamlet?"

"Let's talk about Emory," I said.

"Why?" She tried to focus her eyes.

"She's dead. Somebody killed her. That's the reason the show got shut down."

Hamlet shook her head. "That's just an excuse. The show wasn't doing well. Critics hated it. Audiences agreed."

"I thought you were pretty good," I told her, but mostly because I'd heard that actors responded well to compliments.

Hamlet looked me in the eye. "Really? Did you really think so?"

"You're the best female Hamlet I ever saw." It was a true statement in that she was the only female Hamlet I'd ever seen.

"Well." She smiled.

"Emory was a pain in the ass," I prompted.

"There's not an actor in the cast who wouldn't have minded sticking that pencil *somewhere*," Hamlet agreed, "but actors *complain*. They don't kill people."

"John Wilkes Booth was an actor."

"Don't know him. Was he in anything that I might have seen?"

"Right," I said. "You were on stage for the last scene."

"Yes." She blinked. "I kill a bunch of people and then I get killed."

"I remember," I told her. "You couldn't possibly have gotten off stage to stab Emory. But who could have? Any thoughts?"

She took a second.

"Polonius stays in the shadows," Hamlet said, "because she's supposed to be dead. She could have slipped away. Same for Rosencrantz and Guildenstern. Everyone else is kind of prominent."

"Because they end up slaughtered on the stage," I nodded. "Mostly by you."

"Why are you doing this?" she asked. "Why are you trying to get Phoebe out of jail?"

"Because she didn't do it." Simple.

"No, but, I mean," she went on, "what's your motivation?"

"Oh." I smiled. "Sammy Two Shoes is my friend, and he's in love with Phoebe."

"That's all?" She squinted. "Helping a friend?"

"When a cop was whacking me with a club one night," I explained further, "Sammy kicked the cop in the head. When I got shot, he took me to a guy and got me patched up. When my mother was sick, Sammy brought her soup. When I was in jail once, Sammy bailed me out. Should I go on?"

"I'd rather you didn't," Hamlet said.

"What else can you tell me about the three actors who might have slipped away to pop Emory?"

"Emory hated Polonius," Hamlet told me. "Every night there was some complaint about how Polonius didn't understand the relationship with Ophelia."

I nodded. "I saw one of the things Emory wrote about Polonius in that little spiral notebook she kept."

"Anyway, with Rosencrantz and Guildenstern it might have been more personal. They're dating, and I think Rosencrantz used to go out with Emory."

"Jealousy is always a good motive for murder, they say."

"Your problem is," she said, "that everybody hated Emory. I mean, if you're asking me, my money would be on Nan. If somebody shot up my door, I'd be the worst kind of mad."

"The worst kind of mad?" I asked.

"You know, *scared*-mad. The kind where you're not thinking, you're just reacting."

"Oh." As it happened, I did know scared-mad. Like when a cop was beating you with his club and you're pretty sure you're going to die.

Rosencrantz and Guildenstern lived together in a one-room flat. The place was a wreck. Piles of clothes on the floor, no bathroom door, dozens of takeout containers everywhere. Guildenstern came to the door in her underwear. Rosencrantz appeared to be asleep on the mattress on the floor. The blinds were drawn against the sunlight, exacerbating the atmosphere of chaos and gloom.

"What?" Guildenstern demanded.

"I was at the theatre last night," I said. "I'm trying to get Phoebe out of jail."

Rosencrantz rolled over in bed and there was a gun in her hand. It was too dark to be sure, but it looked like a .38 Special.

I stood very still.

"It would go like this," Rosencrantz told me. "'There was a strange man at the door, Officer. He menaced my roommate and tried to force his way in. You don't know what it's like to be a young girl in this part of town. We were terrified.'"

I nodded. "It's a plausible speech."

"So maybe you should get lost," Guildenstern suggested.

"Don't you want to help Phoebe?" I asked. "Because you know she didn't kill Emory."

"I don't really know anything," Guildenstern answered belligerently.

"The cops know what they're doing," Rosencrantz added.

"Just let me ask you one question," I said. "During the last scene, when everybody on stage gets killed, did you see anyone slip out? Because I think that's when Emory was killed. During the last scene."

Rosencrantz lowered her gun. "Polonius always splits when Gertrude dies. She's dressed as a courtly lady, right, and she makes like it's too much to see the queen dead. She, like, flees."

Guildenstern agreed. "That's right. She flees."

Rosencrantz nodded. "She goes out in the back alley for a smoke. She's got a real nicotine problem."

Guildenstern shrugged. "It's a real problem."

"You both stayed on stage for the whole scene," I said.

"Of course," Rosencrantz said, a little offended. "You can't just walk out of a scene. It's not professional."

"It isn't professional at all," Guildenstern echoed.

I apologized for bothering them, because it's always a good idea to apologize to a person with a gun, and I left.

***

Polonius lived in a sort of a dorm room at Tisch with three other students. She was tall and weighed in at about ninety-five pounds. Stringy blond hair, bloodshot eyes, she came to the door in a large mechanic's shirt that said "Ralph" on it, wearing it like a dress.

"You're that guy who saw the show last night," she mumbled. "The nosy one in the dressing room."

"Right," I said. "Can I come in? I'm trying to get Phoebe out of jail."

She stepped aside. "I love Phoebe."

The roommates were all at a table having breakfast. At a little after noon. Polonius sat down on the sofa next to the door, and I joined her. She lit a cigarette and closed her eyes when she inhaled.

"I didn't kill Emory, if that's what you want to know."

"You left the stage during the last scene," I said. "I'm pretty sure that's when Emory was stabbed."

"I went out for a smoke," she complained. "If I go more than a half-hour without, I get itchy. I left the stage, zoomed out the back, smoked in the alley, and was back in time for final bows. Sue me."

"Sue you? You're an actor. How much money could I get?"

"Good point." She took another deep drag. "You *should* be talking to the guy I saw in the dressing room when I ran by. That guy might know something."

I sat up. "There was a guy?"

"I figured it was one of Emory's boyfriends. She was always complaining about her exes."

"Boyfriend?" I blinked. "Even though she used to date Rosencrantz?"

"She was an equal opportunity employer."

"Did you get a look at him?" I asked. "The boyfriend?"

She shook her head and flicked ashes all over the place.

"But he was wearing a suit, I could see that. None of her other boyfriends *owned* a suit."

I had a sudden, very bad feeling.

"I think they call it a salt-and-pepper," she went on. "Double-breasted. Great big lapels."

***

I found Sammy at Izzy's Deli, near where he lived. He could tell by my face that the jig was up. I should have known right away that he was the one. It was the biggest cliché in the world: the best friend did it. They're clichés because they happen all the time, and they're always true. I just didn't see it coming,

"I only wanted to help Phoebe," he said softly. "This Emory was a nightmare. I didn't mean to ice her. I only wanted to scare her."

"You couldn't think of something better to do than stab her

with a pencil?"

"It was handy." He shrugged. He finished his bagel. He stood up. "Let's go."

"Where do you think we're going?" I asked him.

"To the cops," he told me.

"I'm not taking you to the cops," I assured him. "I'm just going to tell them what I know. Except I'm going to leave out your name, and you're going to blow town."

"I can't do that," he began. "I'm in love with Phoebe."

"How do think she's going to react to the news that you killed somebody?" I asked. "You were nervous about even *introducing* her to your hoodlum friends. Her world's all make-believe and playacting. Your world is...you know."

He nodded. He did know.

***

So, that was that. I took my information to the cops. They found Sammy's fingerprints on a part of the pencil he hadn't wiped. They found a tiny fiber from his suit crushed in Emory's fist. They found Polonius credible as a witness.

But they never found Sammy.

Phoebe was released. She was freaked out, scared, and relieved all at the same time. I didn't speak with her for a long time, but I ran into her at Izzy's about a year later. She showed me a letter from Sammy, postmarked Reno. He'd copied a couple of lines from *Hamlet*. "Doubt thou the stars are fire; Doubt that the sun doth move; Doubt truth to be a liar; But never doubt I love." She said she carried it around in her pocket every day. She said she always would.

Reno Sweeney's was sold in 1979. Blossom Dearie and Bob Dorough are both gone. Phoebe got a long-running gig on Broadway. Some show about cats. And Sammy Two Shoes is just a story now, the kind you tell when you want to remind yourself about the strange things some people do for love.

DEATH PLAYS THE PALACE
By Margaret Dumas

It's 1930 and the Frolics are all the rage, featuring great vaudeville acts, including The Magnificent Mysterioso. Local girl Betty is thrilled to get a job as seamstress, but finds that not all magic is as it seems.

"Gee, Betty, this is the most exciting day of my life!"

My kid sister Trixie scampered beside me as I walked quickly along the sidewalk, but I wasn't looking at her. I was looking at the rose-colored beacon of the Palace Theater's marquee, its magical glow visible from blocks away in the San Francisco mist.

"*Your* life?" I said. "You didn't get the job. This is the most exciting day of *my* life."

"Oh, sure," she agreed. "But once you're in, you'll be able to get me in, too. At least when I'm older."

I shot her a look. She was only thirteen but already star-struck. She thought working at the Palace would be the most glamorous thing in the world. I, on the other hand, was seventeen. I knew darn well it was going to be the most glamorous thing in the whole universe.

Outside the theater we stopped to take in the giant poster that had appeared the week before:

Frolics of 1930
15 All-Star Acts!
Comedy! Music! Magic!

The poster listed some of the performers—The Magnificent Mysterioso, Polly Pink and her Prancing Poodles, Singing Sensation Dickie James—and promised a Spectacular Finale featuring The Famous Frolics Girls.

"Gee," Trixie sighed. "And you're going to meet them all!"

I gulped. Not only was I going to meet them all, I was going to dress them all. The manager of the Palace had called on my home economics teacher, Mrs. Erickson, just the night before, pleading for her to come fill in for the seamstress who had quit the show in Sacramento. Mrs. Erickson had an ailing mother to tend to, so she'd recommended her star graduate—me—for the job.

A job! I had a job! And it was in show business! I was wearing a work smock over my dress and carrying my sewing kit. I was ready. I took a deep breath and glowed brighter than the Palace marquee.

"Hello, beauties."

A tall lean man in a green plaid suit stepped out from the walkway that led to the lobby doors. Trixie elbowed me. He looked exactly like the kind of man Mama had warned us about. A Fancy Man, like the one we'd seen in *The Broadway Melody* just last month. He leaned against the wall, next to the poster, and looked at us like we were cream cakes in the window of Wilson's Bakery.

"Excuse us." I grabbed Trixie's hand and brushed past the man, turning to go up the alley to the back entrance. The employee entrance.

"The show starts at seven," he called after us, sounding amused. "You girls be sure to come see me."

I didn't answer. I wasn't there to see a show or to become a Fallen Woman at the hands of some smooth-talker. I was there for a job.

***

"Get all the costumes lined up on the racks in the right order. Make sure the girls have their quick-change outfits here in the wings when they come off the stage. Help them with the changes and check to make sure everyone looks right before they go on, then collect all the costumes after the show, check each one, and press them or repair them—whatever they need—so they'll be ready for the next show. Got it?"

The stage manager regarded me with beady brown eyes that knew full well I didn't have it. Then he shook his head, mumbled "Lord help us," and hurried away, leaving me blinking in confusion.

I'd sent Trixie home before entering the theater, on the theory that professional show-business people didn't bring their kid sisters with them to work. Now I wished I'd let her stay. It looked like I could use all the help I could get.

"Don't let Pops get to ya," I heard someone say.

I turned to find a blonde woman in a wrap coat looking at me, her rouged lips curved into a smile. "He's always a pill the first night in a new town." She had a tiny puff of a dog in her arms, and shifted it to hold out her hand to me. Her nails were lacquered pink. "I'm Polly. This little cutie is Bits. How's about I introduce you to the rest of the girls?"

I didn't know if she meant the rest of the poodles in her act or the rest of the showgirls, but either way it would be an improvement over standing around backstage with no idea what I was supposed to do next. I nodded.

She led me down a narrow stairway to the basement, where there seemed to be a hundred people rushing around. Some were shouting, some were laughing, and at least one unseen soprano was singing an aria from *Carmen*.

"It isn't that complicated," Polly explained, moving through the chaos as though she didn't even notice it. "We've all been on this bill for six weeks now. The girls know their changes. Mainly what you'll do is darn tights and mend seams—that, and stay out of Dickie's dressing room." She turned to give me a meaningful look, then threw open a door to a long narrow room filled with feathers, sequins, and half-naked showgirls.

"Hey, kids. Meet the new dresser..." She turned to me, one eyebrow raised.

"Betty," I said, managing to remember my own name, if nothing else.

"Betty," Polly repeated. "Betty, meet the Famous Frolics Girls. Ladies, I'm sure you'll be your usual sweet selves to Betty."

This was greeted by hoots and laughter. Polly turned to go. "I'm just down the hall—name's on the door. Come find me if this crowd gets too rowdy."

The crowd, a dozen or so showgirls who didn't seem that much older than me, flocked around the minute Polly left.

"Hey, kid, can you tack this flower back onto my hat?" A redhead thrust a spangled cap into my hands.

"My waistband's a little too tight—," said a brunette with huge dark eyes.

"So, lay off the potatoes, why don't ya?" another girl said to her.

"I'll lay off when I can afford something other than potatoes." The brunette deposited a pair of satin dance shorts in my arms, while her friend—or enemy, it was hard to tell—draped a dressing gown over my shoulder. "There's a rip in the hem, hon," she told me.

I was rapidly disappearing under a pile of sparkling clothes. Every single girl had something for me to do. Eventually, because I was afraid I'd topple over if I didn't, I spoke up.

"Say, can you give me a chance to catch my breath?"

The girls quieted, surprised, I suppose, that I could speak. I looked at them, each wearing some form of colorful printed kimono over their scanties, and I knew if I didn't stop them now, they'd drown me in sequins before the night was over.

"Okay," I said, dumping their clothes onto someone's dressing table. "Let's try this again. Does anyone have something that she can't wear onstage tonight without a repair? Anyone?"

There were a few shrugs and startled looks. One girl raised her hand, then lowered it again, biting her nail and looking around at the others.

"Good. Then there isn't a crisis." I took a breath. "Now, let's have everything that needs a fitting here," I pulled out a chair. "And everything that needs a repair over here. And this..." I plucked the dressing gown from the pile. "Isn't a costume, right?" The girl who'd called me 'hon' shook her head. "I'll be happy to mend it for you, but only after I've done my actual work. Any questions?"

What they'd seen when they'd met me was a five-foot-nothing schoolgirl with unruly brown hair. What they hadn't seen was the eldest of five demanding sisters. I'd dealt with their kind before.

"What did you say your name was, kid?" The brunette with the big eyes regarded me.

"Betty."

She nodded. "Well, welcome to Vaudeville, Betty. You're going to fit right in."

***

I wasn't sure if I fit right in, but after I got the Famous Frolics Girls sorted out, I worked my way down the corridor of dressing rooms, feeling more confident with every mended ruffle and rescued feather. I met the *Carmen*-singing soprano, who was having corset problems, a sister act who wore black and white outfits that were mirror images of each other—with wigs to match—and a three-man acrobatic act who only spoke Italian but managed to reassure me that they did their own mending. I was just about to knock on a door labeled *The Magnificent Mysterioso* when the stage manager yelled at me from the stairs at the end of the hall.

"Hey, you! Dresser! Mysterioso and Rose are onstage, and she just tore her petticoat. Get up there!"

I got up there. Of all the acts on the bill, the magician Mysterioso was the most famous. Trixie had read a breathless account of his legendary Disappearing Sweetheart trick in the paper just that morning. The accompanying picture had shown a darkly handsome man with thick brows and mesmerizing eyes. When I got to the stage, I looked for him with no small amount of nerves.

What I saw was a slightly pudgy bald man moving from point to point on the stage and calling out numbers every time he paused. It took me a moment to figure out that he was walking through the magician's act so the lighting operators would know exactly where to point the spotlights. It took me another minute to realize with a start that the pudgy bald guy was in fact Mysterioso. Wait till I told Trixie that The Magnificent wore a toupee! And possibly a corset.

At first, I didn't notice his assistant. She'd been hidden behind a red and gold cabinet big enough to hold a person. It would hold her, I realized. She was the Sweetheart he would make disappear from the cabinet and then magically reappear seconds later in the balcony.

She caught sight of me and came over. "Are you the new seamstress?" She wore a silver beaded dress with straps that left her arms and décolletage bare. It was loose and fell to just above her knees, the gores of the skirt filled with a sheer white chiffon that floated when she moved. White stockings and silver shoes completed her costume.

The dress was the most beautiful thing I'd ever seen. And the girl was lovely. All the showgirls downstairs were tall and glamorous, but this girl was fresh and pretty, with flawless skin and a dimple when she smiled. "I'm Rose."

"Betty," I said. "They told me you ripped your petticoat?"

She made a face. "Not ripped—cut. And I haven't worn a petticoat since I was nine years old." She swished her skirt until she found two small slits in one of the floaty chiffon panels.

"Oh, gee." I was good, but didn't think I'd be able to mend them without leaving a trace.

"Don't worry," she said, apparently reading my mind. "I've got a scrap of the chiffon down in my dressing room somewhere. You can use it to replace the panel."

"I suppose this isn't the first time your costume's been damaged," I said.

"Hazard of the job." She shrugged. "We were trying out the new box and Mel got a little too close with the five blade." She nodded toward the back of the stage, where a dark green box the size of a small coffin stood next to a stand displaying an alarming number of swords.

"Who's Mel?" I asked, crouching to get a better look at the tear. The five blade, which I assumed was one of the swords, must have been extremely sharp to make a cut that clean.

She laughed. "Mel is Melvin Fine. Otherwise known as The Magnificent Mysterioso."

I gaped up at her and she looked over at the pudgy bald man.

"A bit of advice," she said. "Don't get him mad. Especially when he's got a blade in his hand."

"Rose? Rose!" the magician bellowed. "Get back to your mark!"

"Hold your horses!" she called across the stage. "I've got to run down and change. I'll be right back!"

I'd stood up at the first shout, looking from one yelling performer to the other.

"Get over here now!" Mysterioso was turning an impressive shade of purple.

An icy calm seemed to come over Rose. "Fine!"

She deftly unzipped her dress and let it fall, stepping out of the puddle of silver to stand facing the magician shamelessly in just her scanties, her chin held high. "If you can't wait two minutes for me to get a wrap…"

A deathly silence had come over the theater, everyone stopping what they'd been doing to watch the real-life drama play out. Mysterioso swallowed, then stormed across the stage toward Rose.

"You little tramp," he growled as he approached.

Without stopping to think, I whipped off my smock and thrust it over Rose's shoulders just as Mysterioso reached us.

She turned from him to me, and when we made eye contact, I realized that all her bravado was masking something else. Fear. Had she gone too far? Then she thrust her arms into the sleeves of my smock and turned to view the magician coolly.

"Mel, I'd like you to know Betty, the new seamstress. Betty, meet the Magnificent Mysterioso. My husband."

***

I practically ran back down the stairs, clutching Rose's costume in my shaking hands. I ignored the flurry of performers getting ready for the show and went straight to Rose's dressing room. I knew she and her terrifying husband were still onstage so I opened the door without knocking and entered to find that I'd lost my mind.

Rose was in the room. And she wasn't alone.

It was impossible, but the girl I'd just seen onstage was now reclined on a faded velvet sofa, pulling on her dressing gown and doing her best to disentangle herself from the amorous embrace of the tall man in the green suit I'd met outside the theater that morning.

"Jesus!" he yelped when he realized why Rose—Rose?—was suddenly pushing him away. "I thought you locked the door!"

"I thought you locked the door!" she snapped back, then she shot me a look. "Close the door!"

I should have stepped out, but I stepped in, closing it behind me. "Rose?"

"Jesus," the man said again, adjusting his clothing before turning to glare at me. "Who do you suppose you are?"

"Dickie," the girl said, resting her hand on the back of his neck. "Run along, now. I'll take care of this."

He blew out a breath, then stood and reached for his jacket, giving me a hostile look as he left.

The girl tied the belt of her dressing gown, fluffed her hair, crossed her legs, and patted the couch next to her. "I think you'd better sit down, kid. You look like you've seen a ghost."

***

"Twins!"

Trixie was waiting outside the dressing room door when I left half an hour later. I'd sent her home hours ago, but there she was, my kid sister, staring at me with huge wide eyes, practically shimmering with excitement.

"What are you doing here?" I demanded, darting a look around to see if anyone was paying attention. They weren't.

"I've been here all day," she told me, as if it were perfectly normal. "I snuck in after you, just in case you might need me—which you do. And I heard everything!" She pointed at the closed dressing room door, then pointed up at the stage above. "Twins," she mouthed.

I grabbed her by the sleeve and hustled her down the hall and around the corner. I wasn't sure where I was taking her, but I'd just been sworn to secrecy and I didn't want Trixie to ruin everything.

I spotted an open door to some sort of electrical room and pulled Trixie in after me, shutting the door behind us.

"What exactly did you hear?" I demanded.

She beamed. "I heard that there is no Rose. There are twin sisters, Ruby and Rita, and they pretend to be one girl named Rose so nobody will figure out the Disappearing Sweetheart trick."

Okay, so she'd heard a lot.

"Also," Trixie said. "Rita is the one who's married to Mysterioso, and she's the one playing hanky panky with that singer Dickie James." She made a face. "He stepped on my foot when he came barreling out of there, and he didn't even apologize. Rude! I'd like to give him a swift kick."

"Trixie, you shouldn't be here. And you really shouldn't know about Rita and Ruby!"

She waved my concern away. "Oh, I won't tell. And you'd have told me anyway, you know you would."

"Not until next week when the show leaves town," I said, wanting to believe I'd have been able to wait that long.

"What's one week?" She clasped her hands together dramatically. "Oh, I think it's grand the way Ruby covered for her sister today, don't you? I promise I'll cover for you if you ever sneak around behind your husband's back someday—if you ever get a husband. Who else knows about them, besides that stinker Dickie? Do you think Mysterioso really can't tell the difference between them?"

Sometimes following my sister's thoughts gave me whiplash. "I don't know," I answered the last question. "But how could he not know?" Maybe he'd been so mad at "Rose" onstage because he'd known that she was Ruby, covering for his cheating wife, Rita. "It's all so confusing."

Trixie nodded solemnly. "That's why it's good I'm here to help."

***

That night Trixie did help, hovering in the wings with me as the acts came and went, straightening hats, adjusting feathers, and ruffling tiny little tutus for all of Polly's poodles. We were in the wings together when The Magnificent Mysterioso and "Rose" took the stage. She winked at me just before she stepped out into the lights, swishing the dress I'd mended. Unless it was an identical dress. I couldn't tell if she was Rita or Ruby.

Even knowing it was all illusion, the magic act still had the power to amaze. I winced when the swords went into the casket. I squealed when doves flew out of the empty box. I gasped when the red and gold cabinet was opened to reveal that "Rose" had disappeared. I looked up to the balcony, to the spot where I knew the other twin had been hiding throughout the whole performance. I held my breath as I waited for her spectacular appearance. I waited. And waited.

"Where is she?" Trixie whispered.

The audience began to murmur.

"Something's wrong," I said. Mysterioso, onstage, was beginning to sweat.

I turned and dashed for the stairs down to the dressing rooms, knocking into miscellaneous Frolics Girls who were coming up for the Spectacular Finale. Trixie was right behind me as we rushed to Mysterioso's dressing room door. She was the first to scream when we opened it to find one of the twins lying on the faded velvet couch, a sword plunged through her heart.

***

Melvin Fine, the Magnificent Mysterioso, was arrested for the murder of his wife Rita that night. Ruby was inconsolable. All the Frolics Girls gathered around her as her brother-in-law was taken away, shouting of his innocence. They formed a spangled barrier around the bereaved twin, who ultimately wound up sobbing in Dickie James' arms as poodles yipped, Italian acrobats muttered darkly, and policemen asked everyone questions.

"Hey, kid, you okay?" Polly sought me out after I'd told the police everything I'd seen. Well, almost everything. I was still downstairs near the dressing rooms, where all the performers were milling around, exchanging gossip and telling stories about Rita, Mysterioso, and other deaths in other theaters they'd known.

"I'm fine," I told her. "I'm just worried about my sister." And worried that Mama would kill me for letting Trixie get involved with show people and their glittering, sordid lives. "She's still talking to the police."

"Here." Polly handed me the tiny poodle Bits. "Hold him. He'll make you feel better." So, I sat on the narrow stairs and hugged the warm puff of fur. Once Trixie joined me, I hugged her, too, then handed her the fluffy dog.

"Are you okay?" I asked her.

"Sure, I'm fine." She was about as convincing as you'd expect for a thirteen-year-old who'd just seen the body of a murdered woman.

We should have gone home then, but instead we stayed and watched how the cast of the Frolics responded to the death of one of their own.

One of them must have responded by calling a bootlegger, because as soon as the last policemen left bottles started appearing.

"To Rose!" one of the showgirls toasted, raising a mug.

"To Rita," a man's voice corrected her. It was the horrible Dickie, still wearing his stage makeup and tailcoat, the carnation in his lapel crushed from Ruby's sobbing embrace.

I looked around. "I wonder where Ruby is."

"She's in Dickie's dressing room," Trixie said. "I heard someone say that the doctor gave her a sedative, and they couldn't exactly put her in her own dressing room."

I shuddered, seeing Rita's body again in my mind's eye. She was wearing her costume, the white chiffon of the skirt spread out elegantly over the velvet couch, a dark stain spreading from the sword in her chest.

"What?" Trixie was watching me.

"Nothing. Let's go home."

"Mama's going to kill us." We both said it at the same time, then both smiled, and then both felt terrible for smiling in the horrible circumstances.

We found Polly and handed her dog back to her.

"'Night, kid," she said. "See you tomorrow?"

I stared at her. "Tomorrow?"

"Sure." She looked around at her fellow actors. "The show

must go on, right?"

"But Mysterioso…" Trixie said.

Polly shrugged. "The producer's probably calling New York right now, lining up another magician. Meanwhile, I know someone who thinks he's going to be the headliner."

I followed her glance. Dickie James was looking far too pleased with himself for someone who had just lost his lover to murder.

***

I was trying to figure something out as Trixie and I walked home in the glow of the streetlights. I must not have done a very good job of hiding my thoughts because before we'd gone three blocks, she put her hand on my arm to stop me.

"What is it?"

I shook my head. "It's probably nothing."

She stared at me. "You know something."

I wasn't sure about that. But maybe saying it out loud would help me work it out. "I think I saw something," I said. "With Rita. With the…"

"With the body?" Trixie asked. "What? And don't say 'It's probably nothing.'"

We'd stopped on the sidewalk in front of Finkle's Fine Clothing. The mannequins in the window seemed to be straining to hear.

"Not with the body; with the dress," I said. "I think the girl who was killed was wearing the dress I repaired. I think I saw my own hand-stitching on one of the chiffon panels. But I couldn't have. That would mean the girl who was killed wasn't Rita, it was Ruby. She's the one who got her dress cut, the one I met onstage while Rita was fooling around with Dickie in the dressing room."

Trixie gaped at me. "But that would mean Mysterioso killed the wrong twin!"

I nodded. It would mean a lot of things. "It's not just the dress," I said. "There's something else. But it's probably—"

"It's probably *not* nothing!" Trixie said, sounding just like Mama. "Just spit it out!"

"Dickie," I said. "Dickie was comforting the surviving twin, holding her in his arms…but why would Ruby cry in his arms? Only Rita would have turned to him."

Trixie's jaw dropped. "Do you really think Mysterioso couldn't tell which one was his own wife?"

I shrugged. "Maybe it all happened fast. Maybe he was blinded by rage—"

"Or a fit of jealous passion!" Trixie said, much too

enthusiastically. She grabbed my hands. "How do we find out? How do we know for sure?"

"I think there's only one person who could be absolutely sure."

Trixie's eyes grew huge. "Ruby!"

"Unless she's Rita," I nodded. "In which case…"

"In which case, why didn't she say anything?"

That was what I'd been trying to figure out.

"There's only one reason not to speak up," I said grimly. "And that's because she wants the world to believe she's dead. And I can only think of two reasons why she might want that."

"Because she's afraid Mysterioso will kill her when he finds out he got it wrong?" Trixie asked.

"That's one. The other is that she was in on it with him."

"Oh, Betty! Her own sister?"

"It's only one theory," I reminded her.

Trixie thought about it. "So, either Rita needs our help…"

"Or she needs to be behind bars," I said. "Wait—where are you going?" Trixie had turned back toward the Palace.

"I'm going to see which it is. Come on!"

***

The alley door was still propped open, and from the sounds of it most of the performers were still around. But when we slunk down the stairs, we found the hallway empty.

The Famous Frolics Girls were apparently throwing a wake. We heard music and voices and laughter, cigarette smoke practically billowing from their open dressing room door. We slipped past quickly.

At Dickie's door we exchanged a glance. Trixie nodded and I turned the knob quietly. Rita—if it was Rita—might still be under the influence of a sedative. Which wasn't a bad thing. We might be able to get to the truth faster if she didn't quite realize who she was talking to. That was our plan, at least.

I opened the door slowly, peeking inside. Then, when I saw what was happening, I threw it open and yelled.

"Stop that!"

Dickie James had his hands around Rita's throat. She was conscious and fighting him off, but she was drugged and he was a lot bigger.

Trixie dashed past me and began pummeling the singer's back. He grunted in surprise and pushed Rita away to turn around and swat at Trixie, but I got there first, holding his arm back. "Oh, no you don't! That's my sister!"

Then Trixie kicked him hard in a place that Mama had instructed all her daughters was a man's weak point. His face turned deep red and he collapsed to his knees, making an odd sort of squealing noise.

Trixie stared in amazement. "Did I do that?"

The woman he'd been strangling moaned. She'd fallen into a heap on the floor. I went to her. "Rita?"

She looked at me blearily, then nodded.

"Why didn't you tell anyone it was you? Why did you let them think…"

She shifted her glance to Dickie, now curled up and holding his hands over his weak point. Trixie stood over him, ready with another kick should the need arise. Probably hoping it would.

"I was afraid he'd kill me, too." She put a hand to her throat. "And he almost did."

"Wait," Trixie said. "Him? *Dickie* killed your sister?"

She nodded. "He wanted to frame Mysterioso so we could be together."

I knelt by her, looking into her eyes. "Did you know he was going to kill Ruby?"

She looked horrified. "Of course not! She was my sister!"

Behind me, Trixie gave a satisfied snort.

"When he told me what he'd done I wanted to kill him," Rita said. "We fought, and that's when you came in."

Dickie snarled and reached for Trixie's leg, but she darted away and grabbed a nearby lamp, holding it like a club. "Just you try something, mister."

My heart swelled with pride, but there were parts of this story I'd never tell Mama.

***

The police came back, and we had to talk to them again. They were very nice about everything, although they did point out rather strenuously that in future, should my sister or I think we knew of a murderer wandering around loose, we should probably inform them rather than stroll blithely into his dressing room.

"Yes, sir," we both said solemnly. But I suspect Trixie's fingers were crossed.

And still, the stage manager told me, his eyes now bloodshot as well as beady, the show would go on tomorrow.

"Maybe we should go get some sleep," Trixie suggested. We were sitting on the edge of the stage, looking out over the empty seats of the theater. "We have another day in show business tomorrow."

I could have reminded her that it was still my job, not hers, but I was too tired to argue. Also, I probably wouldn't have won.

"I don't think I want to be in show business after all," I said.

"In fact, once the show leaves town, I don't think I'll want to come back to the Palace for quite a while."

"Why, you're crazy." Trixie grinned. "I'm getting a job here the very minute I can. I want to stay here forever."

THE HOMICIDAL UNDERSTUDY
By Elizabeth Elwood

Never underestimate the ingenuity and determination of an understudy who wants a chance at stardom.

I never trust understudies on principle. Let's face it, every one of them dreams about that magical evening when the star gets struck by lightning, collapses from bronchial pneumonia, or literally breaks a leg. It's not natural to sit back patiently, performance after performance, without hoping for a bolt from the blue to strike the leading lady and allow a new star to be born. Every unknown waiting in the wings longs for the day when she gets the opportunity to step in and wow audience, producer, and critics alike, and any actress who tells you otherwise is lying through her whitened teeth.

However, much as aspiring performers may daydream, very few have the gumption to take matters into their own hands, so it took me a while to comprehend that the minimally talented toady who was understudying the role of Elvira had evil intentions towards the lovely Laura Grant around whom the current Broadway revival of *Blithe Spirit* had been mounted. Geneva Sands was not only Laura's understudy; she was playing the uninspiring role of Mrs. Bradbourne, and it was obvious that she was itching for the chance to abandon her wimpy part and step into the limelight to take over from Laura. However, it was less obvious that her dreams were more than wishful thinking. It was several weeks into the run before I realized that she fully intended to make her dream a reality.

Of course, I had a great deal of opportunity to observe the other players since I was cast as the humble maid, so the most time-consuming part of my evening was the hour spent in my dressing room each night, transforming my svelte figure and gleaming blonde mane into the dumpy Edith. Whilst I'd had some very nice mentions in the reviews, the most genuine admiration I received was from my fellow cast members who were impressed by my ability and willingness to go from glamorous to plain and to disguise the RADA-trained tones of my stage voice with an unappealing nasal twang.

"It's called acting," I pointed out to the toady—Geneva was stunned as well as mean. Having used her vital statistics horizontally to acquire her current part, she couldn't understand how anyone would want to be on stage and not be recognized by her friends in the audience.

Unlike the toady, I didn't hover around the principals. I was courteous and professional, both on stage and off. However, I had great admiration for Laura Grant and I was gratified when she singled me out to praise my work. Over the course of the run, we became, if not exactly friends, like mentor and student. She gave me tips and advice, and seemed genuinely proud when anyone else noticed my skills. If we hadn't become close, I probably would not have noticed what Geneva was up to. Before the show, I was far too busy with my makeup to pay attention to anyone else, and even though my actual stage time was minimal, I still had to hover in the wings as I was constantly bobbing on and off. However, one day as we waited to go on for the final scene, Laura made a comment that surprised me by its frankness.

"I wish David wouldn't hang around the theatre quite so much," she said.

David Garrison, our director, was also Laura's husband.

"It does so undermine the role of the stage manager," Laura continued, "and it puts the other cast members on edge. Particularly poor Geneva. He must be driving her crazy with all those notes. I know she isn't doing that well, but harassing her won't help." Laura sighed. "Of course, I can see why David suggested Geneva be my understudy because she did a quite creditable Elvira in summer stock last year, but she is totally wrong for Mrs. Bradbourne. Why on earth he gave her the part, I can't imagine."

I could. I'd seen our venerable director with his nose in Geneva's cleavage on more than one occasion, and the noises that emanated periodically from her dressing room when he called in to give her extra coaching suggested that he was familiar with a great deal more of her anatomy. However, Laura was one of those rare professionals who is not only totally focused on the job at hand, but also a perfect lady who never listens to or indulges in gossip. Furthermore, her dressing room was at the end of the corridor closest to the stairs that led to the stage, so she never had any reason to wander down to the junior players' neck of the woods. Not that she'd have suspected anything even if she had. Laura was such a sweet and unobservant soul that it was a miracle that she'd managed to find her way to the top of her profession. But then, perhaps her three-wise-monkeys approach to life was what gave her the necessary insulation to survive in the wild jungle of professional theatre.

"Of course," Laura went on, proving my assessment of her

naiveté correct, "Geneva's a very sweet girl, and she's no end of help to me. It's like having a private maid, secretary, and delivery girl, all in one. Nessie"—that was Laura's dresser—"feels quite redundant most of the time. Geneva even comes in early now so she can bring in my dinner from the deli."

Now that was a surprise. Laura was renowned for her disciplined lifestyle. When performing, she ate a hearty late-morning brunch, exercised dutifully in the early afternoon, rested in mid-afternoon, and then, two hours prior to curtain time, walked the ten blocks from her apartment to the theatre. There, she would have a light meal, usually a salad with sandwiches or wraps, gulp down an evil-looking health drink that tasted disgusting but appeared to energize her for hours, and get ready in leisurely fashion, knowing she had plenty of time to digest everything before going on stage.

Nessie was always there to help. The elderly dresser had been with Laura for twenty of the star's forty years, and according to the less kind, she had already been a hundred and three when she began in the position. Other than a three-week holiday every year to visit her sister in Scotland, Nessie was always on hand to cater to her employer's every whim. There was no doubt that the dresser was getting on in years, but I had managed the occasional conversation with the old girl and, in my opinion, she not only had all her marbles, but probably possessed a few more than many of the people that I worked with on stage. Nessie was also ferociously protective of her charge and took great pride in making Laura's life as easy as possible, so I was surprised to hear that Geneva had made such inroads on her territory.

"I had to be terribly tactful," Laura went on, "because Nessie has always seen to my pre-show meal, but I think she's getting a bit past it. I had terrible cramps one day after eating some wraps, and Geneva told me later that she'd popped down to my dressing room that day and Nessie had been watering and deadheading the chrysanthemum that David gave me. While they were talking, Nessie was setting out the food—she always insists on putting everything on plates so I don't have to eat out of the deli boxes—but she hadn't washed her hands first, even though there'd been some dirt under her nails from the flower pot. I was horrified to hear that. I mean, it's so unlike Nessie, but she is getting on, and if she's losing it…well, I was in so much pain I wasn't sure if I could go on. I did manage to get through, but I can't possibly risk that happening again, so I told Nessie that David had asked me to encourage Geneva by letting her take on little extra jobs, and I'd said she could see to my dinner for the next while." Laura frowned.

"I'm afraid Nessie didn't take it too well, though. She's been in rather a huff ever since."

I could well believe it. On the other hand, I didn't for a minute believe the story about Nessie and the flowers. The wiry little Scot was one of the most fastidious old crones I'd ever met, and in my opinion, she'd still be instructing the nurses in the hospital on hygiene when she lay on her deathbed. The story simply didn't ring true. And that's when I began to wonder just what Geneva's purpose was in sidelining Nessie. Come to that, what had caused Laura's upset stomach? It was time to abandon my superior attitude and toady up to the toady. I wanted to learn just what she had in mind.

***

In order to cultivate Geneva, I had to start coming in early, too. Otherwise, between my own professional responsibilities and Geneva's propensity for disappearing with our libidinous director when Elvira was safely on stage and Mrs. Bradbourne was off, there was no time for chatting. However, after a couple of weeks of assiduous effort, liberally larded with flattery, Geneva began to confide in me. It was worse than I thought. Not only did she covet Laura's part, she seriously coveted Laura's husband. Geneva was quite set on the fact that David Garrison was going to dump Laura in the near future. She was sure, if only she had the chance to shine in that title role and demonstrate what she could do, that that would be the final push that would ensure her advancement to Wife Number Two.

If Geneva had actually had any talent, that wouldn't have been a bad theory. David Garrison had ridden to success on the back of his wife's quicksilver talent. He was only a journeyman director, and his pick of the top jobs only happened because Laura insisted that they work together. If Geneva had had the potential to be the next shining star on Broadway, he might well have traded Laura in for a model with a better sell-by date, but for all that David was a parasite, he was not a fool. He knew that Laura was the goose that laid the golden eggs. Geneva's assets were strictly for offstage entertainment.

Still, I didn't point that out to her. There was no benefit in disillusioning her, and I wanted to find out if she was actually planning harm to Laura. Finally, after a week of comments about how wonderful it would be if she ever got the chance to go on in the lead role, she opened up. Having finished getting into costume early, I was visiting in her dressing room and watching her put on her makeup. I dropped a lead-weighted hint.

"Such a shame you never get to go on as Elvira. It really

wouldn't be such a big deal for Laura to have the odd sick day. I couldn't believe the way she hung in there that day she had a tummy ache. She could easily have stepped aside and given you a chance."

Geneva's Botox-enhanced lips emitted a breathy sigh.

"I was so disappointed. There I was, all ready to go on, and my own understudy was primed to do Bradbourne, then up popped Laura and said she was going to carry on. It was such a letdown. David told me later that he thought it was very unkind of her. She was determined not to give me a chance."

"That's pretty hard," I said, egging her on. "When leading actresses have that kind of attitude, they almost invite people to pop something into their coffee to make sure they do have the occasional day off."

Momentarily Geneva looked startled, but the flash of alarm disappeared as quickly as it had manifested. She turned and looked at me blandly, but I wasn't fooled. I had seen the flare of guilt and I knew she'd been responsible for Laura's indisposition. Geneva smiled.

"Oh, darling," she said, "I'd never do anything like that."

It was amazing how her baby-blue orbs could combine cunning and sweetness in one gaze. No wonder she wanted to play Elvira. An amoral, homicidal ghost—it would be type casting. I took the opportunity to search her dressing room during the Sunday matinee when I was guaranteed a clear ten minutes during the Act One séance. My first thought was that there might be something toxic hidden away in her makeup case, but everything there was innocuous enough. I checked her purse and the pockets of her coat and clothing, but those were empty other than the odd Kleenex that had found its way there from the box below her mirror. There were no suspicious items on any of the shelves or in the drawers. All that remained was the counter with her coffee maker and accoutrements. Here I also found three plastic containers that I assumed were for Laura's health drink. The largest of these contained Vega protein and greens, optimistically declaring itself to be chocolate-flavored. The other two—and this I found curious—were both labeled powdered collagen. Why the duplication? I took off the lids and stared at the contents. Both flasks contained white powder, but was it my imagination, or was there a slight difference between the two? I dipped my finger in each powder and tried a taste test. The flavors were distinctly different, and as I returned the lids to the containers, I noticed a tiny black X on the inside of one of the rims. I reached for the box by the mirror, whipped out two Kleenexes and quickly spooned out a few grains of each powder, carefully writing an X on the tissue that contained the contents of the marked flask. Then I hurried out of the dressing room, secured the samples in my own room, and went up to the wings in time for my next entrance.

***

My friendly local pharmacist operates out of a tiny independent corner store in Greenwich Village. Norman is an avid theatre lover and as seasoned a critic as the pundits who write for the most prestigious New York newspapers. When I took my sample in on Monday morning, he was in full flight, having spent Sunday afternoon sitting through the latest revival of *My Fair Lady*.

"My dear," he trilled, "what a lesson in how not to cast your leading men. Henry Higgins was an Old Vic ex-pat who's done *Pygmalion* so many times he looked bewildered every time the orchestra struck up a tune, and Freddy played his role as if he were auditioning for Lancelot in *Camelot*—and he was such a hunk that the audience went out totally bewildered why Eliza went back to Higgins when she could have settled for him."

"Oh, dear. How was the Eliza?"

"A body like a telephone pole and a hat like a UFO with a roof garden. Between the weight of her hat and the width of her hobble skirt, she walked like a geisha with backache. What's more, her makeup sucked. I swear she had twin spiders stuck to her eyelids."

"So not a go on my night off?"

"Definitely not, unless someone gives you a freebie and you're absolutely destitute of anything else to do. Now, I also saw *The Ferryman* last week and that's a totally different story…"

I let him rattle on. One can never do business with Norman until he has been given full rein to air his opinions on what is or is not worth seeing. Having heard his summary of the past two weeks' viewing, I managed to bring him back to the purpose of my visit.

"Oh, my dear," he said, once I had explained my problem in making my too trusting leading lady realize her danger, "how too, too exciting. Yes, I can do that for you, and I shall be as silent and unseeing as those three wise monkeys that the lovely Laura emulates. Will Wednesday do? I shall phone you as soon as I get the results."

Pleased with my morning's work, I thanked him and left the shop. The theatre was dark on Monday and I was quite sure Laura was safe until Wednesday. If Geneva were going to try anything, she wouldn't settle for a paltry weeknight audience. She would wait for an occasion where she could make a splash.

Two days later, Norman called and confirmed that I was

irrefutably right about the toady's ill intentions. The samples were different and the one marked with an X was definitely not collagen. There was now no doubt in my mind that the contents had been responsible for Laura's terrible bout of cramps. The powder had probably been substituted for the collagen in her health drink, which was the item most likely to disguise the taste, though there was also a risk that the food had been tampered with. I was also certain that Geneva was planning another, even worse attack to occur in the future. And I suddenly realized when it would be. There was a fundraising gala scheduled for the following weekend. The theatre would be filled to the gods with influential citizens and reviewers. Geneva wouldn't be able to resist.

It was time to intervene.

As the evening approached, I felt distinctly anxious. What if I were wrong? Accusing a colleague of poisoning the star of the show could backfire horrendously if the charges proved to be mistaken. I certainly couldn't afford to get myself blacklisted for making trouble. I decided the safest course was to talk to Nessie. She was as irritated with Geneva as I was, and I was sure she would take the matter seriously and deal with it discreetly.

Nessie did not disappoint me. She was aghast to hear how Geneva had badmouthed her in order to gain a position of trust with Laura, and she swung into action with the determination of Robert the Bruce approaching the Battle of Bannockburn. She assured me that she would deal with everything. She would alert Laura of the possibility of tampering, wait until Geneva had left Laura's dressing room, and then provide a substitute meal and drink. Once Geneva was safely on stage, Nessie would slip into her dressing room to retrieve the marked container, which she would later take, along with the discarded meal and drink, to *her* pharmacist—if I were to be kept out of it, Norman could not be approached—and get the contents analyzed. All would be done without Geneva's knowledge, but if my suspicions proved correct, then the producer would be told right away.

Come the evening of the gala, I did not need a pharmaceutical report to know that Geneva was guilty. Her bewilderment spoke volumes as the evening wore on and Laura soared to radiant heights without any sign of distress. But sure enough, when the analysis came in the following week, Nessie had the proof she needed. The marked flask contained Orthene 97 and the health drink had been liberally laced with its contents.

Once the producer was made aware of what had been going on, Geneva was sent packing. She tried to deny it, of course, but everyone was aware that there had been a complaint about a missing tin of weed killer at the farm where she had been billeted for the summer stock production, so her sobs and pleas were in vain. Still, there were no charges laid. Laura did not want a scandal. And whether it was because of my talent, or whether dear old Nessie put in a word about who was actually responsible for exposing Geneva's evil intentions, I ended up as Laura's new understudy. I don't mind people feeling that they owe me, but I would prefer to think my promotion was due to my suitability for the part. With my long blonde hair, RADA stage voice and sylph-like figure, I am a natural for Elvira if I do say so myself.

The last I heard of Geneva, she had caught the eye of a visiting Los Angeles business magnate and was heading for Hollywood, where her aptitude for casting-couch negotiations should serve her well. I have no sympathy for her. She was not only selfish and mean-spirited, but she was also stupid. Her method of sidelining Laura was guaranteed to fail because, even without my interference, Nessie would have wised up sooner or later. A simple traffic accident would have been far more sensible. The streets are always crowded when Laura makes her nightly walk to the theatre and it would be so easy, amid the bustling throng of people, for someone, carefully disguised, of course, to bump her off the sidewalk and into the path of a car.

Still, Geneva wasn't actually trying to murder Laura. She only wanted to make her ill. She had only filled the collagen container with laxative. I was the one who substituted the weed killer. (Did I mention that I was billeted at the same farm as the toady for the summer-stock *Blithe Spirit*?) Geneva could easily have pleaded that the laxative was for her own use and had got into the drink by mistake, and Laura is such a gentle soul, she might have given her a second chance. However, I needed the toady out of the way permanently. Now the possibilities are endless, and that simple traffic accident could happen any night. Probably in a month or so when the actress playing Ruth is leaving the show and the reviewers will be there to stamp their seal of approval or disapproval on the new performer stepping into the role.

Yes, as I've always said, every understudy dreams about the star of the show dropping dead. It's not natural to sit back patiently, performance after performance, without hoping for a bolt from the blue to strike the leading lady and allow a new star to be born. Why should I be any different from any other hopeful who wants to tread the boards in a leading role on Broadway?

NO FINAL ACT
By Daryl Wood Gerber

You can always rely on lifelong friends when you need them—even in the world of theatrical competition.

I could count on one finger the person to whom I owed my life—Serena Jergens. In seventh grade, she tried out for and won the role of Luisa in *Sound of Music* so I wouldn't have to kiss icky Jimmy Simms. In eighth grade, she snagged the lead in *South Pacific* so I wouldn't have to embarrass myself by singing "I'm gonna wash that man right out of my hair" when I hadn't even kissed a boy. In high school, she steered me toward sidekick roles. Playing sidekicks, she assured me, would look great on my college application. Who needed to be a leading lady? There were plenty of those to go around. And in college—yes, we went to the same college—she starred in every show: *Cats, Rent, A Streetcar Named Desire, Barefoot in the Park, Agnes of God*. You name it, she could play it. However, in senior year when she auditioned for and won the role of Velma Kelly in *Chicago*, knowing that it was the one role I'd coveted more than any other, it galled me. I told her, of course. To her face. She laughed and knuckled me in the arm saying "As if." As if I could have performed that part or even the role of Roxie. In fact, she championed her sister for that role. Yes, Tilly, Serena's younger sister, joined us at college. When Serena suggested I take on the role of stage manager for *Chicago,* because working backstage would benefit me in years to come, I agreed. Doing backstage work, according to Serena, was character building, and who couldn't use a bit more character?

In the end, I wasn't upset with her decree. During the run of *Chicago,* I met Joe Westin, who became my all-time best friend. And I did star in a couple of local theater productions after college—once when Serena was suffering from pneumonia, and another time, when Serena came down with a severe case of laryngitis.

"Katie, Katie, pretty lady, don't die on me now." Joe nudged me with his elbow.

"I'm not dying." I was standing in the wings of the Crescent Theater having done all my checks and crosschecks for tonight's tech rehearsal of *Wicked*. Tech rehearsals could be a bear, but I wasn't faint of heart. I would get through it one cue at a time. "I'm concentrating."

"Aha. The yawn fooled me."

"I didn't yawn."

"Did so."

Two hours ago, after finishing my shift at Café Olé where I worked as a manager of over two dozen baristas, I'd walked into the Crescent ready for action. I'd strolled down the main aisle, climbed onto the stage, and inhaled the scent of the theater. How I loved the aroma of dust and gel lights and greasepaint. Heaven. I'd gazed at the last row of theater seats and imagined myself singing to the audience. Okay, I didn't have the chops to stand up to Serena years ago and vie for leading roles—I wasn't willing to sleep my way to the top—but I could sing.

"Did you eat?" Joe asked.

"I never miss a meal." While sipping my smoothie dinner, I'd listened as a few early orchestra members warmed up their instruments, and I'd crooned along with them. "Are you excited about tonight?" I asked.

"Every night in theater is intoxicating. You never know what might happen. How about you?"

"Over the moon." No doubt about it, being a part of community theater thrilled me. Amateur actors, musicians, and crew were much more enthusiastic about the art than professionals. We did it for the honor. For the fun. For the friendship.

"How's your mom doing?" Joe asked as he rolled a cable using his shoulder and forearm as braces.

"In pain. Ha-ha." My mother ran a pain clinic. Like her, I enjoyed helping people out of their pain, which was why I served up coffee. For some reason coffee, or rather caffeine, relieved people. I was partial to water. Serena always made fun of me for that. Fish liked water, she joked, not people. Water, I countered, was good for the vocal cords. "She misses Dad," I added. If only she could have ended his pain sooner.

"Give her my best."

"You do it. She's coming to opening night."

"Even though you're not in the play?"

"She's supportive of whatever I do." I pulled a bottle of nasal spray from my pocket.

Joe eyed it, concerned. "Allergies?"

"A minor irritation." I stuck it back in my pocket without using it.

"Hiya, Katie," Tilly Jergens said as she stepped onto the stage. She was beautiful in a white-bread way. Pretty blond hair, symmetrical features, light to Serena's dark. I was the *in between*, a redhead with freckles. "Think I could do a few warm ups?"

I gestured for her to have at it.

Tilly moved center stage and started *a capella* singing the song "Popular" made famous by Kristin Chenoweth. Gracefully, she bounded left and right, hitting each mark perfectly. I knew her performance was faultless because I'd memorized every step, every line. That was my gift as a stage manager.

When she ended the song, she winked at me. "Dressing room mikes on?"

I nodded.

Again, *a capella*, she proceeded to sing the signature song of *Wicked*, "Defying Gravity"—Serena's number. As in her previous routine, Tilly hit every note flawlessly. When she finished, she thanked me and pranced off the stage.

Oh, boy. I could just imagine Serena in the dressing room, boiling mad as she listened to her sister knocking the song out of the park. Glad it wasn't me who had to face her a half-hour before *places*.

Joe sidled up. "Well, that was something. Who knew Tilly had a mean streak?"

"I know. Right?"

"Cards after rehearsal?" he asked.

He liked to play gin with me even though I cleaned his clock. My father taught me to be merciless. "Absolutely."

"Okay, then, off to the old grindstone."

Joe was kidding. He adored doing theater as much as I did. He knew every inch of every theater he'd worked in—each lever, trap door, and rope. On my first visit to his apartment, I discovered he was quite the collector. In addition to records and books, he had amassed hundreds of theater programs over the years and perused them so often that the corners were oily from his fingerprints. If any theater suffered a blackout and all the actors fled to the safety of their homes, I was certain Joe would tuck in his oversized shirt, hitch up his jeans, and recite or sing the current play for the audience. By candlelight, if necessary.

"Places," Vaughn Hill yelled. Vaughn, our director, was as dashing as Mr. Perfect could be. Lean and tall with mesmerizing eyes...and about as shallow as a koi pond. When Serena threw herself at him to get this role, he was toast. "Katie, check the cables."

Why? I wondered. Serena had taken flight as Elphaba over a dozen times. Each time, the cables had worked like a charm. *Heh-heh. Charm.* Funny choice of words for a show about witches. I nipped my warped sense of humor in the bud and said, "On it, boss," and then to Joe, "Man the levers."

"Will do."

Joe and I had been friends for so long, we completed each other's sentences. He'd never had a lover. Neither had I. A couple of years ago, we considered taking the plunge but decided against it. Why ruin a friendship for one roll in the hay? Joe possessed a mischievous sense of humor. A couple of times, he'd pranked me. Once in junior year, when I played second fiddle to Serena, I asked for tissue in the dressing room. He said it was there; I was blind. Unbeknownst to me, sensing I would ask for tissue, he coerced a cast member to remove it and replace it in a matter of minutes. When Joe confessed to the ploy, he said it was because I was acting like Serena. *Moi*? I replied like a diva; he was right. A week later, I asked for a special tea with a particular honey. Tea and honey, like water, helped my vocal cords. Employing the same game plan, he asked a cast member to do his bidding. When I figured what was up, I retaliated. Knowing how he adored his collection of original Elvis LPs, I stole into his apartment and absconded with them. When he mentioned they were missing, I told him he was dreaming; he'd never owned any. After I reduced him to tears, I returned them...and we both laughed. Our friendship meant the world to me.

"Cast on stage," Vaughn called. By day, he was a stockbroker and very conscientious as to time and money. He liked to be in control.

When the cast assembled and Serena wasn't among them, Vaughn yelled, "Serena, love, let's go."

"I'm here." Serena sashayed onto the stage while tying an ornate obi around her royal blue kimono.

Tilly joined her and linked her arm through her sister's. Serena shrugged her off.

Vaughn said in a booming voice, no megaphone necessary, "You all know that tech rehearsals can be trying. Getting the lights right. Pinning down the cues. This show is not easy. Timing is everything. So, let's be on our best behavior. Help each other out." He clapped his hands and blew a kiss to Serena. "Break a leg."

She returned the kiss and hiked up her kimono to reveal her thigh. "You don't mean this one, do you?"

Puh-lease. I rolled my eyes. If I were honest with myself, I was tired of Serena getting role after role simply because she had no compunctions about having sex with anyone. Vaughn, like all the others, fell for her promise to be true. In that way, she was a great actress. Her day job of selling real estate made her a pretty good liar. *This house is the one for you. Termites? No way.* There were always termites.

I cleared my head, positioned myself at the light board, and focused on the tasks at hand.

Act one started with a big opening. The orchestra was brilliant. The cast was spot on with energy and vocals.

However, when Serena appeared on stage as Elphaba for the first time, although she was charming, she wasn't hitting her marks or getting the lines right.

Vaughn stopped the action. "Serena, love, you're messing up the lines."

"They sound better the way I say them," she argued. "More natural."

"But there are cues for the cast as well as the tech people, love, and if you don't say the lines right, they'll miss them."

"Joe and Katie know to go off me. I'm the star of the show."

"Yes, but—"

Serena waved a dismissive hand, done with Vaughn's notes. His face pinched in an unnatural way. He drew in a deep breath and let it out slowly. If he could have hummed a calming mantra without anyone thinking he was nuts, he would have.

An hour later, as Serena and Tilly were singing the duet "For Good," in which Elphaba and Glinda realize they love each other but can't be a team, Vaughn jumped onto the stage. "Stop! Ouch. My delicate ears. Serena, love, you're way off key. What's the problem? Did you forget to hydrate?"

"Of course, I hydrated." Serena stamped her foot. "It's my stupid sister's fault. She isn't blending with me."

Tilly's mouth dropped open. "Yes, I—"

"And Joe smacked his gum," Serena continued. "I heard him."

I shot a look at Joe, who shook his head and opened his mouth—empty.

"No, Serena, it's you. You know what you need to do." Vaughn rolled a hand in front of him as he moved toward her. When he reached her, he caressed her diaphragm with his fingertips. "Work it. C'mon. Work it."

As he coached her, Serena's eyes blazed with indignation. I noticed Tilly listening in, hand fisted. She seemed ready to pop her sister in the nose. Everyone on either side of the stage held a collective breath.

After a long moment, Vaughn released Serena, patted Tilly on the shoulder, said, "Breathe, both of you," and then he turned to the orchestra and jutted a hand. "Maestro, let's proceed. Katie and Joe, we'll start again, top of the scene."

It went on like this for three hours. Serena being right and everyone else being wrong. My cues were *off.* Joe's lights and machinations were *late, early, whatever.* When we finished the rehearsal, I was drenched with sweat, Joe was exhausted, and poor Tilly looked ready for blood. I considered having a chat with Serena to see if she might soften her edges but knew in my heart she wouldn't take my suggestions well. Not to mention I couldn't remember a tech rehearsal when she had been easygoing. Why waste my breath?

After rehearsal, I moved about the theater picking up props that the cast left in the wrong places. A green fan here, an emerald pair of spectacles there. I wished they would put their things back, but they weren't being paid a dime, and I was. A meager fee, but a fee nonetheless. I was their stage manager. They expected me to bring order to their world.

As I neared the costume room, I heard a man and woman arguing.

"Vaughn, listen to me," the woman snarled. "She's going to ruin this show."

The door was slightly ajar. Lights were dim, but I could see Tilly, not Serena, pacing the room. Vaughn was leaning against a table, arms folded.

"What do you expect me to do?" he said. "We open tomorrow."

"She dismissed you in front of the cast and crew. She demeaned my vocals. You know I was on key. You know it." She shot a finger at him.

Vaughn gripped her finger, pulled her to him, and planted a kiss on her mouth.

I stifled my shock.

"Babe, be reasonable," he rasped. "We have sold out the show. We have to open. And we don't have understudies."

"Katie could do it."

"And what would we do for a stage manager? No, love. We can't replace your sister last minute, but I promise, after this show, she will never star in another one. Ever."

As they kissed again, I sneaked away. Talk about a plot twist.

***

Opening night and the theater was buzzing with energy. The actors circulated backstage. A trio vocalized in three-part harmony. A pair of performers sitting on the floor, legs spread, toes touching and hands connected, stretched each other. They pulled forward and back while chatting about what they were wearing to the opening night party. A few actors, already in costume, greeted each other with "Break a leg."

A costumer bustled around a few actors who needed her to sew on a last-minute snap or button.

"Pins!" cried a second costumer as she whizzed past me. "I'm out of pins."

Quelle horreur, I thought and bit back a laugh.

We rented the costumes, wigs, and props from a well-known supplier to theaters. Top notch, but occasionally there were snafus.

As for the tech crew, Joe had spent all afternoon reviewing his list with them. Levers were oiled. Trapdoors were squeaky clean. Curtains and backdrops glided smoothly into place. Teamwork. I loved teamwork.

"Looking good, Katie," the wig mistress said as she checked and double-checked her station. She also served as the prop mistress. "Excited?"

"Over the Yellow Brick Road."

She giggled.

The orchestra started warming up as the oboe provided the A440, a particular frequency that all instruments matched. On a few occasions in high school, I'd played the flute. How I'd loved the trill and thrill of the orchestra finding unity.

"*Psst*. Katie." Tilly beckoned me from the wings. I was standing center stage checking a few light cues. "Have you seen Serena?"

"No. Isn't she here?" I glanced at my watch. She wasn't late, but Serena was always early. She liked to vocalize for a full half hour.

Tilly shook her head. "I've texted her. She's not responding."

"She's nervous. That's all. This is a big role for her."

"For me, too."

"Of course." I patted her shoulder. "And you are killing it."

"Am I?"

"Between us"—I checked to make sure others weren't listening in—"you're a rock star."

Tilly blushed and squeezed my hands. "Thank you. You have always been a bellwether for me. Serena is wrong about you."

"Wrong, how?"

"She said you were jealous of her success, but I can see you're not. You cheer on everyone. Even the Munchkins."

"I don't have a jealous bone in my body. Okay, maybe I do." I sniggered and elbowed her. "This one."

She giggled. "*Hals und beinbrüch*," she said with a German accent. *Break a leg.*

I echoed the sentiment and gave her a hug. "Go get 'em, Glinda."

As she trotted off stage, a frisson of worry skittered up my spine. Where was Serena? I checked the greenroom. Her dressing room. The parking lot, in case she'd decided to neck with someone out of Vaughn's eyesight. She was nowhere.

Ten minutes later, she bolted into the theater. "I'm here!" She looked frazzled, her hair knotted in a messy bun. "You won't believe what happened. My car broke down and then Triple A took forever to get to me. But don't worry. I vocalized in the middle of Main Street to the delight of the entire town." She made an overly theatrical bow. "Let's have a great show." She hoisted her arm and shouted a loud, "Hurrah!"

The cast and crew cheered.

Serena strode to Vaughn, who was standing on the apron conversing with the conductor, and kissed him on the cheek. She ruffled his hair.

He batted her away. "I'm busy, and you're late."

"Didn't you hear? It wasn't my fault."

"Get in costume."

"Well, I never." Serena stomped away like a true diva.

Joe sidled up to me. "Trouble in paradise?"

"Clearly, Vaughn has endured enough of her antics," I whispered.

"She doesn't deserve to be the star," he muttered.

"But she is." I pecked his cheek, which caused him to blush. "Let's make this a night to remember."

"Yes, let's."

***

Twenty minutes into the show, everything was going off without a hitch. Every cue perfect. Serena on key. Tilly acting as though she adored her twin, unless, as Glinda, she wasn't supposed to. All was right with the world.

A short while later, I held my breath as Serena started singing "Gravity." This was the moment when she would soar into the air, her billowing witch costume spreading wider and wider until she encompassed the entire stage. It was a grand technical feat. I glanced at Joe manning the contraption. He didn't look my way, his gaze focused on the cables and levers, his tongue wedged between his teeth.

Up, up, up.

And then suddenly, down.

Elphaba—Serena—plummeted. To the stage. And then beyond because a trap door gave way. She shrieked as she fell through it. Then there was a thud.

The audience and crew gasped. The musicians stopped playing.

What the heck? I left my post yelling, "Call 911," and raced down the rear staircase to help. But it was no use.

***

For the next two hours, the police were as non-judgmental as they could be. Stoic was probably the best choice of words. Detective Christie snooped in every corner of the theater looking for clues and taking photographs. Detective Doyle asked everyone questions.

Serena was dead, her neck broken. She'd died on impact. What went wrong? If Serena's death was ruled as foul play, I feared Joe would be the main suspect because, as it turned out, the cable used to raise Elphaba was shredded. Faulty equipment or deliberate sabotage? The detectives weren't saying.

I sat on a folding chair as they interrogated Tilly and then Vaughn. The questions were routine. Where were you when it happened? Did you notice anything peculiar? How was your relationship with Serena?

Joe stood near me studying his cuticles. I tried to catch his eye but failed.

"Mr. Westin?" Detective Christie said. "May we have a word?"

Glumly, I listened as Doyle said he'd heard rumors that Joe was tired of Serena getting role after role because she'd slept with a variety of directors.

"What about talent?" Joe murmured, not denying the scuttlebutt. "What about integrity?" Even so, he swore he didn't have a hand in her death.

"Ms. Kalitsky," Doyle said to me when he finished with Joe. "Your turn."

My insides turned to jelly. I took a seat and eyed Detective Christie, a sweet-faced forty-something with a warm demeanor. Doyle was her polar opposite. Sharp features. Beady eyes. A casting director couldn't have cast good cop, bad cop better.

Doyle asked me to give my account.

"I was at my post at the light board when I heard what everyone else did. A snap and then a crack. Then Serena shrieked. Seconds later she flew through the trap door and landed in the basement with a thud. I knew it couldn't be good. I dashed down the rear staircase to help." I pointed to it.

"Who opened the trap door?" Doyle asked.

"No one. It had to be a glitch."

"Why didn't anyone help you?"

"The cast and crew were sort of frozen. When I got to Serena, she was…" My voice broke. I asked for water.

Christie bounded to her feet and fetched a cup. She handed it to me. I drank all of it and handed the cup back.

"Serena lay there, her head cranked to the side."

"Which side?" Doyle asked.

"The right. Her left leg was at an odd angle to the rest of her body." I shook my head. "It was so sad. Shocking. She and I were good friends. Lifelong friends." I pressed my fingertips to my lips to fight the tears.

"Anything further you'd like to add?" Christie asked.

"No, ma'am."

"Do you think your crew member, Mr. Westin, did this on purpose?"

"What?" I gasped and cut a look at Joe who was standing in the wings looking dumbstruck. "No way. Never. Joe is a gentle soul. The gentlest on earth. Now Vaughn..." I said leadingly.

"What about him?" Doyle asked.

"He and Serena went at it yesterday."

Christie consulted her notes. "According to others in the cast, they often argued."

"But not in front of everyone. They kept it private, and speaking of private..." I shared the event I'd witnessed between Tilly and Vaughn. The kiss. The passion.

Christie jotted that down. Doyle drummed his fingertips on his leg. After a few more ordinary questions, they excused me.

I strode to Joe and stood there stoically. I would never tell the police that when Joe and I played cards last night, I went into his kitchen to pour myself a cup of coffee and saw a pair of clippers sitting on his kitchen counter. Wire clippers unlike any we stocked at the theater. Joe caught me staring at them. He begged me not to tell anyone. He said he'd been contemplating killing Serena for over a decade. Because of me. When *Wicked* came along, he'd wanted me to become the star of the show. I reminded him that I didn't even audition. He said that was because Serena had made fun of me and made me feel like I shouldn't. Joe promised he wouldn't do anything. I added cream to my coffee and promised him that I'd keep his secret.

An hour later, when Detectives Christie and Doyle deemed the incident was indeed an accident, I breathed easier.

I would never turn Joe in. How could I? I loved him. Yes, if I was finally honest with myself, I loved him. I couldn't imagine life without him. He was my soul mate. I'd learned the meaning of the term from my parents. Besides, if I mentioned the clippers and the police dug deeper, they might realize the fall didn't kill her.

***

I reached Serena in a matter of seconds. She was alive. Her

head was twisted to the right and one leg cranked to the left. It was messy. But she wasn't dead.

She blinked in pain. "Katie, help me."

Looking at her, I realized she'd never walk again, let alone shuffle off to Buffalo. She'd never sing off key again, either. She would be a vegetable.

"Help me."

How could I not? After all, I had been prepared to help her cross over to the great beyond after the final curtain.

"*Shh*," I whispered. "You're going to be fine."

I donned the pair of latex gloves I'd carried for tonight's event, pulled the bottle of nasal spray from my pocket, removed the top, and sprayed two squirts into each of Serena's nostrils. Using a tissue, I blotted the moisture from her upper lip.

"What is that?" she asked.

"Something to help you rest."

As I removed the latex gloves and returned them and the nasal spray to my pocket, the fentanyl from my mother's pain clinic that I'd added to the nasal spray worked its charm. Serena's eyelids fluttered and closed.

I yelled for help, but in less time than it took for the others to join me below stage, Serena died.

I didn't feel any remorse. It was an act of kindness. Pure and simple. Her pain, and everyone else's pain, was over. There would be no final act for her.

DEUS EX MACHINA
By B. J. Graf

*When stagecraft goes wrong, it could be simply a
technical failure—or murder.*

7:48 p.m. October 30, 2038 – Malibu, CA

As the audience began to fill the Getty Villa's outdoor theatre,
Homicide Special Detective Eddie Piedmont squirmed in his seat.
It was a hard, stone seat six rows back from center stage of the
theatre modeled on those of ancient Greece and Rome. The leg
room had been designed for people shorter than Eddie's six-foot-
two-inch frame. And he should have rented himself a seat cushion
like he had for his girlfriend, Jo, but Eddie'd thought the
discomfort might keep him awake during the performance of the
Greek tragedy *Medea*. Eddie wasn't excited about spending one of
his rare nights off watching some Bronze Age domestic dispute
with a high body count. He saw enough of that in his day job, 2038
style.

But Jo was keen on it, and Eddie was more than keen on Jo.
The relationship was new, three months to the day new, and he
didn't want to blow it. So here he was, in his best Brioni suit, his
black hair cut to perfection, thumbing through the program and
pretending an interest in the play as the concession stands' mini-
drones flew overhead, delivering pre-ordered snacks.

"You want something?" Eddie gestured to the drones dropping
orders of Starbucks coffee snuff, wine pops, and cultured kabobs
made from lab-grown, slaughter-free chicken into the outstretched
hands of seated Getty theatre-goers.

"I'm good." Jo tilted her pale blonde head and gave his arm a
little squeeze that made Eddie momentarily forget his discomfort.
"Oh." Jo reached into her purse and extracted the two small laser
pointers given to her by the ushers and handed one to Eddie. The
pointers reminded him of cat toys. "Before I forget," she said. "It's
an interactive performance. We're supposed to take part when
cued."

"Cued how?" Eddie flicked the laser pointer on and off with a
skeptical look.

"The chorus will cue us. Probably when the murders happen, or the *deus ex machina* rolls out at the end." Jo indicated the altar at center stage and the strange twenty-foot-high contraption behind it. The machine was some kind of a crane made out of wood and wires. "Ancient playwrights used it as a plot device," Jo said, "where the gods were flown in at the end to resolve an unsolvable problem."

"And nobody found that contrived?" Eddie said, resisting the urge to roll his eyes.

"It's supposed to be," Jo said, nodding. "When there is no satisfying answer on the mortal plane, jerry-rig one."

"How do you solve a problem like Medea?" Eddie sang the line to the tune from *The Sound of Music* in his sing-song baritone. He and Jo had gone to the Hollywood Bowl for the movie sing-a-long two weeks ago.

"Exactly," Jo said, pulling a face. "I mean, do you really think a mother can kill her own kids and still be sane?"

"Define sane." A couple of the more gruesome cases Eddie had closed two years ago flashed to mind.

"Point taken." Jo smoothed the folds of her sensuous vicuna and silk outfit around her elegant five-foot-nine frame. Jo was an intellectual property attorney. She dealt with different kinds of insanity than Eddie.

"I gotta say when you told me Kyle Lopez was the star of this production," Eddie said, leaning toward her, "I pictured something different. Something…"

"Less tragic?" Jo shot Eddie a sly grin.

Kyle Lopez was a B-List actor who'd had considerable success in the *Fists of Fire* franchise, online mixed-martial arts virtual reality games Eddie liked. But Lopez had never made the grade in the big-time action tent poles that brought real fame and money, and now he was pushing fifty. And he certainly wasn't Oscar or Tony material.

"My theory is Kyle Lopez's working on his acting chops in hopes of moving to the A-List," Jo said. "But don't worry, Eddie. No matter how he does, a happy ending is in your future tonight."

Jo's ocean-blue eyes, so different from Eddie's own pale blue orbs, flashed with merriment. He could drown in those eyes if he wasn't careful, and Eddie didn't want to be careful.

"You're going to make me a fan of Greek tragedy," he replied.

"That's my secret agenda." She flashed him a fleeting wicked grin. Then, Jo's eyes went wide.

Eddie followed her line of sight. Jo was staring at a stunning brunette with a prominent baby bump taking her seat dead center in the first row. The young woman had a familiar face, but it took

Eddie a moment to connect it to her famous name. She was a social media star who'd become infamous for her sex tape made four years ago when she was just eighteen. The brunette had leveraged that tape into a reality show that took off and led to a successful fashion line or something like that.

"Tamara Lopez," Jo whispered. "Kyle's wife."

"Whoa," Eddie said. Lopez might not win an Oscar, but he'd scored at home.

"Imagine," Jo said in a hushed voice. "The old buzzard gets the AARP discount, but they still card his wife at bars. *Not* his first wife, obviously."

"Good to know intellectual property lawyers keep current on the tabloids," Eddie said with a grin.

Jo was about to respond when the warnings to turn off all glove phones signaled the play was about to start, so she gave him a playful punch to the arm instead.

The actors performed on the simple stage, but there were big screens overhead and on both sides of the stage itself which gave the audience close-ups of their faces.

It was a contemporary adaptation of Euripides' play, but despite the current-day lingo, Kyle tended to mumble. Still, Eddie followed the plot. Jason was this famous hero who'd sailed on the Argo and brought home the golden fleece in order to get ahead. Eddie could relate to that. But to hear Jason's wife Medea tell it, he'd gotten a lot of help in bringing home the gold. Most of that help was due to her. And now that their life had taken a turn for the worse and they'd had to leave their country, Jason was dumping Medea for a younger woman who could score him a green card in El Norte. As a foreigner on her own, Medea was about to be deported. The couple had two sons together, and Jason wanted to keep the boys with him. Medea had other ideas. Ideas that started with knives and ended in blood.

As for Kyle Lopez's performance, Eddie thought maybe he should stick to online VR games. The actor scored high marks for how he looked in the shirtless get-up they had him in, but the delivery of his lines, not so much.

The chorus, a group of eight actors, sang and danced their way around the stage at various intervals giving the audience the scoop on Jason and Medea. Their faces in close-up on the screens, the chorus cued the audience to signal 'likes' or 'dislikes' by using the light beams from their pointers. Eddie feigned interest as he flicked the laser over the 'like' spot on the screen to his right. He glanced at Jo to see if she'd noted how civilized he could be, but Jo was absorbed in the play.

On stage Medea killed the fiancée, the girl's moneybags father, and even her own kids, ending Jason's hopes and legacy in the process. And then there she was at the climax, flying above Jason on that crane like a goddess, screaming at him that someday a beam of the Argo would fall on his head and kill the cheating bastard. The crane moved Medea closer to him. The production had floated a hologram of blazing light over the wooden structure which made it look like Medea was riding a chariot built from the sun's burning rays.

The chorus was cueing the audience to respond. Hundreds of red dots of light flickered all over the stage and surrounding screens.

And then Eddie heard a low groan and whine, and suddenly the thick beam of wood from the crane now directly over Kyle Lopez's head crashed down on him.

It was a pretty cool stunt. There was a collective gasp from the audience. And then the pointers' lights hit the 'like' buttons at an even faster rate and the prohibited glove phones came on along with cheers and applause.

But Jo wasn't clapping. And the actress playing Medea was frozen with a terror-struck expression on her face.

Then the screams started. And Eddie bolted for the stage.

***

Kyle Lopez was dead before the ambulance landed on the museum's helipad. Thirty minutes later, after the crew had helped the terrified actress playing Medea off the crane, Eddie met his forty-year-old partner Shin Miyaguchi on the edge of the stage. The play's rattled director made an announcement informing the audience to remain in the theatre until the official release had been sounded. ME/coroner Soledad Garcia and forensics tech Bobby Kubinsky had already arrived and were examining the body.

"Massive cerebral hematoma," said Dr. Garcia, pushing back a lock of her flaming red hair as she knelt by Kyle's body.

Shin's dark eyes roamed over the heavy wooden beam which the uniformed officers had shifted off the corpse. "Talk about cutting short life and career." Shin ran his broad hand over his shaved head.

The screams of Kyle Lopez's pregnant widow had given way to wrenching sobs in the arms of the deceased star's only slightly calmer manager, Michael Lowenstein. Lowenstein had a meticulous comb-over and sported a sharp designer suit. He shepherded Tamara back to her seat in the front row and took the seat next to her where he rubbed the widow's back and spoke in a low reassuring tone.

"What a terrible accident." Director Jessica Nguyen tried to suppress the tremble in her voice. Attired in a simple black sheath, she grabbed hold of one of the Corinthian columns to keep her slim frame from shaking. Eddie pulled her to the right side of the theatre just outside the cordon where they could speak in private.

"You checked all the beam's support wires at the tech rehearsal?" Eddie said.

"We observed *all* the security protocols." The director's worried gaze was focused on the widow, who'd started to yell.

"How could you let this happen?" Tamara Lopez screamed. "How?"

Shin headed over to Eddie. The partners exchanged a glance. The Getty was looking at a major liability lawsuit.

"We need to check the rigging." Eddie pointed to the *deus ex machina* twenty feet overhead. A steep climb.

"A job for young bones." Shin made a face as he cupped his suddenly-sore elbow.

"A sign you need to hit the gym, old man," Eddie said with a smirk.

Shin just wagged his eyebrows. His appreciative glance landed on Jo, now seated in the first row. With her long legs and blonde hair, she looked like one of those models in the ads for flying chopper-cars, hover-yachts, and other expensive trinkets for the very rich. "Is that her?" Shin's gap tooth grin grew wider. "Whoa. No wonder you deleted your Tinder account, partner."

"Better get started on those witness interviews, Shin." Eddie smiled as he started walking toward the rig. Seeing that SID tech Kubinsky had finished taping the scene on his glove phone, Eddie tapped him to follow along and headed up. The image of the dead actor lingered for a moment in the L-shaped space between Kubinsky's thumb and forefinger before the tech closed his phone.

It took Eddie only seconds to climb up into the rigging of the *deus ex machina*, but the nervous tech followed much more slowly. Seated on a t-shaped outcropping of the main trunk of the crane twenty feet above the stage, Eddie grabbed hold of one end of the main support cable with gloved hands. This was the wire which had snapped and let the beam crash onto Kyle Lopez's head.

The cable itself was a quarter inch thick and made of braided steel wire.

"Should easily be strong enough to hold up a beam that size," Bobby Kubinsky said in a quaking voice and trying not to look down from his perch twenty feet above the ground. "So, what happened? Did a bolt come loose? Shoddy construction? Wear and tear?"

"You tell me." Eddie held out the cable end for the tech to examine. Bobby gingerly inched himself closer to the break in the steel.

There was no sign of fraying. All the braided wires had snapped clean at exactly the same point. And the break was sharply angled.

"It's been cut," the tech agreed, his knuckles white as he clung to the wooden machine.

"Yeah," Eddie said, snapping pictures on his glove phone. He borrowed the pasty-faced tech's wire cutters and cut off the ends of the cable, dropping them into an evidence bag along with his own gloves. "Good news for the Getty. Bad news for our caseload." God had not jerry-rigged Kyle Lopez's demise. Somebody very human had.

"Not an accident," Eddie said as he jumped the last few feet back down from the crane onto terra firma. He showed Shin the ends of the cleanly cut cable.

"Homicide?" Shin sputtered. "How's that even possible? If there's no fraying, the cut wasn't done in advance. That means the killer had to slice the line during the performance in full view of over a hundred people—including you."

"Who operated the machinery during tonight's performance?" Eddie asked.

"I did." The voice belonged to a tanned, heavily muscled man in his late twenties who identified himself as Shane Travers. Travers had porcelain veneers and a bleached blond man-bun showing two inches of dark roots. He worried his bottom lip in a nervous way.

"How do you maneuver the crane?" Eddie asked.

"From the console." Shane walked them over to what looked like a big sound board off stage. The buttons on the console worked a series of motorized pulleys that maneuvered the machine back and forth on tracks.

"Can you cut a support cable from this console?" Eddie asked.

"Cut?" Shane's caterpillar eyebrows shot up in surprise. "No. You'd have to do that manually from the rigging itself."

"Which he didn't do," Shin said, eyes glued to his glove phone. "I got the security footage right here." He tilted his glove-phone so Eddie could watch as they ran through the taped performance on fast forward.

Shane hadn't gone near the place where the wires were cut during the performance. Neither had anyone else.

It looked like they were back at square one, and by now the audience was getting restless. Angry complaints were growing.

They'd have to release people soon. Eddie held over all those who were part of the production or directly connected to the murdered star while Shin instructed the uniforms to collect contact information from the rest of the audience.

"What if the cable *wasn't* cut with wire cutters," Eddie said. He was staring down at his gloves in the evidence bag. On the tips of two of the blue latex fingers where he'd held the wire there were tiny black smudges.

"Scorch marks?" Shin leaned in to look. "What are you saying? Somebody used a tiny blow torch on this sucker? How would anybody do that in plain sight?"

"A small IED set for remote detonation?" Eddie cocked his head at the SID Tech, handing him the evidence bag.

"Explosives don't cut that clean," Bobby Kubinsky said. "And there'd be residue. It's not there."

"What else could cut clean in plain sight without anybody suspecting?" Eddie glanced at the now blank screens of the production. Then he froze. Eddie drew his laser pointer from his suit jacket and held it out to Bobby Kubinsky. "What about..."

"A laser?" Kubinsky said. He bobbed his head in a slight nod. "Yeah, that'd work if it was concentrated enough. To cut steel from a distance you'd need a 4kW disk, fiber or CO2 laser. They aren't cheap."

"Could you miniaturize it?" Eddie said. "Like the audience laser pointers?"

"If you used chirped pulse amplification on the C02 laser." Bobby burbled on a detailed technical description of the process.

"But our pointers are harmless," Ms. Nguyen protested.

"These are," Eddie agreed, flicking his on and off. "But what if the killer brought a potent laser to the show? He could use it during the performance to cut the cable, and nobody would suspect a thing because everybody in the audience was waving their pointers around."

Shin and Eddie hustled to get the word to the uniforms and security guards posted at the exits. "Nobody leaves until we confiscate and test each laser pointer," Eddie said.

General audience members gladly complied, handing over pointers and contact information in hopes they could head out sooner.

"Who had it in for Kyle Lopez?" Eddie stared at those who'd been held over for special questioning as one of the blue-suiters asked each of them for their pointers. "*Cui bono?*"

"Who *doesn't* benefit?" Shin said, ticking off suspects on his outstretched fingers. "Shane Travers was Kyle's understudy. If the death had been ruled an accident, Shane would have gotten the starring part the next day. The production will benefit because of the ghoul factor. People will want to come see the play where the actor really died. And his widow inherits the estate."

"Did Kyle have much in the way of an estate?" Eddie asked.

"Yesterday he didn't," Shin said. "But his manager told me they'd been negotiating a new deal with Disney-Warnerflix for Kyle's body of work. That deal is worth five times more now that the actor's a dead celebrity."

A commotion at the side exit made the detectives spin around. A balding man with a bad case of steroidal acne was yelling, his arms flailing as two uniformed officers restrained him. The man got free and swung a hard right at the officer's head. Eddie and Shin hustled over as the uniforms cuffed the guy.

One of the uniformed officers held up a laser with gloved hands. "We found it on him, Detectives." The officer flicked it on and pointed it at a piece of steel cable. The laser started to burn through the metal.

"Good work," Shin said.

"I don't know how that got into my pocket," the balding man protested.

"We can talk about it downtown," Eddie said.

The man's name was Renny Macallum, and a quick rundown of his social profile revealed him to be the opposite of a Kyle Lopez fan. Macallum had been stalking Tamara Lopez and posting deranged comments about her husband online. He also had one prior for domestic abuse.

As the uniforms read the man his rights, Jo joined Eddie offstage. He was reviewing the security footage which showed Macallum leaving his theatre seat and heading for the exit. Staring at the video, his stomach gave a sideways lurch. Eddie paused the footage and pointed at the image of an older woman bumping into Macallum just before the ruckus erupted.

"Is that…?"

Jo leaned close and glanced at the image. "Emily Lopez," Jo said. "Kyle's ex-wife."

***

Two days later Eddie was sitting on Jo's couch, watching the Santa Ana winds lash the branches of the jacaranda outside her Venice house. The cultural expeditions had given way to a night of Indian takeout and an online movie.

The story of Kyle Lopez's murder at the hands of his ex-wife was all over the web. The news pundits played up the theatrical angle of an actor murdered on the opening night of the Getty's production of *Medea*.

"I get that she was jealous," Jo said. "What I don't get is why she'd take it as far as murder. Even if you hadn't caught her, Emily would have lost her alimony once her husband was deceased."

"Wasn't about money," Eddie said, stretching his legs. As a senator's daughter, Mrs. Lopez was more than comfortable in the financial department.

"But don't crimes of passion happen in the heat of the moment? This was planned—an execution."

"That's exactly what Emily Lopez told me," Eddie said. "An execution. Justice served."

"Poetic justice, maybe," Jo said. "But it's awfully extreme. He dumped her, so she goes all Medea and kills him?"

"The play only gave her the idea," Eddie said. "In her mind the date of the opening was more significant."

"An anniversary?" Jo said.

"Yeah, but not the happy kind. Apparently, Emily got pregnant before she and Kyle were married. But he didn't want kids. Flash-forward all these years later. Emily's too old to have kids when Kyle dumps her for the young *mamacita* and their rug rat on the way."

"And the anniversary? Was that when Kyle married Tamara?"

"No," Eddie said. "Opening night was the anniversary of Emily's abortion. Kyle made abortion a condition of his marrying her in the first place. She was never the same after."

"OMG." Jo's face paled and she looked stricken. "It really is tragic. I almost feel sorry for her."

"Yeah." Eddie nodded. "Guilt, justice, there aren't any good answers here."

"No *deus ex machina* either," Jo said, putting her head on his shoulder.

"No?" Eddie kissed her blonde head. "Mrs. Lopez has already lawyered up with the best criminal attorneys a senator's daughter can buy. They'll pull all the strings in a system already rigged in favor of those with money and connections. Bingo—*deus ex machina* 2038 style."

"You're very cynical for one so young," Jo said. "We'll have to work on that."

"Does that mean I'll get that happy ending you promised?" Eddie's grin returned.

Jo winked. "Watch the movie."

THE NINE DEATHS IN HAMLET?
By A. P. Jamison

*Can Gus, with the help of Marshmallow, sniff out who
brought the performance of Hamlet to a deadly
conclusion?*

I was a liar and I wasn't proud of it. Okay, maybe more of a fibber,
but still. See when dusk descended on our ranch, one of the most
beautiful sights in all of Texas was the way the Roseate Spoonbills
glided onto Tear Drop Lake. I kept riding out with my dog by my
side, to see the place where my parents had died. I couldn't tell
anyone that I come here every day because they wouldn't
understand, so I lied.

My name is Augusta DeWitt, but my friends and family call me
Gus. I live on a ranch about two hours outside of San Antonio with
my aunt and sister. As an eleven-year-old cowboy-boot-wearing,
pecan-pie-loving cowgirl from the great State of Texas, I was
raised to tell the truth, but this truth hurt too much. Since their
death I had been eating sorrow by the spoonful and the only ones
who really understood were my Golden Retriever, Buddy Holly the
Marshmallow, and my Appaloosa, Lonesome Dovey.

Standing before the lake, I hit play on my phone and the song
"Not a Day Goes By" by Lonestar began. Once it was over, I
wiped away any trace of tears. Cowgirls didn't cry. Then, I hopped
back on Dovey and the three of us headed back home for supper.
My sister, Susana, was having some friends over. It was what my
aunt called a "command performance" attendance.

I kept seeing my parents in my dreams and my nightmares. And
I wasn't too sure how my aunt was coping—she put all her
energies into cooking and me. Worse, she kept trying to pretend
that my parents were away on some fancy-dancy European cruise,
when I knew dang well they were buried right next to each other
out in the family cemetery at the edge of our property.

See, Miss Lemon Meringue was normally the most delicious
dessert of an aunt anyone could ask for—and no, that wasn't her
real name, but in all my eleven years, it was the only thing I had
ever called her. And, aside from always wearing white and
yellow—Miss Lemon Meringue was our very own ray of

sunshine—she was so soft and sweet, yet tart when she needed to be...

But lately she kept trying to pack Marshmallow and me up in her yellow pickup truck and take us to do fun things that I secretly hated...like The Water Park. Why would I want to hang out in a warm pool full of some other kid's pee? I knew Miss Lemon Meringue liked yellow, but not that much! Then there was The Playground Park. Why would I want to get on a merry-go-round ride when the pony I had didn't need a pole? But the worst so far was The Build-A-Better Dress Store. My Aunt knew I hated wearing dresses so why in the dang world would I want to make one? I mean, what the heck!

I gathered the reins in one hand, but before I could tell Dovey it was time to giddy-up, a big fat brat of a rat—the rodent kind—ran across our dirt pathway. That sent Marshmallow on another great chase down and around the bluebonnets. He didn't like rats in human or animal form. That gorgeous Golden Retriever must have had a little cat in him. And when I say cat, y'all know I mean the lion kind. As he raced to catch up to the rat, I galloped closely behind, hot on their tails.

See, in addition to cattle, oil, and cotton, we run a tiny vineyard and rats love our grapes. They also adore grain, meat, vegetables, seeds, but most of all they go hog wild crazy over the food from the chicken coops.

And once we got back home, we checked to see if any vermin had invaded the coop. Marshmallow had succeeded in keeping the rat from the chickens.

Back in the stables, I gave Dovey a quick brushing and some hay, then Marshmallow and I walked up to our kitchen door and I breathed in a Texas-sized sigh of relief after seeing that hot pink Ford pickup truck parked out front.

Pepper, one of my sister's Best-Friends-For-Life (BFFL), had arrived, so there was no way Miss Lemon Meringue was going to be able to rope me into another "cheer Gus up event road trip" or "homemade cooking or sewing class" tonight. Giddy-up. I was hoping that Pepper's friend Luke was with her. I liked Luke in the way a cowgirl adores her cowboy big brother. See, Luke didn't act his age despite being something like thirty years old. He wasn't the kind to get grossed out by bodily functions like passing gas and vomit, in fact he exceled at both of them. I liked that in a cowboy. He was actually a large animal veterinarian, so there wasn't much he hadn't seen in the puke, pee, poop, and pass gas department. I liked that about him. A lot.

I just wished my aunt understood that. I didn't need her fussing all over me; I just needed someone who laughed at what I laughed at like my daddy once did…

Oh goody. I could hear voices as Marshmallow and I stood just outside the side door by the kitchen window. Pepper *was* here with Luke. I wasn't sure what to think. Luke was sweet on Pepper but her heart was as confused as a fart in a fan factory. To be fair, I was told that whom we fall in love with is one of life's great mysteries, and she was also one of the kindest people I knew. She would *shoot* you, but not kill you. I liked that about her. A lot.

I opened the door and quietly entered the kitchen with Marshmallow by my side. I was smacked in the face by the heavenly aroma of butter, brown sugar, molasses, and maple syrup. Giddy-up. That could only mean freshly baked pecan pie for dessert, thank you, Miss Lemon Meringue!

Pepper, Luke, and Susana were gathered around our oversized marble island in the center of the kitchen. Pepper liked to have all her clothes match from her pink broomstick skirt to her pink boots. She was all girly girl on the outside right down to her bubblegum pink lipstick but on the inside, she was 100% hardcore Texan. "Guess what, y'all," Pepper said with unbridled joy. "I've been keeping a secret, but it's time to tell you that I was cast as Ophelia and Luke here is going to be Horatio of *Hamlet*. Opening night is next Friday at The Roxie Theater. Y'all have to come. You just have to. I got you tickets and that includes you, Marshmallow."

He wagged his plumed tail at her.

Now THIS was an "event" road trip we could embrace. I rubbed the top of Marshmallow's sweet blond head. I loved *Hamlet*.

When I wasn't out riding with the cowboys or playing with Marshmallow, I read everything we had in the library. Sure, we had a TV in the house, but it was reserved for one thing, and one thing only, Texas Football. Shakespeare was my Daddy's favorite author, so of course he had introduced me to all his stories. My mouth got me grounded an awful lot, so at an age younger than most, I had already finished reading all of Austen, Christie, Twain, Tolstoy, Dickens, and Nancy Drew. There were only so many times I could read the dang dictionary. What? I sort of started reading at the age of five.

And now I was going to see *Hamlet*. I could just hug Pepper and Luke! But Lordy Lou, what would Miss Lemon Meringue say?

"That is so wonderful," Miss Lemon Meringue said with the ease of an entertainer, "so wonderful, but there is no way we can go. We have to think of Gus. *Hamlet* is the story about a young man insanely haunted by the death of his father. I just don't think

Gus is ready for that."

Boom. There it was. I *was* haunted by the death of my parents, but I wasn't haunted by Hamlet's! This was a story where actors pretended to die. I exhaled and felt like steam was coming out of my nose.

And I could tell by my aunt's sweet smile that she was up to something more than making her famed pecan pie. But cowgirl boots on the ground, I was going to this play!

"Gus." Miss Lemon Meringue turned to me. "We're going to a puppet show that night."

I ignored her and went straight to my sister, Susana, who was sitting on a barstool by the kitchen island. I needed time to think. And my sister was a comfort. She was one of those Texas beauties whose lush black hair, violet eyes, pale skin, and petulant pout could start or stop a speeding bullet. She hugged me. She did that a lot these days.

As I tucked my head against Susana's shoulder, Luke smiled at me. He was a bit thinner than I remembered, but he was still tall, dark, and Texas handsome. Normally, Pepper was attracted to guys that were so country they thought a seven-course meal was a possum and a six-pack, but Luke was different. And he still had that twinkle in his mischievous eyes and looked like he was just about to fake barf on me. I was besotted.

Then I turned to Miss Lemon Meringue. "A puppet show?" Give me a good Shakespeare play any day. So, I said, "As long as it's the *Murder of Gonzago*, Hamlet's play-within-a-play puppet show, I'm game." I mean, where else can you get that much desire, murder, revenge, and treachery all wrapped up like a gourmet Tex-Mex taco, aside from right here in the great state of Texas…

Miss Lemon Meringue suddenly seemed drained of all her sweet sugar and, instead, all her tangy tartness was on full display. "No, darling Gus, it's a real puppet show, with a tiny stage and finger puppets. It will be so fun!"

I wanted to shout that fingers should not do any walking or talking or two-stepping. Period. But instead I said, "Why do you still treat me like I'm just five years old when I'm two years away from being legally able to drive a John Deere?"

Miss Lemon Meringue put her perfectly manicured hands on the ties of her yellow apron. That was a bad sign. I had to act fast. So, despite the fact that my mouth was so dry that if I were a catfish I'd have to carry a canteen, I blurted this out. "You always taught me that we must show our support for our loved ones through action and I can't think of a better way of showing our support for Pepper and Luke than by attending their opening night." Then I put on the biggest beaming smile ever. Oh, I was so close to ending up with a big bar of saddle soap in my sassy mouth.

Instead, Miss Lemon Meringue's jaw slacked. She looked as if it was going to drop right into her buttery pecan piecrust. Then she recovered and closed her mouth, but in a moment, she would open it again. She was as lemon pie sly as they come. The puppet showdown wasn't over. "Okay, Miss Augusta DeWitt. If you can tell me how many characters in *Hamlet* die, you can go."

"Dang. Dang. Dang." I had to let her think that she had me. But then I slowly went on and said, "One drowning, two beheadings or hangings depending on your interpretation, one simple stabbing, two simple poisonings, and three aggravated stabbings." I wanted to end by saying 'and a partridge in a pear tree,' but that saddle soap was too close for comfort. "So, to sum it up, there are a grand total of *nine* deaths in *Hamlet*." The only major character to survive the play was Horatio, Hamlet's best friend, because *someone* had to tell the story. There it was: Ding. Ding. Ding. All that I was missing was the wrapping paper and the big bad bow. Or lasso depending upon how you liked your gifts wrapped.

The room went crazy silent. Even Pepper and my sister, Susana, who could talk the ears off of an elephant, weren't saying a word, but then I thought of my daddy and momma. They would've wanted to go to this play, too!

Then all eight eyes were on me. "What?"

I hopped off the saddle barstool and as my boots hit the wood floor, I said, "They had better show Ophelia's death. Good ole Bill Shakespeare, arguably the greatest writer, writes one of the greatest deaths and it is not on the page. Dang. Just dang."

Writers are always banging on about show don't tell. Why didn't he show Ophelia's death on the page or in this case on the stage? I wanted to know if she really climbed a tree and, as its branch snapped, Ophelia fell into the water and drowned. But what if it was a suicide? Or what if Ophelia was really murdered? Why was Bill so obtuse? I know—a big word. I found it in the dictionary.

***

On Friday night, the electricity of anticipation crackled through the rows of The Roxie. Built in 2005, The Roxie was like a 14-year-old teenager, albeit, a cool one. The room was small, but charming. Miss Lemon Meringue liked to use the words "cozy" and "intimate" to describe this theatergoing experience. Each guest was seated just a few feet from the stage, so everyone had a good seat and I liked that.

My sister, Susana, sat on one side of Miss Lemon Meringue

while Marshmallow and I sat on the other. He technically rested on his traveling checkered dog blanket at my feet, but before us was the stage.

***

By Act V, Scene 1, I had to confess that up until the last scene, the actors had riveted me. Especially Xavier, who starred as Hamlet. Pepper said the rumor was that the next stop for him might be Hollywood. I understood why. He was a star in the making. But after this rendition of *Hamlet* also decided not to show Ophelia's death, I was madder than a puffed toad learning that the frog he had just kissed was not a princess, but an alligator.

***

I stared at the grave of Ophelia and watched as Laertes, her brother, gently lifted her dead body out of the wooden casket to show the mourners—us—his dead sister.

Just then, something flickered at the outside of my vision and I spun my head. Fading away at the side of the stage were two ghosts. But these ghosts weren't in *Hamlet*. Then I looked closer at them. It was the ghosts of my parents and they were soaking wet! I gasped as they faded away.

Then before I could make sense of what I had just seen, I spied Luke, playing Horatio, come out of his hiding place by the trees in the forest, stagger over to the gravesite, and promptly fall on top of Pepper, playing Ophelia.

The audience gasped.

But I knew that wasn't part of the play. Horatio had to live to tell the tale. What the H, E, double toothpicks, was going on? Were they rewriting Shakespeare?

Suddenly Pepper, still playing the dead Ophelia, rose up from her coffin and tried to wake Luke, but he wasn't moving.

All the color had drained from his ashen face. He was either an Oscar-worthy actor or…

Pepper screamed three words that were as powerful as anything Shakespeare had ever written. "Luke is dead!" Then she fell back into her coffin and started wailing.

In the blink of a jackrabbit's eye, the theater went from silence to chaos. The show's director looked like he had not only lost the plot, but one of his best actors. Now the stage was in turmoil, full of cast and crew racing around, so I had to act fast. Marshmallow and I took this opportunity to go on stage and see for ourselves.

We hurried over to Luke. Big gobs of blood had formed around his mouth. I didn't like this vomit. And I normally don't mind the dead—the only adults who had ever scared the daylights out of me were still living. But this was bad. Very bad.

Luke was really dead.

Texas-sized tears formed in my eyes. I quickly wiped them away with my arm. I had to focus. Miss Lemon Meringue couldn't see me sobbing. Marshmallow sniffed Luke and his supersonic nose began twitching. He smelled something. Something awful. What had Marshmallow found?

Then a security guard appeared and said, "Please make room for the doctor. And, unless you are a medical professional, please leave the stage." But Marshmallow didn't listen—he sat right down. I just stared at him; I hadn't given him the command. See, Marshmallow only sat like that when he had found rat poison. I had trained him to point out that odor. I bent down and rubbed Marshmallow's belly and his head. That was the silent "good boy" sign we had developed on the ranch. But poison, this was bad. I was so angry I wanted to stomp something to smithereens in my buckskinned boots, but instead, Marshmallow and I left the stage immediately. We had to find a killer before we were kicked out, discounted, or dismissed. It was the only way I could deal with Luke's tragic and untimely death.

***

If Marshmallow smelled rat poison on Luke, was there another place in the theater that he could sniff it out? It was something... and we needed to start at the beginning. The dressing rooms.

Marshmallow and I went down a set of steep stairs to the basement. Given that it was a small theater, there was one large men's dressing room and one large women's dressing room. While I headed to the men's dressing room, Marshmallow veered off straight toward the women's. Why was he taking us here? I opened a door that had a Texas star on it. Marshmallow went straight to Pepper's spot. I gulped. Did Pepper have something to do with Luke's death? Oh, Lordy no. It couldn't be...

But in the trashcan by her chair, I found the remains of a piece of cake. Again, Marshmallow sat down in the "I found poison" position and I knew this could be evidence. One of the main ingredients of rat poison causes internal bleeding. That's how they died. They bled to death. Was rat poison the cause of Luke's death?

I had to find Pepper.

So after carefully bagging the entire trash can, we headed back upstairs to find Pepper being comforted by my sister and aunt.

"Pepper, I'm so sorry about Luke." I really was. I understood the searing pain of death. The finality of it. One minute you are laughing with your loved ones, and then what seems like the next minute, they are six-fricking-feet down under covered in Texas dirt and their ghosts start haunting you. "But I need to ask you a few questions, is that okay?" Not many people respect an eleven-year-old's questions, but she always had. "Can you tell me more about this cake?"

"Cake?" was her one-word reply.

"Yes, please."

"It was Gertrude's birthday, I mean, Adelaide, so Luke got me a piece. He knew I loved buttercream frosting. But my tummy was doing flips with first-night jitters, so I passed."

"Do you know who brought the cake?"

"No. But Luke had a piece and then he ate mine. Then he threw the plates in the trash."

"Do you know who gave the pieces to him?" I asked. This was key.

"I have no idea." Pepper replied while tears sat on the brims of her eyes.

Dread was fixin' to fill my lungs.

"Gus, you're scaring me," Pepper said. "What happened?"

"Luke ate a piece of cake that was meant for you. Marshmallow thinks it was filled with rat poison. If it is, I think someone may be trying to kill you."

"Kill me?"

"Yes. Do you have any enemies?" I asked.

"No!"

"Anyone you tied up recently using your lasso?" Pepper was an expert with a lasso and men didn't always like being tied up when she got mad at them.

"No."

Sometimes people die and we don't know why. This wasn't going to be one of those times!

Miss Lemon Meringue, Marshmallow, Susana, and I went back downstairs. On the way to the men's dressing room, I almost collided with the stunning actress named Adelaide who played Gertrude—that was Hamlet's mom—as she hurried down the hallway sobbing buckets of sorrow toward the ladies' room. Gertrude shut the bathroom door with such force she might as well have been a high plains hurricane.

Susana stopped halfway down the theater hallway, leaned in, and whispered to Miss Lemon, Marshmallow, and me, "Adelaide had a mad crush on Luke and hated that he was sweet on Pepper."

"Didn't she know about Pepper?" I whispered back.

Susana shook her lovely locks. "No. Since Pepper was playing Ophelia, who was supposed to be in love with Hamlet, she decided not to reveal she's gay. No one knew."

That meant everyone knew Pepper wasn't into Luke. This

wasn't making sense. Pepper wasn't a threat to Gertrude.

But I had noticed Adelaide's gait—I'm a cowgirl so I'm attuned to all manner of walking, trotting, running, and galloping; that's how you detect horse injuries—and her gait was off. Was she crying about Pepper, Luke, or was her leg in some serious sort of pain?

I knocked on the bathroom door and said, "Are you all right?"

"No," was her sob-filled reply in a full-on Australian accent.

Was her shortness of breath from crying or lack of oxygen? I didn't know.

"Can I get you anything?" is what I said out loud. Manners still mattered even during a murder investigation.

Adelaide opened the door slightly. "Can you get my purse, please? It's in the dressing room. Right next to my toy kangaroo."

This I had to see before Marshmallow used the kangaroo as a new chew toy. In a moment, the kangaroo was safely tucked away and I was back with Adelaide's purse, but I slow-walked the last part of the way so I could peek into her open bag. I stopped when I saw the pill bottle.

She had a prescription for Coumadin for her deep vein thrombosis.

The murderer could have used that instead of rat poison. They share the same ingredients. That's why doctors prescribed this medicine in very small doses. The surgeon prescribed it for my granddaddy after his hip surgery so he wouldn't get a blood clot.

Just then the man in a suit reached out his hand. "I'm Detective Martinez. This is Miss Adelaide's purse? Did you remove anything?"

"No," I said, stunned.

***

Five minutes later, the San Antonio police escorted Adelaide back upstairs in handcuffs. It wasn't a good look on Gertrude, the Queen of Denmark. Yes, she had a bottle of Coumadin, which I'm betting was used in the cake, but I saw the genuine shock on her face when the police arrested her on suspicion of murder. She wasn't faking her surprise at being handcuffed. But how could I prove it? Before they took her away, I had to be sure. What could I do? Think. Think. Think.

With the help of Marshmallow, I had just moments to sniff this answer out. What if the motive was all wrong? What if Pepper wasn't the target, but what if Horatio was? Then the famous words of Hamlet came floating back to me. "The play's the thing, wherein I'll catch the conscience of the king."

I glanced over at the case of our family's Texas Tear Drop wine by my aunt's chair. It was to be uncorked at the after-party celebration. I snuck over to Susana and whispered in her ear. Miss Lemon Meringue gave me the "a smart ass just don't fit into a saddle" look. But I wasn't going to let that or a mouthful of saddle soap stop me from moving forward with my plan. Besides, my sister had already agreed to help me.

Susana stood in the middle of the stage. "Before the Queen of Denmark is led away, I think we need to toast to our beloved friend, Luke." She grabbed one of the bottles of wine. It was a vintage year on the ranch.

I smiled at my awesome sis, but Detective Martinez was having none of it. "This is neither the time nor the place."

Susana put a hand on her hip just like Miss Lemon Meringue had. "We want to honor our friend in a place he loved. Wouldn't you want that for a loved one who had just been murdered?"

There was nothing more Detective Martinez could say.

"This *was* Luke's favorite wine," I added for good measure.

"That was before his ulcer," Ben, the actor who played Laertes, said.

Boom. Bang. Dang. Then it all made sense. The weight loss, the vomiting, the gas, the nausea. Luke had been acting to cover up his ulcer. Someone here knew he had an ulcer. Someone who knew he couldn't pass up a piece of cake. Someone who knew that the Coumadin would only kill someone with a bleeding ulcer.

Susana, my sister, who knew how to tap a keg or open a fine bottle of wine, was already pouring the wine into plastic cups that were being passed around to Miss Lemon Meringue, Adelaide, Ben, Pepper, Xavier, and even Detective Martinez. I watched closely to make sure that everyone had a glass. Why? Because someone in the cast aside from Gertrude could also be taking Coumadin and set her up. You couldn't drink alcohol while taking a blood thinner. I learned that from my granddaddy when he was taking Coumadin.

"To Luke," Susana said as she raised her glass.

I watched each face, standing in a circle on the stage. All but one took a drink.

Then I knew. But in this instance, it was the conscience of a *future* king that gave him away.

Marshmallow and I hurried over to Xavier, the actor playing Hamlet. I finally decided that the truth was what I needed to lead with. "You knew Luke had an ulcer. You knew that Adelaide had deep vein thrombosis. You just took advantage of their illnesses. You wanted Luke's death to go viral and put this play on the map. You wanted to be famous and now you will be. Damn. See, there is no way you can launch your acting career in Los Angeles when you will be rotting like a rodent in prison for the murder of Luke."

The veneer of a smile slid off Xavier's blindingly white teeth. Then he lunged at me, but before his hands could get to my neck, Marshmallow's teeth got to his jeans at his ankle.

The rest was silence…except for Marshmallow growling at him until the police could take Hamlet away.

***

I finally understood why Shakespeare never showed us how Ophelia died. Sometimes these things haunt us because we will never know all the answers. And I did finally feel Hamlet's famous line:

When sorrows come, they come not single spies, but in battalions…

The full saltwater fireworks finally started down my face. Marshmallow moved in closer. He knew. It wasn't just about death. It was about loved ones being taken too soon. Before their time. And those of us left behind who have to live with that emptiness in our hearts every hour of every day.

My thoughts drifted back to the ghosts of my parents. Had they been murdered, too? It would explain why I still saw them. Unlike Hamlet or Xavier, I didn't want revenge or fame. I wanted justice. But how does an eleven-year old get justice?

The only way I know how, one-cowgirl-boot step at a time.

HEAT WAVE
By Maureen Jennings

*When handsome Julian Cross comes seeking help to
find his missing brother, the enterprising Charlotte
Frayne proves up to the task—and more.*

The city was sweltering in the hottest July in recorded memory.
For five days in a row, temperatures had reached over 90 degrees
Fahrenheit and the nights weren't that much cooler. The
newspapers reported two hundred deaths across the country, all
attributed to the heat. Rumour had it that a man had cooked an egg
on the sidewalk in Winnipeg. I didn't believe it. Nobody would
waste a perfectly good egg on such a stunt. Not these days. In
Toronto, a milkman's horse had dropped dead on his rounds. That
one I believed.

Monday, I went in to work even earlier than usual to take
advantage of the slightly lower morning temperature. My boss, Mr
Gilmore, rents two rooms on the second level of the Yonge street
Arcade. I had the front, he had the back, neither had windows. It
was artificial light winter and summer. The rooms tended to be a
touch cooler in summer with no sun to beat in, but today I'd hardly
been there half an hour before I was sweating. I discreetly
unbuttoned the neck of my blouse. I'd already slipped off my
stockings, but nobody could see my bare feet underneath the desk.
Mr Gilmore wasn't due until ten o'clock, and I expected on a day
like this he might come in later. The hall was, shall we say, under
carpeted and I could always hear him clumping down the hall so
there was plenty of time to make myself presentable. "We have to
create an immediate impression of decorum and good breeding,
Miss Frayne. Our clients see a polite and pleasant young woman as
well-dressed as any of Mr Eaton's salesladies. They will feel at
ease, knowing they can expect to be treated with the utmost
decorum." *Decorum* was one of Mr Gilmore's favourite words.

I'd picked up copies of the three morning newspapers on my
way over and I was about to skim through them. My job was to
take note of particular items that might bring us business. Lost and
Found of course. You'd be amazed how easy it was to link people
together. Those who had lost and those who had found. Sort of like
being a matchmaker. I kept a file on all the missing dogs, purses,

and bits of jewelry. By now I had developed quite a circle of acquaintances who kept an eye out for me. Kidnapped dogs were easy to identify. We were usually able to get in before the kidnapper contacted the owner. Joyous reunions resulted. Generous rewards were always shared.

However, I'd say the obituary column was the most lucrative. I would track down the address of the people mentioned as 'is survived by,' and send them a note. The letterhead said, **T.GILMORE AND ASSOCIATES. Private Investigators. Utter Discretion; reasonable rates guaranteed.** In fact, Mr Gilmore had no associates unless you counted me, which he didn't. But he said it gave more respectability to his work. As if he were a solicitor. My job was to write a short note to the grieving widow or occasionally widower. *Please accept our most sincere condolences. We are here if you need us.* Unscrupulous people were known to keep track of the death notices in the newspapers and send a letter to the bereaved one, claiming dubious connections with the dear departed. Blackmail really. You'd be surprised how common this was. Getting to the bottom of such claims was how we earned our bread and butter.

I swatted a reckless fly who had decided to explore my desk. This morning's *Star* was as leaden and dispirited as the weather itself. Europe in an upheaval as usual. I was about to switch to the Globe when a terse notice caught my eye.

The body of a man was washed up on Cherry Beach late last night. According to police he was probably in his mid-twenties, blonde haired. Medium height. He was clothed only in his swimming trunks. The cause of death was drowning. The police believe he must have gone into the water to escape the heat and got into difficulties. Given the condition of the body, they estimate he had been in the lake for a couple of days. To date the body has not been identified although the police did conduct a search of the beach and discovered a neat pile of clothing near the shore. No wallet was present.

If there had been, it would have been a miracle indeed. Dozens of people jammed into broiling squalid houses were spending nights on the beach. An unguarded bundle of clothes would have been too tempting to resist.

I heard somebody coming down the hall and quickly buttoned my collar and slipped my feet into my sandals.

There was a knock on the door. You can tell a lot by the way prospective clients knock. There's the timid, uncertain sort of knock from those who would rather not be consulting a private detective but feel they must; always a woman, usually in search of her dog; most often afraid of risking the disapproval of her husband who had to pay the bill. A sharp and prolonged rat-a-tat was ninety percent of the time an aggrieved man who suspects his spouse is cheating on him.

This current knock was somewhere in between. Firm and confident but not aggressive. Male I guessed.

"Come in."

He did so and I met Julian Cross. My life was never the same after that.

Let me backtrack a little. I'm looking down the wrong side of thirty and I'm not spoken for. I had a couple of tries that didn't go anywhere so I suppose you'd say I was on the verge of giving up hope. My gran, who I've lived with since my mother ran off with a roadie when I was three, is always telling me I'm too picky. 'No such thing as the perfect man,' I know that, of course I do, but my range of possibilities is limited by my height. I started growing taller than all my peers when I was a teenager. Gran used to say, jokingly, 'I'm going to put a brick on your head. No man wants to get hitched to a woman who can look down on him.' I think I would have sat in a trouser press if it had worked, but there didn't seem to be anything I could do about my legs getting longer and longer. When I passed twenty-one, I could almost look a six-foot-tall man straight in the eyes. Others, I could indeed look down on. And just as Grannie said, they seemed not to like that.

The man who had just walked into the office was at least six foot three. I was surprised to see he was leaning on a cane which reduced his height somewhat. He was elegantly dressed in a tan coloured linen suit. When he removed his panama, he revealed crisp dark hair cut short. He had brown eyes and a smile that would light up your life.

"Can I help you?" I asked. To my own ears I sounded breathless.

"I can see you're not Mr Gilmore. You therefore must be Miss Charlotte Frayne."

He nodded in the direction of the name plate on my desk.

I returned his smile. Who wouldn't?

"Correct on all counts. I am expecting Mr Gilmore later this morning."

"That's fine. I'd just as soon talk to you."

"Please have a seat."

I indicated the solitary wooden chair and he limped over to it. He groaned slightly as he sat down, and I could see his leg was stuck straight in front of him. No mobility at the knee from the look of it. I glanced at his hand. I wished men would wear wedding rings the way we women did so everybody could know what was what. He had long fingers, tanned and slim, bare of jewelry.

"My name is Cross, Julian Cross. I heard about you from a neighbour, Mrs Harley," he said. "She was most impressed with your ability."

I remembered the case well. Luring Mrs Harley's cat from the roof with an open can of sardines didn't exactly require much ability, but Boots had certainly impressed himself on me. The marks had only just started to fade.

"Thank you," I murmured. "How can I help you, Mr Cross?" He looked vaguely familiar, but I couldn't quite place him.

"I would like to find my brother. My mother is gravely ill and it would bring her much comfort if she could see Stephen before she passes on."

I raised my eyebrows.

"He disappeared about two years ago. We have not had a word since."

"Did you report this to the police?"

"Eventually we did. Stephen left home more than once when he was a teenager, so at first we didn't think much of it. He was always back within the week, hungry and dirty. This time two weeks went by, then a month. I went to the police and filed a missing person report."

He paused and his eyes drifted away. An unhappy memory, I thought.

He came back to earth, gave me a little grin. "Sorry. I got distracted. The police could find no trace of him whatsoever. After a year they closed the case. As one officer said to me, 'Kids leave home every day of the week. He'll show up when he's ready.'"

"Was he a kid?" I asked.

"He'd just turned eighteen. Not exactly a kid, but I suppose not an adult either."

"Was there a reason he might have run away? Trouble in the family for instance?"

Cross began to rub his knee. It was an unconscious gesture that I'm sure he wasn't aware of.

"He didn't get along with our father. Ever since I remember, Steve was rebellious, mouthy my father called him. They were always arguing."

Again, his thoughts drifted away.

I called him back. "What about you? Did you have the same kind of relationship?"

"Oddly enough I didn't. I'd say Father was rather strict, but he wasn't around much when I was growing up, so I was left to my mother's ministrations."

He held up his hand to halt my comment although I hadn't been about to make one.

"I know what you're thinking. That I was spoiled rotten." He smiled that light-up-your-life smile. "I confess I was. My mother was a lot younger than my father and she was full of fun."

I got the picture.

"Come the war, I joined up as soon as I could, and Father liked that. Made him proud. Unfortunately, I didn't last long. Ypres did for me." His voice tailed off.

Since the war had ended, I'd had occasion to talk to several returning soldiers and without fail they seemed to run out of words very quickly. They'd get a strange expression on their faces as if the physical pain and the heart pain were indistinguishable. Julian Cross had just such a look.

He began to fish in his pocket. "Do you mind if I smoke?"

I minded, but he was a prospective client, so I simply shrugged. He tapped a cigarette out of his silver case, lit it, and drew in the smoke as if it was keeping him alive. A lot of ex-soldiers consumed cigarettes in that way. While he was doing all that, I inserted a fresh sheet of paper into the typewriter and moved my chair into position.

"You don't mind if I take this down, do you?"

"Not at all."

"You said your brother disappeared two years ago when he was eighteen."

"That's right. October 30, 1934. It was a few days after his birthday."

"And you say your mother is gravely ill?"

"Yes, unfortunately she is. The doctor has given her three months at the most."

"And your father?"

"He died last year."

"Did he want to find your brother?"

Julian drew deeply on his cigarette. "I'd say no. Not at all. He was only too glad to be rid of him."

"So other than informing the police, this is the first time you have independently tried to discover his whereabouts?"

"Yes."

Another drag on the cigarette. The tiny office was rapidly filling up with smoke. I suppressed my cough.

"Actually, I am here at my mother's request," said Cross. "She knows her life is coming to an end and she hopes to get some information about Stephen that is conclusive one way or the other."

"That is understandable. Otherwise one finds oneself in a perpetual state of waiting."

He flashed me a look of surprise. "Exactly. Mother won't give up hope." Out of the corner of my eye I could see the newspaper notice.

"Have you tried advertising yourself?"

"Frankly no. We are a fairly wealthy family and I was afraid we'd have to deal with too many fraudulent responses. My mother cannot take it. She is dreadfully frail at the moment. If we do find him alive, I will make sure she sees him."

"And if he's dead?"

"I will have to tell her. She is insisting on setting up a trust fund in his name in case he does deign to return."

"I see."

I'd meant to keep my voice neutral, but something must have seeped through.

He flushed. "Perhaps you think that's crass of me to even care, but it seems a waste to tie up money for a ghost. Don't get me wrong, Miss Frayne, I loved my little brother. Nothing would give me greater pleasure than to see him again, but he has caused my mother much grief. Why should he saunter back in say three- or four-years' time and simply pick up a hefty sum of money that he hasn't ever earned?"

He couldn't keep the bitterness out of his voice. So much for his claim to being spoiled. It seemed like mom had been asking for a payback.

I reached for the newspaper and handed it to him.

"Did you happen to see this notice about a missing man?"

"No. I make a point of not reading the paper. Too depressing. Sometimes I wonder what we fought a war for. I don't know if it changed much."

A lot of veterans felt the same way and I sympathized with them. I gave him a moment to read the notice.

"Could it be your brother?"

He shrugged. "Possibly, but it's a very general description."

He stubbed out his cigarette in a little metal pill box which he took from his pocket. Another holdover from being in the army.

He sighed. "I'll need to actually see the body before I can be sure. Do you know how I should go about doing that?"

"As a matter of fact, I do. Let me make a phone call."

He continued to stare at the newspaper as if it might suddenly speak up and give him answers. I dialed the morgue.

"Operator, will you put me through to Mr Craig. It's Charlotte

Frayne calling."

Within a minute, Joe Craig came on the phone.

"Charlie! Where've you been? You owe me a lunch as I recall."

I'd known Joe Craig for a couple of years and liked him a lot. He was the head mortician at the city morgue and knowing him had proved to be useful on more than one occasion. Our relationship might have gone further than friendship but even standing on tip-toe, Joe couldn't push five foot five inches. He swore it didn't matter to him, but it did to me, so we hadn't progressed past the flirtation stage.

"Mr Craig, I'm calling on behalf of my client. He thinks that the body that was taken from the lake yesterday might be his brother."

"He's within earshot, I gather?"

"Quite so. We were wondering if you could give us any more specific details. Save him an unnecessary visit to the morgue."

"Sure. You won't want to come here if you don't have to. The fish and the water have had a go at the corpse's face. It's a mess. We did all the usual x-ray checks but there were no traces of previous injuries or diseases that we could see. The body was thinner than it should be but otherwise normal. Early twenties probably. Blond hair. Blue eyes." He chuckled. "Do you want to do the usual test?"

"Yes, please."

Julian Cross was now watching me intently. I didn't really like what I was about to do, but it was a good way to sift out the truth.

"Here goes," said Joe. "Ask him if his brother had a small crescent-shaped scar above his left ankle?"

"Does he?"

"Nope, smooth as a baby's you know what."

It's surprising how many people want to claim bodies that don't really belong to them. Sometimes, sheer longing, sometimes in the hope of recompense. Joe and I had devised a little trap to catch the liars and cheats or the misguided.

"Thank you, Mr Craig. I will pass this along."

"All righty. How about lunch on Friday?"

"Thank you. Much appreciated."

"Is that a yes?"

"Quite so. Good-by."

I hung up and faced Julian Cross.

"Did Stephen have a crescent-shaped scar on his left ankle?"

He started. "Good Lord. He did. He fell off a swing when he was a kid. Gave himself quite a bang. Oh my. Don't tell me I've found my brother at last."

"The best thing to do is go to the morgue and make a personal identification. Do you feel up to doing that?"

He slumped in the chair. "I suppose there's no help for it. We must get this settled. Were there any other marks on the body?"

"Nothing really significant. Apparently, the young man was rather emaciated."

Cross shook his head. "Stephen was always a skinny runt... he'd drink rather than eat."

He reached into his jacket and took out a cheque book. "How much do I owe you?"

"Good heavens, Mr Cross. I haven't done anything. You could have seen that notice yourself."

"But I didn't and you did. Please! If you don't tell me, I shall be compelled to improvise and that probably isn't a good idea."

He was right about that. I named our usual consultation fee which he promptly doubled. Then he took out a small envelope from his other pocket.

"Please allow me to give you these tickets. I'm appearing in a play at the Strand."

So that's why he looked familiar. I'd gone past the billboard poster at the theatre.

He smiled at me again. "I know, an unlikely profession considering where I come from, but it's what I always wanted to do. My father didn't agree with my choice at first, but Mother has been wonderful."

I accepted the tickets. He struggled to his feet with another groan. "Thank you so much, Miss Frayne. Please come to the stage door and say hello when you come to the performance."

He limped off.

I waited until I knew he had left the floor and I rang Joe. He answered immediately.

"Well?"

"He's on his way."

"What's up?"

"He's looking for a body. He'll take whatever fits the general description of missing sibling."

"Why?"

"His mother says she's going to leave a trust fund for the missing brother unless he's proven dead. Take a big chunk out of Julian's inheritance most likely."

"Got it."

"I'm guessing he'll ask for a prompt cremation to save his mother the pain of having to see the corpse of her son."

"What do you want me to do?"

"Make it really difficult for him. Lots of red tape to go through. Nothing can proceed until the mother sees the body."

"OK."

"And by the way, Joe. You'll notice that sometimes Mr Cross will limp and sometimes he won't."

"Playing for sympathy, is he?"

"Something like that. I heard him coming down the hall and he wasn't using a cane then, but when he came into the office, he acted like a crippled war veteran. In fact, he is an actor. He's appearing at the Strand in that new play. *Night Must Fall.* He plays a charming killer."

"Typecast?"

"At least maybe the charming part."

"Is he tall?"

"What does that have to do with anything?"

"Nothing. It's just that you've got a certain tone in your voice."

"That's ridiculous. I do not."

"Yes, you do."

"Joe. Get out of here!"

"OK. See you Friday?"

"All right."

"We can pick up sandwiches and bring them here."

"What? To the morgue?"

"Probably the coolest place in the city."

I knew what he meant, but it's not just the weather that determines the temperature of the human heart.

Oh, I mentioned earlier that after encountering Julian Cross my life changed. What happened was that Mr Gilmore, on hearing the story (and seeing the cheque), decided to promote me to acting partner. He said he was very pleased with my work.

And Joe and I did have dinner in the morgue. It was indeed wonderfully cool. I have to say it did eventually get warmer.

THUS WITH A KISS
By Margaret Lucke

In community theater, there's often as much drama offstage as on, and that's definitely true during the Pleasant Valley Players' staging of Romeo and Juliet.

Spoiler alert: At the end of the play, Romeo and Juliet are dead.

You're probably not surprised to learn that. After five-plus centuries of theatrical productions and a couple hundred movie versions, pretty much everyone knows the story.

But once the curtain falls, Romeo and Juliet are supposed to get up from their bier and take their bows with the rest of the cast.

If only that had happened last night.

***

"Places, everyone," I said into my headset. This was the device that connected me to the stagehands, the sound-and-lights guy in the tech booth, and the actors waiting in the greenroom for their moments of onstage glory. The lights were about to rise on what was, thank goodness, the final performance of the Pleasant Valley Players staging of the bard's classic tragedy.

Usually our group knew better than to tackle such ambitious plays. We stuck to musicals and screwball comedies—sure crowd pleasers. But this was the last show that the director, Harwood Sweeney, would do with us. Next week he and his wife, Zelda, were moving to New York, where the faculty recruiters at a large university had taken leave of their senses and hired him to head their theater department. Directing *Romeo and Juliet* was Harwood's longtime dream, and he'd been such a stalwart of our group that the play selection committee had agreed to indulge him.

A farewell gift. And probably a mistake.

We were a small community theater, a company of amateurs. Lots of enthusiasm and some talent, too, though the talent was—I'm trying to be kind here—unevenly distributed. Frankly, Shakespeare was a stretch for this bunch.

It hadn't been a smooth run. Lots of botched cues, flubbed lines, and late entrances. Too many speeches sounded stilted—Elizabethan English was a foreign language to most of the cast. And to be honest, Harwood wasn't up to the task of making them bilingual.

As the stage manager, my job was to make sure each performance ran smoothly. Talk about challenges. I sat on a high stool in the wings at stage right, just out of sight of the audience, with the script open on a notebook-sized table in front of me.

My front-row seat to disaster.

I felt a tap on my shoulder and caught a whiff of Harwood's tobaccoey, beery breath. "Break a leg, Roni," he said.

"Thanks." *Break a leg* is how theater people wish each other good luck, something I expected to need. I nodded but didn't look up from the script, where all of the cues were written—instructions for what the lights crew, sound crew, props crew, and actors were supposed to do, and probably wouldn't.

"Juliet's doing especially well, don't you think?" he said.

"Of course," I replied. Getting past the fact that she was an insufferable twit, Juliet was the most talented actress we had, despite her tendency to chew the scenery. She snagged the lead in every play she tried out for. No surprise that Harwood had cast her in this role, even though she was close to thirty—my age, and twice the age of Shakespeare's heroine. "Go sit down, Harwood. It's time for Act One."

He ignored me. "Romeo's doing okay, too. As I'm sure you've noticed." He aimed a smirk in my direction.

I felt redness flare into my cheeks. Had I been that obvious? Romeo was new to us, an unknown quantity when he showed up for the *R&J* auditions. That he was given the coveted role had rankled some of the actors, in particular Count Paris, who'd considered himself a shoo-in for it. The women—including me, I admit—were much more welcoming. Which had set up a lot of competition and jealousy between the smaller-minded among us.

In community theater there's often as much drama offstage as on.

"Coming to the cast party?" Harwood asked. His hand lingered on my shoulder. I shrugged it off. He pointed to the first row, where his wife was making her way to her usual seat. "Zelda made snickerdoodles."

"Wouldn't miss it." The cast party would be held at Harwood's house right after tonight's show. Everyone was looking forward to it. A chance to let off steam, toss back a few drinks—more than a few for some people—and toast the end to all the little things that had gone wrong during the three-weekend run. And eat lots of snickerdoodles. Zelda's were legendary, and this would be our last chance to enjoy them.

And for me, the cast party would be a chance to corner Romeo and see if he really meant the kiss he gave me last night in the greenroom after everyone had gone home.

***

Despite my nervousness, tonight's show was going better than I expected. The actors entered and exited when they were supposed to, none of the costumes hung askew, nobody tripped over the scenery. Only Mercutio totally flubbed his lines, but he got sent to meet his maker before the intermission, so I didn't have to worry about him after that.

We'd reached the final, climactic scene, which takes place in a crypt in a churchyard. I crossed my fingers that we would finish without a mishap.

To prevent her parents from marrying her off to Count Paris, the good Friar Laurence gave her a potion that would let her fake her death until Romeo could arrive to run away with her. Now Juliet lay comatose on a slanted platform, which was higher at its upstage end so the audience could see her clearly. She'd arranged herself in a dramatic pose, one arm flung up over her head. Even in a scene where she did nothing but lie there, she couldn't resist overacting.

Romeo, by contrast, did a fine, restrained job of expressing his grief. Drinking the poison he'd brought to the crypt, he delivered his last words with just the right flourish:

"Thus with a kiss I die!"

Then he joined Juliet in the "palace of dim night" called death. But of course she woke up, and was so distressed to find Romeo's corpse that she grabbed his dagger from its sheath and stabbed herself.

Love is complicated.

When Prince Escalus uttered the play's closing lines—"For never was a story of more woe/Than this of Juliet and her Romeo"—I let out a huge sigh of relief. We'd staggered through all eight performances without totally embarrassing ourselves. Let the party begin!

I gave the cue to cut the lights, and the theater plunged into darkness. The only illumination came from the exit signs and the tiny glow of the reading light clipped to my desk. A smattering of applause began. I heard the actors scrambling blindly into position for their bows.

"Okay," I told the tech booth through my headset. "Lights up."

Nothing happened. The tentative applause faltered, then turned into rhythmic clapping and stomping—audience-speak for *get this show on the road.*

"Hey, wake up. We need lights!"

"What's going on?" Harwood's whispered voice. He had snuck

up behind me. His hand fumbled for my shoulder and I swatted it back.

"I don't know." Panic was creeping in. The stage was supposed to be dark for only a few seconds. From the cast I heard muffled noises: a moan, an *oomph,* a *hey-watch-it,* a patter of running feet.

Finally, the stage lights flickered on. I heaved another sigh and the audience began to applaud again.

Then came a collective gasp. Although Count Paris, who's also killed in the final scene—really, the body count in this play is over the top—was on his feet, the star-cross'd lovers still lay on their platform, entwined in each other's arms.

Oh, great. Hijinks during the last performance weren't unheard of, but this was not the moment for a love scene. Not between those two. Not after the way Romeo had acted toward me last night—

Harwood let out a sound. A wheeze? A sob?

The applause stopped, to be replaced with a growing murmur of confusion and dismay.

Lady Capulet shook Romeo's shoulder. Then, lifting the dagger with which Juliet had stabbed herself, she let out a shriek.

"Oh my god! The blood is real!"

***

It fell to me to try to create order out of the ensuing chaos, because no one else stepped up. Most of the audience was fleeing for the exits, though a few, like Zelda Sweeney, had pushed onto the stage for a closer look. The cast members milled around helplessly. Lady Capulet was sobbing. Harwood had vanished.

I hurried to the platform where Romeo and Juliet lay in their lifeless embrace. Count Paris helped me pull them apart.

Lady Capulet was right. Juliet's packet of stage blood had been pierced and spilled, but the corn-syrup-and-food-coloring wasn't all that stained her costume red. The show called for her to stab herself in the heart with a rubber knife. But the gash ripped through her gown had been made by a real dagger, which, along with the prop one, was nestled in between the ill-fated sweethearts.

Romeo is supposed to die by poison, but he too had blood all over him. My heart skipped a beat. Juliet's blood, his own, or the fake stuff? I couldn't tell.

Paris picked up the dagger. "Don't touch that," I warned.

"Look at this, Roni." He held it out to me. The hilt showed engraved letters: *A.C.*

My initials! "What the heck? I've never seen that thing before."

I took Juliet's wrist in one hand and Romeo's in the other,

trying to find the beat of their pulses. Romeo's was there, faint and thready, and he gave a low moan at my touch. Thank goodness, he was alive. But Juliet—

"Someone call 911," I said.

"Already done." Mercutio, proving he was good for something after all. In the distance I heard sirens.

***

Way past midnight. No cast party. No snickerdoodles.

Instead, the cops had herded the cast and crew into the greenroom. The Capulets gravitated to one corner, the Montagues to another. Harwood still hadn't appeared. The officers tried to keep us from comparing notes and concocting stories. But you can't keep theater people from talking.

"Romeo killed her," was the buzz among the Capulets. "He was jealous of all the attention she got from other guys. He stabbed himself so he'd look innocent."

"It was one of the women," whispered the Montagues. "Somebody who was angry that those two loved each other and wanted Romeo for herself." Was I imagining it, or were they staring at me?

A lanky, redheaded man in an ill-fitting sports coat came into the room. He introduced himself as Detective Ketcham and asked which of us was the stage manager. I raised my hand. No way to deny it, with everyone pointing in my direction.

"Come with me," he said.

He led me to the stage manager's station, where my script lay askew on the table. On the stage, crime-scene techs were hard at work. Romeo and Juliet no longer sprawled on the funeral platform. They'd been whisked away, Romeo to the hospital, Juliet to the morgue.

"Your name is Aronia Cates," Ketcham told me.

I nodded. "Everyone calls me Roni."

"Initials A.C."

"That dagger isn't mine."

"I supposed this isn't yours either."

He handed me a clear plastic envelope. Inside was a sheet of paper. "Read this."

My eyes widened and my heart started pounding.

I'm sorry I have to kill her. But now that I've finally found my true love, I refuse to lose him to that evil little witch.

Plain paper, Helvetica font. Anyone could have written it. The hand-scrawled *Aronia Cates* at the bottom proved nothing.

"This is totally fake. Where did you find it?" The envelope slipped from my trembling fingers, landing on the floor in a puff of dust.

"Tucked right into these pages. Act Two, Scene One." Ketcham tapped the script.

"It's a forgery. Someone's trying to frame me."

"Yup, figured you'd say that." He bent and retrieved the incriminating document.

"I'll prove it. Give me a pen."

He did. I wrote my signature across the top of a script page.

"There. See how different those signatures are?"

Ketcham lined up the plastic bag and the script. My heart pushed into my throat. The handwritten names looked remarkably the same.

At the detective's insistence, I accompanied him to the Pleasant Valley Police headquarters. When we got there, he sat me in a small, bleak room and asked me lots of questions. I answered truthfully for the most part. I wanted this horrible crime cleared up as much as he did.

Should I have insisted on having a lawyer present? Maybe, but I had nothing to hide. Besides, I didn't know any lawyers, certainly none who would welcome my call at three a.m.

Finally Ketcham told me I could leave. He said he didn't have enough evidence to arrest me—yet.

***

The sky was turning pink with dawn when I walked out of the police station. I summoned a ride-share to take me to the theater, where my car was parked. Yellow crime-scene tape festooned the building. My car and a police cruiser were the only vehicles in the lot. Apparently everyone else had gone home, or maybe they were at PVPD HQ, being interrogated in grim little rooms.

I went straight home, in desperate need of the "sleep that knits up the raveled sleeve of care," as the Bard called it. I fell onto on my bed, but my tear-filled eyes refused to close. So I stared at the cobwebs on the ceiling while questions took turns jumping on the trampoline that was my brain.

Who would want to kill Juliet? Well, that answer was easy. Just about everyone. The people who were jealous of her talent, those who envied her beauty, the others who were sick to death of her arrogant, officious attitude.

But why would that person also try to kill Romeo? None of us had met him before the *R&J* auditions. He was as good-looking and talented as Juliet, but he shared none of her drawbacks. I offered a prayer to Dionysus, Greek god of the theater among other things, that Romeo would survive.

The villain was one of us, a member of the cast or crew. That thought would have sobered me if I weren't sober already. To accomplish the dastardly deed, the killer had to be onstage or backstage when the blackout delayed the curtain call. Until then, everything was going according to the script.

Which raised more questions.

How had that blackout happened? The guy running the lights was our most competent tech. It wasn't like him to fumble the cues and controls.

Where had Harwood disappeared to while the cops were questioning the rest of us?

Who'd get to eat Zelda's fresh-baked snickerdoodles?

And last, but far from least: who hated me enough to frame me for murder?

Finally, exhausted, I indulged in a couple of hours of fitful rest. When I woke, morning had brightened the world beyond my bedroom curtains. I showered, spritzed on some jasmine-scented body spray, and carefully made up my face. An improvement, though nothing hid the redness in my eyes. I practiced a few smiles in the mirror and left the house.

***

Normally on the day after the last performance, I'd head straight to the theater, where we'd all get together to strike the set—dismantle the scenery, put away the costumes and props, and make the place ready for the next production. But today I had things to do first. Anyway, the theater was off-limits, being a crime scene.

First stop: a coffee shop for some urgently needed caffeine.

Second stop: the Pleasant Valley Hospital. I arrived at Romeo's room just as a hatchet-faced nurse was coming out. She stopped in front of me, hands parked on her hips.

"No visitors." Her glare told me she expected me to go in and start a hootchy-kootchy dance.

"How is he doing?" I asked.

"Can't tell you."

"But you must know. You just came out of his room. Is he all right? He's going to live, isn't he?"

"Are you family?"

"Sort of." A theater community is like a big family, with all of a family's love, loyalty, and petty squabbles.

She shook her head. A sort-of kinship wasn't good enough. "I can't say anything. Patient privacy. Maybe he'll have visitors later.

You can sit in there." She pointed toward a waiting room.

I peeked in. Two women occupied a shabby vinyl sofa, fiddling with cameras and notepads. Probably reporters—murder was big news in our little town. A tired-looking cop leaned against a wall. I had no desire to chat with any of them, so I didn't stay.

A waste of body spray and makeup. But at least I knew Romeo was alive.

Third stop, or I should say 3.A: a florist, where I purchased a bouquet of purple blooms suitable for someone in mourning. They were slightly wilted, but then so was I.

On to 3.B: the cottage where Juliet still lived with her mother. We all knew her mom—she came to every performance. I'd seen her in last night's audience and could only imagine her terrible shock when Juliet failed to rise for the curtain call. I wanted to offer condolences on behalf of the Players and myself. If I happened to pick up some clues as to who had killed Juliet and why I was being framed, so much the better.

I parked at the curb behind a drab gray sedan and walked up to the house. The screen door was closed, but the front door behind it gaped wide, letting me peer into the living room. Juliet's mom sagged on a sofa, paging through a large scrapbook. Tears ran down her cheeks.

My posies were extraneous. The living room overflowed with bouquets. The other main feature of the décor was Juliet herself. The walls were covered with posters of the Players' productions and photos of our star actress prancing and preening onstage. The coffee table was heaped with more scrapbooks, no doubt filled with playbills and newspaper clippings lauding her achievements. I wondered if her mom had saved the local paper's review of *R&J*'s opening night. The headline read: *Players tackle the Bard and fumble.*

Maybe it was the reviewer who should have been murdered.

I was about to call out a hello when a man came into the living room from the back of the house. A lanky, redheaded man carrying a sheet of paper in a clear plastic bag.

Detective Ketcham. Just who I didn't want to see. I stepped to the side of the door so I could eavesdrop without being noticed.

"Ma'am," he asked, "what do you know about this trip to New York your daughter was planning?"

"What? She wasn't going anywhere."

"This is a printout of an airline reservation in your daughter's name. A flight to LaGuardia, a week from tomorrow."

"Impossible. Let me see that." A moment of silence, then a sob. "But…this makes no sense. When's the return flight?"

"Says here it's one-way. And there's some half-filled suitcases in her closet."

"No-o-o-o!" she wailed.

"We're done here, Ketch." A new voice, baritone. If the cops were about to leave, it was time for me to get out of there too. I hurried to my car, trailing flower petals in my wake.

***

Driving away from Juliet's home, more questions leaped onto my brain trampoline. A week from tomorrow—the same day that the Sweeneys were leaving for their new home. No way that was a coincidence.

Could Juliet have been stalking Harwood? She demanded more than her share of his time and compliments, but that meant nothing. She was a prima donna, a limelight seeker; she craved everyone's attention.

But maybe to him, she'd crossed a fatal line.

I began to see what had happened. Juliet always claimed Pleasant Valley wasn't big enough to hold her talent. When Harwood landed his plum job in New York, she saw her chance. She made plans to chase him there and demand he use his new contacts to open the Big Apple's stage doors for her.

She became such an annoying pest, such a threat to his success in his new home, that he killed her so she wouldn't ruin his life. Romeo tried to stop him and was stabbed for his effort. Harwood disappeared from the theater last night to avoid the police.

Fourth stop: The Sweeneys' house. Harwood might avoid Ketcham's questions, but he wouldn't avoid mine.

Not when he was trying to frame me for her murder.

***

Harwood and Zelda lived in a tidy brown bungalow, a far cry from the penthouse overlooking Broadway they aspired to. Beneath the front windows, petunias had been planted to give the place curb appeal. A FOR SALE sign dangled from an L-shaped pole that looked like a hangman's scaffold.

I climbed the steps to the front porch. The door was freshly painted, the brass knocker polished to a gleam. I wondered if the house would still be on the market when Harwood went to prison.

I started to knock, then hesitated. Was I asking for trouble, coming to confront a murderer? Quietly setting the knocker loop in place, I peered through the window beside the door to see what I might be getting into. At the rear of a hallway lined with packing boxes, a door led into the kitchen. Someone was walking around back there. The sound of yelling carried through the windowpane.

I tiptoed off the porch and crept around the house to the

backyard patio. A sliding glass door gave a view into the kitchen. I crouched behind a bush and checked out what was transpiring inside.

Harwood sat at the table. Zelda stood over him, holding a gun to his head.

My breath stopped, and I began to tremble. She was getting him to confess. Holding him there until police could arrive. Probably she'd already called them, but I'd do that now, just in case. I slipped my phone out of my purse.

How awful it must have been for her to realize her husband wasn't just a mediocre director but a good actor, conning everyone into thinking he was an okay guy.

I aimed my phone at the window to snap a photo as proof of the story I'd tell the cops. But it fell from my shaking hand, hitting the patio flagstones with a clatter. I tried to grab it, but tripped over a garden hose and fell, knocking over a metal garden chair. Another loud noise.

But not as loud as the sound of the gunshot inside the house.

I froze, not daring to breathe.

The kitchen door slid open and Zelda yelled, "Who's there?"

She stepped out onto the patio, gun in hand. "Oh, Roni! It's you. How convenient. Come inside. We'll have tea and cookies. I made snickerdoodles for last night's party, but of course that got cancelled."

The direction she was aiming the weapon made her invitation impossible to refuse.

Scooping up the phone, I hauled myself to my feet, brushing dirt off my scraped knees.

"Hurry up," she snarled.

I realized I'd gotten the story wrong. It was Zelda who killed Juliet. I tried to recall if she'd still been in her front-row seat at the end of last night's show. Maybe she'd slipped backstage during intermission.

Was the grip of that pistol engraved with the initials *A.C.*?

Zelda sat me down next to Harwood, whose head rested on the table beside a stack of cookie tins. The top tin was open and full of luscious-looking snickerdoodles.

Harwood groaned. Blood seeped from a wound on his shoulder.

"You shot him!"

"That wasn't the plan," Zelda said. She stayed on her feet, positioning herself so she could easily shoot either one of us.

"I really need to be going. I'll pass on the refreshments." I started to rise, but she nudged me back in place with the gun barrel.

"Not so fast. I need you here while I think of a new story."

Keeping my hands beneath the table, I thumbed 911 into my phone.

"New story?" I said to distract her. "What was the old one?"

"I didn't expect Harwood to figure out it was me who stabbed his little floozy. We were going to go to New York together and get on with our lives. Forget she ever existed."

"But why—"

The dispatcher answered. I hoped I had the volume low enough that Zelda wouldn't notice over the sound of her own voice.

"Don't you get it? He was going to leave me! He thought he'd been so sneaky, but I knew all about their sordid affair."

Harwood and Juliet? Who knew? And how had they kept that secret hidden when theater people are the world's biggest gossips?

"Can you believe he was going to take that trollop to New York and leave me behind? He thought he could make her a star. What a laugh!"

Keep her talking. "Okay, Zelda, that's why you killed *her*. What about your other victim?"

"The new guy playing Romeo? Collateral damage. He tried to push me away from her. Who knew he'd be so noble. Hey, he's going to live. No harm, no foul."

"But why try to pin it on me? The letter, the initials on the knife."

"Because the police would believe it. You've clearly got a crush on Mr. Noble. That strumpet was making a play for him, and you were jealous. She didn't give a fig about him, you know. She just wanted another feather in her cap."

Harwood groaned again.

"Plus," Zelda went on, "you'd have no alibi. Your desk is at the edge of the stage. A few steps and you're in a perfect position to stab her. You can never prove you didn't leave your post."

"Yesshecan," Harwood mumbled. He lifted his head a few inches. "I was...standing...behind her...the whole time."

Zelda frowned, then her face brightened. "I've got it! The new narrative. Murder-suicide. Roni, you're madly in love with Harwood—"

"Harwood! You've got to be kidding."

Harwood sputtered.

"And when you discovered his affair with that bimbo, you were enraged. So you stabbed her last night and came here today to shoot him. Then you turned the gun on yourself rather than face the music."

Zelda came around behind my chair. I felt the gun brush my temple. Before I could think, I grabbed the open cookie tin. Lifted it over my head and backward. Snickerdoodles flew everywhere as the tin connected with her forehead, making a satisfying smack.

She screamed and dropped the gun. We both scrambled for it. Thank goodness, I won.

I held the gun on her as she cowered under the table.

My phone had fallen, too, but the connection hadn't been lost. "Hey, 9ll, did you catch all that?"

The dispatcher said, "Officers are on the way."

"In fact, they're here," said Detective Ketcham, arriving right on cue. He stepped through the sliding glass door, cookies crunching under his feet.

"Mrs. Sweeney, I'm arresting you for murder."

I applauded his outstanding performance.

In short order, Zelda was in the police car, Harwood was in the hospital, and I was back in the grim interrogation room at PVPD. The tone of the questioning was much warmer this time.

***

It was late afternoon when I finally got to the theater. The crime scene tape had come down, and the cast and crew had shown up to strike the set. Not much work had been accomplished, though. Everyone was in the greenroom rehashing last night's events.

Even Romeo was there, looking pale and disheveled and handsome.

"You're out of the hospital!" I said in surprise and delight.

"Yeah." He managed a smile. "The wound wasn't as bad as it looked."

I hugged him. He winced in pain, but he hugged me back.

I took the starring role as I recounted the latest developments.

"Zelda?" Mercutio asked. "It was Zelda?"

"Yes. She's in jail, under arrest."

"Thank goodness it wasn't one of us," said Lady Capulet. Everyone nodded, relieved to know our theater family was without blame. Blame for murder, anyway.

"One thing puzzles me," I said. "Why didn't the stage lights come on when it was time for the curtain call? If they had, Zelda wouldn't have had a chance to kill—"

"I can guess," said the lighting tech. "She flipped the circuit breaker. The box is right there backstage."

"Yeah," said Mercutio. "Flip it off, stab two people, flip it on again, and slip away in the confusion. Easy."

Count Paris went to the fridge and took out two bottles of champagne. "I was going to bring these to the cast party. Let's drink a toast in memory of our Juliet."

Lady Montague got plastic glasses from the cupboard. Count Paris filled them and the lights tech handed them out. We raised them in solemn tribute and took a ceremonial sip.

"Before you drink any more," I told my fellow Thespians, "I have the perfect thing to go with champagne." I produced the cookie tin I'd snuck from the bottom of the stack in the Sweeneys' kitchen and opened it with a flourish.

"Snickerdoodles!" someone cried, and everybody laughed.

After all, the show must go on.

SUCH TRICKS AS THESE

(Othello, Act 2, Scene 1)

By Jaquelyn Lyman-Thomas

Green-eyed jealousy lurks in suburbia.

Jeanette Franklin-Gardner had died eighty-seven times in her nearly life-long acting career, including as many of Shakespeare's tragic heroines. As she listened in stupor to her neighbor Meg's latest delusions, Jeanette relived every one of those stage deaths—and Blanche DuBois's insanity as well.

"I *know* what's going on," Meg repeated for maybe the fourth time before giving yet another bit of 'evidence': "For god's sake, she parades naked past her bay window when Randy's working in the front yard."

Jeanette murmured noncommittally as she stirred stevia into her decaf coffee and contemplated the glow of late afternoon sun on the roses outside her kitchen window. There was always someone lusting after Randy. Last year it was the female postal carrier, more recently a visiting niece of the neighbor on Meg's other side. Now it was the blond thirty-something Amanda, who'd just moved in across the street with her older husband, Gavin. Jeanette had met Amanda only in passing, but she'd chatted with Gavin the other day over her front fence. He'd seen her play Lady Bracknell in *The Importance of Being Earnest* in D.C. last summer. He had lovely brown eyes and a bit of silver at his temples. Reminded her a bit of Harrison Ford in *Extraordinary Measures.*

Jeanette realized Meg had gone silent and jerked herself back to the present. "But, hon," she said, "has Randy done anything to indicate he's even remotely interested in her? He's not that kind of guy."

Meg frowned. "He's *attractive*," she insisted. "You know how men are—all ego and libido."

Yes, Randy was attractive. But he was taciturn—definitely *not* a "ladies' man" given to flirting with random females, no matter how vivacious.

Meg ran a hand through her too-dark page-boy hair, her persistent grey recently expunged with a bit of Clairol. She reminded Jeanette of the Artful Dodger she'd worked with in Oliver Twist as a young teenager. But Meg was in her fifties, like

Jeanette—way too old for the schoolgirl angst she was always exuding. The "Everyone's Trying to Steal My Husband" show had been running for most of the twenty-some years they'd been neighbors in their cozy Chesapeake Bay hamlet of Canterbury Close, and it showed no sign of closing any time soon.

Meg started to describe the "shocking mini-skirt" Amanda had been wearing the previous day, but broke off when the back door opened. Jeanette's husband Denny came in, escaped strands of his grey ponytail framing his ruddy, still-handsome face. Randy appeared behind him, slightly taller, dark hair flecked with gray, sleeveless shirt clinging with sweat to very respectable abs.

"You won't have to worry about your boat stranding you," Denny said to Meg. "She's seaworthy again."

"It's more work than it's worth." Meg shot her husband a dark look. "We're going to sell the stupid thing anyway."

Randy's jaw tightened, but he said nothing. He clapped Denny on the back and slipped out. Jeanette and Denny exchanged stunned looks.

"I'd better get dinner," Meg said and followed Randy. Obviously, she couldn't leave him unsupervised even briefly with Manhunter Amanda on the prowl.

"Thanks for keeping her occupied." Denny cracked open a beer, sat down, and took a long drink.

Jeanette dumped her cold coffee and poured herself cabernet. "I just stay in character and try not to slit my wrists."

He sighed. "Is there anyone or anything she *isn't* jealous of?"

"Ironically, *you*." When he nodded sadly, she went on. "And maybe some anonymous starving orphan on the other side of the world."

"Just until the poor kid gets featured on a UNICEF ad. Then she'll say he's exploiting his poverty for personal gain." Denny crumpled the can and tossed it a little too forcefully at the trashcan.

It bounced off the rim and landed at Jeanette's feet. She picked it up. "I've tried to talk to her. It's like the world's a mirror, and she only sees herself."

"Rand and I wouldn't get time together if it weren't for you." Denny managed a smile. "You make our lives bearable. I wish we could do something in return."

She waved a hand dismissively. "I've had a wonderful career, and I have the world's best friends."

"Your career isn't over. You're too young to retire."

"I've got my students and my computer clients."

"The computer crap's for hard currency. The mentoring's for the future of the theater. *Acting* is for *you*."

Jeanette raised a brow. "There's the pot accusing the kettle, for sure."

"I was only good because I played opposite you so often." He got up for another beer. "There's a rumor the Shakespeare Company's going to cast for *Othello*."

"I'm too old for Desdemona."

"Not for Emilia. I could audition for Brabantio."

Jeanette let her gaze go soft. She sipped her wine and stared into the past. No one could have rivaled their Portia and Brutus in *Julius Caesar* all those years ago.

"I'll think about it," she said and turned to pull the pork chops from the fridge.

***

After dinner, they retired to their respective rooms upstairs. Jeanette settled in her stuffed chair in the window alcove with an Agatha Christie mystery but didn't turn on the light. Dusk greyed and finally erased the vibrant pinks and scarlets of the rhododendrons and azaleas in the yard below—and in Gavin and Amanda's yard across the street. Beyond their house a slice of the bay glittered, and moonlight silvered the rigging of Gavin's sailboat. While all the houses on that side of the street had Chesapeake waterfront, most were modest ranchers and bungalows that had begun as summer retreats and, over decades, been remodeled into year-round dwellings. Gavin and Amanda had bought the only large house on the street, a tidewater home with a wrap-around veranda, built when the land had been a tobacco farm.

Suddenly the light in the dining room of the big house clicked on. From Jeanette's elevation, the infamous bay window became a bright fishbowl in which Amanda and Gavin ignored each other over what appeared to be a recently delivered pizza. They'd lived there only a month, but already rumors slithered around the neighborhood: Amanda demanding the house be put in her name; Amanda declaring she wanted children, then, after they were married, changing her mind; and Amanda, in general, executing a brilliant plot to go from Annapolis waitress to rich man's wife. Jeanette wondered how much was true, how much the wishful thinking of the envious. They certainly made an odd pair: Gavin was friendly and seemed to enjoy people, but conversation with Amanda amounted to breathy 'Hellos' and 'Sorry—gotta runs.'

In the fishbowl of light Gavin said something, his gaze earnest. Amanda scowled, stood up abruptly, and slapped him. She stomped from the room, leaving him motionless, staring out the window into the dark. Then he got up slowly, as if exhausted, and cleared the table. The fishbowl went dark.

Jeanette remained at the window, grateful for her relationship with Denny—even though their marriage had been necessary for reasons that hadn't mattered for almost three decades: it banished her volatile ex who'd been stalking her, and it saved Denny's family relationships at a time when attitudes toward being gay were much different. She and Denny were best friends.

But Meg and Randy were different. Over the years, Jeanette and Denny had watched Meg rob Randy of all the things that made him happy: oil painting, playing the piano, even running—anything that competed with her for his attention. Jeanette smiled sadly at the irony that Denny was the only one Randy was allowed to spend time with. He and Randy were the ones who should have been together all along. She mulled opportunities and choices, fate and accident. The mystery novel slid unnoticed to the floor.

Jeanette finally turned the light on, morphing the windowpane into a black mirror in which she stared back at herself, the faint mist of grey in her long chestnut hair and the fine lines around her mouth rendered indiscernible in the murky reflection. She was still Portia to Denny's Brutus, Beatrice to his Benedick.

She was Juliet, Cordelia, the Scottish Lady. The Duchess of Malfi. Fastrada. Blanche. Desdemona. Every character she'd ever played still lived inside her.

Was there room for at least *one* more?

Jeanette got up and went to the repurposed bedroom they called "the library." The floor-to-ceiling shelves contained the lifetime collection of two avid booklovers, and the closet brimmed full of theater paraphernalia—wigs, makeup, costumes, even a few old props. She came back with a worn paperback *Othello* and sat down to read.

Once Jeanette made up her mind about a part, she invited the character to possess her. When she finished reading, she got up and walked around the room, felt how the character moved, let the character speak through her until she was a living, breathing embodiment.

She was up very late.

***

Monday dawned brilliantly—the perfect June morning on the lip of the Chesapeake: warm but not yet off-the-charts humid, with a breeze just strong enough to ruffle hair and oak leaves. Randy came to help Denny haul the Boston Whaler to the community dock, and Jeanette trimmed the roses that cascaded over the arbor at the front gate. Across the street, Gavin was on a ladder cleaning out gutters—in cutoff shorts and a tee shirt. She wondered why someone with his wealth didn't just hire a handyman. Come to think of it, he always mowed his own lawn as well.

He waved from the top of the ladder. She waved back.

Amanda stalked out of the house without a glance at either of them, slid into her red Porsche 911 Cabriolet—Denny always sighed with envy when he saw it—, and roared out of the drive and down the street. She barely missed old Mrs. Brolin walking her terrier, screeched the tires as she turned onto the main road without bothering about the stop sign, and nearly ran down the kids waiting for the bus their last week of school. An older one flashed her the finger.

Jeanette had barely fifteen minutes of peace and birdsong before Meg's voice started in behind her. "You're not going to believe this, but she was prowling under our bedroom window in the middle of the night!"

Jeanette turned slowly. "You're kidding."

"I *heard* her, and the shrubbery was moving. It was too dark to see anything else."

Jeanette took a slow breath and committed herself. "Amanda's out of control," she admitted. "She almost ran down Mary Brolin this morning—not to mention the kids at the bus stop."

"Something's got to be done. Randy just says I'm imagining things."

Jeanette sighed. She knew the core of the situation wasn't Meg's fault, but some things simply were what they *were*—and Meg had never been interested in any reality but her own anyway. "Have you considered talking to Amanda?"

"It's not my problem—it's *hers*," she snapped and left. Jeanette rolled her eyes and went back to her task.

By the time the red sports car returned, loaded with high-end shopping bags, Jeanette had finished the roses and weeded the daylily bed, and Meg had left for her part-time job at the public library. Jeanette walked across the street and invited Amanda to lunch the next day.

Amanda tossed her honey-blonde hair over her shoulder. Her dazzling smile didn't reach her eyes. "I'd love to have lunch. We saw you at the theater last summer. Acting must be very exciting."

Jeanette shrugged. "It's not as glamorous as people think, but I enjoy it."

"I'll look forward to hearing about it." Amanda closed the car door, three bags in each hand. "See you tomorrow."

Jeanette walked back across the street, musing that Amanda wasn't as good an actress as she apparently thought she was.

But, fortunately, Jeanette's student Laura *was* a good actress. They'd worked together in *You Can't Take It With You* a couple of years before. She arrived on time for her mentoring session but stared in shock at the suggestion she audition for Desdemona. "I'm not ready," she insisted.

"Nonsense." Jeanette opened the paperback. "Let's work through it. Then you can decide."

They spent the afternoon reading, Jeanette taking the other characters' parts and coaching as they went. "Confidence without arrogance at this point. She believes she's doing a *good* thing... think bafflement here—she's clueless about Othello's behavior... Remember her innocence as she dies—she's merely a pawn in Iago's scheming."

By the time they finished the session with their usual cup of tea, Laura was feeling more confident. "Iago's really an evil genius, isn't he?" she said as Jeanette saw her to the door.

"Best manipulator ever," Jeanette replied.

When Denny came home, the boat snug in its summer slip, Jeanette was on the screened porch with a glass of wine. He joined her with two fingers of Tullamore Dew and picked up the battered *Othello* from the table. "Got you interested, huh?"

"I've convinced Laura to audition for Desdemona."

"Don't evade the question," he chided. "It would be great to be onstage together again."

She smiled. "'*Thou know'st we work by wit, and not by witchcraft,*'" she said as she got up to make dinner, "'*and wit depends on dilatory time.*'"

***

Amanda arrived fashionably late for lunch the next day, dressed in very tight shorts and a sleek top revealing a valley of cleavage. Jeanette had made a variety of finger sandwiches and a salad, about which Amanda offered a nasal "How lovely" as she sat down. She accepted a glass of chardonnay and commented on how "charming" everything was.

"So—are you all settled in?" Jeanette asked as she passed the relish tray.

Amanda sighed loudly. "Mostly. Thank *goodness* we have a housekeeper. I don't think I could keep up with everything. My course load at the university is *killing* me."

Jeanette glowed with interest. "What are you majoring in?"

"I *was* studying social work, but I've switched to computer science—so I can help Gavin run the company." She toyed with an egg salad sandwich before taking a bite.

"You're such a lovely couple," Jeanette said. "How did you meet?"

"I was waitressing at the Keel & Rudder in Annapolis and

taking classes at the community college. My dad had just died, and my mother is, well…" She looked at the table and swallowed. "She has a drug problem. I was putting myself through school. Gavin used to come in a lot, and we started talking. He encouraged me to apply to the University of Maryland. When I got accepted, he asked me out."

"Very romantic," Jeanette said. Slowly, she steered the conversation toward other neighbors—few of whom Amanda seemed to have met—and finally, Meg.

"Is there something wrong with her?" Amanda asked. "She's always staring at me."

Jeanette topped off their glasses. "When you're unhappy, it's hard to see people who are enjoying life." She leaned in confidentially. "You're young and pretty, and you've got a beautiful house"—she raised her eyebrows suggestively—"*and* a handsome, *very* successful husband."

"You mean she's got a crush on *Gavin*? He's a bit out of her league." Amanda wasn't incredulous so much as derisive, but then she remembered herself and murmured, "Not to be rude, of course."

Jeanette shrugged. "Middle age does weird things to people who are already depressed and insecure."

"That's so pathetic," Amanda said, shaking her head.

"Isn't it?" Jeanette concluded, then smiled again. "So, tell me more about your classes. I'll certainly know where to come for computer help."

Amanda talked about stupid and immature classmates (Jeanette nodded in sympathy) and about bumbling professors whose mistakes in coding she'd pointed out in front of the class (Jeanette chuckled appreciatively). When Amanda left, she gave Jeanette an air hug, thanked her for lunch, and invited her to call if she ever needed computer help.

Jeanette watched her click across the street in her stiletto heels, then went to her own computer. She attended to business first, solving a few issues for clients, then delved into things closer to home. She was still working when Denny came back from the marina with Randy—in time for Meg's arrival from work, of course—and she took a cup of coffee back to the computer with her after dinner.

***

The next morning Jeanette was groggily making coffee when banging on the back door made her jump. She opened it to admit Meg.

"I have proof," Meg declared and held up her phone.

Jeanette motioned her to a chair. "What's happened?"

Meg tapped on her smart phone and held the video for Jeanette to see: a barely discernable shadow lurked in shrubbery below the camera. There was a flash of blond hair, and an arm moving in a repetitive arc, accompanied by cracking sounds. "She was throwing pebbles at our window last night. The video's time-stamped. Nobody can say I'm imagining things now."

"True, but you can't tell who the person is."

"Maybe the police can get fingerprints off the pebbles. They're all over the ground under the window."

Jeanette hesitated. "I probably shouldn't tell anyone this," she said, "but you know how everyone's saying she's a gold digger? She *really* doesn't seem to like her husband very much." Jeanette described the drama she'd witnessed that night in the bay window.

Meg's lips flattened into a thin, angry line. In a tight voice she said, "If something happens to Gavin, she'll have a ton of money and be free to go after anyone she wants."

Left unspoken was the inevitable conclusion that Amanda's prey would be Randy.

***

A couple of days later, Jeanette woke to shouting outside. She stumbled to the window and blinked at the invading sun. Amanda and Meg were hurling obscenities at each other by the hedge next door. Jeanette pulled on sweats and took the steps two at a time. Downstairs, Denny and Randy were staring out the living room window, coffee in hand.

"What the hell's going on?" she asked.

"My money's on Amanda," Denny said without taking his eyes from the spectacle. "No slapping or scratching yet, but I'm hopeful."

Randy shook his head miserably. "Meg went to Amanda's last evening. Said she needed to talk to her. This morning Amanda's pounding on the door screaming Meg keyed her car in the middle of the night."

"Damn shame," Denny said. "I snuck a peek with the binoculars. Someone scratched 'Bitch' on the driver's door."

Jeanette went for coffee and returned to stand beside them. The shrieking was loud even with the windows closed, but she caught only occasional words: the f-word figured prominently, as did "bitch" and various synonyms, with "whore" and "adulterer" thrown in for variety.

"Should we intervene?" Jeanette said as they watched the combatants.

Randy and Denny looked at each other, then at her.

"If you want to jump into the fray," Denny said, "go for it."

Jeanette scowled. "Thanks, boys. '*Mere prattle, without practice*,'" she snapped, making Denny snort.

But the yelling stopped suddenly, replaced by a blaring police siren. Gavin came running from his house as the police cruiser pulled up. The siren died abruptly.

Jeanette put her coffee down with a thud and headed for the front door. She called "Cowards!" over her shoulder at the men.

"I'll photograph the damage," the police officer was saying, his tone calm, but Amanda and Meg both started in again—Amanda claiming Meg was "deluded," Meg that she hadn't touched the car. The officer—"Cpl. P. Metzger," according to his uniform—held up a hand for silence, announced he would talk to them individually, and led Amanda several paces away.

Meg grabbed Jeanette's arm, her eyes blazing. "All I did was *talk* to her," she hissed. "She's a lying bitch."

"Just tell him the truth about *everything*," Jeanette said. "We know you didn't do this."

When the officer finished with Amanda, he wrote on his pad while she retreated to stand with Gavin. Jeanette patted Meg's shoulder. "Get it over with," she whispered. "I'll find Randy."

Meg gave a determined nod and approached the officer. Jeanette went up the walk into Meg and Randy's house, out to the backyard, and through the connecting gate to her own house. She found the men where she'd left them and pointed at Randy.

"Get out there and play the supportive husband," she commanded. "Go the back way so Meg thinks you were home."

Randy nodded and left reluctantly, as if on his way to the scaffold.

Jeanette and Denny watched Randy arrive on the scene and put his arm around Meg, who continued her explanations, punctuated with gestures at Amanda who held Gavin's hand and watched haughtily. Gavin stared at the ground. The officer finally went to photograph the Porsche, then sat for a while in his car before leaving. Gavin and Amanda went back into their house, and Randy and Meg disappeared into theirs. The rubbernecking neighbors vanished back into their holes like prairie dogs.

"I'm sorry," Denny said into the silence. "You're always fixing things." He kissed Jeanette's cheek.

He looked so sheepish and sad that Jeanette let him off the hook. "You can make it up to me by fixing dinner tonight," she said. "I think I deserve steak on the grill."

He grinned. "Rare, with mushrooms and baked sweet potatoes?"

"'*I know my price. I am worth no worse a place.*'" She looked at the exquisite oil painting of the Chesapeake waterfront that hung over their fireplace. Randy had painted it almost twenty years before. "I'm just sorry about how things are. Randy's given up so much for her, and it's never enough. I'll apologize for snapping at him."

"I was lucky," Denny said. "I knew who I was very early on. And I had a best friend who cared more about me than herself."

She shook her head. "We cared about *each other*. You know I've had my fun here and there, but I haven't met anyone I want to commit to permanently sharing a bed with. So, you're probably stuck with me a while longer." She smiled. "You better start on *Othello*—I'm *way* ahead of you."

They had a quiet dinner—the steak was perfect—and retired to their bedrooms early.

* * *

The next morning, Jeanette went to the mailbox and was returning to the house, absently flipping through the stack—bills, postcard from friends in Oregon, car registration renewal—when she heard a yelp from next door. Meg stood frozen on the sidewalk near her own mailbox, mouth open, staring at a creased paper she'd apparently just unfolded.

"Are you okay?" Jeanette called.

Meg mutely held up the paper, and Jeanette hurried over. In huge letters from a high-quality printer, the note read:

YOU DON'T DESERVE YOUR HUSBAND. HE HATES YOU AND HE'S GOING TO LEAVE YOU TO BE WITH SOMEONE WHO REALLY LOVES HIM. IF YOU DON'T LET HIM GO, YOU'LL BE SORRY.

"Oh, my God," Jeanette said. "Have you gotten anything like this before?"

"No." The shock on Meg's face morphed into resolve. "But we know where it came from, don't we?" She turned on her heel and went into her house.

A couple of days later, Meg started getting nasty emails from "avenger@xdz7.com," calling her various names and accusing her of everything from adultery to pedophilia. Then came the cease-and-desist letter from a lawyer on behalf of Amanda, who accused Meg of sending *her* nasty letters and emails.

The room was still dark when Jeanette awoke to pounding on the front door. The red numbers on her clock read 2:27. She got downstairs seconds before Denny to find Gavin, pale and shaking, on their front porch.

"She's *dead*," he gasped. "Amanda. In her car. Blood everywhere." He swayed, and Danny caught him and helped him inside to the couch. Jeanette brought a glass of brandy while Denny called the police.

"She must have just gotten back from class when it happened," Gavin whispered. "I got up to use the bathroom and happened to look out the window. I saw her in the streetlight."

Jeanette didn't tell Gavin that Amanda had never even been a student at the community college—let alone the university; that when he thought she was in class, she was clubbing in Baltimore or D.C. with various young men; or that her father wasn't dead and her mother wasn't a drug addict. All that could wait.

***

Since much of the neighborhood had witnessed the escalating animosity between Amanda and Meg, and the police had already been called in once, it didn't take long to focus suspicion. Meg soon abandoned her denials and admitted—quite triumphantly, Jeanette thought—that she'd "stopped that bitch from killing Gavin *and* stealing Randy." They found Meg's bloody shirt and the steak knife that had severed Amanda's jugular buried haphazardly under a rhododendron in the backyard.

As impending dawn lightened the eastern sky, Randy stared after the retreating squad cars, tears glistening on his cheeks. "I know she's difficult, but oh, my God," he murmured. "How could she have done this? I can't believe…"

They coaxed him into their house, gave him a large brandy, and put him to bed in the spare room. It was still too early for coffee, let alone alcohol, but Jeanette poured two Macallans and told Denny what she'd discovered about Amanda. "Her mother's a nurse, and her father owns an auto repair business. But according to some rather nasty media posts, Amanda's a scheming social climber. She was enough of an actress to fool a kind, recently bereaved man initially, but not good enough to sustain the role."

"Then she butted heads with Meg," Denny said. "Arrogance versus Insecurity. Bad combination." He swirled the whisky and stared into his glass. "Part of me can't believe anyone I know could have murdered someone."

Jeanette raised a brow. "But the *other* part?"

"She made Randy miserable. He told me it was like the frog in boiling water thing—she turned up the heat so slowly he didn't realize he was losing himself a piece at a time until the only things left were what Meg wanted. He was just the nonentity who shared her space." Denny sipped the whiskey, looked at her finally. "But to *kill* someone?"

"'*The wine she drinks is made of grapes*,'" Jeanette murmured.

Denny studied her, brow furrowed. "I've just realized something. Those lines you've been quoting—they don't sound like Emilia's."

"You can't play *any* of the parts in *Othello* without keeping one eye on Iago," Jeanette said. "He pulls the strings." She forced herself into a convincing smile, making sure the corners of her eyes crinkled appropriately.

Denny's eyes mirrored hers—curious, terrified, guilty, relieved, exhausted. He set his glass down, put his hands on her shoulders, and kissed her forehead. Then he went wordlessly up the stairs.

Jeanette poured another whiskey and stared out the front window at the slice of water between Gavin's house and his neighbor's. Pink dawn crawled toward her over the Chesapeake. The whiskey scalded her throat. "'*Demand me nothing*,'" she whispered to the rising sun. "'*What you know, you know*.'" Tears sliced hot furrows down her cheeks.

Two Years Later

After three curtain calls and a standing ovation at the conclusion of opening night, the cast of *Mrs. Warren's Profession* retired to the dressing rooms to strip off heavy makeup and heavier costumes. The jubilation of success played out in hugs and slaps on the back, congratulations all around, presentations of flowers, and the popping of champagne corks. Finally, the merriment subsided into comfortable bonhomie, and Jeanette sat in her fuzzy robe between Denny and Laura, stripping the last of Mrs. Warren from her eyes with baby oil.

"He's here, you know," Denny said as he divested himself of Sir George Crofts' caterpillar eyebrows.

Jeanette tossed the cotton ball in the trash and reached for the moisturizer. "Who is?"

"Don't play dumb, girlfriend."

"A secret admirer?" Laura said as she got up, fully morphed from Vivie Warren back to normality, ready to meet her boyfriend for the party at the director's house.

Jeanette patted her face with a damp cloth and rose as well. "Apparently not *that* secret," she grumbled. She took off the robe with an actor's nonchalance, pulled her evening dress on over her slip, and lifted her hair so Laura could do the zipper.

"See you guys at the party," Laura said and smiled mischievously. "Hopefully with the 'secret admirer.'" She escaped before Jeanette could even frown.

Denny buttoned his shirt and stood to hug Jeanette. "Give yourself permission to be happy, girlfriend," he whispered in her ear, "and give the poor guy a break at the same time."

He broke away to open the door at Randy's knock, threw his arm around his husband, and sauntered away.

Jeanette gathered her belongings with a smile, glad her friends were so happy. When she turned to leave, Gavin was standing in the doorway with a large bouquet.

"Hi," she said. Denny's words lingered in the room.

"I'm not asking for anything other than to share this evening with you," Gavin said quickly, as if preempting objections. "You were astounding tonight." He held out the flowers. "Could we *please* just spend some time together and see what happens?"

Close up he was even handsomer than Harrison Ford.

"'*I would not deny you,*'" she said, "'*but, by this good day, I yield upon great persuasion.*'"[1] She accepted the flowers.

---

[1] From *Much Ado About Nothing*

FINAL CURTAIN
By Sharon Lynn

When death descends along with the final curtain,
backstage romance, gambling, and money play into the
motivation.

When Sally Swanson saw the body dangling from the black velvet curtain, she thought it was Devon Shaffer. The lead actor's ego was enough to drive anyone to murder.

The bubble she had just blown deflated, gum sticking to her lips. She stared. No, not Devon. The flop of hair, the tattooed forearm pointing an accusing, bloody finger at the wooden stage floor belonged to her wayward light board operator, Charlie Foster.

With shaking hands, she pressed the Talk button on her headset. "Kyra," Sally croaked to backstage. "Pull up the curtain."

"Check." The word echoed around the mostly empty 250-seat theater. Kyra Azul must have pushed Announce instead of Talk. "Sorry 'bout that," the stagehand said into the headset as the curtain rose to reveal the simple set of a table and two chairs. "Why?"

Ignoring the question, Sally bolted toward the production booth exit only to be yanked back as her headphones tore through her purple hair.

She managed to untangle herself before the door of the shotgun shaped booth burst open, and Flash Richard barreled in.

"Sally! What's going on?" he demanded. His round, bald head was beaded in sweat, his breathing fast. As he collapsed onto one of the chairs, the casters moaned in protest.

Wide-eyed, she squeezed her petite frame past him and clomped her engineer boots into the soon-to-be-gutted theater.

The meager audience continued to shuffle out through the garishly painted doors, stale cigarette smoke wafting in on the sound of slot machines and construction drills. Most patrons were already facing the back of the theater and had missed the spectacle. But two or three playgoers looked around, pointing their phone cameras at where the curtain had been.

"Oh, hey," Sally called, smacking her gum frantically in an attempt to look casual. "Sorry about the mannequin. With all the casino reconstruction, we piled a bunch of props in the fly system above the stage."

The explanation seemed to satisfy the patrons and they left, Sally at their heels.

Sealing out the sound of bells and whistles with a slam of the doors, Sally allowed herself a sigh which turned into a yelp as Margery Sotoyea's sturdy form bustled in. Her thick dark hair and bushy eyebrows gave Margery a stern look at odds with her sweet nature.

"What's this about a body? Richard called me. I think he's hyperventilating."

Not able to help herself, Sally turned on her new boss. "You hired me to stage manage during drunken, drug-fueled concerts," she accused. "Not..." The horror of what she had seen crystallized. Dropping to the floor, she put her head between her knees to keep from passing out.

"What's puddled on the stage?" Kyra's voice called from backstage as she emerged.

Before Sally could stop her, Kyra looked up at the source of the dripping blood.

Her scream faded into sobs punctuated by "How could this happen to me?"

***

Two days later, the Tribal Police reconvened the actors and crew in the Pima Ballroom, one of three directly across the hall from the theater.

Sally reluctantly held a sobbing Kyra, awkwardly patting her shoulder.

"How can you be so calm?" Kyra wailed at her. "This is the worst thing that's ever happened to me."

Refraining from rolling her eyes, Sally explained, "One time, I disguised a roadie as a bass guitarist who was too drunk to stand. I'll panic once this nightmare is over."

Devon approached in an attempt to console Kyra, but it only made her moan louder. The lead actor hung his head, taking the role of wounded victim.

Sally was the newcomer and had gotten different gossip from every member of the small troop. She'd heard that Charlie and Kyra had dated, then broken up when Kyra had an affair with Devon. Or, the affair had been between supporting actor Tripp and Charlie. Or both.

Sally didn't know who to believe or who she could trust. Searching the faces of her new co-workers, she wondered if a murderer was among them.

Devon towered over Sally, his handsome face creased with worry. Was Devon concerned because he thought he was the intended victim, or did he have something to hide?

Flash Richard, the lighting designer, paced along the wall like a caged bull elephant. Sally recalled the fury he had flung at Charlie for playing the wrong flashing sequence during the show the night of the murder. Was a missed cue enough to kill over?

Gorgeous supporting actor Tripp Jordan, in a leather jacket and chewing on a toothpick, staged himself to look casual, but kept looking to see if his performance was being appreciated. Did Tripp take his fling with Charlie too seriously? Perhaps love had tipped to hate.

Quiet for too long, Kyra let out another ear-splitting woe-is-me cry. Margery relieved Sally from comforting duties.

Just as Sally mouthed "Thank you" to her boss, a friendly-looking blond man threw open the double-doors of the Pima Ballroom. The scent of stale grease from the buffet and the crashing bells of a jackpot followed him in.

He declared with a grin, "It seems I only get to the theater when the show mustn't go on."

The tension in the room released, and Sally managed a wan smile, instantly liking him. Even Kyra's sniffles slowed.

"Special Agent in Charge Johnathan Nelson, FBI," he said, shaking hands. "But you can call me SAC Jack."

Eying her hair, he asked Sally, "What do you call that color?"

"Eggplant," she said, pushing one side of her bob behind her ear. "With magenta highlights."

He stepped back, appraising her. "You look like a petunia!"

Sally could tell he meant it as a compliment.

Softly clapping once, he informed everyone, "We've canceled the matinee today. But the evening show is on. Our forensic team will be done shortly. Right then," he said, smiling. "Who's in charge?"

Devon stepped forward, drawing attention to his full height. Once all eyes were on him, his shoulders slumped under the weight of the world. "Devon Shaffer."

"The leading man, as they say." Jack checked his notes. "Can you tell me about the victim?"

Devon looked on the brink of tears. "A charming young man. Everyone liked him. Everyone."

Jack turned to Tripp, who continued to lounge against a wall like a 1950s teen idol. "Supporting actor?" He waited for a begrudging nod from Tripp before asking, "What was your feeling?"

Tripp drew a breath to answer, but Devon interrupted. "Charlie was the best. Right, Tripp?"

Snapping his mouth shut hard enough to splinter the toothpick, Tripp glared thunderously at Devon. "It's Sally who is in charge during shows," Tripp said, pointing at her while glaring at Devon.

Sally threw a pleading look to Margery but not before Jack said, "I'll start with you, then." The agent indicated that she follow him from the ballroom.

The wide hallway was under construction. Most of the ghastly orange carpeting was torn out, the flocked wallpaper peeled away in large strips. The cacophony from the gaming floor which opened wide at the end of the hall drowned out any chance at a conversation.

Jack aimed straight across the ballroom hallway to the theater. A tribal officer opened it, but Sally's feet froze, images of Charlie's body clicking through her mind. She rubbed her arm where her latest tattoo prickled.

"Agent Nelson? Why is the FBI here?"

The agent reversed direction to shepherd Sally inside. "Jack, please. Reservation land," he answered. "Part of the pact with Native American nations in the Southwest was that the FBI would deal with homicide. Sort of a rent-a-cop deal."

Sally glanced at her feet to hide her reaction, not sure if he was joking.

He hunched over to look in her face. "It's okay to laugh," he offered. "Emotions run high." Straightening, he continued, "Besides, I'm a fun guy. Just ask any mushroom."

She shook her head in disbelief at his pun as they entered the back of the theater.

Her eyes laser-locked onto the fly system over the stage where Charlie had been hanged, but no sign of the crime remained.

"Where were you?" Jack asked, his voice quiet.

Mutely, she tore her gaze away and stared at the window-fronted production booth behind the last rows of seats. Her fingers worried at the scab of the tattoo, a double-neck guitar, the same ink that the band she had stage managed got at the end of their tour. Sally had thought herself lucky to land this gig so quickly. But after a murder, she was rethinking her life choices.

As he guided her into the booth, the agent fired questions without giving her time to answer. "What is your title? What does Kyra do? Has Devon always been the lead? Is Tripp jealous? Is he trying to look like James Dean? Does Margery work for the theater or the casino?"

"Devon," she began, "What does…Who?"

"What's the square root of sixty-four?"

"Eight," Sally said with such confidence that she surprised

herself. "What did you just ask?"

Jack smiled indulgently. "Jumpstarting your brain. Most people forget square roots, but if you take them by surprise, it spills out. Are you okay now?"

She nodded.

"Show me what was happening when you saw the body."

The theater's single security camera positioned above the exit door caught her eye. "Was there anything on that?"

Jack followed her gaze. "It looks as though the body was attached from the catwalk above the stage. Unfortunately, this device didn't capture it. Why aren't there cameras backstage?"

"Sometimes costume changes happen there," she explained, turning the house lights up to simulate the end-of-show lighting. She untangled the headphone cord. "I called the cue through these," she told him, indicating the Talk button. "Kyra lowered the curtain after the applause. Most of the audience was out already. When I saw him,"—a shudder passed through her—"I called to Kyra to raise it again."

"Can't you control it from back here?"

She shook her head. "They're lifted by hand. This theater was originally built for community outreach. It only seats 250, and we rarely have a quarter of that. As part of the casino redesign, this space will be expanded, updated, and we'll get tribute bands instead of experimental theater," Sally explained as they left the booth, walked down the inclined side aisle to the stage, and stepped up the stairs. Pushing the curtain aside, she added, "Margery brought me on board last week because of my experience with rock concerts."

Backstage they examined the ropes and pegs holding each pipe of the fly system in place. "We lower the curtains by hand. Their weight is counterbalanced with pig irons."

As he hoisted one of the iron, rectangular blocks, Sally removed a peg and lowered the backdrop. "Once the pipe is balanced, anyone can move it."

"Why couldn't Kyra see the body?"

Sally shrugged. "She's behind the curtain. Charlie was in front."

"Was Charlie in any trouble?"

"No."

Sally's expression must have betrayed something because Jack immediately asked, "But?"

"Well, he messed up the cues the night he was killed. Flash read him the riot act."

Jack flipped through the pages of a small notebook he kept in his jacket pocket. "Flash?" he asked.

Sally made a nervous twitch with her hand. "Sorry. Richard, the lighting designer. Everyone calls him Flash."

Jack narrowed his eyes at her. "Richard is, if you'll excuse the description, the portly gentleman?"

"Flash is about his lighting, not his speed. I guess he puts a flashing strobe sequence into every show. His light designs are evocative the first time you see them, but it's become a joke here."

Richard's face had been purple with rage when he discovered Charlie's miscue. "Richard was furious because Charlie had messed with the strobe effect. I don't know why he cares so much. He has nine or ten sequences programmed in for this show alone."

"Did the victim play the wrong one or add in a new pattern?"

Her shoulders pumped up and down. "Flash is the only one who can tell the difference."

A memory surfaced in Sally's mind. "I thought it was Devon when I first saw the body. They're the same height, same build, same color hair. In the dark, from behind, it would have been easy to confuse them."

"Would anyone want to kill Devon?"

An involuntary snort came out of her. "I'm sorry, but I've only been here a week and have heard everyone's complaints."

Jack raised his eyebrows, encouraging her to explain.

"He broke Kyra's heart." She ticked off Devon's transgressions on her fingers. "He belittles Tripp at every turn. And he asked me to fire Margery and replace her with someone younger, like I have that kind of power."

Jack's eyes widened at the suggestion.

"I know. And Margery is the senior tribe member on our payroll. If she wanted him out, she could arrange it, but not the other way around."

"And you?"

Jack was so disarming Sally almost confessed her threats of violence if Devon called her a pixie one more time. Instead, she admitted, "When he asked me to get him coffee, I may have put soy sauce in it."

"Nothing more sinister?" he asked, hefting a pig iron in his hand.

Mouth sealed tight, she shook her head, no.

"These are heavy," he observed, handing her a weight.

Taking it in both hands, she slipped her middle fingers into the troughs at each end where the ropes of the fly system slide in. The positioning allowed even her little arms to hold the counterweight comfortably.

Jack looked impressed. "You handle that pretty good."

Shrugging, she told him, "We all do. Everyone has to chip in when the theater staff is small."

"Everyone?" The sharp interest in Jack's eyes made them brighten. "Even the actors?"

Sally set the counterweight down and looked at him. "I guess. Why?"

Instead of answering, Jack pulled a folder from his briefcase with a series of black and white photos and handed her one. "Does this look like anything to you?"

The image was mostly splatter, with a round blob and two straight lines coming out of it. "The lines could be a little kid's bunny drawing. But why would..." It slipped from her trembling hands as she figured out what she was looking at.

"Is that blood?"

Jack stooped to pick up the picture. "It looks as though Charlie was subdued by a whack on the skull with one of your counterweights." Tucking the photo away, he added, "The splatter is probably random."

Sally shivered as Jack led her back to the Pima Ballroom.

***

After a tense afternoon, cast and crew readied for the last performance of *The Final Curtain*. Jack joined Sally in the production booth. Richard filled the third chair, sitting in as light board operator.

"There aren't many cues, so I'm handling sound myself," Sally informed the agent as she settled into the center chair. Pressing Talk on the headset, she called the cues to dim the house and raise the curtain. She faded out the overture.

Richard stood, stripping his headset off. "I'll be back before the strobe sequence." His curt tone stopped the protest in Sally's throat.

"Did Charlie leave the same way?" Jack wondered.

Sally shook her head. "No. He disappeared after intermission, but he only had one cue in Act II, turning up the house lights. I just did it myself."

Jack shuffled through a stack of papers. "How big is the audience?"

Sally peered into the darkness. "I'd say forty-five."

"And this is normal?

She bobbed her head. "From what everyone says. Again, I haven't been here that long, but we've never had more."

He tapped a reconciliation sheet. "The ticketing audit shows a sold-out show."

Sally squinted at the sheet in the dim light. "Yeah. I double-check the reconciliation, and Margery deposits the money. The tickets are sold through kiosks or online. A company will buy a large block and hand them out as perks to employees." She shrugged. "Most people don't show up. It's not why they come to a casino."

Jack's faraway look made Sally nervous for a reason she couldn't pinpoint.

"Have you seen the bank statements?"

Suddenly wary, Sally stated, "Yes. Margery gave me very thorough training. The ticket sales match the deposits even if the gate doesn't."

"Gate?"

Pointing to a handwritten notation on the ticket audit, Sally explained, "It's the number of tickets torn at the door."

Richard burst in, and papers flew everywhere as Sally jumped. Squeezing past her, he spun the dial on the light board, selecting a strobing sequence at random. He'd been so concerned about the pattern on the night of Charlie's death. Why not now?

Turning to Sally, he asked, "Can you take care of the final cues?"

He was out the door before she had a chance to agree.

"He doesn't really light up the room, does he?" Jack indicated the light board dial. "Is that what Charlie was supposed to play?"

Sally scrolled through the sequences. "It should be the last one."

"Play that, instead," Jack suggested.

Sally gathered the stray papers together and handed them to Jack, giving her time to think about his line of questioning. It sounded like he suspected someone of embezzling, and since Margery handled deposits, she would be his chief suspect.

Sally liked Margery, and her own casino-funded salary. She knew where her loyalty lay. "No one could be stealing money," she assured him. "It all balances."

Jack's eyebrows went up. "What makes you say that?"

"I mean..." Sally wanted to take it back, but couldn't think how.

A scheduled confrontation between Devon and Tripp on stage provided the distraction she needed. The violence of the scene seemed so real. Were either of the actors drawing on actual experiences?

Shaking her head, she said, "Pardon me," and pressed Talk on the headset. "Cuing strobe sequence," warning Kyra backstage that the lights would be changing. She reached across to the console and hit the button.

Richard's strobing lights normally looked random. But as Sally watched the flashes, a pattern emerged. Short, short, short, long, long, long, short, short, short, pause, repeat.

A foggy memory surfaced, but Sally couldn't pinpoint it. Closing her eyes, she tapped along with the cycle.

Her eyes flew open to find Jack's dawning recognition.

"It's an SOS, isn't it?" Sally yelped, excited.

Jack tilted his head toward her. "How did you know?"

"*Pirates: Beware.* A play about a stranded sailor I did in school used Morse code." Her brow furrowed in confusion. "But I don't get it. If Charlie was in trouble, why would he reprogram the lights? Wouldn't he just leave?"

Shaking his finger back and forth, Jack said, "But he played the wrong sequence, remember?"

He waited while Sally worked at the problem. "Flash Richard was furious because Charlie played the wrong sequence," she recalled. "So, this was the right one." Shrugging, she admitted, "I still don't get it. Why would Flash want an SOS? Who was he signaling?"

"Who was Richard signaling?" Jack's gaze was unfocused until he clapped his hands.

Holding up a finger, he rolled back in his chair, rose and went to the door. "I'll be on the gaming floor," he whispered.

The chimes of slot machines mingled with construction drills when the theater doors opened. A couple of audience members looked around at the siren call of gambling.

Stuffing a piece of gum in her mouth, Sally waited for the applause. She called for the final curtain, dread dancing along her spine as it lowered, but everything looked okay. She blew a bubble.

Kyra's voice came through the headset. "All clear back here."

"Me, too."

"I don't know if I could have survived another scare." Kyra sighed, a sob catching in her throat.

Sally decided not to tell Kyra about the SOS. But it got her thinking. What if other nights had coded messages in the lights?

Once the patrons were gone, she opened the second-to-last sequence in the light board and played it, watching carefully. Another pattern emerged, longer, and harder to find. Short, long, long, long, long, short, short, short, short, long, short, short, short, long, long, pause, repeat.

No wonder it seemed random at first glance.

Using her phone, she opened a Morse code translator and typed in the pattern.

The translation returned, "One-hundred-forty-three."

As she double-checked her work, Margery came into the booth.

"Jack and I found a coded message," Sally blurted out, unable to hold onto the news.

"No," Margery exhaled, taking a seat. "What did it say?"

Sally told her about the SOS, then added, "But that's not all. I found another one."

Margery's palm slapped the counter in short, rapid whacks. "Well? Don't keep me waiting! What does it say?"

"One hundred-and-forty-three."

Margery slumped in her chair. "What's it mean?"

Sally's face fell. "I was hoping you'd know."

Scooting to the stack of papers Jack had been examining, Margery grabbed the ticket audits. "What night was the one-hundred-and-forty-three message played?"

Sally confirmed, "The night of Charlie's death and the one before. Although the last one was supposed to be the SOS."

As Margery scanned the ticket audit, Sally recalled Jack's questions. "Do you think someone could be embezzling?" she inquired in a small voice.

Margery shook her head. "Not possible. I always have the stage manager double-check the audits and deposits so that one person is never solely in charge." Grabbing a pencil, she marked two sets of numbers, then turned the paper toward Sally. "The gate count was fifty-seven."

"Total tickets sold was one-ninety-six which matches the bank deposit," Sally pointed out. "But..." She subtracted the gate from the tickets sold. "One thirty-nine. Rats. I thought it would be our coded number."

Margery's pencil scanned the sheet. "Four comps," she stated, looking at Sally triumphantly.

Sally nodded. "Four complimentary tickets were counted in the tickets torn at the door, but not sold. If we don't include them—"

"We get one-hundred-and-forty-three." Margery grinned. "We figured it out!"

Sally shook her head. "But we still don't know what it means."

Standing, Margery hugged Sally and told her, "That's not our job. I'll go find Jack."

Staring at the audits, Sally couldn't understand why the numbers were one night off. One-hundred-and-forty-three matched the tickets for the performance after the sequence was played. While she pondered, she doodled in the margin: 143, SOS, and finally an R for Richard. The R drew her attention. Tilting her head and turning the paper sideways made the R look like a rabbit. Very much like the blood splatter Charlie created with his dying breath.

A knock caused her to jump, and she bounced out of her chair to open the door for Jack.

Only it wasn't him. It was Richard.

Teeth bared, he advanced on Sally. "I saw you messing with the lights."

There was no way for her to avoid his bulk. She backed away, spinning a chair in front of her to separate them.

He batted it away, and it ricocheted into her.

Stumbling, she moved the other two chairs between them, pinning her against the back of the booth.

"You don't understand what they'll do to me," he practically whined.

Using the wall for leverage, she pushed a chair at him with all her strength.

It connected with his stomach causing him to bellow. He backed off to catch his breath, but Sally was still trapped.

Desperately she flipped the closest switch she could reach. The eerie flashes of Richard's design flooded into the theater and booth, causing his movements to appear in slow motion as he came at her. The slab of his arms slashed toward her head. She avoided the blow by scrambling onto the counter, pushing electronics aside.

Balanced on hands and knees, she scuttled over the equipment and past Richard as he stumbled from the force of his missed swipe.

Her hand reached for the doorknob as her legs slipped off the counter and slammed into the floor. She twisted the knob before being jerked back by her neck.

"They'll kill me." Richard's hot spittle rained across Sally's back. "That idiot Charlie sent the wrong message."

Clawing at the strap around her throat, Sally kicked her foot backward, hoping to smash her boot into Richard's shin.

He easily stepped out of reach, but the distraction allowed her to work one finger between her neck and what turned out to be the cord of her headset. She managed a gasp before her finger went numb.

Letting her free hand follow the cord to the soundboard, she found the pre-show announcement button and flicked it.

Richard slapped it off before two words had gotten out and yanked her around to face him. "Everything was supposed to be gone by now."

Sally had no idea what he was talking about. She opened her mouth and pushed her gum out to fall on Richard's arm.

He convulsed, allowing her to get two more fingers between her neck and the cord, but it wouldn't help for long.

The coded lights Richard had created made his face monstrous, forcing her to fight away panic.

"I had to send a message. It was him or me!" As Richard ranted, his grip tightened.

Holding his gaze steady, Sally's free hand searched for the Announce button on the headset. She couldn't yell, but the house would fill with static when it was pressed.

She pushed rhythmically. Short, short, short, long, long, long, short, short, short, pause repeat.

Jack burst into the room, gun drawn.

"Drop the pixie!" he shouted.

***

"But it can't be embezzlement," Sally insisted to Jack after Richard had been hauled away.

"Correct you are," Jack agreed. "Money talks, but all mine ever says is goodbye."

She rubbed the raw skin of her throat. "But—"

"Money laundering. Ill-gotten gains being cleaned with your little show," he explained. "On the night before the murder, one-hundred and forty-three tickets sold for cash were deposited and accounted for. At this rate, the theater is cleaning fifteen thousand dollars per week."

"Where is all the cash coming from?"

In answer, Jack escorted Sally past the large plastic sheets hiding construction and to the gaming floor. The raucous song of slot machines beckoned in a crowd. Half of the slots sat dark, roped off by officials in suits.

"All those,"—Jack indicated the inactive machines—"are owned by CredCom, Inc., and are leased to the casino. CredCom is in turn owned by ShareCred which owns your ticket distributor. And Richard works for ShareCred."

She was still confused. "Aren't those legitimate slot machines?"

"Completely," Jack assured her. "Slots with credit card skimmers on them. The casino was getting rid of all these outdated machines and replacing them to avoid this kind of scenario. Membership cards are safer." He held up a casino membership card and pointed to a slot machine with a matching icon.

"The credit card was read by the casino's machine and had a normal transaction. But the card was also transmitted to CredCom who put a small cash advance on it. So small most people wouldn't notice. Then CredCom took the extra cash and bought tickets to your show. The cash was deposited from the show into the bank, squeaky clean, with no one the wiser."

As they wove their way back to the hallway and the theater, Sally's brows knit together, concentrating as Jack spoke. "Richard coded in how much money was skimmed and flashed the code. The next day CredCom would buy that number of tickets in cash. No paper trail."

As they entered the theater, Sally returned to something Richard had said. "'Everything's supposed to be gone by now.' He meant the slots." She snapped her gum in realization. "The SOS was the signal to clear out the skimmers so the casino wouldn't find them when the machines were removed."

Jack held up his hand, and Sally slapped a high-five.

Jack continued, "Since the signal wasn't launched, Richard was in danger. He had to pay for his mistake. Charlie was his sacrifice, serving as signal and apology."

The theater doors closed, muffling the sounds of the casino.

A cold shudder rattled Sally. "Who was he signaling?"

Jack shook his head. "Bad guys. You don't want to know more than that."

Sally didn't need Jack to tell her twice.

Jack pointed to the technician setting a ladder under the theater's sole security cam. "A webcam was installed next to the closed-circuit system. We wouldn't have found it if we hadn't been looking. Every show was monitored via the internet."

The camera came loose, and the technician handed it to a waiting agent who wrapped it carefully in an evidence bag.

Jack eyed it. "I shutter,"—he winked—"to think what that camera has seen."

"One thing's for sure," Sally grinned. "It's curtains for this scam."

THE MASK
By Cheryl Marceau

*Misty Mountains Morris means masks,
music, and ancient mysteries.*

Andy Roberts had never been this excited in his life.

For seventeen years in a row, Andy had taken vacation time from one cubicle-farm job after another to attend the week-long English-Scottish sessions at the Mist-Covered Mountains Folk Music and Dance Camp. Popularly known as Misty Mountains, the camp was situated along a lake deep in the White Mountains. For seven glorious days and nights, Andy reveled in traditional dance and music, transported to long-ago and far-away places.

During his third summer, Andy and his friend Bill Forbes had joined the Misty Mountains Morris Men. Morris dancing, a centuries-old tradition meant to ensure bountiful harvests, had long since become a kind of ritual theater. The Misty Mountains team was invited to dance at events all over New England. The performance that Andy always enjoyed most, in the place where he first learned to dance, was the team's act at the camp ceilidh, or talent show, on the final night of camp.

For the first time at Misty Mountains, the Morris men planned to perform the Abbots Bromley Horn Dance, named for a village in England and believed to be an ancient invocation to the gods for a good stag hunt. The team would dance into the darkened common room in the camp recreation hall at midnight, carrying rustic deer antler masks meant to represent stags' heads, while a member of the troupe played an ancient modal tune on a tin whistle. Tonight was the summer solstice, a time of magic and mystery. The dance would be eerie and beautiful, evoking ancient spirits, perfect for the solstice. It would knock 'em dead.

Andy hummed the traditional tune they would use for the dance as he moved around his cabin, anxiously preparing for his big moment, imagining every step of his performance. His roommate Graham, a fellow Morris dancer, had gone ahead, but Andy took his time. He had something very special planned. Goosebumps covered his flesh as he imagined the first person who'd…well, that was for later.

He pulled on a hunter-green vest over a red shirt and khaki

green knee breeches, then donned a floppy green beret. One final glance at the mirror inside his closet door and he was ready. He set his antlers on the cabin porch while he secured the latch. The last thing he and Graham needed was a hungry animal sniffing out their stash of munchies.

He'd just started down the porch steps, carrying the antler mask as he would a priceless treasure, when he realized his flashlight was still inside. Even after walking these paths for seventeen years, he didn't trust himself in the dark. Especially not tonight. He set the antlers on the small front porch of the cabin and turned back inside to get the flashlight.

The cabin door slammed shut behind him. Andy spun around. Must have been the wind. He pressed the latch and pushed the door to open it. Nothing. He leaned against the door with all his weight. No luck.

Uneasily he peered at the latch. It opened, all right, but the door didn't move.

"Help! Somebody, get me out of here!" he hollered, pounding on the door. The team's performance would start in a few minutes. He went to climb out the window, pushing aside the curtains, but the heavy wooden shutters were latched from the outside. How could that have happened? They'd been open before he went to the gala that evening.

He hollered and hammered on the door with his flashlight until he was exhausted. It was hopeless. Everyone at camp would already be at the rec hall, a five-minute walk along the lake. There wasn't much chance anyone would hear him.

***

Bill Forbes peered into the rec hall from outside, and looked again at his watch. Andy was late. The act right before them wailed away on his bass singing "The Naked Meditation Blues," the crowd jiving to the beat and snapping their fingers with the rhythm.

Bill barely heard the music, worried about the dance. He had no idea how to adapt it if Andy didn't show up.

The blues song ended and the audience burst into raucous applause. It was time for the Morris team, but Andy had yet to appear.

He was never late.

"Hey guys," Bill said to the team, "stall for time. I'm going to look for Andy."

Just then a figure in black materialized from out of the night. Unlike the simple antlers carried by the rest of the Morris troupe, his mask was a full skeletal head of a deer, its large crown of antlers looking very much like the sharp weapons they'd been when the animal was alive. The dark dancer's face was smeared with an inky black paste.

"Where have you been? Get going!" Bill waved the figure forward as he herded the rest of the troupe to the door. "What's with the face paint? And you aren't in costume." Bill allowed the others to pass him as they lined up for their entrance. "Geez, Andy," he whispered as the dark dancer passed him in a pungent wake, "you didn't even take a shower!"

One of the Morris men tiptoed across the back of the rec hall and dimmed the lights as a plaintive melody arose from a tin whistle. The troupe entered from the side of the hall and danced toward the empty floor in front that served as a stage, weaving and bowing, twining around each other in the faint light. The only sound in the hall was the tin whistle and the deliberate tread of eight men in soft-soled shoes.

The dancers moved forward and back, imitating charging stags as the stylized hunt progressed. Suddenly the dark dancer swooped forward, nearly skewering Graham, who faced him at that moment. Graham jumped back, struggling to keep his balance and avoid the lethal horns.

Bill glanced over to see what had happened. The dark dancer, eyes glowing from behind his mask, rushed toward him with antlers lowered, as if fighting another stag for dominance. He narrowly avoided running one of his spear-like points through Bill, who realized with a shock that the near-misses were intentional. One by one, as the troupe moved through the dance, the dark dancer charged at each man. The measured steps they'd rehearsed grew more frenzied as the dancers raced ahead of the malevolent figure.

The audience sat in total stillness, enthralled.

The dance concluded as the men moved into "curtain call" position. All but one. The dark dancer wound past the others and out the door.

The team looked around, dazed. The whistle player took the dark dancer's lead and stepped behind him, continuing the ancient tune. The rest of the troupe followed. Soon the mesmerized audience stood, forming a strange procession in pursuit.

The lone dancer made his way around bushes and under branches, followed by his entourage. As they made their way along the lake shore, Bill stumbled on a tree root, barely avoiding a nasty fall. The quarter moon wasn't bright enough to light the trail.

The bizarre parade continued a short distance to a spot where the path disappeared into the woods.

Okay, Andy, Bill thought. *Your little joke has gone on too long.*

Time to turn around.

The whistle player fell silent. No one moved. Bill watched nervously to see what Andy would do next.

The dark dancer stepped between two pine trees, twisting and turning, keeping his mask from snagging on the branches, then disappeared into the deep black forest.

"Andy!" Bill called. "Enough already. C'mon back."

Except for the snapping and rustling of the underbrush that grew fainter with every moment, there was no sound in response.

Fighting a lingering unease, Bill returned to the rec hall where the after-party would soon start. The spell had been broken. Campers' murmurs surrounded him as everyone drifted toward the hall.

The Morris team stacked their antler masks at one end of the room while other campers set up tables where the stage had been, and put out food and drink. "What the heck was that all about?" Bill asked the others. "Graham, did Andy tell you he was planning something?"

"Nah, he seemed a little hyper this afternoon, but he didn't say anything."

Bill was furious, but he wasn't about to be Andy's babysitter, especially after that stunt. It was a miracle they'd gotten through Abbots Bromley at all, much less without serious injuries. He hoped Andy wouldn't fall into the lake, but Bill refused to go looking for him.

***

Andy sat on his bunk, fighting tears. The performance would be over by now. This was probably his only chance to perform Abbots Bromley and he'd missed it. And his antler mask was on the porch, unprotected.

A whiff of something reached his nostrils. He sniffed the air, peering through the sliver of open space between the shutters, and caught a glimmer of light. A flashlight?

"Help! I'm stuck!"

Nobody answered. He sniffed again. Fire!

The decades-old wooden cabins were nestled among pine, birch, and oak trees. Dried leaves and needles carpeted the ground. The leaves would burn in a flash, and soon the cabins could ignite.

Andy pounded harder. "Help! Fire! Help!" He screamed louder than he thought possible.

***

Bill swigged some Scotch from a silver flask that Graham passed around. Still no Andy. This was not like the man at all. Bill's anger turned to worry. He really ought to see if his friend was all right. By now Andy might have returned to his cabin.

Sad to be leaving in the morning, he took in the faint glow of moonlight on the lake. A loon called and he stood bewitched by the ghostly sound until it died out over the water.

What was wrong with Andy? He hadn't been drunk or acting strangely at the gala ball earlier in the evening. Graham confirmed that Andy'd been in the cabin getting ready just before the ceilidh. So what happened between when Graham left the cabin and Andy turned up at the rec hall?

Bill's musing was shattered by screams from somewhere near the cabins. He smelled smoke and broke into a run. As he rounded a curve in the trail, flames licked the sky in front of Andy's cabin. He sprinted toward it, racing up the steps, and stumbled against a boulder.

"Andy?"

"In here! Something's blocking the door!" Andy hollered back.

Bill shoved the stone, grunting with the effort. "It won't budge! Climb out a window!"

"They're shuttered," Andy yelled.

The fire grew hotter and brighter. Bill found the window latch. He yanked the shutter out of the way.

Andy dove out the window and darted to the porch. He aimed his flashlight where he'd left the antler mask, and found only empty steps and the boulder lodged in front of the door.

"My mask!"

"Never mind that. Get help!" Bill said as he took off toward the fire extinguisher mounted on the outside wall of the communal bathroom. In his haste, he barely noticed that the flames threatening the cabins bore a striking resemblance to the ritual bonfires that were lit for the solstice in many ancient cultures.

***

Andy rushed into the rec hall. "Help! Fire at the cabins!"

Graham stared at him. "What the hell was that nonsense all about?"

"Get as many fire extinguishers as you can and head to the cabins," Andy said. He ran to the piano and pounded the keys, interrupting a jam session. "Fire at the cabins!"

The crowd in the rec hall ran to the doors. Graham took off, giving Andy a middle-finger salute as he left.

Andy's head throbbed. Why had someone barricaded him in the cabin and set a fire? Where was his mask? It couldn't be gone. Stupid, stupid, stupid, he thought, as he raced back to his cabin to help put out the fire.

He gasped when he arrived to see the cabin smoldering. The

others had been saved, but his was a loss.

Bill seized Andy's shoulder as Andy approached the chaotic scene. "We need to talk," Bill said.

"This is a bad time." Andy shrugged him off.

"Like hell! That was some insane stunt you pulled. Showing up at the last minute. Screwing up the dance. That crazy chase into the woods."

"What?" Andy poked Bill's chest. "You got me out, remember? You think I put that rock in front of my door? That I locked the windows from the outside?"

Bill stepped back. "But...if that wasn't you..."

Andy felt queasy. "If who wasn't me?"

"You were late, then you turned up. Black clothes, dark face paint, completely out of costume. I couldn't figure out what you were up to." Bill shook his head. "I thought it was you."

"What about the stag mask?" Andy asked, on the verge of panic, his voice rising.

"Yeah, and that mask. Not at all like ours, which really ticked me off. Full skull, real ghoulish."

Andy grabbed Bill's arm. "You have to show me where it is!"

Bill shook off Andy's grip. "I can't. That guy took it into the woods past the rec hall, where the trail ends. He hasn't come back."

Andy paled. "I'm dead." His head swam. "I have to find him." He took off running with Bill close behind.

Andy was grateful for even a tiny glimmer of moonlight. It was hard to run and aim a flashlight beam, and he wasn't a great runner. Breathless, they reached the place at the end of the trail where the dark dancer had vanished into the woods.

"Now what?" Bill said.

"We go after him, what did you think we were doing?"

"No way! It isn't safe."

"Suit yourself." Andy turned away from Bill and shone his flashlight into the woods.

"This is nuts," Bill said. "You can buy another mask. If you go in, you'll get lost. You could die of hypothermia. Happens all the time up here in the Whites."

"It won't happen."

"Andy, I mean it. Stop!" Bill grabbed Andy's arm and tugged hard, pulling Andy back toward him. "Look at me. What is so important about that damn mask?"

Andy's voice quivered. "You wouldn't believe me if I told you."

Bill's voice softened. "You haven't been yourself this week, and something truly weird happened tonight. What is going on?"

Andy felt Bill looking at him like he'd been invaded by body snatchers. "Before I tell you anything," Andy said, "you have to swear you won't repeat it to a living soul."

Bill nodded and made a cross-your-heart-and-swear gesture.

"So I was in England last September. At Abbots Bromley."

"For the dance?"

"I wanted to experience the whole thing where it began," Andy said. "I met a chatty guy at a pub that night, after the main event, and bought him a couple of pints. After a while he knows I do Morris dancing. Knows I'm going to do the horn dance. Tells me where the ancient masks are stored. Those masks only ever leave the village church one day every September, for the dance."

Andy dropped his head, mumbling.

"What was that?" Bill asked.

"Suddenly I couldn't imagine anything more exciting than dancing with one of those masks. They're reindeer skulls brought over to England by Vikings. Thousand-year-old masks, Bill. Think about it! So I've had a few pints. I figure maybe I'll sneak in and take a look. The next thing I know, I've got one in my hands and I'm running back to my hotel. Shocking how easy it was to ship the thing home as a theater prop."

"Now what?" Bill said. "They'll notice their mask is missing in September when it's time for their next performance. Think they'd be able to trace it back to you?"

Andy stood up. "I really have to find that mask."

"If I can't talk you out of it, I'm coming with you."

Andy headed into the woods first, aiming his flashlight at the ground, desperately looking for trampled grass, broken twigs, any sign of the man who'd come this way.

He and Bill bushwhacked through thick growth. Broken branches clawed at Andy, scratching his face and hands. A splintered branch carved a gash on his right arm, but he pushed forward.

Abruptly he stopped, listening. "What was that music?"

"What music?" Bill said. "I didn't hear anything. Probably a jam session in the rec hall."

Andy held his breath to catch any sound that might be carried on the night air, but heard only tree frogs. He sighed and stretched, then tromped a few steps forward.

"There it goes again!" he whispered.

Bill straightened and cupped his hand around his ear. "Sounds like peepers."

Every sound took on new meaning. "There!" Andy swiveled to

the right, pointing deeper into the woods. "A tin whistle." He charged into the forest, shoving branches out of his way and jumping over fallen logs, pulling farther and farther away from Bill.

He was closing on the stranger who stole his mask, he knew it. A faint hint of a tune teased him forward. He tripped and pitched face first onto the jagged limb of a fallen tree. The broken end caught him near his left eye. He reached up and felt a warm trickle that had to be blood. At least his eye was working. The pain would slow him down, but it couldn't be helped now.

As he traveled in the direction of the music, Andy picked up a foul scent. A bear? He braced for an attack, trying to remember what to do if a bear charged him. Minutes passed. The forest grew increasingly still, until Andy realized he no longer heard the night birds, or the peepers. Fog filled his head. Must be the loss of blood. He slogged on, desperate to find the mask.

The rank odor grew stronger. Without warning his feet went out from under him. Something seized him by the back of the neck and lifted him into the air. Terrified, he twisted around to see what kind of creature held him, but in the blackness he could barely make out the gleam of its eyes as the grip on his neck tightened and he was thrust out over a deep ravine. He struggled fiercely to free himself, screaming for help, but the thing was too strong.

Andy wrenched away and plunged down the abyss, clutching in vain at whatever his hands scraped against, battered by rocks and roots. The last thing he heard before he lost consciousness was the Abbots Bromley tune.

***

Bill tried to follow Andy as he ran toward the music he said he heard, but it was as if his friend were suddenly superhuman, racing through undergrowth in the dark, outrunning the light from his flashlight.

An inhuman shriek filled the night air.

"Andy?" Bill shivered. Mountain lion? "Andy!" He listened desperately for any sound that would point him to where the screech came from, but all he heard over his furiously pounding heart was the chirp of insects and the call of tree frogs. "Andy!" If his friend had been attacked by a big cat, wouldn't there have been some kind of commotion? Damn! He'd told the man not to go, but Andy was never one to listen.

Exhausted, disoriented, and terrified for his friend, Bill planted himself at the base of an oak tree and pulled his knees to his chest. This would have to serve as his shelter tonight. Nobody would be able to search for them in the dark. As Bill listened to myriad unsettling night noises, he tried to turn his thoughts to all the wonderful times he'd had with Andy, of their years of friendship. "Please, please let him be okay," he breathed in prayer to whatever spirit might be listening.

***

Bill woke to voices calling his and Andy's names. Morning had finally come, foggy and dark. "Over here!" he hollered, struggling to straighten his chilled and cramped body. He had a flash of a strange dream, hearing the horn dance tune as Andy reached out to him.

Two strangers emerged from the trees nearby. "Stacy Appleton," one of them said, extending her hand. "New Hampshire Fish and Game. Are you Andy Roberts?"

"Bill Forbes. I guess that means you haven't found Andy yet?" The hope he'd felt on hearing the searchers flickered and died.

"Nope, but don't worry," said the other warden. "With any luck your friend has your good sense and parked himself somewhere once he realized he was lost."

Hope turned quickly to despair. Andy's behavior had been so bizarre and out of character, it seemed unlikely that he'd suddenly stopped his wild pursuit to hunker down for the night. If Andy wasn't back at camp, he could be anywhere.

The three backtracked to where the tracks indicated Andy had taken off without Bill. One of the searchers radioed their location to the rest of the team. "I'll head back with you," Appleton said. "Mike here will wait until the others show up to continue the search."

"But—" Bill started to argue. He couldn't just leave while Andy was out there.

"There's no point in you coming with us. We've done this a time or two, we'll take it from here. Get yourself some breakfast and wait at camp in case your friend shows up on his own."

***

Later that year, Bill watched the dancers wind their way along the English country lane in Abbots Bromley. He imagined Andy in this place the previous September, as his friend had described it, seeing the horn dance in its original setting. He ached for Andy, wishing they could enjoy this beautiful fall day together.

The search had been called off a couple of weeks after Andy's disappearance. The Morris troupe tried to get the search and rescue teams to keep looking, but there were too many hikers with bad luck or worse judgment who needed saving. There'd been no sign of Andy in the area—no torn clothing, stray shoes, or other clues to show he'd passed that way.

That evening Bill sipped a beer at the bar in a pub called The Crown Abbots Bromley. Was this the place Andy had talked about?

A cluster of men at the end of the bar looked familiar, and he realized they were four of the Morris dancers who'd performed that day. He looked away, unwilling to make eye contact, unable to talk about their dancing for fear of telling them about Andy and the mysterious dancer. Even so, he felt compelled to eavesdrop.

"Strange, wasn't it?"

"I'm just glad that old mask is back. Wouldn't be the same with a new one."

"Didn't Freddie say something about a terrible stink in the storage room? What was that about?"

"Mwa-ha-haaaaa! They say it was the old Viking, returning his mask to its rightful place."

The men laughed loudly and ordered another round.

Bill's skin prickled. He gripped the bar to keep from falling to the floor.

He knew with terrifying certainty that Andy Roberts would never be found.

THE ULTIMATE TIE-BREAKER
By Deborah Maxey

Is the true evil the threat of what a Broadway play might bring to the Holler, or is something far more fundamental?

"This is gon be the biggest thing to ever come to Hickory Hoke Holler. I don't see how in the world we kin say no." Etta Belle Taylor shook her head in disbelief. She had imagined the whole town thoroughly impressed that she'd applied to President Franklin D. Roosevelt's Works Progress Administration and won a grant to bring a live Broadway Play to their little town tucked tight in the peaks and ridges of the Blue Ridge Mountains of Virginia.

She presented the offer from the Federal Theatre Project to the six members at last month's town council meeting, and to her shock, all three males vehemently protested the idea. After a lot of heated discussion, they decided to delay the vote and display the President's letter in the local library for a month, allowing the town folk to see it, and offer their feedback informally to any of them.

Now time was up. The deadline was looming. If the motion carried, Etta Belle would have to quickly write the acceptance letter, attach it to the President's offer, and send it by post the very next day in order for it to reach Washington, D.C. on time.

Etta Belle was confused and disappointed by any negative reactions. She had anticipated being praised, not challenged. But as her beloved housemate, Beulah Mae Oaken, reminded her, besides quilters, the two of them were the only "artsy people" in all of Hickory Hoke. Etta Belle was the first person to ever offer art lessons, and Beulah Mae, an aspiring writer, gave poetry readings in the local library.

Both women spent long evenings discussing how exciting it would be to have the real stars of theatre from New York City walking the streets, staying at the Hickory Hotel, and dining among the locals at Lula's Lunch Counter. Both women were eager to greet and escort the big-named talent all over their little town.

But the council had to approve.

As rotating chair of the committee, Etta Belle's parlor was the site of the vote. She straightened up in her chair, hoping to gain stature and garner more influence as she offered a chance for final discussion. "It peers to me from what I hear in town, most folks seem ta be all fer it. Not all of um. But them that don't want it, don't have to come. If'n we approve it, we got a lot to do. We got to start a committee to pick the play and one to get the outdoor stage built. What we have here is a chance to be the council that brings history ta the Hoke. Somethin folks'll be talkin bout fer all the rest ah time."

"I never in all my born days heard such nonsense," Otis Dimpson growled. He stopped to readjust the corncob pipe sticking out of the front pocket of his bib overalls. Since he was as round as he was tall, the angle of his belly caused the pipe to lay flat against his chest and point to his throat. Frowning, he looked around the room at the committee, shook his head, and continued, "If we pass it we gon make history alright and I'm gon be ashamed to say I was part of it. The Hoke ain't no place fer all that. I said it last month, now it looks ta me like I'm gonna have ta chaw my cabbage twict and say it agin. I ain't fer it. Kain't see as how we want them city slickers comin in here. Them persnickety Yankees look down they noses at us and act like we's all catawampus. I ain't fer it. Not even a drab."

"Hurrumph...." Sheriff Delbert Dodge cleared his throat, as was his habit before he issued statements that he thought were important. It had the intended effect and drew the attention of the four members present his way. "I agree with Otis. And another thing, if we say yes, we just heppin our own govment to throw good hard-earned money down the drain. The US of A don't need ta spend money on no New York City actors with they uppity ways just so they kin go places and put on phony baloney play actin. Govment needs ta give the people that money fer what they need. Money fer roads. A little post office. A real doctor. I make a motion ta go ahead and vote right now." The sheriff ended by sniffing loudly through his nose, his customary way of letting his nostrils imply, "And that's all I got ta say bout that."

Etta Belle quickly interjected, "We gotta wait ta vote. Miz Nettie ain't here yet and she ain't never missed a meetin, nor been late befo. She'll be along dreckly."

"Well now." Annalese Jimson started. "As the mountain granny who tends ta the sick in these parts, I gotta agree with the sheriff that we could use the hep of a doctor with all the farm accidents, flu, and baby birthin going on here and yonder. But ya'll all know, that ain't what the govment is offerin us. And I don't see nary thin wrong with that there play comin to Hickory Hoke. It might be good fer us to try some real entertainment, not just church picnics, and buck dancing ta fiddles. Heck, I wish we had us the money to put up a movie theatre like the one over to Dry Fork Junction."

The room was silent.

Annalise continued, "And another thin, ain't we bein selfish if we say no? That letter said the whole reason was to give them outta work theatre people jobs. I don't see how we kin deny um. The Depression musta been hard on them just like it was us." Annalise finished her thoughts by moving a strand of stray white hair behind her ear.

Etta Belle looked over to Chester Chimes. He'd arrived covered in sawdust from his grist mill. Every meeting he used body language to demonstrate his resentment for the intrusion on his time. But since he worried about any changes that could happen if he weren't present to dissent, he stayed on the council. Chester sat with his arms crossed over his midsection. He was customarily stone-faced and silent with civic duty. Until it came time to vote.

"Till Nettie gits here, tell us what you thinkin, Chester?" Etta Belle prompted.

"I'm thinkin I got me a long line ah loggers at the mill waitin on me whils't we sit here spinnin wheels. Where I am with it ain't a durn site different than where I was last month. No. We don't need our young'uns influenced by no big city foolishness."

A rustling sound in the foyer of Etta Belle's house drew their attention. When the door to the parlor swung open, all three men rose halfway in their seats showing respect, as Nettie Nelson, the town librarian, entered the parlor.

Collectively the group stared at the disheveled sight of her. Always fastidious about her appearance, Nettie's black dress was covered in dust. Her brown ice cream cone hair bun was knocked sideways and beginning to unthread from its usual tight perch atop her head.

Just inside the parlor, a maroon horsehair settee faced the center of the room. Slender as a willow branch, the young widow walked over to it and placed her shaking hands on its back for support, opened her mouth to speak, then shook her head and looked down at her hands.

"Miz Nettie, what in the world is wrong?" Annalise asked.

Nettie looked up, tears welling in her eyes. They spilled over, running down her porcelain cheeks as she began, "I am...so...so sorry." She swallowed and took a deep breath. "I know I was supposed to bring it, but the letter from the President...it's...gone. Just gone. I've searched everywhere. It was in the display case in the front of the library all month. I think almost everyone in town came to see it." She looked down at the white knuckle grip her hands had on the settee. "It was there just an hour ago." She shook her head. Her loose bun wiggled, dangerously threatening to spill her long shiny hair out completely. "It's my fault. I should have watched it more closely. I've searched everywhere. I've looked over and under everything. It's just not in the library. Someone must have taken it."

The parlor was quiet as they each tried to make sense of her news.

Etta Belle shook her head in disbelief. "Somebody musta wanted ta own a letter from the President. And now if we kaint find it we ain't got no invitation, cause I was sposed ta return it with our reply."

Nettie shook her head, "I am so sorry. It never occurred to me someone would take it."

Suddenly the entire council became aware of swift, hard footsteps ascending Etta Belle's veranda. The screen door squeaked open, then slammed shut. In seconds Wilbur Agee, the Postmaster of Hickory Hoke, appeared at the parlor room door, his normally tan face white as a sheet. His eyes were big as saucers and he was holding a bloody piece of paper with holes in it close to his chest. "Sheriff! Sheriff!" He looked around the room catching sight of four-hundred-pound Delbert Dodge, holding his hat, struggling to stand.

"What in tarnation, Wilbur?" Delbert asked.

"We got us…we got us…"

"Out with it," Delbert urged.

"We got us…a murder. A cold-blooded murder. This here proves it." Wilbur turned over the paper he was holding so the group could see. In bold letters the heading *Office of the President of the United States* stood out, despite the blood stains. Across the breadth of the letter in large black print, someone had written *Over her dead body*. They each recognized the holes in the paper were where the contact information for a reply had been.

Everyone gasped.

Wilbur's normally deep voice was two octaves above normal. "This was on the body. I didn't see who done it, but when I seen what they wrote I picked it up so it wouldn't blow away."

For a moment the room was deathly quiet. The six committee members were dumbstruck, their mouths open, their eyes unblinking.

Sheriff Dodge sprang into action, adjusting his suspenders and putting on his hat as he demanded, "Where, Wilbur? Where's the body? And who'd they kill?"

"I went ta take out the trash behind the post office…and thar she was…." He looked over to Etta Belle, shaking his head slowly, lowering his voice. "I'm so sorry, Miz Etta Belle, I know you two is close…it's Miz Beulah Mae."

Etta Belle screamed, "Oh no! No! Please no!" She stood so quickly the cane-back rocker she had been sitting in tipped dangerously backward before righting itself into a violent rhythm.

Annalise and Nettie sped to her side. The women flanked Etta Belle, each grasping an arm as the grieving woman crumbled in upon herself.

***

The next few days all of Hickory Hoke buzzed with the story of the most horrible murder anyone could ever recall. Folks at the General Store lingered on the topic as they stood on the porch. Patrons having meals at Lula's Lunch Counter held hushed conversations as they commiserated and speculated on who could have committed such a violent act. The sidewalks, normally filled with shoppers along Hickory Lane, now seemed clogged with folks stopping to confer on the murder instead. For the first time anyone could ever recall, there was true evil afoot in the quiet mountain holler.

The sheriff began his investigation by asking Nettie for the names of everyone she had conversed with in the library about the President's letter. Nettie made a list of almost every resident of Hickory Hoke. The sheriff quickly eliminated anyone in support of the play and concentrated on the naysayers. His focus became those whom Nettie said were open about resenting the idea, felt the play was foolishness, or expressed their distrust of theatre professionals or northerners. He compiled another list of those who disliked Etta Belle and her close relationship with Beulah Mae.

Over the years, because of her exceptional memory and insight, Annalise had become pivotal to the sheriff. Although he never liked to admit it, Sheriff Dodge often called her in to consult, always under the guise of asking her about an anonymous town person's medical issue. Because Annalise had provided care for almost everyone anywhere around, and been midwife to almost every birth, she was the person who knew their fellow citizens best.

When the sheriff asked Annalise to come to the jail, she suspected he was stuck in his investigation but would never be willing to admit it. She was prepared with an idea. She was aware that having ruled and reigned as Hickory Hoke's only officer for many years, Sheriff Delbert Dodge initially balked at her suggestions. Annalise noted, however, that the sheriff always listened.

Annalise met with him at the jail and answered his question about "someone's" strange rash, then she offered an idea. The sheriff made no comment. After giving him a day to think about it, Annalise returned to see if the snow globe of his resistance had settled.

"So, Delbert. I know you. I'm figuring being the brilliant law man that you is, you don figgered out how to make my little idea even better."

Annalise was well practiced in sidestepping his ego.

Delbert took a deep breath, pushing out his chest so that his suspenders expanded. "Hurrumph...I don give it right smart thought all right." He sniffed through his nose.

"I knew I set that brilliant mind ah yours ta thinkin. So, I figger what you probly gon do is ast me to get that group a folks you have on your list in here so I kin be the one ta talk to um, since they gon think I ain't near as smart as you. And they probly gon let go ah some clues they wouldn't let go of in front of no lawman with yo history. Is that what you come up with?"

Delbert's eyes went blank a second, then he nodded.

"I knew you'd think ah somethin sneaky like that. You gon ast um ta meet here? Or are you thinkin somewhere like the libury so they get all thrown off thinkin it's just a friendly set to?"

Delbert blinked a time or two, paused, then said, "I was thinkin the libury."

"Dang, Sheriff, you aint nothin but brilliant. You gon be there? Or are you thinkin the sight ah you might just hush um all up?"

Delbert reared back in his chair and took a deep breath, then nodded. "Hurrumph...I'm gon sit right cheer cause if they see me down to the libury, they gon know they in a heap a trouble and clam up tight." He sniffed hard through his nose.

Annalise nodded, her face solemn. "You smart as a whip. No wonder the Hoke ain't got much crime."

From the list of folks the sheriff came up with, Annalise asked to start with the Right Reverend Dennis Strait from Avoid the Devils Harvest Church; Horris Beasley, sponsor of the buck dancing jubilees; Lester Nolan, a logger who hated all outsiders; and Otis Dempson from the council, who was told he would have to move his smelly hog parlor if the play was approved, since it was next to the town property line where the amphitheater would be built.

Annalise ruled out a woman murderer when she saw how deep the knife wound on Beulah Mae's neck had been. She also calculated that since there was only one cut from behind, the murderer didn't have a personal relationship with Beulah Mae or may have been afraid she would avoid him if they were face to face.

The sheriff had no trouble getting the men to attend. Annalise had suggested he tell them she wanted to get some ideas from each of them about who they thought might have committed the murder.

The evening of the meeting, Nettie closed the library early and Annalise arranged chairs in a circle in the front room. She didn't want a table for them to lean on for support. She wanted to see if the conversation made them squirm. Annalise knew anxiety when she saw it and she figured the person with the most anxiety was her lead suspect.

After coughing to get their attention, Annalise started. "So, I'm sho ya'll know why we are here. Since Beulah Mae was killed by somebody what didn't want that play to come ta town and ya'll meet a lotta folks in yo line a work, I figger if we get ta talkin, ya'll might come up with a good list a folks fer the sheriff to go see. One man might make another man think ah somebody else." Annalise looked around. The men nodded.

"Reverend, would you go first?"

The reverend tilted his head full of shiny dark, slicked back hair to the left. Using long fingers, the thin, middle-aged man adjusted the jacket of his black suit and took a deep breath before speaking with great authority. "I'll be pleased ta. Ain't no secret I been preaching fer a month that it ain't fittin fer that play ta come here. And you ain't gon find nary soul in my flock that'll disagree with me. It's the devils work. We don't need them demons loosed on our good godly people here in the Hoke." He crossed his legs after he spoke, folding his arms over his chest.

Though he may have been posturing to look relaxed, Annalise recognized that he was closing up his body like a fort, covering all of his vulnerable parts for protection.

She looked to Horace Beasley, a portly man whose dancing days were over due to a plowing accident that left him with a wooden leg. Horace sat slumped in his chair, avoiding eye contact. Along with raising tobacco, he made ends meet by holding buck dancing festivals in every county around. People eagerly waited from one event to the next to throw down a piece of wood and show off their fancy flat foot stepping to lively mountain music.

"Horace, you know folks from ever where. You got any ideas who coulda don this?"

The middle-aged man looked up and stroked his long grey beard with a hand that only a hard worker could earn, calloused and yellowed with tobacco stains. "Not nary one. Anybody kill a woman in my book is lower'n pond scum. Don't know um. Don't wanna know um." He took a deep breath. "I know folks gon spend what little extree money they got buying souvenirs and what not, even if the play part is free. Probably gon leave um doodly squat to pay fer the next few buck dances. But I sho ain't one ta kill over nothin like money or no big city actors comin neither. And I don't know nobody that would."

Annalise felt the truth of his words, eliminating him from her mental list.

"Lester?"

Lester Nolan grunted. The burliest logger in the mountains, Lester dwarfed the other men in the group with his huge arm muscles and massive shoulders. Twice the size of the library chair, he shifted uncomfortably. But because of his calm demeanor Annalise suspected the small seat was the reason, not anxiety.

Lester, with a voice deeper than hickory roots, spoke slowly, stretching his words out at a languid pace. "I agree. Ya'll all know how it is with them city slickers. When they hear the way we talk, they figger they's smarter'n us and better'n us. Them highfalutin ways gnaw at me like a beaver with a stick. But ain't no reason to kill. And I don't know nobody that would murder neither. Fer me, I'll just stay up in my holler so I ain't got no call ta see um."

With no emotion in her voice, Annalise asked, "Did *you* kill her?"

The power of her words surprised Lester so much it seemed as though they pushed his head and shoulders slightly backward.

"No," he said sharply. After some thought he stated louder. "No, you hear me? I ain't never killed a livin human soul in my whole life." His words echoed around the library walls.

"Otis? That leaves you." Annalise looked over to the older man.

"I don't know nobody that would kill Beulah Mae neither," Otis replied.

With the same calm tone Annalise asked, "Then, Otis did *you* kill Beulah Mae?"

"No," Otis shouted. The indignity of her question sank in. He leaned toward her. "No. I ain't even blevin you ast me that. You ah all people. You don knowed me and my family since day one and heped ta birth all nine ah my little uns. I ain't no killer. And it's a insult ta even ast me." Otis looked at Annalise with a scowl. "I fer durn sure didn't want ta move my hog parlor, but the real reason I'm agin it is I don't want them comin here and pollutin our young folks, putting uppidty ideas in they minds. Them big city ways don't blong here."

Annalise nodded her head in understanding.

Three of the men sat glowering at her. But not the reverend. His chin was tilted up and to his left. She knew that posture. It was one he took when he assumed he was on high moral ground.

"So, Reverend…" Annalise started, looking into his dark brown eyes. "I kaint help but wonder if what Otis said might be true. Would a New York City Broadway play pollute our young'uns?"

The reverend sat up straighter and took a deep breath, ready to offer his expertise. "Yes. I kin quote you chapter and verse ah the Holy Bible what will tell you it would."

Annalise tilted her head to one side like she was still curious. "You know, Reverend, I been wonderin somethin fer a long spell and ain't never had no chance ta ast you. It's bout Beulah Mae and Etta Belle. Some folks say they are just salt-a-the-earth. But I spect you don heard how other folks say it didn't seem fittin them two women livin together in that big ole house, paintin and poem writtin and such." Annalise shrugged her shoulders slightly. "I guess this ain't got a thing ta do with the play and all, but since we's here and I ain't had no other chance to ast you, do you mind tellin me what you think ah all that there. Unless a course the Bible ain't got nothin ta say on it, in which case I'd shorley spect you to go quiet as a church mouse."

While she was speaking, Annaliese noted that the reverend's eyes narrowed, his nostrils flared, the veins on his neck stood out, and he clenched and unclenched his fingers into tight fists.

"The Bible has plenty to say bout the wrongs ah that way ah livin. Man and wife, the Bible says." He hammered his right fist on his knee. His voice got louder. "Man and wife. That's what lives together. Them women was livin in deep dark sin. Damnation and sin."

Annalise was careful not to react. She nodded as though she understood, frowned with curiosity, and using the same measured, casual tone, continued. "I'm specktin bein the Bible expert that you is, you might know if the Bible's got somethin to say bout two women livin in sin and workin to pollute our good mountain folk by bringin in that New York City play."

"Bible has plenty. Sodom and Gomorrah. Lot's wife…"

Annalise interrupted, "So, Reverend, did you kill Beulah Mae to save our good people from all that pollutin?"

The reverend stopped short, took a breath, and lowered his voice. "You ain't got no right to ast me."

"You sho?"

He looked down, inspecting his cuticles. "You all done here, Miz Annalise? I got me some sick folks in my flock that need tendin too with a pastor's call."

"No, Reverend. Not yet. You see I ain't so sho you ain't the one we need to thank fer savin us from all that sin, damnation, and pollutin of our youngsters. Peers to me you are the very one that would see the evil in it and how it was gon affect us if it won't stopped. I think you stepped in to save us from it. I think you could be our hero."

The silence was deafening.

The reverend tilted his head to the left, studying Annalise.

Annalise continued, her voice even and soft, "Way I see it, we got *somebody* we need to thank. Ever thin in the Hoke was bout ta change fer the worst. Mo women, or God forbid even men folk, might start livin together and our chilren would be restless with them city slicker ideas and evil ways comin from that play. That there takes a real true understandin ah the Bible. And a man worth his salt to defend it." Annalise shook her head in acknowledgement, "I just kaint say how grateful all ah us would feel bout somebody who would take kere of our very souls fer seein it that-a-way." Annalise moved forward in her chair, her eyes never leaving the reverend's. "That sounds ta me like something a good man like you would do. A man who if they was to ast him to put his hand on the Bible and swear, would never tell nothin but the God's honest truth. Reverend, do we all need ta be thankin you? Did you do it fer us?"

The reverend took a deep breath and sat up straighter. "Yes. Demons was bein loosed in Hickory Hoke. Them evil women and that play actin had ta be stopped."

Annalise sat back. The other men in the room looked one to another in disbelief.

"Thank ye, Reverend. I figger the whole town is gon respect you tellin the truth about what you did." The reverend stared at her and Annalise glanced around the room nodding her head as though the others were in agreement.

The reverend sat up straighter. "I did what was right. Beulah Mae or Etta Belle, one needed ta die to put a stop to *all* of it."

Annalise nodded her head, taking slow breaths and casually reclining her back against the chair. "Well, Reverend, theys so many truths that don come out since you kilt Miz Beulah Mae. I spect you acted on the truth you thought you knew."

"I acted on *God's* truth. Bible truth," the reverend said forcefully.

"I hear ya. I hear ya. But see won't nothin writ in the Bible to tell you the truth bout Etta Belle and Beulah Mae. Who they was and why they lived together. Looks like to me you got a way ah seein right and wrong the way you *want* to see it. Etta Belle was Beulah Mae's mama, but she never tole nobody till after Beulah Mae died. Then she tole me. She didn't even tell her daughter. See,

Etta Belle got in a family way when she was only twelve years old. A bad man, all likkered up on moonshine, drug her into the woods when she was walkin home from school. She was kickin and screamin and he beat her good fer it, too. He almost kilt her. She didn't want her innocent little baby to know the horrible way she come about bein born, so she give Beulah Mae to some good folks to raise, wantin her to have a real family. When Beulah Mae turned eighteen, her dopted folks tole her to go lookin fer Etta Belle, tellin her that all her life Etta Belle had felt called to send money to help raise her. They figgered Etta Belle would tell her the truth, that she was her mama. But Etta Belle just didn't have the heart to tell her flesh and blood that turrible story, cause she worried the shame of it would change her daughter forever.

"The two ah them took to each other right away cause they was so much alike. When Etta Belle's sister, Florence, what lives here in the Hoke, tole um they should move here, she said Hickory Hoke was a place where folks get along, foller the Ten Commandments, don't judge each other, and love one another like family. Just the way it's preached to most ah us ever Sunday in church. And it's what we read in the Bible, too." Annalise looked at the reverend. "Way I see it, you musta skipped studyin up on them parts, Reverend."

TRUE CRIME
By Adam Meyer

*In Hollywood, relationships are everything. But as
one veteran TV director finds out, tough times can put
a strain on both professional—and personal—
relationships. Desperate for a new gig, he takes an
unlikely meeting ... but the job he's offered isn't quite
what he had in mind.*

I looked down at the body, the woman's arms jutting out like sticks
from the sides of a snowman, eyes staring sightlessly up at the
ceiling. She looked utterly and completely dead.

"Okay, quiet on the set," I said. "Roll camera and...hold on,
hold on."

I stared at the monitor, shaking my head. The light angling in
from the right side of the bedroom was too harsh, creating a
patchwork of shadows across the woman's face.

"Tony, what's going on with her? She looks like something out
of a Fritz Lang movie."

My director of photography stared at me blankly. Just two
years out of Los Angeles City College, Antonio Martinez had more
than proved his worth on the set of our true-crime docuseries
Deadly Vows. However, his ignorance about references to German
Expressionism betrayed his youth.

"She must've moved, boss."

As if to prove his point the actress turned her face a little,
clearly uncomfortable from lying there for so long. I couldn't say I
blamed her, as we'd already spent a twelve-hour day following her
as she ran down a hall, nearly fell down a staircase, and was shot in
the chest. All of this based on the actual case of a woman in
Muncie, Indiana, who'd been stalked by her ex-husband after the
police neglected to enforce a restraining order.

"Okay, you should be good now, boss." Tony moved in beside
me at the monitor, checking the shot for himself. "What do you
think?"

"Looks good. Only...who's that in the background?"

I turned from the monitor to see someone in the back corner of
the set. Unlike the ragged jeans and stylish T-shirts that were the
unofficial uniform on set, he wore a crisp blue button-down and
pleated khakis. His tanned face was striking beneath a sweep of

white hair, but his expression was hard to read.

Burt Swift, my boss, almost never came to set.

I glanced back at the monitor for a minute, but by then Burt was gone.

"You know what, we've got plenty in the can," I said, feeling rattled but trying not to show it. "Let's wrap for the night."

***

Less than an hour later, I crossed the small studio lot where we shot *Deadly Vows* and headed into the stucco building where Swift Productions had its offices and edit bays. Burt was a notorious hard-ass, pushing his researchers and writers and editors to work long days, but it was well past eleven p.m. and all the deskbound employees had left. I saw a light glowing through the narrow gap beneath Burt's office door, however. He must've been waiting for me.

"Hey, Burt, you in there?"

I knocked softly, half-hoping he wouldn't hear it.

"Come on in, Kevin."

Burt had his feet up on his desk and his iPad in his hand. He continued to look at the screen as I crossed the room, then finally put the tablet down and faced me.

"How long we been working together?" he asked.

"Eighteen years. Be nineteen in October."

"Amazing. You remember when we started, how it was just the two of us?"

Of course, I did. I'd been in my early thirties then, a few years out of grad school at UCLA, where I'd studied film. Film studies, that is, not the world-class MFA program where guys like Coppola had honed their craft. Back then I was working as a producer/ director on local commercials and doing part-time shifts at a second-run movie theater. Then I answered an ad looking for a director in the *LA Weekly*, and that was how I met Burt Swift.

He was about the same age as me but had more swagger and a bigger bankroll, thanks largely to the small chain of mattress stores he inherited from his father. Of course, what he really wanted to do was be an actor. Unfortunately, that hadn't worked out too well. He'd auditioned for years and gotten nowhere. One of his father's connections told him maybe he'd have more luck as a producer, and gave him a chance to make six episodes of a low-budget true crime show called *Murder in the Neighborhood*. Trouble was, Burt had no idea how to make a TV series and he'd already spent a third of his budget on some barely watchable footage. He needed help.

So Burt paid me a thousand bucks a week—twice what I'd been earning—and I taught him the difference between a gaffer and a grip, showed him how editing software worked, and directed reenactments of crimes that always looked cheap but were compelling, too. The network liked the six episodes and bought six more, and before either of us knew it, Swift Productions was off and running.

I suppose I could've pushed Burt for an ownership stake in the company, but being management wasn't my style. I'd always aspired to be a great filmmaker, a Martin Scorsese or a Francis Ford Coppola, and even if all I actually did was make low-end crime shows, hey, I was still a director. As Burt sold a stable of true-crime series to various networks, I was his top guy. He paid me well for what I did and gave me almost total autonomy, and the arrangement worked for both of us. At least I thought it did.

I looked at Burt, trying to meet his gaze, but he kept looking away. His eyes landed on a framed wedding photo of him and his wife Alissa on a Malibu beach, hand-in-hand. She was his third wife, fifteen years his junior, and whenever he mentioned her to me, he was usually complaining about how much money she'd spent.

"What's going on here?" I asked.

"Have you seen the overtime reports for the crew?" Burt leaned toward me, elbows on the desk. "They're bleeding me dry."

"I know we ran long tonight but we had some technical issues."

"Technical issues? For the last six months?"

"I'm just trying to do these shows right."

"'Right'? What's that mean?" Burt shook his head at me. "You're not Steven Spielberg here, okay?"

As far as I was concerned, Spielberg was an overrated hack. But I kept that to myself.

"Look, the point is, more and more people are cutting the cord and the networks don't pay me what they used to," he said. "Budgets are smaller, margins are thinner. The streaming networks, they want high-end stuff, not the kind of shows I make. So, I'm feeling the squeeze here."

"I'm just trying to do the best I can for you, Burt. I know there's financial pressure but I'm not just going to be a hack."

Without warning, Burt leaned closer and said, "I'm sorry things have to end like this."

A cold hand squeezed my lungs until they were empty. "What do you mean 'end'?"

"You're fired, Kevin."

I stared at Burt in disbelief.

"You've done good work. But it's time for you to move on." He stood up then and so did I, but I didn't feel quite steady on my feet. "You've always wanted to go off and make a real movie, something great. Maybe it's time you just went and did it, huh?"

***

At first, I thought maybe Burt was right. I had a script I'd been dabbling with for years and hoped to make, and maybe this was my chance to finish it. It was dark and brooding, a cross between early Tarantino and the Coen brothers, something full of violence and rage. But I wrote a few pages and then I checked my bank account and, just like that, the words stopped flowing. Sure, Burt paid me well, but I had a mortgage on my Santa Monica condo and alimony for my ex-wife and a payment to make on my Jaguar. My bank account seemed to drain right before my eyes.

Of course, even though I'd been holed up at Swift Productions for years, I still had plenty of contacts around town. Lots of people agreed to meet me for coffee, but no one seemed to have any work. Finally, one friend—more of an acquaintance really—pulled me aside and said, "Look, Kev, I'll be straight with you. You're pushing fifty and you've been doing second-rate shows that no one really respects, so they're not gonna hire you. My advice? Get a teaching job or something, or maybe try your hand at the nightly news. 'Cause that's the best you're gonna do."

I told my so-called friend what he could do with his unsolicited advice, and I kept looking. I had a couple of close calls on projects, but nothing panned out. Two months after getting fired, I was desperate.

Then the phone rang.

A number I didn't recognize came up. It was a 323 area code, so I assumed it was about a job. I let it ring a couple times before answering, just so I didn't seem desperate.

"This is Kevin," I said, trying to project confidence. But I sounded like I'd spoken no more than two words to another person all day except to order myself some coffee, which was true.

"Kevin, this is Alissa Swift. Burt's wife."

I'd seen Alissa at the office a few times a year and we usually chatted at the Christmas party, but that was about it. I was at her wedding, but if she saw me on the street, I wasn't sure if she'd recognize me. She certainly had never called me to chat.

"Did Burt give you my number?" I asked.

"No, he didn't—and please don't tell him I called you."

"In case you haven't heard, Burt fired me."

"I have. That's exactly why I thought you might be interested in a...business opportunity."

"To do what? You producing some projects of your own?"

As far as I knew, Alissa was a woman whose only job was

being Mrs. Burt Swift. But then this was Hollywood, and everyone was either an actor or a producer or a director, or wanted to be.

"Maybe we could talk more in person, all right?"

She gave me the name of a bar on Wilshire about a half mile from where I went to grad school and told me to be there at nine-thirty.

I showed up at a quarter after nine. The bar was the kind of hangout that was too high-priced to be frequented by students but too down on its heels to attract upscale twenty-somethings. It was the kind of place that would make a good set for an episode of *Deadly Vows*, I thought, before reminding myself that wasn't my problem anymore.

I found Alissa in the last booth in the back, wearing black jeans and a dark red sweater, cradling a glass of something brown with ice cubes in it. She took a long sip, studying me over the rim of her glass.

"You're early," she said, putting her hand out to me. "I didn't know if you'd come."

"You're the boss's wife. Why wouldn't I?"

"Like you said, he's not your boss anymore."

She finished the rest of her drink in one long swig. The waitress brought her another and a beer for me. When she had wandered off, Alissa leaned in across the table and said, "I want to leave Burt."

I sipped my beer, trying to decide what to say. "I'm sorry. He always seemed crazy about you."

"When we got married, Burt had me sign a prenup. If I divorce him, I'll get hardly anything. After almost eight years of marriage, it's just not fair. And the things I've put up with from him…" She looked away, tears glinting in the dim barroom light. "You have no idea how Burt's treated me."

"I'm sorry. That's awful, Mrs. Swift. But honestly, I don't have any idea what this has to do with me."

"You've worked with him for years. You've done…how many of these true crime shows?"

At first, I thought it was a rhetorical question, but she seemed to be waiting for an answer. "I don't know. Hundreds."

"All those murders…you must have a pretty good idea of how it's done."

I felt that same icy grip in my chest as when Burt had been about to fire me. "What are you trying to say?"

I shifted uncomfortably, picking up my beer so I'd have something to do with my hands besides hold them up and try to hide behind them.

"I'm not sure what you're asking here, Mrs. Swift, but I should really go."

"Fifty thousand dollars."

"Stop. What you're asking, it's just—"

"All right, then. A hundred K. But that's my final offer."

I sat there, letting the number roll around at the edge of my brain. A hundred thousand dollars. I thought of all the bills I could pay. The months I could spend working on my script without worry. Then I came to my senses and shook my head.

"Goodbye, Mrs. Swift. That's a very generous offer, but I can't."

I stood and she stood with me, reaching out with a perfectly manicured hand and grabbing my wrist. "Please, just think about it, okay?"

I promised that I would, and then I got out of there as fast as I could. Whatever I was or might be, even in my darkest moments— a hack, a washed-up director, a loser—I still wasn't a killer. At least that was something.

***

For the next two weeks, I didn't hear from Alissa Swift and I didn't reach out to her either. I tried working on my script, but I didn't make any progress. I spent several long days reaching out about work, but the friendly replies I'd gotten at first had dried up. Frustrated, I plopped down in front of the TV and was channel surfing when I saw one of the first shows Burt and I had done together, *Swift Vengeance*, come on.

At first, I was going to flip away, but the more I watched, the more I liked it. This episode was about a woman who believes her husband is cheating and decides to lie in wait to murder him. The acting in the re-creation was mediocre, but the shots were well-chosen and the writing solid. Suddenly, I remembered how good it had felt to shoot quickly and without a lot of pretense, using a handful of crew members and working on a limited number of sets.

Maybe I could get back to that way of working. Maybe Burt was right, that I'd gotten too full of myself, let the budgets and schedules get too bloated. Maybe I could get back to basics.

Without thinking much about it, I picked up the phone. It rang a few times and then a voice I knew as well as my own answered.

"Hello?"

An icy wave rolled down my back. He didn't know who was calling. He'd taken my number out of his phone and he didn't even recognize it.

"Burt, it's me." A long pause, and now I felt a knife twist in my belly. "Kevin Longley."

"Kev, how are you? I can't talk long, I'm on set." Faintly, I could hear a voice in the background, one I knew quite well.

"Is that Tony? My DP?"

"He's directing for me now. Doing pretty good, too." A brief bit of faint chatter, then Burt said, "So what do you want?"

"I want to talk to you. I really thought about what you said, and I can see how I could make some changes. I really feel like—"

"Look, we're about to roll here. Let's talk some other time, okay?"

"Sure, I'll talk to your assistant and—"

I stopped speaking when I realized that Burt had already hung up. I put the phone down, watching my hands shake. A moment later, I picked up my cell again, and dialed a number that wasn't stored in there. I had it printed in my memory banks, however.

It rang only once before a woman's voice answered.

"Hello?"

"It's me. I'll do it."

***

I spent the next two weeks poring over all the old cases I had done re-creations for. I also went through the police reports and interviews stored on my hard drive, and watched as many of the old episodes as I could find on Netflix and cable. I made notes and drew charts and analyzed all the cases of killers gone wrong.

I tried to make a plan for how to do it, to kill Burt. I looked at different weapons and locations, using every scenario I could imagine, but every time I came up with a possible hole that could lead to my arrest. There had to be a perfect murder, but if so, I hadn't found it. Not yet, anyway. Besides, was I really cold-blooded enough to kill a man? Even after the way Burt had treated me, did he really deserve this?

I wasn't sure. But I needed the money and I wanted revenge.

Then one night it came to me, the way a unique shot sometimes did a day or two after looking at a script, and I could perfectly envision it in my mind. I knew what I had to do and just how to do it.

The next day, I drove out into the Valley, miles from home, and bought a burner phone. No more calls related to this on my personal cell. Then I reached out to someone who could help me get a weapon and told him exactly what I needed. I had a few more calls to make, and one in particular was critical. But first, I cued up one of my favorite episodes of *Deadly Vows*, and watched and re-watched the murder scene, where a man got stabbed by his jealous ex. A smile broke across my face. This was definitely going to work.

The next night, I used my burner phone to call Alissa Swift.

"I've got a plan to kill your husband," I said. "But I'm going to need your help."

Part of me wished she'd say she changed her mind, she didn't want me to go through with it. But another part hoped the opposite.

"Anything," she said.

I couldn't say I was surprised. After all the shows I'd made about killers, nothing about human nature shocked me.

**

Three nights later, I was walking up to the Swift house in Beverly Hills. It was a two-story box made of stucco and red roof tiles, and though it looked modest I knew it would go for at least two million dollars on the open market.

There was a fence around the wooded property, but I was able to scale it quickly. Alissa told me that the motion sensor light on the northeastern corner of the roof was broken, so no one would see me creeping in toward the bushes. Not that it was much of a risk; the neighbors were at least fifty feet away on either side.

I took the bolt cutters I'd bought as a prop for an old episode of *Deadly Vows* and cut off a chunk of low-hanging branch, then laid it across the driveway. Finally, I checked the time on my burner phone, found a quiet spot behind some thick bushes, and took the rubber-gripped knife out of my jacket.

Then I waited.

Alissa had told me she and Burt would be home from their date night by no later than eleven, and sure enough, it was 10:47 when the Range Rover pulled into the driveway. I adjusted my fingers around the knife and took a deep breath of the night air. I felt a tingling in my belly, that familiar mix of anticipation and fear that I knew from being on set.

As the SUV approached the house, the garage door started to roll up. I pulled the ski mask down over my face. About fifteen feet away, the vehicle edged along the driveway, then stopped with a sudden lurch. Burt must've seen the large branch blocking his way. A moment later, the overhead light went on inside the vehicle. I only saw Burt's face for an instant as he slipped out into the dark.

"Gimme a sec," he called to Alissa, who sat up straight in the passenger seat. I could see her face quite clearly: her eyes glinting with anticipation, her tongue shooting out to moisten her lips.

I hurried across the lawn, knife in hand. Burt was wrestling with the branch and didn't look up. When I was just three feet from him, his eyes met mine and he said, "What the hell?"

"Shut up," I growled, charging toward him

He stumbled back, clutching his chest, as I brought the knife in against him. The brightness of the headlights blasted us for a moment as we crossed the driveway and then it was dark again. He groaned loudly, falling backward, a pool of redness spreading across his oatmeal-colored sweater.

"You shouldn't have screwed me over," I said, straddling him. "You made a huge mistake."

He made a gargling sound, the words caught in his throat, bringing one shaking hand to his chest. I had to admit, I was enjoying this more than I'd thought.

I stood over him for a full minute, watching as he thrashed on the ground, the knife still clutched tightly in my right hand. I heard boots crunching as Alissa got out of the Range Rover and walked toward me.

"Stay there," I said sharply, and she did as she was told. I'd never felt more powerful than in that moment, though I knew the feeling wouldn't last.

Finally, when Burt had stopped making sounds, I pulled off the mask and crossed toward Alissa.

"It's over," I said, wiping the knife on the mask's dark wool. "You should call the police."

Alissa seemed slightly out of breath, as though she'd crossed a longer distance than just the length of her driveway. "I didn't really think you'd do it."

"Are you sorry?" I asked.

"Hardly. He got what he deserved."

"And you'll pay me what you promised?"

"Absolutely." She looked down at the ground and spat. "It's worth every penny, knowing Burt's gone. Now you better go. Before someone sees us."

"Too late." Burt had only just started to sit up, and he was groaning a little as he did. Not from being stabbed, since the knife I'd used was a prop, supplied by the same guy who'd been selling me weapons for TV shoots for years.

"You're alive," Alissa said, running toward him. "It's a miracle!"

"Save it." Burt dusted himself off as he rose to his full height, glaring at his wife. "Kevin told me exactly what you tried to hire him for, and like a fool I told him he was crazy. I said you loved me, and you were a good person, that you'd never contract someone to kill me. But I was wrong."

"I don't understand…"

"It's a setup," I told her. "Burt said he'd pay me double what you were if I could prove I was telling the truth about you."

"But how…I saw you stab him…."

"We do this for a living, remember?" Burt smiled with pride.

"Remember when I went to the bathroom after the movie? One of my guys was in there with a squib full of fake blood. I knew what you had planned because Kevin told me everything…well, almost."

I nodded. I'd told him it would seem more realistic if he didn't know every detail of my plan. But then, his acting had turned out to be better than I gave him credit for.

"You set me up." Alissa looked at me, nothing but pure hatred in her eyes. "You've been lying to me."

"If it makes you feel better, I really did want to kill him."

Burt snorted a laugh. But that was the truth.

"Trouble was, I looked at all the murder cases I've done reenactments for over the years, and I realized there is no such thing as a perfect crime. People never get away with it. So, I called Burt and spilled the beans and offered to help prove what you were up to."

"So what?" Alissa practically hissed the words at me. "You two think you're going to get me arrested for what, attempted murder? There's no crime. Some kind of conspiracy charge, then? It'll never hold up."

"All I want is for you to agree to a quiet divorce. One with terms that are way more favorable than what's in the prenup."

"I'll tell a judge all kinds of stories about you, just like the ones I told him." She looked at me, arms folded smugly. "You think you're the only one in this family who can act a little?"

"Alissa, I'm not an idiot. You think I went to all this trouble and didn't record everything?" He reached inside his front pocket, pulled out his phone, and tapped the screen. A high angle shot played, her coming up to me, a smile on her face, while Burt's "dead" body lay on the ground.

"You're unbelievable," she said, looking from Burt to me and back again. "Both of you."

"Goodbye, Alissa." Burt put a hand to his chest, right where the biggest spatter of fake blood had spread, and glanced at me. "Jeez, you didn't have to hit me so hard with that retractable knife."

I shrugged. "Just wanted it to be believable."

"Well, you got the job done," he said, and I smiled.

***

A couple months later, things were back to normal—well, almost.

Burt told me that Alissa had moved out, and within a couple of months she was dating an investment banker down in San Diego who ran a billion-dollar hedge fund. According to what Burt had seen on Facebook, she was wildly happy. Burt was showing up on the set of *Deadly Vows* more and more, and had even taken a small role in front of the camera. Apparently, he was thinking of relaunching his acting career.

As for me, I still directed the occasional episode of *Deadly Vows*, but that was it. I could've pushed for more work, but I didn't. That kid Tony was doing a good job in my place and besides, I had plenty of money to tide me over.

On my days off, I was busy writing. I printed the pages out daily, after I finished working, and soon I had a good-sized stack on the desk next to my laptop.

It wasn't the hard-edged thriller I'd spent years working on, however. It was a light-hearted romantic comedy, the kind of thing that was rarely made anymore. Burt told me I was crazy to write it. I didn't care.

I'd had enough of death for a while.

A STAR GOES DARK
By Raquel V. Reyes

Milagros Valesquez may be the comedy star at Teatro Cómico, but some of her antics are more tragic than comic.

I hadn't signed up for death threats when I applied for an internship at Teatro Cómico. Nor had I signed up to be an understudy. But here I was, in the fifth row of the historic Mediterranean revival El Gallo theater on the legendary Calle Ocho in Miami, Florida, checking the company's email account while listening to the director and Milagros Valesquez bicker. The troupe's headliner to whom I was an understudy and to whom the director was yelling with code red exasperation was a genius at comedic timing. She was also a diva of the highest order.

"Maestro, listen to me." Milagros struck a pose under the center stage Fresnel light, her fist jutting like it held a sword in a Wagner opera. "It would be more funny if—"

The stage went dark. It was tech week. Who knew if the lighting crew had done it on purpose, but their timing was comedy gold. I muffled a laugh.

When the lights came up, Milagros was frozen in position, challenging a void. Her adversary had left the stage. The director, Willy "Chico" Gonzalez, stormed by me and waved for me to follow. I grabbed my messenger bag, tossed my script and phone into it, and chased him to the lobby. He punched the eye of the golden cockerel in the ornate wood relief and a hidden passage opened. The wrought-iron-grate stairs to his tiny office were narrow. I walked on my tiptoes so my heels wouldn't get stuck in the quatrefoil holes.

"What do we have today?" He slumped into the cracked leather chair behind his desk.

With no place to put anything, much less sit, I pulled my phone from my bag and leaned casually against the door jamb, half in and half out of the room.

"The usual request for comps, and actors wanting to audition," I replied.

"No. The other thing," he said.

"Only one." I scrolled through the emails.

"Let me hear it." He rubbed his fingers on his forehead before reaching into his shirt pocket for a cigarette.

"You can't smoke in here. El Gallo is owned by the city."

"What are you, a government employee?" He tapped the red packet of cancer sticks with a dare-me vibe in his eyes.

"Also, nicotine will kill you. And the fire alarm will probably go off." I pointed to the sprinkler over his head.

"It's never gone off before. But, fine." He put the pack back in his shirt pocket and opened the little drawer under the lip of the desk. Things rolled and rattled. He withdrew an e-cigarette and took a hit. There was a faint smell of vanilla and clove. The LED tip glowed an unnatural orange. "¿Feliz? Now, read me the letter."

"You are a disgrace to all Cubans. You don't deserve a star," I read from my phone.

"That's it? No threats? No vows to shut the production down?" He exhaled a plume of scented water vapor. "Gracias a dios."

"But still, I should report it to the police, no?" I asked.

"No! Definitely not." He exploded from his chair, lifting off the ground, his weedy body too light and unprepared for such energy. "We don't want the media to get wind of it." He reached for a folded *El Nuevo Herald* that had dislodged from its pile and shook it like he was swatting gnats. "You didn't say anything about the other ones, did you?"

"I haven't done anything." I took a micro-step backward. The cold of the plaster wall on my sleeveless arm stopped me from a successful retreat.

"Good." He looked at the newspaper in his hand and made a face. He stuffed it into the shallow drawer, then sat. "Why does she have to be so difficult?"

His words were a rumble through closed teeth and not meant for my ears. I'd recognized the photo in the article. It was a review from last season. I'd read it. Everybody had read it. Well, maybe not everybody, but most of Miami. And probably every university theater department, African American studies department, and Latin American/Caribbean studies department across the U.S.A. I remember Professor Alleyne went off syllabus to hold a group discussion on minstrel shows. It might have even made it to NPR. Milagros Valesquez, star of stage and screen (the small, telenovela screen), defending her blackface character as being tradition and not racism. She hadn't won the argument. The coverage nearly shut the company down. Willy's apology ran on the five o'clock news on both Telemundo and Univision. He apologized in an English version for the American stations. He promised Milagros would wear makeup that matched her actual warm-beige skin tone for the remainder of the run and in any future productions with the company.

"You know your lines, right?"

"Sure. I mean as much as I can know them. Why?"

"Maybe you should stay after Milagros leaves and run the opening scene with the rest of the cast." He scratched his beard stubble.

"How late will we run? I have a date with my boyfriend. He just won a grant to continue his botany research."

"No más que nine or ten. You'll make your date." Willy took his wallet from his pants and threw a five-dollar bill on the desk. "Get two colada, one for me and one for the cast."

"Anything else, Director Chico?" I used his nickname purely to annoy him. He wanted people to forget his previous career as a half-rate band leader of the marginally successful Chico and the Miami Salsa Machine. Why had I chosen a Miami internship over a Broadway one? I could be in the costume and makeup department of *Hamilton* right now, but instead, I was getting coffee like a secretary from 1962.

Coming out of the stairwell, I smacked into Milagros.

"Where is he?" Her amber-blonde hair was coming out from under her wig cap. She looked like a scarecrow that had seen better days.

I pointed upwards. I thought to ask her where she'd thrown her wig because she'd certainly thrown it. Into the seats? Into the wings? Into the orchestra pit? She always threw it. And I always had to find it and brush it back to beauty. I almost asked, but I was awed to see her in natural daylight. The three o'clock sun was streaming through the glass doors and arched windows of the lobby. I looked from her to her headshot in the locked glass display over her shoulder. Her skin was darker. In the photo, she was a golden oak color and in front of me, she was a dark walnut. I checked the cast photo that had been taken four weeks ago at the start of rehearsals. She was lighter in that one, too.

"What are you staring at?"

I blinked. "Ummm, your mic is coming untaped," I said.

She peeled the cloth tape from her widow's peak, unplugged the mic's wire from its battery pack, and threw it at me like she'd found a garden snake in her blouse. Before stuffing the equipment into my bag, I compared her makeup on the tape to my own skin. It was almost the same.

"Are you going to La Esquinita?" She didn't wait for an answer. "Get me a cortadito. No sugar. Three blue packets." I lip-synced the words as she barked them. As understudy, I'd not only memorized her stage lines but her coffee order.

***

I perched the brown bag from the café window around the corner onto the long horizontal bronze door handle and vainly scanned the lobby. With no one in sight to let me in, I clicked on Willy's number. Before I could hit send, Milagros yelped and stumbled out of the office stairwell with one shoe missing. Willy rushed after her. They were both cussing in Spanish. I pressed my ear closer to the gap between the doors.

"Hay dios. Are you okay?" Willy cupped Milagros' elbow to steady her.

"Estoy perfecta, no thanks to you." She yanked her arm away.

"I hope you didn't twist your ankle. I'd hate for you to miss opening night."

"Don't be stupid. I'm fine!"

"Here let me help you." He cradled her arm. "Take a few steps on it."

Milagros walked on her bare foot. The first step was wobbly, but the second was sure. "You cannot get rid of me that easily," she said.

I rattled the doors to get their attention. Willy pushed the heavy door open.

"Milagros, are you alright?" I asked.

"Do you have my café?"

I took the small Styrofoam cup with the X on the lid from the bag and gave it to her.

"No sugar?"

I nodded yes. "No sugar. Three blues. What happened?"

"She tripped on the stairs," Willy said.

"I wouldn't have tripped if you hadn't been pushing me to get out of your office." Milagros took a curt sip from her cup.

"Did your heel get caught?" I asked before noticing Milagros' one shoe was a platform mule. I offered Willy his colada.

"I'm sure that's what happened," Willy said. "You must be more careful." He patted Milagros' forearm. "I can't lose my star before the show even opens." He took his drink and the thimble-sized serving cup I'd held out to him.

"You can't get rid of me," she said with a Cheshire Cat smile.

Willy pinched the colada cup into a spout and poured himself a serving. A drip bubbled at the edge with gravity winning. Willy threw back the sweet and dark espresso like it was tequila then he took another. "Take the rest to the crew." I was handed the sticky cup before he returned to his roost.

"Don't forget your shoe." The errant mate flew from a high angle out the corridor and rolled to a landing on the faux-malachite tiled floor.

"Get my wig. Act two starts in ten minutes." Milagros slipped her foot into her shoe and sashayed into the dark theater.

***

In the control room, I gave Manolo and Fiona the opened colada. The house was dark and only one light was lit at center stage. The control panel, with its toggles and dimmers, was a modernist version of a night sky, little red lights for stars and glow tape for moons and comets.

"I have to ask. Did you cut the lights off on Milagros on purpose or by accident?"

Manolo looked at Fiona. She looked at him. Fiona shrugged and jutted her chin at him. He shrugged in return and tilted his head. They weren't a romantic couple, but they were longtime work partners who clearly shared a silent language.

"Well?"

"Maybe," Manolo said.

"I knew it! It was too perfect a timing. So funny." I leaned over the control panel and surveyed the darkness. "Any idea what row la bruja threw her wig to?"

"Don't give witches a bad name. She's more like a spoiled toddler," Fiona said. She raised one of the dimmer slides and the house lights came on. "Second row. Stage left."

"I don't know why Willy keeps hiring her. She's hell to work with and after last season's fiasco… Milagros should be on stage." Manolo erased some numbers and symbols in his call book.

"Well, wasn't that Willy and the makeup department's fault, too? Somebody should have called her out on it during dress rehearsal," I said.

Fiona and Manolo exchanged a look.

"It was a surprise to all of us. No one knew until she walked on stage opening night." Fiona grimaced, full teeth and furrowed brow. "The lights weren't leveled for such dark makeup. She looked like an oil slick. Shiny and goopy. I was professionally embarrassed beyond the obvious stomach-turning racial stereotyping."

"Wow. Why did Willy take her back this season?"

"She has something on him. I don't know if it's money or dirt," Manolo said.

Fiona glanced at her partner. "It's both from what I've heard. She put up most of the money for this season. Plus, Willy and Milagros go way back. Like to Miami Salsa Machine days."

"Do you think she is going to pull the makeup trick again?" I asked.

"No," the pair said in unison.

"She's already doing it. She's using tanning spray…"

"Not spray. Cream. Tan accelerator cream. It's light activated. Can you say blackfishing?" Fiona rolled her eyes.

"Whatever it is, she is darker today than she was two weeks ago when I hung the lights and started testing levels," Manolo continued. "I've changed the gels twice already, trying to get a natural tone on her."

"Wow. Does she think it's 1889 and this is a teatro bufo?" I looked at my phone. Five minutes until act two's run through. "This coffee's probably ice cold by now but I should get it to the actors anyway." As I left the booth, I heard them talking about trying a gobo of stars for the talent show scene. It was the last scene and my favorite of the play. Estrella, Milagros's character, a housewife and mother, enters a televised contest and blows the judges away with her singing. The rest of the play is domestic humor and slapstick. Milagros couldn't hold a note so they were using a recording, but it's still a powerful and happy ending. If I had to step into the role, which I really didn't want to do because I'm a behind-the-scenes kind of person, at least I wouldn't need the recorded song. I plucked her wig from the second row and hurried to the dressing rooms.

The cast was small. Four others besides Milagros: the husband that doesn't want to lose his housekeeper and cook so he constantly cuts down his wife; the best friend that is light in the common sense department; the mail carrier that always listens to her singing before he knocks on the door; and the landlady that complains about the noise. There is one scene where Estrella is singing by a window and the landlady soaks her with a garden hose. Willy expects that to get the biggest laugh.

"Sorry, this might be cold," I said, putting the cup on the white Formica table that lined the mirrored wall. I got a wave and a smile, but the cast didn't stop their conversation for me. Nothing can stop a good chisme session. Gossip was a staple of the acting world and Cuban breaktime. It was usually harmless and TMZ level.

The cast shared the big dressing room and Milagros had a private room. Her door was open and she wasn't in, so I put the wig on the mannequin head and combed the black hair into shape. Thank goodness the wig was a 2-B wave and not a tight 3-C curl. Milagros's blackfish game was more Ariana Grande subtle than Rachel Dolezal transracial. I looked around the room for evidence of the self-tanner that Fiona had mentioned. It wasn't in plain sight, so I checked in the plastic storage dresser below the counter.

Bingo. Maori Mama Browning Lotion. About half of the sixteen-ounce bottle was gone. Apparently, Milagros hadn't learned her lesson last season. Empty promises with an extra serving of no self-examination.

I'd stayed local so I could contribute to the Miami arts community. Grow where you are planted, they say. There is so much talent in Miami, but the city loses out to LA and NYC. Those cities have more jobs and more chances to get noticed for the right reasons. All press is good press, they say. But really, Teatro Cómico and Miami did not need the kind of press that Milagros's minstrel act would garner. I had to have faith that the universe had a plan. Maybe that's why I was the understudy.

"Places. Act two, dry tech. Places." The stage manager's voice crackled over the loudspeaker. I joined the cast as they walked to the wings.

"Where is Milagros?" I asked the stage manager. She shrugged. I looked across the stage to the other wing, but she wasn't there either. I walked onto the worn wood stage and shielded my eyes from the lights. "Where is Milagros?"

"I sent her home," Willy said from the darkness. "She wasn't feeling well. So I told her to get some rest. You can take her place. It will be good practice just in case."

Milagros had been just fine twenty minutes ago, but who was I to question the universe's grand plan. The cue to cue run-through went smoothly. I sang the closing number so that the crew could set the mic levels for my pitch and projection. Then, Willy had us practice act one. My comedy wasn't as physical as Milagros's, but I got a few laughs from the crew with my line delivery. Willy released us a few minutes after eight with a call of five p.m. for dress rehearsal the next day.

"I told you you'd make your date," Willy said to me as I descended the stairs into the audience.

"Thanks, it's kind of an important night for him. Do you have any notes for me?"

"None. You sing better than her and you know your lines. ¿Qué más quieres?"

"I don't know. Was I funny enough? Should I try to be funnier? Maybe trip over the vacuum cleaner or do a big sneeze when I'm dusting?"

"You were funny. Don't overdo it. It will work. We are better than gag laughs. We are real comedy not Saturday morning cartoons. Teatro Cómico de Miami no es muñequitos. We are serious comedy." Willy wagged his finger like a principal addressing an office of truant students.

"Okay. So, I'll see you tomorrow. Buenas noches."

***

The next day I arrived at the theater an hour early to ensure Milagros had what she needed. Fiona was center stage straddling a ladder. She spoke into her headset and Manolo brought up the light she'd been working on. It was the special stars gobo. It added a nice touch.

"Is that light only for the big song?" I asked Fiona.

"Yep. Just that one scene. You like it?"

"I love it."

"Pass me that yellow gel, right there."

I carefully stepped on the second rung and reached it up to her. She loosened the frame holding the stencil and fed the polycarbonate sheet into it. With a hand signal, Manolo brought the light back to full. The stars were an intense yellow. I twirled in the circle of stars. "Perfect!"

I had Milagros makeup, wig, and costume laid out along with a room temperature bottle of water and her Thayer's dry mouth spray before she arrived.

"What are you doing in here?" Milagros plopped her purse on the upholstered chair in the corner.

"Getting things ready for you. Are you feeling better?"

"What?" She took off the Japanese style silk robe she had on over a black shell and skinny jeans.

"Willy said you weren't feeling well yesterday. That's why you missed the rest of tech."

Milagros pushed passed me and grabbed a hanger from the rolling costume rack. She hung the robe and then sat to remove her ballerina strap flats. "I left because tech is boring. You don't need the show's star for that. That is what understudies are for. An understudy does the unimportant things and you are my unimportant understudy."

I couldn't believe Milagros was living up to her diva status. I mean, I could believe it, but still, it was harsh to be on the pointed end of it.

"Get out of here," she said, shoving me out the door. "I have to do my makeup and get dressed. Do not disturb me."

"Yes, Mrs. Valesquez," I replied with a minute bow of my head. She might have noticed my mockery because she slammed the door and turned the lock.

A few minutes later, Willy texted me to meet him in his office. I smelled real cigarette smoke when I got to the lobby.

"You can't smoke in historic buildings," I yelled up the stairs.

"Calmate. I can't find my electronic one and this is only half a cigarette to calm my nerves. And I have a fan on."

I heard the whirl of a small fan, the kind everyone had in case the AC broke or a hurricane took out the power.

"Want do you want?" I asked while pinching my nose to the smell and the second-hand carcinogens.

"Any more emails?"

I had forgotten to check the company account. "Not since I last checked. Let me take a quick look." I typed in the password and waited a second for the page to generate. "Nothing new."

"What about the other thing?"

It took me a moment to glean what he was asking. The threats. "No, nothing new," I reassured him.

"Hm. Every day a message and today nothing? Maybe they heard about your singing yesterday and stopped worrying." Willy laughed. "I know I did."

"Is that all you wanted? I should get backstage."

"No, wait." He went into his office and returned carrying a thermos with lime slices in a small plastic bag tied to the handle. "Give this to Milagros. It's my mother's chicken soup."

I climbed to meet him. "But she says she's not sick."

"Por favor, give it to her." Willy pushed the container into my hands. "My mother adored all of Milagros's telenovelas. And, so, she makes Milagros this special good luck soup before every performance. It a tradition."

I nodded and left to perform a task that I knew might get my head bitten off. I knocked on Milagros's door and stepped back in anticipation. The door cracked open.

"What do you want?"

She was hiding behind the door.

"Willy sent me to give you this soup," I replied. I could see Milagros's backside reflected in the little bit of mirror visible. There was a tiny thong-sized triangle of beige skin at the base of her spine. The rest of her was dark brown.

"Leave it," she barked. "I have to finish dressing."

I left the thermos by her door then waited for curtain call with the other actors. Willy had me sit in the audience with him and a reviewer from the small Little Havana weekly paper. I thought it was supposed to be a closed dress rehearsal, but it seemed I'd been wrong. The reviewer, an attractive middle-aged woman, was a friend of Willy's, maybe even a more-than-friends friend.

The play began. There were the normal drags in pace that happen when not performing in front of a live audience. Actors needed the energy feed from a packed house. All in all the show went smoothly. The light and sound cues were on time and the rest of the cast were making their entrances. Intermission was only as long as a bathroom break. When Milagros came back on in act two, I swear she was even darker than before. She also looked a little sweaty. I glanced at the reviewer and Willy to see if they noticed anything, but they were smiling at one another like high school sweethearts. It was time for the big song finale. I held my breath. It could all go terribly sideways. The stage was dark as an announcer, a pre-recorded Manolo, introduced the contest's last performer. Milagros gripped the microphone stand and swayed. This was not how she had rehearsed it. The music hadn't started. The first notes of the piano tinkled and the starry spotlight came up. Milagros looked green rather than brown. Her lip-syncing was wildly off, too. I moved to the aisle seat in case I needed to catch her from falling into the orchestra pit.

At the climax of the song, at the longest and highest note, Milagros was supposed to look up to the trusses and hold the note. As she tilted her head skyward and the gobo light began to rotate, a C-clamp fell from the truss and beamed her in the forehead. Milagros collapsed just as the music stopped and the stage went dark.

"*Brava! Brava!*" The reviewer applauded and laughed.

But Milagros's accident was not a sight gag. The cast and I rushed to Milagros. She was unconscious and clammy.

"Call an ambulance!" I yelled.

***

Opening night, I took over Milagros's role. She was still in the ICU. The hunk of steel that hit her skull gave her a hairline fracture, but the nicotine poisoning was the reason for the intensive care unit. Somehow, Milagros's self-tanning lotion had been laced with a heavy amount of nicotine.

My phone rang.

"Hola, mi amor," I answered the call.

"I want to wish you good…"

"Aaaa," I chided.

"I meant to say, break a leg. That's what you drama people say, right?"

"Yeah, break a leg. Thanks, honey."

"Sorry, I can't be there tonight. I promise I will make every show next week."

"I know, love, you don't have to explain."

"But, I do. I want to be there for you and your theater career, but my hands are tied. The harvest is this week. It's my only chance to take blood samples from the workers before and after the cutting of the leaves. Comparing the concentration of transdermal nicotine absorption from the green tobacco will give us the data we need to push for safer working conditions. I'm the only one on the team fluent in Spanish. They can't get the field data without me."

"Baby, it's alright. I understand. Your work is important. It's the intersection of migrant justice and social justice. I'm so proud of what you do. Don't worry. I'll be fine. And you can see me in next week's shows."

"I love you, my Afro-Cuban reina."

I loved it when he called me his queen. Instead of a star on Calle Ocho's walk of fame maybe I'd get a crown with the title Social Justice Queen.

NOT YOUR LOLITA
By Merrilee Robson

A cautionary tale, for young—and old.
You can learn a lot from books.

My mom calls me Molly, but in this new school, I'm going to be Jade.

It's not a lie. I'm Mary Jade, Mary after my grandmother and Jade because when I was born my mother must have had some never-repeated impulse to do something different and give me a name that wasn't from a family member or a saint.

I don't know why she picked that name but I'm glad she did. I've always been Molly but Jade seems right for this school

The town is bigger than the place we lived before, and so is the school.

And the school has a real theater, with tiers of seats covered in deep red velvet and a stage with a proper curtain, also red velvet.

It isn't like my old school, where the stage was a platform at one end of the school gym, with the audience in folding chairs set out grudgingly by the janitor.

And, instead of old Mrs. Callas, who taught English and ran the drama class as grudgingly as the janitor put out chairs, this school has Mr. Pooley, who has actually been in plays and even had a few parts in movies.

Mr. Pooley of the bronze hair. Mr. Pooley, who somehow manages to keep a tan even in winter, so that his face is almost the same bronze as his hair. Mr. Pooley who wears loose cotton shirts and faded blue jeans, and moves like he might be a dancer. Mr. Pooley, with eyes the color of those jeans he wears.

Mr. Pooley, who'd given me a part in the new school play.

"I'm the only kid in my grade who has a part in the play," I tell my mom. "Mrs. Callas only ever cast seniors in speaking parts." Last year I'd been one of the speechless villagers on that stupid platform in the gym.

"That's lovely, dear," Mom says. She's in the bathroom, plucking her eyebrows. "I'm sure you'll be really good. Douglas and I will look forward to watching you."

I can see both our faces reflected in the bathroom mirror. We look alike. Same chestnut hair, same green eyes. Sometimes people think she's my older sister, not my mom.

But her face wears a dreamy little smile and mine has a huge frown on it. Partly because I don't want Douglas to come and watch me in the play. And partly because I want to ask why she doesn't go to a brow bar like everyone else.

But I know that will just lead to the talk about how we don't have any money.

I try to avoid those talks.

"You'll love it," I say. "It's really fancy. It'll be like going to a real theater, not a school play."

I can tell she's not really listening. She's brushing blush on her cheeks, carefully smoothing color on her lips, and then using that trick my grandmother had taught her when Mom was my age, spraying perfume into the air so the mist envelops her and the whole bathroom smells like Chanel. She's still smiling, thinking of Douglas.

She gasps when the apartment door buzzer sounds. "That'll be Douglas. And I'm not ready. Would you let him in, honey, and tell him I'll just be a sec."

I don't like Douglas.

And not, like my mom thinks, because I want her to get back with my father. I don't think I'd even recognize my father if I saw him, so I know that's not happening.

But I think she could do better than Douglas.

Sure, he's some big executive in the place she works. And he takes her to nice restaurants and brings her flowers.

But his fancy suits can't really hide that gut he has. The peppermints he uses can't cover up the alcohol on his breath.

And he always stands way too close to me, especially like now when Mom's not here.

"How's the new school?" he asks. The peppermint smell almost makes me gag.

"It's good. But I've got a lot of homework. I should get started. Mom will be ready in a minute."

I try to move past him to go to my room. But that's a problem. This town is bigger than the place we used to live. Mom says there are better jobs here. And the school is bigger and better, with a proper drama department, which I like.

But our new apartment is way smaller than our last home. And I don't have a real bedroom. Just an alcove off the living room with a screen in front of the bed.

So basically, there's no place to go to get away from him.

"I'll just go check on Mom," I say.

He grips my wrist. His hand is sweaty, although it's cold

outside and we sure don't keep our apartment very warm.

"I just thought we should get to know each other a bit, now that I'm spending so much time with your mother."

That seems okay. So I stop walking away.

But I do pull away from his sweaty hand. I fold both arms firmly over my chest.

"Your mother says you like reading."

That's totally true. My new school has a much better library than the old one, where I'd already read almost all of the books. And there is big public library in town. I already have a library card and there's a bunch of books sitting on my nightstand.

"I brought you a book. I thought you might like it."

He hands me a book with a pale cover. The title, *Lolita*, is printed in a dark script.

I can't resist glancing through a few pages. There's some sort of forward, which makes me think it might be boring but I skip over that and then there's a chapter that seems to be set in the south of France. It looks like it might be some sort of romance or an adventure story.

"Thanks," I say, grinning at him. Maybe he's not so bad after all.

He winks at me.

Then Mom's perfume proceeds her down the hall and he turns to greet her.

Mom looks beautiful in that green dress that brings out the color of her eyes and makes her hair shine like fire.

"I won't be late, Molly," Mom says.

"I'm Jade," I say, but they're already out the door.

I do have homework to do. But first I'm going to learn my part for the play.

I'm playing a housemaid. It's a small part but I've got some funny lines.

I want to learn them perfectly for tomorrow's rehearsal.

Mr. Pooley told me I have natural talent. And, with some training, I could be a star.

So I want to learn my lines to impress him.

Mr. Pooley.

Or Steven.

He said we could call him Steven.

Not in drama class, where we have to be more formal.

But, in the play rehearsals after school, then it's fine.

"We're a team," he told us. "The cast of a play is something special."

My new friend, Ethan, refuses to call him Steven. To his face, he just says "you" or sometimes "Mr. Pooley."

"Drooley Pooley" is what he calls him behind his back.

Ethan is my counterpart in the play. He plays the hired man on the farm next to where my character lives and we have quite a few scenes together.

"Do you call him that because all of the girls in school drool over him?" I ask.

"Or vice versa," Ethan says.

I don't know what he means. But I don't bother to ask him.

We need to get on with the rehearsal.

I like Ethan. He's even kind of cute, with dark hair that he tosses back out of his face and brown eyes with the longest lashes. In the play he likes my character, the maid, but she has a crush on the owner of the farm next door.

But it all works out in the end. My character finally falls in love with Ethan's. And the gentleman, a burly senior on the school football team, ends up with the lady in the house where I'm the maid.

"No class struggle in this play," Ethan growls, but he always seems happy to grab me in the final scene, when the two couples embrace.

The football player seems equally happy to embrace Chelsea, who plays the heroine. I don't blame him. She's in 12th grade and she's awfully pretty, with long blond hair, eyes the color of cinnamon, and a smile that reveals just one dimple in her flawless cheek.

She looks just exactly like the heroine in the play should look.

And that must be why Mr. Pooley cast her in the part.

Because she sure can't act.

She simpers prettily but she delivers her lines in a flat tone and her face is wooden, expressionless, except for the occasional flash of that one dimple.

And she can never remember her lines.

I've taken to whispering them to her whenever she suddenly freezes, a look of panic on her face. I soon know her part as well as my own.

I know Mr. Pooley is trying to help her. He asks her to stay late after the rehearsal so he can help her.

I think I'd give everything for that kind of attention from Mr. Pooley—Steven.

But I can see that Chelsea needs it more than me. Steven says I'm doing a great job, that I have real talent.

And then, suddenly, Chelsea is gone.

Her grades are bad and she needs to spend more time on her classwork, Mr. Pooley tells us. She's dropping out of the play.

And he gives me that blindingly white smile, and says, "What do you say to taking on that role, Jade? You seem to know all the lines."

I say yes, feeling like I'm floating above the stage.

But I feel bad for Chelsea. Maybe I'd been too obvious in feeding her the lines, showing off that I knew them all.

But I'd only been trying to help.

I see Chelsea in the hallways from time to time. She must still be having trouble in her classes because I never see her smiling. Her dimple is gone.

The football player grumbles a bit, saying I look too young. But Mr. Pooley says that, in costume and with my hair up, I'll look perfect.

Another girl is cast in my part as the maid. She's in the grade ahead of me and she thinks she should have gotten the lead. She's being a bit mean about it.

So I'm happy when Steven asks me to stay after rehearsal. I know I might need to do a bit of extra work to make sure I do a really good job. I mean, I've never had a speaking role before, let alone the lead.

I thought we were going to rehearse my lines but he asks me to go backstage. I follow him downstairs to where the costumes and props are stored. He lifts down the pink dress that Chelsea had looked so pretty in.

"Try this on," he says.

I start to walk over to the dressing rooms. That's something else the theatre has, real dressing rooms with makeup mirrors surrounded by lights, just like a theatre in one of those old movies my mom likes to watch.

"Oh, don't bother going in there," Steven says. "We're not prudish in the theatre world. In that off-Broadway play I was in, we all just dressed in one big room."

I don't want to seem prudish or babyish, but I still hesitate.

"I'll turn my back if it makes you feel more comfortable."

I don't feel comfortable but I slip into the dress anyway, turning my back on him too, as if it is better if neither of us can see the other.

The dress is so pretty, a pink brocade with a low neckline. Chelsea had looked like a princess in it. I spin around to look on the mirror.

I'm so much smaller than Chelsea. The bodice, which had barely contained her white breasts, hangs loose on me. The waist, which had so neatly defined her curvaceous figure, is equally loose.

"I'm sure it can be taken in," I say. The girl who works on all the costumes is a whiz with her sewing machine. I wonder why she hasn't stayed too, if we were going to look at costumes.

"Hmmm, maybe something else," Steven says. "Try this."

It's another pretty dress. How did this school manage to have such pretty costumes? In my old school we had to make do with cast-off clothes that people donated.

This dress is emerald green, a slim, short sheath with narrow straps and a slit up one side.

When I turn around I notice that, while Steven had turned his back while I undressed, I can see his eyes in the mirror.

Was it just a mistake? Or had he been watching me?

When he smiles at me, it doesn't matter.

"No one will complain that you don't look old enough now," he says.

He walks over so I can see us both in the mirror. He stands behind me and lifts up locks of my long hair.

"I think we'll put your hair up," he says. "What do you think?"

I can smell his cologne, a blend of spice and lime. He's only a little younger than Douglas, I think, but his body is so different. And his smell is so different from Douglas' peppermint.

He takes me by the shoulders and turns me around.

"Pretty Jade," he says. "Jade of the jade eyes."

And then he kisses me.

It is so different from the only other time I'd been kissed.

That had been last year, a boy in my old school who'd slobbered all over my chin.

This is so different. But I don't have the words to describe it.

His arms come around me and I reach up to touch that bronze hair.

And then I hear a noise, a clattering sound.

Steven pulls back. "That's the janitor. He'll want to lock up. See you tomorrow, pretty Jade.

I must have floated home.

And, even though I have lots of homework, I can't concentrate. I picture myself on stage and everyone in the audience applauding for me.

And then I picture Steven telling me he loves me.

I try to read. I can always lose myself in a book. I pick up that book Douglas gave me.

It starts off okay. There are some kids in love in the south of France. But then it gets weird, with some old guy with a funny name. I guess he isn't all that old. Maybe the same age as Steven. But he doesn't sound handsome at all.

I throw the book on my bed and start to do my homework after all.

I see Chelsea the next day.

I smile at her, expecting her to pass me by.

But she grabs my hand and pulls me into the girl's washroom.

"I hear you got the lead," she says.

"Yeah," I say, smiling at her in what I hope is a kindly way. "It's too bad you had to quit. I won't be as good as you, but I'll try my best."

"I thought that other girl had the lead."

"No, she's in my old part." I scuff my sneaker on the tile floor. "There's not as many lines to learn and I know the lines for the lead already."

She reaches over and shoves open the door of each stall, checking that they are empty.

"Has he told you that you have natural talent and that with the proper training you could be a star?"

My face tells her she's right.

"Look, Jade. Don't be as stupid as I was. Stay in the play if you want to. But don't be alone with him."

I'm not floating anymore.

"Did he… Did he kiss you too?" I can hear a tremble in my voice.

She glances at the door of the washroom. I hear voices in the hall but can't tell what they're saying.

"Yes, he kissed me."

There are tears in her cinnamon eyes. "He kissed me but…. I don't want to say. But don't go downstairs with him."

I can tell I am blushing.

"Just," she went on, "I…there's a space under the stage. They have some mattresses there. There's a trap door in the stage and the mattresses are to catch you if they have a scene that uses the trap door.

"Don't go there with him. I…I've never…. And I kept begging him to stop. I told him I didn't want to…. Just don't, okay, Jade?"

She rushes out of the bathroom.

I just stand there, stunned.

And then I start making a plan.

Ethan is willing to help.

He knows where the keys to the backstage area are kept. We unlock the area under the stage. It's creepy under there, filled with cobwebs. The janitor obviously doesn't clean there very often. That's good.

Ethan knows how to remove the supports from the trap door.

We shove the mattresses away from that area, leaving the bare concrete floor exposed.

We lock the door that leads to the area under the stage.

I race upstairs when I hear Mr. Pooley's footsteps on the stage.

"Oh, there you are, pretty Jade," he says. "Were you backstage? Let's go back there. I have something I want to show you."

"Oh, Mr. Pooley," I say. "Let's just stay up here. Can you help me with my lines a bit? I'm just not sure how I should say them."

"Steven, remember?" he says. His smile looks more wolfish than handsome now.

He reaches out to smooth my hair. "And I'm sure your lines are perfect. I said you had a natural talent, didn't I?"

He embraces me, kissing me, sticking his tongue in my mouth.

"You're so beautiful," he says, running his hand up under my sweatshirt and touching my breasts.

I remember what my mom taught me after she'd taken that self-defence class, and bring my knee up.

He doubles over and I jump away from him.

"You little bitch!" he yells. "You're always prancing around in those tight leggings and flashing those little apple-sized tits at me. What am I supposed to do? You know you want it as much as I do."

"It doesn't matter what I want," I say. "You're my teacher and I'm only fourteen."

I think his face pales a little at that.

"And my tits are covered by a sweatshirt," I say. "I don't know how I can flaunt them through that."

"Aw, come on, Jade."

He reaches out to grab me and I turn from him. Racing across the stage, I thank my mother for sending me to those ballet lessons, even when we couldn't afford them, as I leap over the trap door.

I can hear Mr. Pooley's heavy footsteps behind me, running across the stage. He might have taken dance lessons too but he doesn't know about the trap door.

I hear the thud as it drops open and another thud as he hits the cement floor.

There is silence for a moment.

Then I hear his voice.

"Jade," he sounds more worried than angry. "You have to help me. I think my leg is broken."

I walk over to the stage door where Ethan is waiting for me.

Maybe the janitor will find Mr. Pooley soon.

Then again, it's the start of a long weekend. He might be tempted to skip cleaning in here.

The door swings shut behind us.
I don't think he'll say anything when they find him.
And now I have to figure out what to do about Douglas.
I'd ended up reading more of that book.

A DEATH IN SHUBERT ALLEY
By Lee Sauer

*It seems an impossible crime. No one was seen
entering or leaving the area; there's no evidence to
follow up. Can the detectives crack the case? If only
time could tell.*

Saturday, April 20th, 2019. 2:10 a.m.

When I arrived on the scene, the uniforms had already corralled witnesses, cordoned off the area with crime scene tape, and done basic crowd control, moving the looky-loos (and reporters) out of sight of the body, although at 2 a.m., there weren't a huge number of voyeurs after a cheap thrill. As almost always (even in summer), a cold wind whipped down Shubert Alley, making it about 20 degrees colder than adjoining streets.

My partner, Detective James Martin, was ten blocks uptown, completing an assault investigation, and would follow as soon as he was free.

The body was lying on the ground in Shubert Alley beside a tipped-over electric wheelchair. You didn't need a physical examination to tell he'd been strangled.

If you're not familiar with Manhattan, Shubert Alley is a block-long pedestrian mall in the heart of the Theater District. It connects 44th and 45th Streets and runs parallel to Broadway and Eighth Avenue. Shubert Alley gets its name from the Shubert Theater whose entrance is at the intersection of the Alley and 44th Street. Frankly, it's not a high-crime area, and I can't recall so much as an armed robbery here, let alone a murder. Even at this hour, it was reasonably well lit from streetlamps and the illuminated posters for Broadway shows running its length.

I recognized the uniform managing the Crime Scene Log, so I walked over and asked him if we had an ID on the victim.

"No, Sergeant, none of the witnesses knew him."

The first thing you need to know is that the way we process a murder scene is *nothing* like you see on TV. For one thing, you'll never see any police official except a coroner touching a murder victim. Period. We can't go through his pockets to find his wallet. Most of the time, we identify the victim from someone at the scene who knows who he is, but if not, we have to wait for the coroner to arrive.

"Okay, I'm doing a walkthrough of the scene."

He handed me the log and I entered my name, rank, and purpose for entering. I walked over to the victim and took a closer look. From his neck, he'd obviously been strangled with a chain, since ligature marks of the links were evident. No murder weapon was in sight.

He seemed in his 50s or 60s and was casually, but neatly dressed. The wheelchair looked expensive and, while not new, looked well-maintained. If I'd had to guess, I'd have pegged him as reasonably well-to-do, definitely not homeless. I could see a cell phone in his shirt pocket.

I turned to Officer Sanchez, following behind me. "Okay, Luis. Tell me what you know."

"Okay, Sarge. The time of the incident was approximately 12:15 a.m. We have five witnesses, but none of them actually saw it happen. There were two couples, one coming down 44th and the other coming into the Alley from 45th. The vic entered the Alley from 45th, seen by our witnesses who were about midway through the block. They turned the corner into the Alley about three minutes or so later, saw the tipped-over chair at the other end of the Alley, and thought the vic had an accident. They ran down to offer assistance, saw his face and called 911. At this point the other couple turned into the Alley. Neither saw anyone else enter or leave Shubert Alley. It's possible the killer could have gotten away down 44th, but they don't remember seeing anyone."

"When did you get here?"

"I was in the first car and we got here at 12:22. My partner called for additional officers and for paramedics to pronounce the victim while I corralled the witnesses. I put a babysitter on each of the witnesses, mainly to keep them from talking to each other. And I took photos."

"You called in the evidence techs?"

"Right."

"Have you started the canvass yet?"

"No. I was waiting for a detective."

"Fine. Get a couple teams of officers working the buildings on the Alley and everything on the block on 44th and 45th. There are two or three restaurants and bars still open, and the closed businesses might have some employees still around, or maybe a janitor or a night watchman."

As I finished speaking to Luis, James showed up. I shared what I'd learned, and he did his own walkthrough.

He pulled me aside. "Did you notice the chain marks on the neck?"

"What about them?"

"They're really large. He must have been strangled with something the size of a motorcycle chain."

I took a closer look. "You're right. I wonder if the killer could have been on a motorcycle? That might explain how he was able to get away without anybody seeing him. Somebody on foot carrying a chain that large would have been pretty noticeable."

"Makes sense. And a big chain like that is something a biker might have."

This was an encouraging sign. A motorcycle meant a good chance that traffic cams might have captured a license plate.

"Right. Okay, let's get busy. Start the canvass. Wake people up. Make sure the uniforms ask if anyone saw or heard a motorcycle, and ID anybody who owns or drives one."

After a "Will do," James headed off.

I'd seen pretty much all there was to see, so I walked over to speak with the witnesses. The first one I came to was a woman in her 20s, presumably half of one of the couples Luis had described.

"Hello, I'm Sergeant David Richards. Thank you for waiting. I'm going to have this officer drive you down to Manhattan South where you'll be a lot more comfortable and we can take your statement. We appreciate your cooperation."

I quickly moved on to speak to the next witness, deliberately giving her no chance to protest. The witnesses were going to be waiting for hours before I'd be able to get back to start taking statements, and it was going to be easier to hang on to them there than out here on the street.

As I was repeating my spiel for the final time, I realized that there were five witnesses, but Luis had only told me about four. After I'd moved away from witness five, a man in his 60s, I turned to Luis and asked him about the man.

"Oh, sorry! His name is Juan Avila. He's the overnight custodian at the Shubert Theater. He was locking up when I arrived on the scene. We think he was the first person to see the victim. He said he was doing his usual closing-up stuff when he noticed the vic in his tipped-over chair. He thought he was just a drunk who'd passed out on the street and didn't pay any attention to him. He went back inside before the other witnesses arrived."

"I take it he didn't see anyone leaving the scene."

"Right."

Our conversation was interrupted by the arrival on the scene of the crime scene technicians. I quickly told Luis, "Surveillance videos are looking more and more important, since it doesn't look like our eyewitnesses saw anything. Get somebody working on finding and securing them."

I walked over to where the techs were getting started. As I was saying hello, I saw one of the officers doing traffic control on 44th Street having a confrontation with a van driver. I went over to see what was going on.

"Sergeant, this gentleman is under the impression he's going to drive his van through the crime scene."

"What seems to be the problem?"

The guy in the van, who'd been screaming at the uniform, calmed down a little. For some reason, a policeman in plain clothes will sometimes have that effect. Go figure.

"I gotta deliver my load to the Shubert. Otherwise, all them thirsty and hungry patrons is gonna stay thirsty and hungry all next week, and I won't get paid."

"Well, sir, I'm sorry to be the one to break this to you, but nobody's going to be driving through Shubert Alley for at least the next six or eight hours. This is a murder scene."

"I know that, but how can I…"

"Sorry, you can't. Not until we're done."

He drove off down the street muttering something I was just as glad not to be able to hear.

Watching him drive off, I felt a tap on my shoulder.

"Dave, how's it progressing? What do you need?"

It was my boss, Lieutenant Donald Wilson, commander of the Homicide Unit.

"Hi, LT. We have an unknown victim and no assailant sightings. Once the crime scene techs are finished, anything you could do to expedite the Coroner so we can get an ID would be a big help. The victim has a cell phone, so getting early attention to a search warrant for his cell data would be appreciated too."

"Okay, Dave, I'll take care of both of those. Let me know once you get the paperwork for the cell warrant done. Let's do a walkthrough."

By the time we'd finished, the evidence techs were packing up. The LT put in a call to the Coroner's office, then turned to me and said, "Dave, I'd like to have a brief private conversation."

I could tell this wasn't going to be a happy chat.

"I want to give you a heads up. This case is going to be very high-profile, because of the location and possibly because of the victim. Take a look. He's nicely and conservatively dressed. Those are expensive shoes. When we ID him, we're probably going to find he's either a tourist or someone else unlikely to be involved in street crime."

None of that was a surprise. Then he dropped the bad news. "I've already had two calls from the Mayor's office. I'm sure the only reason I haven't heard from the Mayor himself is that it's the middle of the night. I'll do my best to keep the official pressure on me and not you, but I doubt I'll be completely successful. You need to be prepared. For God's sake, get this one solved. And damn fast!"

Despite the LT's efforts, it was another three hours before the Coroner arrived. Once he was on the scene, James and I headed to Manhattan South to start witness interviews.

Saturday, April 20th, 2019. 5:45 a.m.

When James and I arrived at Manhattan South to interview our witnesses, they were, unsurprisingly, NOT happy. Cooperating witnesses always end up frustrated with us. They wait many, many hours to be interviewed. Because we can't compel them to wait, uniforms at the station frequently give the witnesses…let's just say unrealistic estimates about the ETA of the detectives, and otherwise coax them to remain at the station.

Too, we need to keep them isolated from other witnesses and from television and other media until they've been interviewed. As a result, they range from grumpy to being out-and-out angry with us.

By time we got to our last witness, Juan Avila, the late-night custodian at the Shubert, he was fed up to the point of open hostility. Understandable, but it made getting the information we needed harder. Our first four witnesses had been cranky, but willing enough. But they didn't really tell us anything we hadn't learned at the scene. Specifically, no one remembered hearing a motorcycle, but weren't sure they would have noticed one.

Expectations for anything better from Mr. Avila were low.

"I already told the first cop everything I know six hours ago."

"We know, but we need to hear it directly from you, for the record. You might have information you don't even know you have."

"Hah!"

"Okay, we'll try to be as quick as we can. Please tell us exactly what you saw."

"What the hell. Okay, I'm comin' out the front door to get everything shut down for the night so that things are set up for the deliveries we're gonna get about four a.m.…."

"Yeah, we met the delivery van. He was pretty unhappy that he wouldn't be able to get to your dock until we were done."

"I damn well bet he was unhappy. So anyway, I come out and I see this guy lying on the ground. His chair is tipped over, and he's just lying there. I'm thinking he's a wino who passed out and fell over. IN SHUBERT ALLEY! We don't tolerate that kind of riff-raff there. And we pretty much never get drunks. I was really pissed off to see him, so I just did what I had to do and got the hell out of there. I just thought he was drunk. I didn't know he was dead."

"When you came out to take in your trash cans and such, was there anyone else in the Alley or on 44th Street?"

"I didn't see nobody. There might have been somebody at the other end and I might not have noticed 'em, but there was nobody at my end."

"Did you hear anything when you came out?"

"Naw. I didn't hear nothing. Like what?"

"Oh, the sound of a car backfiring or a motorcycle, for example."

"No, I didn't hear nothing like that. But there coulda been a noise, and I just might not of noticed it. Are we done?"

James and I locked eyes and silently shared the conclusion that we weren't going to get anything useful from Avila, so I said, "Okay, Mr. Avila. Thank you very much for waiting all this time to talk with us. We really do appreciate it. We'll get an officer to drive you home or back to the theater, whichever you prefer."

This set the guy off on another round of complaining that he'd waited here ten hours to talk to us and for what? He was totally exaggerating. He hadn't been waiting here more than nine hours.

Sunday, April 21st, 2019. 9:00 a.m.

By Sunday morning, the murder had hit the papers, and they were going nuts. Not so much the *Times*, but the *News* and the *Post* were screaming bloody murder (no pun intended) for information and an arrest.

We'd heard from the Mayor's office, and I'd had a heart-to-heart conversation with the Mayor himself, who explained calmly and politely how it was in all our interests to get this case wrapped up quickly. *Very quickly.*

He wasn't telling me anything I didn't already know.

Back at the station, James greeted me glumly.

"We got the basic information from the victim's wallet. His name is Paul Cooper. He was staying at the Holiday Inn Express on 39th, and he was a tourist from California planning to go to the theater for the next ten days. Other than his interest in Broadway, there was no help in his hotel room. He's never been arrested. He's gainfully employed as a computer programmer. Other than a couple of parking tickets, no criminal record."

James and I started working the phones, reaching out to family and friends of Paul Cooper. Everyone we talked with was definite that he was a straight-up law-abiding citizen. He didn't smoke (anything). He drank only the occasional glass of wine with dinner. He paid his bills promptly. Nobody had any notion that someone might have had a grudge against him.

None of this was particularly surprising, but it was all so completely unhelpful that I was really starting to dislike this guy.

"Any word on the tox screen?" I asked James.

"The usual. A couple of days," he replied. "But I'll bet you ten to one it'll be clean."

"No bet," I snorted. "Okay, we assume that the killing wasn't related to Cooper's background. Any indications of robbery?"

"That looks like a dead end," James responded. "Wallet, watch, and one ring on his body. Credit cards were intact, and the wallet contained a little over $200 in cash."

"Likely not a robbery."

"And probably not a drug deal gone bad, both because of the victim and the location."

I sighed. "So, a great big pile of nothing. The search warrants will get us his cell records and his internet search history, but I'm not expecting anything useful there. Was there anything significant in the Coroner's report?"

"The preliminary autopsy report was mostly negatives. No defensive injuries. Nothing under the fingernails. The hyoid bone was broken, indicating strangulation, and his larynx was crushed. We already knew that from seeing the victim's neck. No useful fingerprint evidence from the victim's wheelchair (other than the victim's, of course)."

"Well, if somebody was strangling him from behind with a motorcycle chain and wasn't robbing him, you wouldn't really expect much in the way of fingerprints," I replied.

"There was one thing that was unexpected. The strangulation only involved the front of the throat, not the back or sides. With the wheelchair's headrest, I wouldn't have expected the back of the neck to be involved. But the sides are another matter."

"That is odd!" When someone is strangled with a cord (or a chain), what usually happens is that the perp gets behind the victim and loops his cord or chain around the victim's neck so that he can pull the cord in opposite directions. That means that the cord is tight against the neck all the way around, and the victim has no chance to get a hand under the cord and ease the pressure against his neck.

"Yes, it's strange. The perp was evidently behind the victim, put his chain over the top of the head and pulled straight back. Definitely unusual," said James.

"For one thing," he continued, "it would take a lot of strength to strangle someone that way. For another, the vic should have been able to get his hands under both sides of the chain and pull back against it. But, no defensive injuries on the victim's hands. If he'd been pulling against a heavy chain in a life-and-death struggle, I'd have expected his hands to be pretty well shredded, and they weren't. They were perfectly clean, not even bruised."

"I really hate it when the evidence in a crime doesn't make sense," I muttered as I plopped myself down at my desk.

James and I sat there for about an hour, trying to come up with a scenario that fit the facts, without success. At that point, I got another call from the Mayor's office. I just kept responding, "Yes, sir," every few seconds. James sat watching grimly.

"So what's up, Sarge?"

"There will be a press conference at 2 p.m. this afternoon where a reward and a hotline will be announced. Our presence was requested (meaning it's mandatory), and it's not considered necessary for us to make any statement. Meaning, the Mayor is going to do the talking and we should keep our yaps shut."

That was actually perfectly fine with me. I didn't think it would be helpful to share anything but the basic information about the name of the victim, the location of the crime, and the cause of death. The media wouldn't like that. They already had everything we were planning to give them except the victim's name, but sharing anything else could only hinder solving the murder.

Tuesday, April 23rd, 2019. 7:45 a.m.

Well, so much for the integrity of our investigation.

Sunday's press conference went as planned. James and I along with Lieutenant Wilson served as a backdrop while the Mayor spoke. He didn't give out anything beyond the victim's name, his home city, and the fact that he was an upstanding citizen who was here in New York as a tourist.

Naturally, the media wanted more, much more, but the Mayor got why we wanted to keep the rest of what we knew under wraps, and he stuck to the plan I'd proposed.

Unfortunately, some son of a bitch in the Mayor's Office or

here in the Homicide Unit leaked everything we'd gleaned from the autopsy and from the search of the victim's possessions. I'd love to pin this on the Mayor's office, but there were a couple of details that we hadn't mentioned to the Mayor or his people, so the leak almost certainly came from right under our noses.

And naturally, instead of being satisfied with all the additional facts that went beyond what we gave them in the press conference, it just made the vultures hungrier for more.

I suspect the smoke coming out of my ears when I walked into the office carrying the *News* tipped James off that I was not a happy camper.

"Well, the damn leaks have given our 'journalist' friends a hook for all their coverage. They're calling it, 'The Theatergoer Murders.'"

"What? Has there been another murder that nobody bothered to report to the police?"

"Not that I've heard, but they're already speculating about a serial killer. A muscular, tattooed biker with a giant chain strangling disabled innocents for the fun of it."

"Have you heard from City Hall about this?" James asked.

"Oh, yes indeed. They were on the phone to me at 5 a.m. Needless to say, the Mayor is livid. My protests that revealing this information was the last thing we wanted didn't seem to impress His Honor. As far as he was concerned, we must have leaked it to get attention."

"Right," James responded. "More media attention is *exactly* what we're after. However, the one upside of this, if you can call it an upside, is that the hotline is ringing off the hook. We've already have more than 250 tips from the ever-helpful public."

"And ninety-nine percent of them will turn out to be obvious garbage. But each and every one of them has to be checked out, leaving us precious little time to do any real investigating."

"Although, to be honest," I continued, "we really didn't have much of anything to investigate. Dead ends are pretty much all there is."

"I re-interviewed all our 'eyewitnesses.' All, except Juan Avila, who is refusing to talk with us. Do you want me to lean on him, maybe get a search warrant for his home?" James asked.

"Frankly, I don't think he'll have anything more to tell us than we already know, so let's give him a pass," I replied.

Thursday, April 25th, 2019. 11:25 a.m.

We got the tox screen today. As expected, it's completely

negative. I was still holding out some hope for the results of our search warrant (which James had spent the last hour pouring over).

James threw his pencil down on his desk in disgust. "There's not one helpful item here. The only phone calls were about buying theater tickets and making hotel reservations. He called home just after he checked into his hotel to confirm his safe arrival. His internet searches were all tourist and theater-related. Nothing juicy whatsoever."

"And nothing that could give us a hook on something to investigate," I responded. But we might just have one ace in the hole. We got the surveillance videos just after you started going through the phone and internet stuff, and I've got Joanne in tech services going through them right now."

And, of course, just as with every other development in this... let's just say "frustrating" case, all news was rotten news.

"This is not going to make you happy, I'm afraid," Joanne told us. "The exact location of the murder was in a dead spot between two different cameras. So, we saw the victim making the turn off 45th Street into Shubert Alley, wheeling in his electric wheelchair toward 44th, but he zipped off one of the cameras and never appeared on the next one."

"Damn, damn, and damn! We'd been holding out really high hope from that video," I said, starting to feel overwhelmed with the realization that nothing was going to fall our way in this case. "Please tell me there were some indications of our attacker walking or riding away from the scene."

Joanne seemed reluctant to continue. Not a good sign. "Well, even more unfortunately, because of a combination of malfunctions and dead spots, there were plenty of places where someone (who was either amazingly good at camera-spotting or was just damn lucky) could have gotten out of there without showing up on camera."

She paused, and I knew there was even more bad news coming. "Go on," I said.

"We did confirm that there was no motorcycle on 44th and Broadway, but just because he used a motorcycle chain doesn't necessarily mean he was riding a motorcycle that night." She hesitated again.

"And...?"

Joanne swallowed hard and plunged on. "Worst of all, we couldn't identify anyone on the cameras covering 44th at Broadway or 44th at Eighth Avenue who remotely could have been the perpetrator. In fact, not a single person exited from 44th Street during the critical time-period."

I tried not to be incredulous (or at least appear so), but there's no other word to describe how I was feeling. "You are telling me that our guy vanished into thin air."

"Well, he can't have, but he did. I can only tell you what is on the videos." She was starting to get defensive.

And, then James interjected, "Most likely, he had a way to get into one of the closed businesses on 44th Street after hours."

In any event, without a connection to the victim, catching him was looking less and less likely.

Monday, September 16th, 2019. 10:00 a.m.

We're at a dead end.

We investigated everyone who had after-hours access to every building on 44th Street. Every single person either had an alibi or obviously lacked the muscular ability to have strangled our victim in the way he'd been strangled.

We investigated the pants off every single useless tip that came in on the hotline. Nada. Absolutely nothing.

Unless somebody called in a new lead, or something completely unexpected dropped in our lap (which pretty much only happens on TV), we had nowhere to go.

The case would stay officially open. Unsolved murders always do, but this one was as cold as they come.

The only good news was that after about a week, the media lost interest, and stories about "The Theatergoer Murders" were only used for wrapping proverbial fish.

There haven't been any subsequent crimes with the same MO. I deliberately don't go anywhere near Shubert Alley. In fact, neither James nor I have been within two blocks of it since the night of the murder.

Our failure is just too painful for any reminders.

I know it shouldn't bother us as much as it does. Even in homicide, you get unsolved cases, and not all that infrequently. But for some reason, this one hurt more. We should have solved this one.

Four Months Earlier. Saturday, April 20th, 2019. 12:10 a.m.

"This is my favorite spot in the world," Paul Cooper thought to himself as he sped down 45th Street in his electric wheelchair. "I'm in New York City, the heart of the Theater District. Ten days of fabulous theater ahead. Musicals, plays, and one oddball Off-Broadway revue. This is as good as it gets!"

His plane had been hours late, he'd missed the show he'd expected to see that evening, and he hadn't yet had dinner, but he was on an emotional high.

Turning left off of 45th Street into a deserted Shubert Alley (and hit by the frigid winds omnipresent here), he started to think about where he might get a very late supper. He whizzed past the Booth Theater toward the Shubert, and looked to his right, where the walls were lined with large, illuminated posters of every Broadway show currently running. "*To Kill a Mockingbird, All My Sons, Beetlejuice, Network, Come from Away, Kiss Me Kate, Tootsie, Dear Evan Hansen,*" he ticked off each of the brightly illuminated posters as he passed.

His eyes on the posters and not his path ahead, he didn't notice the large chain stretching across the width of the Alley near the entrance of the Shubert Theater until he struck it at full speed.

The impact knocked his hand off the joystick controlling his chair, but his forearm still pressed it down, continuing to propel him forward. Even as his hand flailed trying to find the control, his forearm continued to force his chair forward, pressing his throat against the large chain. Within a few seconds his larynx had been crushed. As his body struggled against the unbearable pressure of the chain on his neck, his legs began to kick, and his wheelchair tipped over.

Paul briefly hung suspended on the chain, flailing, until he dropped to the pavement.

At that moment, Juan Avila, night custodian at the Shubert Theater emerged from the front entrance to finish his final tasks before going home for the night.

As he spotted Paul Cooper lying there, he muttered, "A goddamn drunk. In Shubert Alley." With one last thing to do before locking up, he removed the chain to let the 4 a.m. delivery van pull directly up to the Shubert's loading dock.

Carrying the heavy chain, he headed back into the theater muttering, "Goddam winos. I shoulda given that lousy drunk a good swift kick!"

On the pavement, lying next to his wheelchair, Paul Cooper died, murdered in and by Shubert Alley.

DANCE ON FIRE
By Shawn Reilly Simmons

An Illinois couple visiting a Mexican resort for the first time find themselves involved in more than just the usual sun-and-fun activities.

"I specifically asked for an ocean view when I booked the villa. You must understand my husband and I didn't fly all the way to the Riviera Maya to gaze at the rear end of a dining hall." Patricia Waller smiled sweetly at the young woman behind the registration desk as she tapped on her keyboard, a faint worry line appearing between her perfectly contoured eyebrows. The porter leaned against the brass luggage cart, resting his head on his forearm, the white collar of his shirt wilting with perspiration. He'd told the Wallers he could meet them with their luggage once they were reassigned a suite, but Patricia insisted their things stay with them until the troublesome matter could be sorted out.

"I'm so sorry, ma'am," the registration clerk said. "This was our error. Just give me one moment." She picked up the phone and spoke softly into the receiver.

"The suite was very nice, Patty," her husband Bill said from behind her. He gave the porter an apologetic glance and twisted his floppy sun hat in his hands. Bill had already apologized to the man half a dozen times as they wound their way back to the main lobby through the topiary gardens of the sprawling beach resort. The young man had nodded and shrugged, but hadn't complained. Fantasy Beach Resorts advertised a perfect customer experience above all else.

"The suite was very nice, Wally," Patricia said. "But not what we asked for."

Bill sighed. He knew better than to press his wife on these kinds of things. Especially when she called him Wally, which after twenty-four years of marriage he knew was code for both "I've got this" and "It's settled then."

The desk clerk slipped an envelope with the keys to a new suite across the wide marble desk. "So sorry for the inconvenience. Eric will show you to the correct lodgings now."

"Nothing to worry about, dear," Patricia said with a gracious smile. "And thank you for making a second trip with us, Eric."

***

"Look at all of these activities," Patricia said, leafing through the brochures on the desk in their suite. "They have live shows every night, and all these classes I can sign up for."

Bill leaned back inside the sliding glass door from the balcony and called her over, a glass of champagne in each hand. "Would you look at that?" he said after she'd joined him on the spacious veranda. "I've never seen an ocean so blue."

"It's beautiful," Patricia said with a sigh. She looked down and scraped a dried palm frond off the edge of the balcony with her white sneaker. "We finally made it to Mexico."

"The dream trip we've been planning forever. Hey, are you sure you don't want to see Chichén Itzá with me tomorrow?" Bill had a familiar hopeful lilt to his voice.

"No, I'm going to stick around the resort," Patricia said. "You know I don't go in for all those excursions."

"I know. I just thought since it's our first time here, and it's one of the best things to do while visiting the Yucatan—"

"As voted on by the internet," his wife reminded him.

Bill squeezed her shoulders and tipped his glass, draining the last of the champagne. "When should we change your name to Patty Stickler?"

Patricia leaned into her husband and tapped him playfully on the chest. "Look, I want you to go and see the ruins. Have a grand old time doing it, too. I'm going to do the morning yoga on the beach and maybe sign up for the pottery class in the afternoon. Or maybe I'll just read my book by the pool all day. That sounds like a dream come true. I have plenty to keep me occupied, Wally."

Bill circled his wife's waist with his arm and pulled her to him. "That's settled then. I love you."

"Of course you do," Patricia said and gave him a peck on the cheek. "Now, which restaurant do you want to try first? I can't believe everything is included, and there are ten to choose from! We're going to put on twenty pounds this week."

***

Bill and Patricia selected a pair of stools at the end of the hibachi station. A chef in a tall toque and white coat was clanging two spatulas on the flat top, scraping large piles of chopped vegetables across the scorching hot metal. Patricia clapped in delight when he balanced an egg on the spatula and flipped it in the air, catching it with the top of his toque.

"Impressive," Bill said after a swig of his beer.

"Welcome to Fantasy Resort Hibachi, where we have a dinner

and a show every night. First it is your dinner. Will you have beef, chicken, or shrimp this evening?" the chef asked.

"We'll take one of each," Patricia said. "Might as well, since it's all included, right?"

"Any allergies?" the chef asked with a smile.

"Not a one," Patricia said.

A young woman accompanied by an older man wandered into the restaurant and took a seat a couple of stools down from the Wallers. The woman crossed her long legs and clasped her hands tightly in her lap as the man glanced around the room at the diners sitting at the tables that lined the walls.

"Cocktail?" the server asked as they got settled. The woman shook her head, her brown bangs sweeping forward to hide her eyes. The man ordered a soda, and the woman a glass of water.

"You should ask for bottled water," Patricia called to them after the server stepped toward the bar. "It's safer."

The woman gave Patricia an alarmed smile, then the couple leaned their heads together and began talking quietly.

"The show tonight looks exciting," Bill said. The champagne and beer and the heat from the hibachi had reddened his cheeks. "The Fire and Ice Show. Sounds intriguing."

"It will be intriguing to see how they manage to keep ice from melting in this hot weather," Patricia said, then took a sip of her wine. "It's downright boiling outside."

***

The main plaza of the resort had been transformed into an outdoor stage, with two dozen rows of folding white chairs facing a concrete band shell. Most of the seats were already taken, but Patricia spotted two empty chairs close to the front. The Wallers inched their way to them with Bill apologizing to each person they walked in front of.

Just as they sat down, a ball of fire shot into the air over the stage, illuminating the faces of the crowd. Mouths fell open as three female dancers emerged from the wings, all with flames shooting up from elaborate headpieces made to look like ancient Inca crowns. A light show sputtered images and flashes onto the band shell behind the dancers as they moved through a choreographed set, then settled into three places at the edge of the stage.

Three male dancers emerged from the wings, all dressed in icy blue costumes, each claiming a fire goddess to woo.

"My word," Bill shouted over the loud music. "Aren't they something?"

"Nothing like our community theater back home, is it? I'd love to see Faye Crumb pull off a fire-on-the-head dance."

"I wonder how that fire keeps alight. Do you see any cords or—" Bill began, but was cut off by a scream. Several people in front of the Wallers stood up from their chairs and pointed at the stage. Bill shot up too, his expression turning from wonder to horror. "Oh, Patty, don't look."

Patricia peered between the two people in front of her, and saw one of the goddesses' heads was engulfed in flames. She was writhing on the ground as the other performers attempted to put the fire out.

"Bill!" Patricia shouted, but he was already gone, pushing through the folding chairs to get to the stage.

***

The next morning the Wallers woke to find a note had been slid under their door.

"It's an apology from the resort about the incident last night," Bill said, walking back to the bedroom where Patricia was having her coffee.

"I feel so bad for the poor girl," Patricia said. "It was very brave of you to rush up there to help."

Bill shrugged. "It's what anyone would do."

"Well, I don't know about that, but your training at the firehouse came in handy, didn't it?"

"I'm just a volunteer fireman," Bill said. "Are you almost finished with your coffee? I'd like to get some breakfast before getting on the bus."

Patricia and Bill went to the Buffet Hall to get a quick breakfast, and it seemed like most of the resort's visitors had the same idea. The Wallers filled their plates with eggs, bacon, and fresh fruit and Patricia found a table for them in front of one of the large windows overlooking the main pool.

"Oh look," Patricia said, waving at someone behind Bill's back. The couple who sat near them at dinner the night before were wandering through the dining room, looking for somewhere to sit. "Won't you join us?"

The couple conferred for several seconds longer than Patricia thought was necessary, and then sat down at the Wallers' table.

"Thanks," the woman said quietly.

"Think nothing of it," Patricia said. "We're the Wallers from Peoria. I'm Patty and this is my husband, Bill."

"Nice to meet you," the man said and shoved a forkful of eggs in his mouth.

Patricia smiled at the woman and took a sip of her coffee. "And where are you all from?" Bill nudged his wife's foot under the table, a signal she knew meant "don't be too nosy with people we've just met."

"Washington," the woman said.

"District or state?" Bill asked.

"State," the man said, not looking up from his plate. Awkward silence fell over the table as the two couples ate.

"Can I get you any coffee?" A waitress had appeared next to the table.

"Two coffees," the man next to Patricia said between bites of bacon.

"Actually, I'd like tea, thanks," the woman said. "Only one cup of coffee for me a day or I get the jitters." The man sighed and finished his bacon.

"We'll have two more, dear," Patricia said. "And do you have any of the green packets of sweetener? Bill doesn't take sugar." The waitress nodded and slipped away.

***

"Come back to me in one piece," Patricia said, giving Bill a kiss just before he got on the excursion bus. His camera dangled from a strap around his neck and he'd painted his nose white with sunscreen.

"You can't get rid of me that easy," Bill said.

Patricia watched him choose a seat and waited until the bus pulled away, her lips twisting into a half-frown when she saw who got up and took the seat next to her husband just as the bus got moving. The mysterious woman from Washington, who never fully introduced herself at breakfast.

***

Patricia went through the motions during the beach yoga class, but her mind struggled to find calmness. Thoughts of the woman on the bus talking to Bill the whole way to Chichén Itzá and back kept distracting her. She was young, much younger than Patricia, and tall and slender, not compact and athletic like Patricia was. During the final resting Corpse Pose when she was supposed to be ridding her mind of all negative thoughts and setting a good intention for the day, all she could think about was Faye Crumb, the aspiring community theater actress and their next door neighbor back home, and the time she found Faye and Bill at her kitchen table drinking tea and talking about roses.

Faye had never been interested in roses before, only acting, and Patricia was convinced her new fascination with flowers was a ruse to spend more time with her husband. Bill was president of their neighborhood garden club and loved nothing more than helping people care for their plants, those fickle flowers in particular. Bill told Patricia she was being silly, that he had absolutely no interest in anyone else, no matter how much more they enjoyed gardening than she did.

But Patricia knew that Bill had only one flaw...he had no idea how utterly attractive he was.

***

The man from Washington was sitting by the pool, wearing a wide-brimmed straw hat and reading a book. His long arms and legs were deeply tanned and his t-shirt was ringed with sweat. He gripped his paperback tighter as Patricia approached his lounge chair.

"I've never read that author," Patricia said, her brightly-colored caftan shifting in the breeze around her legs. "I'm not much for political thrillers. I prefer Dorothy L. Sayers or Agatha Christie myself. I've read all of them more than once."

The man smiled at her then focused back on his book.

Patricia shrugged and made her way to the thatched-roof hut next to the pool to get a towel and order a smoothie.

"Oh, are you okay?" Patricia asked when she saw the young woman behind the counter. Her eyes were wet and she swiped her cheek with the back of her hand to catch a falling tear. The nameplate on her uniform shirt read CYNTHIA.

"Sorry, ma'am," she said. "What kind of smoothie would you like?"

"Never mind about the drink," Patricia said. "Can I help you with anything?"

Cynthia smiled and shook her head. "I'm just...my friend. She's in the hospital. But I shouldn't burden you with bad news. This is your fantasy vacation, of course."

"Your friend, is she the performer from last night?" Patricia asked. She leaned on the counter and lowered her voice.

The woman nodded and fresh tears threatened to spill.

"I am so sorry, it was truly awful," Patricia said. "And I'm sorry for what you must be going through. You look sick from worry."

"Thank you," Cynthia said. "Only it's not just her. The girl before her, Ruthie, she died. My worry now is the show is cursed." She placed a blender jar on top of base and tossed some strawberries and kiwi in, even though Patricia hadn't ordered yet. "When the other girl...drowned, well she was gone from the show, of course, and there was a spot open, so they finally gave Mira a chance."

"Oh dear," Patricia said. "Ruthie drowned?"

Cynthia nodded. "Two weeks ago. Something must have

happened because she was the water aerobics instructor here, too. She was always in the water, out in the ocean swimming. Her boyfriend found her out by the rocks." Cynthia looked behind her at the sea. "Ruthie's parents don't think she really drowned. She'd been acting funny for a week before it happened, like something was upsetting her."

Patrica thought about the young woman's parents and said a silent prayer to keep her own child safe from harmful forces.

"The worst part for Mira is last night was her first time on the stage. She's been auditioning and practicing, wanting to join the performance team. They get paid extra, on top of the maid and restaurant duties, you know?"

"I had no idea it was her debut performance. They were all excellent, all the way up to…"

The blender drowned out her last few words and a shadow fell across the counter next to Patricia. She recognized the big straw hat.

"Ready for a refill, Mr. Smith?"

He held up his glass and nodded.

"Fresh lemonade, coming up."

***

"I'm so sure that's his name," Patricia sniffed, snuggling next to Bill in bed that evening. "Mr. Smith, my foot. Mr. Smith from Washington, no less."

"A lot of people have that name, Patty," Bill said, stiffling a yawn. Patricia had rubbed aloe on the tops of his feet and his knees before they settled under the cool sheets.

"He hasn't turned a page in that book all day, just sits there and ogles the guests."

"And how would you know that?" Bill asked with a hum.

Patricia tapped him lightly on the chest. "So what did you and Mrs. Smith talk about on your excursion?"

"How do you know she's his missus?"

"She's got a wedding band on," Patricia said, considering. "He doesn't, though. And what kind of husband doesn't know his wife only wants one cup of coffee in the morning?"

"Lots of men don't wear wedding rings," Bill said. "And not everyone is as attentive to others as you are, Patty. Maybe he's her uncle and they're on a family vacation. She is quite a lot younger than him."

"Who goes to a romantic all-inclusive resort like this with their uncle?"

"I'm sure at some point in the history of the world, a niece and uncle took a trip together."

"You're just trying to avoid my question. What did you and Mrs. Smith talk about on the bus?"

Bill sighed and rubbed his eyes with his thumb and forefinger. "She asked me about the accident, about the girl on fire."

"Oh," Patricia said.

"She wanted to know if the girl had said anything, who had helped her, just generally what I witnessed after I got on the stage."

"That seems strange, doesn't it? Some young woman digging for details about a terrible accident?"

Bill shrugged and rolled toward her, settling his arm over her waist and tugging her closer to him, his signal that sleep was close at hand. "She's a lookie-loo," he said, his words softening at the edges. "People who hang around the perimeter of a tragedy... gazing with morbid fascination at the misfortune of others." Bill's breaths deepened and he drifted away. Patricia stared at the wall in the dark and said a prayer for Mira, the young burn victim in the hospital.

***

The next afternoon Patricia eyed Mr. Smith from behind her sunglasses, lifting up her book to cover her face whenever he looked her way.

"Another margarita, Mrs. Waller?" Cynthia had come out from behind the bar and was taking orders from the guests sunbathing at the pool.

"Yes, please, Cynthia. Also, have you heard anything more about Mira's condition?"

"Oh it's some good news, ma'am." Cynthia's eyes brightened. "She's doing much better. They don't think the burns caused much permanent damage. Something about the heavy stage makeup protecting her face."

"Well, that is an exciting update," Patricia said. "I'll drink to that. But first I'm just going to head up to my room for one minute to freshen up and I'll be right back down."

***

Patricia climbed the steps to the third floor and stopped short on the landing. Eric, the luggage porter, was backing out of their room, pulling the door closed quietly behind him.

"Excuse me," Patricia said. "What are you doing?"

Eric's shoulders tensed and he turned around, a wide smile on his face. He slipped a small tablet into his jacket pocket and pulled a master key from his front shirt pocket. He held it up for her to see.

"Just cleaning some debris from your veranda," he said. "To keep it nice for you."

"I didn't request anyone come—" Patricia began.

"A courtesy for our guests. Lots of birds and trees dropping things. It can get unpleasant." Eric trotted down the stairs after a quick nod and was gone.

Patricia let herself into the suite and looked around. The bed was still a tumble of sheets and the shower and sink were wet from their morning rituals, so the maid hadn't been in to tidy the suite yet. The twenty-dollar bill Patricia had left that morning as a tip for her was still under the water glass next to the bed. Patricia shrugged and stepped out onto the veranda where she saw two palm fronds near the edge, the same ones she'd seen that morning as she had her first cup of coffee and watched the sunrise with Bill. She looked back over her shoulder at the closed door of the suite and wondered what the porter had really been doing in their room.

***

"How was snorkeling?" Patricia asked, sipping on her second margarita by the pool. Bill had lumbered up, his silver hair damp from his latest excursion.

"Glorious," Bill said. "I wish you had been there to see all the fish!"

"You know I'd get too claustrophobic and have a panic attack," Patricia said. "Anyway, you had company." She eyed Mrs. Smith as she settled onto the lounge chair next to her traveling companion.

"She's a sweet kid," Bill said. "You'd like Sarah if you got to know her a little. She reminds me of Peter. You know, a real go-getter."

Patricia smiled at the name of their son, picturing him in his dorm room at the university, preparing for his final year of college. "So, is Sarah Mr. Smith's niece or what?"

"How do you ask something like that?" Bill said with a yawn. He eased himself back onto the lounge chair. "She doesn't talk about him at all, and it would be rude to pry. She mostly wanted to talk about you and me, where we're from and the places we've traveled."

Patricia waved to Cynthia behind the bar, pointed at her drink and motioned toward Bill. Cynthia nodded and fired up the blender. "Well, what did you tell her?"

A snuffling snore from Bill was her only reply. Patricia sighed and picked up her book.

***

"Bill," Patricia called to her husband, who was in the shower. They were getting ready to head down to dinner.

"Yeah?" Bill shouted, his voice muffled by the water.

Patricia stepped to the doorway of the open-air bath suite. Bill was obscured behind a wet wall of glass as he washed the sea salt from his hair. "Did you rearrange the passports in the safe?"

"Safe?" Bill shouted. "What safe?"

"The room safe, dear."

"No, I haven't been in the safe," Bill said. He turned off the water and stood dripping for a few seconds, shaking the water from his hair.

"I could have sworn…" Patricia began. "No, I know I had mine on top. It's got the lighter cover. Bill, I think someone has been in our safe."

Bill wrapped a towel around his waist and looked at his wife. "What's missing?"

"That's what's confusing," Patricia said. "Nothing is missing."

***

The next morning Bill and Sarah were off to swim with the dolphins while Patricia signed up for a hat-weaving class. Mr. Smith had decided to shake up his routine by moving down a few chairs at the pool. Patricia waved to him as she walked past, her caftan billowing behind her in the breeze.

"Cynthia, dear," Patricia said. "Could you make me an iced coffee, please?"

"Of course, coming right up."

Patricia watched her stir together coffee and almond milk and pour it over a large cup of ice. "Is there any news this morning? About Mira?"

"Yes, she is quite well, ma'am," Cynthia said. "She should be back to work here in the next week or two. It's a miracle."

"It sure is," Patricia said. "I'm so glad to hear it. I was wondering, you mentioned the girl who passed away had a boyfriend?"

"Oh yes, he works here too," Cynthia said as she placed the lid on the coffee cup.

"Is he one of the performers?"

"No, registrations," Cynthia said. Her eyes darkened slightly as Mr. Smith approached.

"That is good news about Mira," he said in a gravelly voice. "Best I've heard in a while."

"Oh, do you know the young lady?" Patricia asked. The hairs on her arm stood up as he sidled closer to her.

"Only by reputation," Mr. Smith said with a smile. He eyed her flowing dress then lifted his gaze to Cynthia. "Lemonade, please."

"Yes, sir," Cynthia said, forcing a smile.

***

Patricia wore her new hat as she sat on the balcony, looking down at the pool. Most of the lounge chairs were occupied, except for Mr. Smith's. He'd disappeared at some point during her class, and hadn't returned.

The dolphin swimming group entered the pool area from the beach, and Patricia spotted Bill and Sarah walking together, Sarah laughing at something Bill had said. A pin pricked the center of her chest as she watched them arrive at the pool, then go their separate ways. Bill shielded his eyes and searched the lounge chairs for his wife. Patricia watched his expression change from happy to concerned, and Patricia followed his gaze. Sarah and Mr. Smith were on the far side of the pool, and appeared to be having words with each other, however quietly.

Bill took a few steps toward them, then seemed to think better of it, and headed to the stairwell. Patricia watched the Smiths, his hand gripping her upper arm. Sarah untangled from him and hurried up the steps to the poolside rooms.

As the door to the suite opened, Patricia fixed her face into a smile and waved to Bill.

"How was it today?" she asked as he settled into the opposite chair.

"Good," Bill said.

"And Sarah?"

Bill's eyes darted to the side briefly, then relaxed into his smile. "She's a good kid. Very curious. She talks to everyone on the trips."

"But mostly to you, it appears," Patricia said.

"I don't know. I don't think so."

"What is she doing here?"

"I think she's on vacation," Bill said. He stepped lightly through the conversation, aware that hidden land mines were always a danger in the well-trodden landscape of a marriage.

"A vacation from what, dear?" Patricia said, a slight edge to her words.

"I don't know...I get a feeling though, the way she asks all those questions. I think she might be some kind of cop."

Patricia surprised herself by laughing out loud, which made Bill laugh in return.

"Drink?" Bill asked, standing up.

"Of course," Patricia said with a residual giggle. The laughter had broken through the dam of tension between them.

Bill went inside to pour them each a glass of wine. Sarah came down the stairs, dressed in slacks and a dress shirt and headed toward the main building of the resort.

Patricia watched her go until she couldn't see her anymore. "Sometimes you say the funniest things, Wally. One of the reasons I love you so."

***

The Wallers decided to spend the next day together at the resort. They took a private tour in a glass-bottomed boat, and reserved a table for two at the French restaurant for lunch. Their bellies full of Coq au Vin and a pricey bottle of Sancerre, the couple headed back to their suite to change into bathing suits for an afternoon lounging by the pool.

"I was just cleaning off the veranda, to make it nice for you. It can get unpleasant." Patricia heard the familiar words as she and Bill reached the top floor and a bitter taste tinged the back of her tongue.

The couple in the neighboring suite were standing in the hall talking to Eric. When he heard the Wallers approaching from behind, he turned, his eyes meeting Patricia's.

A bell sounded and the elevator doors slid open and the maid pushed her cart onto the landing. Patricia glanced at the broom attached to the front of the cart and then at Eric's empty hands.

"Housekeeping?" the maid said.

Eric sprung at the Wallers, shoving them out of the way. A small tablet clattered to the ground as he fled down the stairs.

"Stop!" Patricia shouted as she kicked off her shoes and ran after him.

Eric made it to the ground floor and ran out toward the pool as Patricia rounded the final flight of stairs.

"Stop him!" she panted. When she reached the pool she saw Eric sprinting past the bar, the tails of his jacket flying out behind him.

Mr. Smith stepped out from the side of the bar and put his foot out, tripping Eric and pushing him into the pool. Patricia pulled up short and put her hands on her knees as Eric splashed in the water, his jacket billowing up around his arms. The crowd around the pool stood up to watch as Mr. Smith yanked Eric up by the jacket and produced a pair of handcuffs from his baggy shorts.

"You're under arrest for Ruthie's murder," Mr. Smith said. "And the FBI wants to have a word with you about some other things too."

***

"So, they were cops after all," Bill said over dinner that night. They opted for the Italian spot that evening and were sharing a big bowl of spaghetti.

"Mr. Smith is undercover resort security," Patricia corrected him. "And your Sarah is with the FBI."

"Identity theft is big business, I guess," Bill said. "And Ruthie found out that Eric was scamming the guests so he..."

"Awful, I know," Patricia said. "Sarah rushed off to the hospital earlier to see Mira and ask her about the notes she'd found in the makeup table backstage. She laid out everything Eric was doing, and the network he was selling the information to."

"So he tried to kill her, too?" Bill said, shaking his head. "What gets into people?"

"Greed," Patricia said. "That tablet he dropped had the names, passport numbers, and credit card information of hundreds of Fantasy Resort guests," Patricia said. "Eric was letting himself into the suites and copying the information from the safes. Nothing was ever missing, so no one would suspect...and the thefts took place weeks or months later."

"No one would suspect except my very attentive and lovely wife," Bill said.

The waitress appeared at their table with a bottle of champagne. "From the manager," she said, popping the cork. "This bottle is not part of the all-inclusive. But for you..."

"How lovely," Patricia said. After the waitress poured their glasses and slipped away she added, "Fantasy Resorts has also agreed to give us four weeks stay at any one of their resorts. You know, because we helped uncover the fraud."

"Oh, I don't know if I should be away from my roses for that long," Bill said.

"I'm sure you can get Faye to watch over them for you while we're gone," Patricia said after a sip of bubbly. "And I think four weeks is enough time to teach me to be brave enough for snorkeling."

Bill laughed and touched her glass with his. "There is no one braver than you."

MISSED CUE
By Lynn Slaughter

The world of ballet is a small one. A missed cue ends
up in tragedy, exposing complicated relationships.

Victor Pesetsky, Ballet Études' artistic director, was visibly on edge during the final dress rehearsal for *Romeo and Juliet.* Through his head set, he growled an endless stream of corrections to Matt Gates, his lighting designer.

Gates chalked up Victor's ill temper to pre-opening night nerves. So far, the rehearsal, despite Victor's complaints about the lighting, had gone amazingly well. The chemistry between the leads, Lydia Miseau and Alexander Varese, was electric. And Gates marveled at how Lydia, despite being 39, an age considered ancient for ballerinas, so convincingly imbued the role of fourteen-year-old Juliet. In all the years he'd worked with the company, he'd never seen her dance with such dramatic intensity as she had in Act III after swallowing a sleeping potion to fake her death. Looking increasingly agonized, she dramatically stumbled about the stage until her collapse into slumber.

And then Gates saw Lydia Miseau do something she'd never done before in her twenty-one years as a professional dancer. She missed a cue, the musical cue to awaken. Darlene, the stage manager, frantically whispered to her to get up.

"Cut!" shouted Victor as he charged down the aisle. "God damn it, Lydia, what the hell?"

Darlene ran to the ballerina sprawled on the funeral bed. She gently shook her, but she didn't stir. Darlene bent down, feeling for a heartbeat.

Nothing.

"Call 911," she screamed.

***

By the time Lieutenant Avery O'Connor arrived, the stage area surrounding the funeral bed had been roped off, and Chet Roberts, the medical examiner, had begun his preliminary investigation. Dancers, their faces streaked with black ribbons of mascara, huddled in the wings. They reeked of sweat and hairspray.

O'Connor gestured to two patrol officers. "Clear the dressing rooms and ask everyone to come out and take a seat in the audience. And seal off the deceased's dressing room."

The officers nodded, and O'Connor headed over to examine the body and talk to Chet.

"Anything?" she asked.

"No sign of a wound. Looks like heart failure. We'll know more when we get her on the table."

O'Connor nodded and knelt down to examine the body. Lydia Miseau was beautiful—delicate nose, high cheek bones, and coltish shapely legs. Her lean muscular frame reflected a lifetime devoted to honing her physical instrument. She didn't look like anyone who was ready to die.

The lieutenant moved downstage toward the audience of dancers and theater personnel. The work lights burned brightly, and she could feel rivulets of sweat working their way down her spine.

A distraught-looking man wearing a fedora clambered up the steps onto the stage. "I'm Victor Pesetsky, artistic director. Lydia is my wife. She was in perfect health. I don't understand."

"I'm so sorry for your loss," O'Connor said. "You have my word that we'll conduct a thorough investigation."

"Thank you, but that won't bring her back. She is my muse, my soul mate." Pesetsky's face crumpled, and tears spilled down his lined face.

Must have been a May-December romance, O'Connor thought. Pesetsky was tall and gaunt with piercing black eyes, a long, thin nose, and a shock of gray hair peeking out from his fedora. Her mother would have called him "distinguished-looking." Distinguished or not, he was clearly much older than his late wife.

A wiry guy wearing jeans and a black turtleneck approached O'Connor. "Matt Gates, lighting designer," he said as he extended his hand. "I am a close friend of Lydia's."

"I'll need to talk with both of you," O'Connor said, motioning to Pesetsky and Gates. "But first, I want to say a few words to everyone."

Gates turned to Pesetsky. "I'm so horribly sorry, Victor." He reached for his arm, and the newly widowed director swatted him away as though he were a pesky fly.

Something going on with those two? O'Connor wondered. Or was Pesetsky just a prickly guy? Of course, his wife had just unexpectedly died. She'd known plenty of survivors whose grief took the form of angry irritation at anyone who tried to come close. Sure enough, rather than take a seat in the audience with Gates and the others, Pesetsky held himself apart, pacing up and down the side aisle.

O'Connor walked over to the woman wearing a headset. "You are?"

"Darlene Bott, stage manager."

"Do you have a microphone I can use?"

Darlene grabbed a mike and handed it to her.

"And is there a place I could interview everyone individually?"

"Of course. We'll put you in the Green Room."

"Good," said O'Connor. She moved to the stage apron and spoke crisply. "I know this is a terrible shock. Miss Miseau may have died from entirely natural causes, but obviously we need to do a thorough investigation. Plan to stay here until I've had a chance to speak individually with each of you."

A few groans came from the obviously exhausted dancers.

O'Connor wiped the sweat off her brow. It was going to be a long night.

***

And a spectacularly unproductive one, despite the hours of interviews. No, no one had seen or heard anything or anyone behaving suspiciously. No, Lydia had no enemies. She was revered, not only as a great dancer but as a warm, caring human being. Even the janitor sang her praises. "You know how it is," he told O'Connor. "Some people act like you don't even exist. But she always greeted me, asked about my wife and kids. She wasn't snotty like some of them."

On the drive home, O'Connor couldn't stop thinking about the dead ballerina. Could Lydia Miseau really have been that perfect? She'd risen to the top in a field known for its competitiveness. When O'Connor had taken her niece to see the company's fall production of *Giselle*, she'd been in awe of Miseau who'd performed with fiery passion and reckless abandon. O'Connor doubted you could fake those qualities on stage. No, there had to have been much more to Lydia Miseau than this paragon of niceness everyone had described.

***

The next day, O'Connor consumed an entire pot of coffee while filling out paperwork and fielding media requests for comments about the sudden death of Lydia Miseau. Just as she was about to call Chet to check on the autopsy progress, he texted her: *Found something interesting.*

Thirty-five minutes later, O'Connor stood shivering in the morgue's examination room as she stared down at Lydia's body.

"You're kidding," she said after Chet had given her the news.

"Nope."

"How far along?"

"It looks like she was about six weeks."

Victor Pesetsky certainly hadn't mentioned anything about a pregnancy. Had Miseau not told anyone—even her husband?

"So, what's the cause of death?" O'Connor asked.

"I wish I could tell you. No external wounds. We'll have to wait on the toxicology report, but as of right now, there's no evidence of anything that could have caused her death. It looks like her heart just stopped."

"You're telling me you really have no idea?" O'Connor could feel the beginnings of a headache coming on.

Chet shot her a baleful look. "The weird thing is her heart looks perfectly healthy. There's no evidence of scarring, and she was obviously in great physical shape."

"I don't believe this! So she drops dead for no apparent reason?"

"There's always a reason," Chet said. "We just don't know what it is yet."

***

When O'Connor swung by the theater to see if she could speak with Pesetsky, she found him in the third-floor practice studio rehearsing with Varese and Lydia's understudy, Muriel Gaston.

"Don't hesitate," he cried. Muriel ran and leapt into Varese's arms and he lifted her high above his head. "Good! Better. Now more, more. He is a magnet you cannot resist. You are helplessly drawn to him."

Interesting. She knew opening night had been postponed for a week, but clearly Pesetsky was wasting no time preparing his wife's successor as Juliet. Gone was the tearful, agitated man who'd seemed awash in grief. Today, Victor Pesetsky appeared totally caught up in coaching his wife's very young replacement.

O'Connor stood in the doorway and waited for a break. When Pesetsky's gaze landed on her, she detected a slight stiffening of his shoulders.

"Ah, Lieutenant," he said. "Any news?"

"The investigation is ongoing. I have a few more questions for you."

"You two," he said to Varese and Gaston, "take ten."

The dancers, covered in sweat, toweled off, guzzled water, and collapsed against the studio wall beneath the barre.

"Is there somewhere private we can talk?" O'Connor asked.

"Of course. Let's go downstairs to my office."

O'Connor followed him down two flights of stairs to the basement level. They passed a large costume and props room and rows of dressing rooms, including Lydia Miseau's, cordoned off with yellow tape.

Victor Pesetsky ushered her into his small office at the end of the hall. Pictures of the company's signature productions lined his walls, several featuring Lydia. On his mahogany desk, O'Connor noticed a gilt-framed head shot of his wife, as well as a photo of Pesetsky flanked by two twentyish looking adults, a fragile looking woman, and a sturdy man with Pesetsky's distinctive nose.

"Are these your children?" O'Connor asked.

"Yes. From my first marriage."

"And are they involved with ballet?"

"My son is actually our business manager, but my daughter has stayed as far away as possible. She's seen what a struggle life in the arts is."

"Were they close to Lydia?"

He paused. "To be honest, not especially. Their mother's and my divorce was not a happy one. It wasn't Lydia's fault. Their mother and I had grown apart, but I think they blamed Lydia."

"That must have been difficult."

He shrugged. "Well, truthfully, I have regrets about my relationship with my children. My son and I have gotten closer in recent years, since he came on board to help us out with fundraising and finances. But my daughter? Not so much. I suppose I've always been married to my art. I was much better at making ballets than I was at being a father."

He was being surprisingly forthcoming, O'Connor thought. And he'd just given her the perfect segue. "Mr. Pesetsky, were you aware that your wife was six weeks pregnant?"

He let out a heavy breath. "I take it you've seen the autopsy report?"

"Just the preliminary one."

"Lydia wanted to wait to tell the company until she'd gotten through the first trimester."

"How did you feel about the pregnancy?"

"I'm not going to lie to you, Lieutenant. This baby was a surprise, but we were…elated. Lydia is…was…nearly forty. Dancers don't go on forever, and the baby coming…well, it changed everything."

"In what way?"

"Every year, my wife would say she was probably going to step down at the end of the season. But the end of the season would arrive, and she'd announce, 'Oh hell, let's go for one more.' And who was I to complain? She was still technically solid, and maturity had brought such depth to her dancing."

"But with the baby coming, you think she would have followed through on retiring for good?"

"I think so. The baby gave her something to look forward to, move toward."

"And for you?"

He paused, then said, "This was going to be my chance for a do-over. Be a better father, a better man this go round."

O'Connor stared at the man as his face suddenly turned ashen. He brought his hand to his chest and shut his eyes. "Is there anything else, Lieutenant? I'm feeling a bit woozy." He reached down and pulled a bottle of pills and a water bottle out of his desk drawer. He shook two pills out and guzzled them down with water.

"Are you all right?"

"I will be. Anything else?"

"Just curious. Was your wife's life insured?"

"Yes, of course. We insure all of our principal dancers. Our audiences come to see these magnificent artists. If something happens to any of them, it's a major loss for us at the box office."

"But you weren't concerned that your wife was planning to retire and become a mother? Wouldn't that have hurt the box office?"

"Lieutenant, I love my wife. We both knew she could not dance forever. And we were preparing. She was working closely with Muriel—grooming her, I suppose you might say, to take over her roles. My wife was a wonderful coach. And Muriel is a sponge, a great talent as well."

Mighty convenient to have a ready replacement for your dead star. "So, how much was Lydia's life insured for?" she asked.

Victor stood up and waved his hand. "I can't recall. My son handles all of that. Now, if you'll excuse me, I really must get back to rehearsal." He moved toward the door, then turned around. "Have you learned anything about what caused my wife's death?"

"Nothing definite. We're waiting on the toxicology report."

"My wife did not take drugs, Lieutenant. She was in perfect health. I strongly doubt your toxicology report will show a thing."

"We'll keep you informed," O'Connor said. As he walked out, she couldn't help wondering why he seemed so confident that the toxicology report would reveal nothing.

***

O'Connor's next stop was three doors down, the even tinier office of Frederick Pesetsky, a younger, shorter, and burlier version of his father. He was on the phone when she tapped on the frame of his open door. He motioned her in. "Look, we'll pay you as soon as the funding from the Arts Council comes in…Yes, I know we're overdue. I'm asking for your patience. You do know we're dealing with the tragic death of our principal dancer, don't you?" Frederick listened for several seconds, then reiterated that he'd be in touch soon and clicked off.

"Creditors," he said. "They couldn't care less what we're going through. The joys of being in the arts. So, what can I do for you, Lieutenant?"

"Your father mentioned that Lydia's life had been insured by the company."

"That's true. We insure all the principal dancers."

"Mind telling me how much her life was insured for?"

"As I recall, it was a lot. Let me look this up for you." He began typing on his laptop.

O'Connor waited, checking her phone for texts. Nothing, except for messages from reporters begging for a quote.

"Wow," the younger Pesetsky said. "I didn't recall it was that much, but of course, she was the company's star."

"So, what are we talking about here?"

"Ten million."

"That's a lot of money. I'm curious. How serious is the company's financial situation?"

"Off the record? Very serious. We were worried that we'd have to lay off some of the corps dancers." He pushed his chair back and shook his head. "Ballet is expensive to produce, and for the past three years, the Arts Council budget has been slashed. Every arts organization in the city is feeling the pinch. People don't understand that ticket sales only cover a portion of our expenses."

"I take it then that this insurance money will be very helpful."

He looked pained. "Well, I suppose, but what an awful price to pay for financial solvency. Lydia is...was my father's muse—a genuine star with a huge fan base."

"How did you feel about her?"

He shrugged. "At first, I hated her. My father left my mother for her. And she was so young. But over the years, I think we both softened. I could see that she wasn't the devil—just someone who was very ambitious. And incredibly gifted."

O'Connor nodded, and then asked, "Were you aware that Lydia was pregnant?"

Frederick's mouth gaped open. "You're kidding."

"No."

"That won't be good news for my father."

"Why not?"

"Well, for one thing, he's not in great health—don't know what he'd do without his nitroglycerin. Besides..." He paused, as though debating about whether he should continue.

"Besides what?"

"My father had a vasectomy years ago."

Didn't see that one coming, O'Connor thought, as she carefully kept her expression blank. "And you know this because?"

"Because I overheard my parents arguing about it before they split up. My father told my mother after the fact. He knew she wanted more children, and he didn't care. He could barely tolerate the ones he had."

God, he sounded bitter, and why wouldn't he be? O'Connor pressed on. "And yet you're now working with your father."

He shrugged. "Now that I'm an adult, we get along much better. I grew up watching ballet and fell in love with it. Now I'm in a position to help sustain it. And frankly, I'm useful to my father."

Interesting choice of words. O'Connor had grown up in a large boisterous Irish Catholic family where children were treasured as gifts from God. She'd never felt "barely tolerated" or that she needed to be "useful" to her parents to win their approval.

O'Connor thanked the younger Pesetsky for his time and slipped out of his office. As she walked down the hall, she couldn't stop thinking about Victor Pesetsky's alleged vasectomy. If it were true, the man was one hell of an actor. All those pronouncements he'd made about being elated about the coming baby and looking forward to another shot at fatherhood? Given his lousy record as a parent and his total devotion to his artistic work, how "elated" was he? And if he knew about the baby and what most likely was his wife's infidelity, how angry would he have been about her betrayal?

And then there was the insurance money which would put the company back on a solid financial footing. Get rid of Lydia Miseau, and sure, Victor Pesetsky would lose his star, but Muriel Gaston seemed more than ready to take her place.

How ready had she been? It must have been hard to wait in the wings to become the company's star while Lydia put off retiring year after year. She could have decided to hasten the ballerina's exit. Definitely worth talking to her again. O'Connor headed back up the two flights of stairs to the rehearsal studio.

She was nearly there when the third floor doorway creaked open, and Muriel Gaston and Alexander Varese appeared, looking flushed and weighed down by their dance bags. Funny how dancers often looked so tall and imposing on stage, and in real life, were often on the diminutive side—like these two.

"Ms. Gaston," O'Connor said. "I have a few more questions."

Gaston's crystal blue eyes widened. "For me?"

"Yes. Is there somewhere we could talk privately?"

"Sure. We can talk in one of the women's dressing rooms. The other dancers are off today."

Five minutes later, O'Connor and Gaston were settled on a lumpy pea green loveseat in the corner of the long, narrow mirrored room. A pile of old *Dance Magazines* lay on the floor near Gaston. She pulled off her pointe shoes and winced as she rubbed her feet. "Long rehearsal," she said.

"From what I saw, your practice went well."

"Yes—I mean, under the circumstances." She sighed. "I still can't wrap my head around Lydia being gone."

"I can only imagine. How did you feel about her?"

She abruptly abandoned her foot massage and stared at O'Connor. "Like I said last night, she was an extraordinary dancer and a wonderful human being."

"Did it frustrate you that she kept putting retirement off?"

She pursed her lips and shrugged. "Sometimes. I'm not going to tell you I didn't want the chance to dance Lydia's signature roles. But you have to understand. I was learning so much from her. Lydia believed in me, told me all the time I would someday surpass her as a great ballerina. She helped me believe in myself. And anyway…" She paused.

"Anyway?"

"A few days before…she collapsed…she told me she would soon have a surprise for me, news that would make both of us very happy. And then she pulled me into her arms." Her face clouded over as she lifted a shaky hand to her bun and shoved back a loose hair pin.

"Did you have any idea what she meant? What the surprise was?"

She shook her head. "Of course, I wondered if she meant she was retiring, but…"

"But what?"

"If the surprise was her retirement, I couldn't fathom how that would make her happy. Lydia lived to dance."

"So you didn't think her retiring was the surprise?"

She frowned and shook her head. "No, that's just it. I think this time, she was serious about stepping down. For the last several weeks, our coaching sessions were long, intense. She pushed me hard—brought things out of me I didn't even know were there." Her voice shook as she added, "I will be indebted to her forever."

The young dancer seemed to be genuinely grieving for her mentor. If Lydia Miseau had been murdered, Gaston did not appear to be a promising suspect. O'Connor thanked her for her time and reminded her to call if she thought of anything else.

As O'Connor walked away, her thoughts returned to Victor Pesetsky. From what she'd gleaned so far, he had the strongest motive to harm Lydia Miseau. But if he had murdered his wife, how the hell had he done it?

She paused at Lydia's closed dressing room and decided to take a look. She pushed the door open, ducked under the crime scene tape, and flicked on the light. O'Connor was shocked to discover Matt Gates, the lighting designer, hunched over in the makeup chair, his head in his hands. He raised his tear-filled eyes to her.

"What are you doing here? This area is off limits," she said.

"I'm sorry," he said, his voice catching. "I just wanted to feel close to Lydia. Can you smell her scent? Lilacs—she couldn't get enough of them. I...I just can't believe she's gone."

"You really can't be in here. Did you touch anything?"

"No!"

O'Connor studied his crimson face, streaked with tears. She was starting to lose her patience. "You weren't just close friends, were you?" she said. "You and Lydia were lovers."

"Please...she's dead. What difference can this make now? Let poor Victor grieve in peace."

"What were you planning to do about the baby?"

His chin trembled. "How did you know?"

"Preliminary findings from the autopsy. So what was the plan?"

"We didn't know." He bit down on his lower lip. "Lydia wanted to keep the baby, leave the company. I was afraid Victor could make things difficult for us...The ballet world is a small one."

"Do you think Victor knew about the two of you? The baby?"

"If he did, he didn't let on. Of course, I've known him a long time. He's a hell of an actor. I've seen him smooth-talk blowhard potential donors and act like he's their best friend when I knew perfectly well he couldn't stand them."

"And you weren't concerned that maybe Lydia would change her mind and decide to stay with her husband? Or had she told you that was her plan?"

"God, no!" he exclaimed. "She told me she figured out long ago that Victor was madly in love with her dancing, but he'd never loved her. She was so lonely. He barely acknowledged her presence at home. All he cared about was her usefulness to him."

Hmm, O'Connor thought. *Seems to be a theme here*. If people in Pesetsky's orbit were useful, they mattered. Otherwise, they didn't count.

"Okay," she said, "that's all for now." She gestured toward the door.

"Do you know what killed Lydia?" he asked as he stood up.

"Not yet. We hope to have a final report soon."

After Gates left, O'Connor glanced around the dressing room. Glittery costumes hung on a rack, and a pile of beat up looking pointe shoes lay in the corner. She slid into Lydia's makeup chair and studied the array of cosmetics strewn on the counter: false eyelashes, jars of makeup, cleansing cream, mascara, rouge, eyeliner, and lipsticks. She remembered laboring over her makeup during her high school theater days.

And then she had an idea. She pulled out her gloves and several evidence bags from her suit pocket and stuffed them with Lydia's cosmetics. On her way out, she texted Chet: *Dropping by. Have some questions.*

***

Chet was munching a hot pastrami and Swiss cheese sub from Vinny's when O'Connor arrived. He held up a half and offered it to her.

"I'm good," she said. "I wanted to ask you about whether something could have killed Lydia that might not show up in any tests."

"What do you mean? Like what?"

"Well, I was in her dressing room earlier. She'd applied full makeup for the final dress rehearsal. I looked at all her cosmetics, and it got me to thinking. Was there anything someone could add to her makeup that could have caused her heart to shut down but wouldn't necessarily be detectable?"

Chet rubbed his chin. "Huh—hadn't thought of that, but it's possible. If her makeup was laced with blood pressure medication, for example, it wouldn't have killed her immediately, but it would eventually have slowed her heart to the point where it simply stopped. And the medication flushes through the system pretty fast."

"What about nitroglycerin?"

"Same deal," Chet said.

O'Connor jumped up and practically ran out the door. "Thanks, Chet—really helpful," she called over her shoulder.

***

Three days later, O'Connor's hunch paid off. The analysis of Lydia's makeup had revealed traces of nitroglycerin, enough to kill a person with a healthy heart. And O'Connor knew exactly who had access to the drug.

When she arrived at the theater, she found Victor Pesetsky in his office working on his computer.

He looked up at her expectantly. "Any news, Lieutenant?"

"I'm afraid so, sir. Your wife died as a result of her makeup being laced with nitroglycerin, the same medication you're on. I'm going to have to ask you to come downtown with me as a person of interest in her death."

Victor Pesetsky blanched. "I see. Is this my cue to call my attorney?"

"Best not to miss it," O'Connor said.

* With special thanks to Luci Hansson Zahray, *aka* "the Poison Lady," for her expert advice.

YOU KNOW HOW ACTRESSES ARE
By C. M. Surrisi

Although she should be recuperating from a breakdown, a well-known actress living in a boarding house continues to show declining health, which makes fellow resident Miss Simpson curious...and then suspicious.

Cordelia Huntington suffered a nervous breakdown while on stage playing Aunt Martha in *Arsenic and Old Lace*. It was the Comstock Theater's 1953 Summer Repertory Season opening production, and Cordelia's seventh time performing the role in one venue or another.

The actor playing Mortimer, Marshall Briggs, said his line: "But, how did the poison get into the wine?"

Aunt Martha was then to say, "Well, we put it in wine because it's less noticeable. When it's in tea, it has a distinct odor."

Instead, Aunt Martha babbled, "bu bu bu bu bu."

Briggs was caught up short. This wasn't her next line.

Cordelia crossed downstage center and began to undo her hair pins and let her long locks fall to her shoulders.

The audience thought it was all in the fun of the performance. They started to giggle.

Briggs looked to the stage manager who thrust his hands up in a "what the hell is going on" salute. Then Cordelia started to rip the buttons of her shirt and when a randy fellow in the second row cried, "Take it all off, Aunt Martha," Briggs had no choice but to scoop her up and carry her off stage, yelling, "Kill the lights! Curtain!"

***

Many months later, Cordelia was stable enough to be released from a convalescent hospital. She accepted a position as dramaturg with the Green Briar Players, a repertory company in a nearby town. The day she arrived, the air was clean and crisp and a layer of soft fluffy snow blanketed the white clapboard homes and churches. The actress was a favorite of the local people who showed both sympathy for her frail condition and great affection.

Cordelia took up residence at Milner's Boarding House a block from the playhouse. Next to it was a stand of pine woods that she could see from her window. She sat gazing at the trees each morning.

Initially, she was reclusive. But soon, she indulged in a cup of tea in the parlor in the late afternoon with two other ladies who resided there: a retired bank teller, Miss Swenson, and a widow, Mrs. Williams. She regaled them with one or another of her various speeches, including Regina from *The Little Foxes* and *The Madwoman of Chaillot*. She never mentioned *Arsenic and Old Lace*.

***

Miss Swenson soon grew weary of the tea-time performances, but she enjoyed being in the star's company. Mrs. Williams, on the other hand, appeared endlessly interested, and enjoyed her own version of tea formalities including wearing a netted hat and short white gloves. After Cordelia had retired to her chambers one afternoon, Mrs. Williams sighed and said, "She seems a bit of a fading star, don't you think?"

"She has been quite ill," replied Miss Swenson.

"Yes, I suppose," said Mrs. Williams. "I heard her breakdown was the result of a scandal."

"Really?" Miss Swenson was not typically one for gossip, but she made an exception when it came to celebrities.

Mrs. Williams leaned forward conspiratorially. "Dumped by her married boyfriend—the director."

Miss Swenson raised her eyebrow. "You don't say."

The landlady, Mrs. Milner, was not so enthralled. She was obliged to haul the meal trays up to the third floor and, after Cordelia had imbibed only a nibble, haul them back down. She rather thought she had rented to aging royalty.

Mrs. Milner was also skeptical about Dr. Rudolph, who visited Cordelia once a week. He carried an old, cracked leather medical bag that clinked with bottles. A cloud of cigar smoke clung to his black coat. He hardly presented the picture of health.

Further, his visits did not seem to be improving Cordelia's health. She'd arrived thin, but with some color in her face. His weekly visits left her with an ashen complexion.

Once when Mrs. Milner was picking up her tray, she asked, "Are you feeling alright, Miss Huntington?"

Cordelia answered, "I'm still convalescing, that's all. I'm going to take a tonic now."

On the way down the three flights of stairs, Mrs. Milner muttered, "It's probably all that tonic and not much food that's doing it to ya'. These vain types. Always watching their weight."

Miss Swenson also noticed Cordelia's pallor. She would never have ventured to address it directly, but she did confide in Mrs. Blaine, her good friend who resided down the block. "You know, I believe Miss Huntington is having a relapse."

"Is she babbling nonsense?" asked Mrs. Blaine. "I heard she babbled complete nonsense on stage on the day of the...you know."

"Oh, no. Not that at all. It's more like it's intestinal. She gets thinner and paler with each passing day."

"Maybe it's something she's eating?"

"She eats in her room and takes only a cookie or two with tea despite Mrs. Williams' urging. And she's visited by a doctor every week. I just can't imagine."

Mrs. Blaine could imagine, though, because she was a great imaginer. Her husband was a deputy with the local police, and she had received an unusual degree of exposure to the unimaginable through his tales from life on the force.

"For one thing, the medicine may not be agreeing with her. What kind of doctor is he?"

"I couldn't say. Except he looks a bit of a rumple, he smells of tobacco, his bag is a broken-down old thing, and he sports an enormous amount of hair growing in his ears."

"Gracious! What's his name?"

"I don't know. Do you think I should find out?"

"I certainly do. I'll have my Mr. Deputy Blaine check him out."

***

Miss Swenson could not seem to pry the name of the doctor out of Cordelia, but she did press on. "I see your physician visited yesterday. I don't think I caught his name."

Cordelia sipped her tea and nodded.

When Miss Swenson inquired about his name to Mrs. Milner, she replied smugly, "That's private, I'm sure."

Miss Swenson persisted by taking a winter stroll in the snow around the dwelling. In this manner she acquired the license plate number for the doctor's automobile, which she immediately passed along to Mrs. Blaine.

Mrs. Blaine reported back a week later that the car was registered to Eustis Rudolph, and worse than having the unfortunate name Eustis, no such person was registered in the state as a medical doctor!

"Goodness, what could this mean?" Miss Swenson replied. "I wonder if Cordelia knows he's not a real doctor? Should we do something? Might he be poisoning her?"

Mrs. Blaine was schooled enough in the crime business by her husband to know that this would be jumping to conclusions. What they needed were "means," in other words, a sample of what Cordelia was imbibing; "motive," a plausible reason why Rudolph might be doing her harm; and "opportunity." That they already had. He visited once a week with her privately.

"I don't see how I could get in her room to see what Rudolph might be giving her," Miss Swenson told her friend.

"You may not need to. Look at this." Mrs. Blaine thrust the classified section of the newspaper under her friend's nose.

Miss Swenson read the circled ad: "Part-time maid. Milner's Boarding House. Inquire with Mrs. Milner at 757-3392." She looked at her friend with confusion.

"What do you think? I could apply for this," said Mrs. Blaine.

"Apply for what?" boomed the voice of Mr. Deputy Blaine who walked into the kitchen and set down his hat on the table.

Mrs. Blaine didn't blink. "I'm thinking of taking a part-time job as a maid at Mrs. Milner's Boarding House."

Being a detective, Deputy Blaine also didn't blink. "Is this about that Rudolph fellow who isn't really a doctor?"

"Indeed, it is," said his wife. "We think Cordelia Huntington is being poisoned by him and we have no other way to get evidence of that than to go undercover."

Deputy Blaine looked at his wife, then at Miss Swenson. He scratched his head. "Don't you live there?"

"That's the point, Gerald. She lives there. There is only so much she can do without making Mrs. Milner suspicious and risking her residence. I am not known to the woman."

"Wait just a minute," said her husband.

Miss Swenson spoke up. "I have grave suspicions that Cordelia Huntington is being poisoned by Eustis Rudolph. He has adequate opportunity, being alone with her once a week. I think he is doing it with a tonic that he gives her. Admittedly, I have no idea why, but I ask you, should we wait until she is dead to inquire into that?"

"I could be a detective in the house and gather some of the tonic." Mrs. Blaine pushed the newspaper in front of her husband. "Look, Mrs. Milner is advertising for a part-time maid. It's perfect. You, my dear, can be pursuing the issue of motive using your extensive resources, and I can be investigating inside."

Deputy Blaine's face slowly changed from resistant to intrigued. "No overnight duties."

"Certainly not," Mrs. Blaine agreed. "We shall reconnoiter here at the end of each day."

***

Without any difficulty, Mrs. Blaine secured an interview with Mrs. Milner.

"I don't think I've seen you in town before. Where do you live?" Mrs. Milner scrutinized the application of Molly Beam.

"I live in the Donut Hole," said Mrs. Blaine, whose husband had created an address for her in the poorest part of town, where Mrs. Milner was not likely to visit.

"How old are you?"

"I'm forty-seven."

"Have you worked as a maid before?"

"You could say that. I've been nurse and maid for my ailing mother for twenty years, until she passed away this past summer."

"I see you are married?"

Mrs. Blaine looked quickly at her left ring finger. How silly to have left her ring on. She thought quickly. "My mother's. It's sentimental."

After some consternation, and in consideration of not having any other applicants due to the low pay, Mrs. Milner said, "Fine. I'll give you a try. But it's very active work. You have to carry trays up and down two flights of stairs and not get in the way of our residents, and not fuss about our one special guest."

Mrs. Blaine raised her eyebrows. "Oh, who is that?"

Mrs. Milner leaned in closely and whispered, "Cordelia Huntington."

Mrs. Blaine's eyes shot back and forth, and she whispered, "Who is that?"

Mrs. Milner smiled. "You'll do just fine."

***

So, Mrs. Blaine donned the black dress with the white collar, and she became Molly the maid at Milner's Boarding House.

On the first day, Mrs. Milner pointed to the tray on the kitchen counter. "She doesn't go to the theater much anymore, so you'll be taking her meals up every day. Take it up, knock on the door. She'll tell you to come in. She'll probably be rude and not even look at you. Place the tray on the table and leave."

Molly did as she was told. When she carried up her first breakfast tray, she knocked and heard, "Come in." When she entered the room, she saw a thin woman sitting by the window in a dressing gown. The woman stared out the window and did not acknowledge Molly.

This gave Molly the chance she'd hoped for to check out the room. Her eyes darted in every direction, scanning the table top, the bureau, the small table with the crystal lamp. She raked her glance across the window sill, the nightstand, and a footstool.

"Ma'am, I have a fresh hand towel for you," she said.

Cordelia nodded.

Molly took the towel from under her arm and hurried to the bathroom. There was nothing out on the counter. She dared to open the medicine chest. When it was open two inches, the hinge screeched. Her heart stopped. She held her breath. She felt obliged to say, "Just a quick wipe down, ma'am."

"No need," came a faint voice from the woman in the chair.

It may have been only two inches, but it was enough for Molly to see a row of small brown bottles. A quick count told her there were seven. She squeezed her fists and resisted taking one. Surely, one of seven would be missed.

***

At tea that afternoon, Miss Swenson kept a solemn expression as Mrs. Blaine served. Still, Mrs. Blaine stole a wink at her when Cordelia and Mrs. Williams weren't looking. The plump Mrs. Williams fussed over the cookie she wanted, annoyingly picking them up and smelling them. Miss Swenson didn't mind this for herself, since she never ate cookies, but she felt relieved for Cordelia that Mrs. Williams wore her white gloves throughout this obnoxious exercise. After finally making her choice, Mrs. Williams thrust the plate under Cordelia's nose and was relentless until the actress finally accepted one.

Cordelia nibbled the cookie.

Mrs. Williams set her tea cup in its saucer, brushed crumbs off her mouth with her gloved fingers, took a breath and asked in an affected society voice that she used during tea, "Do you think you will ever perform *Arsenic and Old Lace* again?"

Miss Swenson's head jerked back so abruptly that tea sloshed over the edge of her cup. Her eyes darted to Cordelia. She was about to hush the ridiculous Mrs. Williams when Cordelia surprised them and performed a speech from *Arsenic and Old Lace*. Not one by Aunt Martha, but instead, one by the other poisoner, Aunt Abby.

"'Oh Mortimer, don't be so inquisitive. The gentleman died because he drank some wine with poison in it,'" Cordelia said in a drifty tone.

"Who put the poison in the wine?" asked Mrs. Williams earnestly, urging her on with a cue.

"'We did. I did,'" Cordelia responded. "'All the gentlemen in the cellar.'"

After Cordelia retired to her room, Mrs. Williams looked sadly at Miss Swenson. "She really isn't as good an actress as her reputation would suggest."

Miss Swenson refrained from rolling her eyes. "I don't think she's quite recovered."

"I suppose that would affect one's performance."

Miss Swenson agreed, "I'm sure it would."

"Oh well, you know how actresses are. The show must go on, even if poorly."

***

That night, Mrs. Blaine described Cordelia's room to her husband and Miss Swenson.

"I couldn't take a bottle. There were only seven, all lined up like little soldiers. I knew it would be missed. I didn't see anything else, but I must say I could knock her over with a feather. If she is being poisoned, I wouldn't think she could endure it much longer." Mrs. Blaine rubbed her own stomach and stepped to the counter where she took out a box of baking soda and spooned some into a glass of water. "I must have eaten something that disagreed with me."

Her husband, the deputy, snapped to attention. "Where and what did you eat today, my dear?"

Mrs. Blaine finished swallowing her dose and scrunched her forehead as she tried to remember. "I only ate bits and snacks here and there at the boarding house today. A glass of orange juice. A half of a sandwich. A cup of tea. A pickle. An olive—"

"Did you eat anything that was on Cordelia's tray?" pressed her husband.

Mrs. Blaine reared back. "Of course, I didn't."

"Well, don't," Deputy Blaine barked.

Miss Swenson tried to ease the tension. "The doctor will be there tomorrow."

"I'll try and meet him," said Mrs. Blaine.

"Be careful. And for goodness sake, don't eat anything," said her husband.

Miss Swenson wanted to say "Well, what about me? Should I eat anything?" But she didn't feel the least bit ill.

***

As she was carrying a bundle of dirty linens downstairs the next morning, Molly came face to face with the doctor.

"Pardon me," she said, but she didn't move enough to let him pass easily. She took her time and studied his bag.

He turned his body and bottles clinked inside the leather satchel.

The smell of tobacco was intense. It triggered a recollection that nicotine could be deadly in concentrated doses.

"Molly!" Mrs. Milner said sharply from the bottom of the stairs. "What are you doing? Let the doctor by."

"Of course." Molly hurried down the rest of the steps and off to the cellar to fill the washing machine.

After that, she went about her dusting duties, hovering, listening, waiting for the doctor to leave, then went up to the third floor to collect the breakfast tray.

"Come in," said a drowsy Cordelia. She was lying on her bed with her arm over her eyes. An empty tonic bottle sat on the bedside stand.

Molly walked lightly toward the bathroom. "Getting the tray, ma'am, and refreshing the towels."

Cordelia made a sound like a hum.

Molly squeezed through the bathroom door that stood ajar, and opened the medicine cabinet two inches, being careful not to evoke a screech. There on the shelf, lined up as before, were six bottles.

Molly peeked into the room and saw Cordelia's chest rising and lowering in sleep. She carefully took one of the bottles off the shelf, unscrewed the cap and smelled it. There was no aroma of nicotine as she had anticipated. It smelled more like Earl Grey tea. She poured half of it into a small jar she had secreted in her pocket, and dribbled water from the faucet into the bottle to refill it. A second later, it was back on the shelf, she'd picked up the tray, and was on her way downstairs where she ran into Mrs. Milner.

"I suppose her ladyship is having her afternoon nap."

**

When Deputy Blaine arrived home from work, Mrs. Blaine and Miss Swenson were sitting at the kitchen table with sly smiles on their faces and the jar of tonic in front of them.

"Well, well. What do we have here?" Deputy Blaine asked as he rubbed his hands together.

"The tonic," said Mrs. Blaine proudly.

Deputy Blaine held it up to the light and tipped it to consider its viscosity. "I'm very eager to see what's in this elixir."

"Do you know anything more about the doctor?" asked Miss Swenson.

Deputy Blaine set down his hat and took off his jacket. "Not really. I had someone follow him and he spent most of his days either drinking tea with a withered old Chinese woman or visiting homes—presumably dropping off this tonic."

"It smells like tea, that's for certain," said Mrs. Blaine.

Her husband growled. "Don't go smelling and touching the stuff!"

"Fine. Fine."

**

It took two weeks for the sample to be tested. During that time, Mrs. Blaine hauled the trays, Mrs. Milner sat in the kitchen and sniped about her famous guest, and tea continued with Cordelia muttering lines from *Arsenic and Old Lace* while Miss Williams fussed over the cookies.

Finally, they had the results.

Deputy Blaine laid a paper on the kitchen table and Mrs. Blaine and Miss Swenson bent over it. "It's not poison," said the deputy. "It's mostly bergamot oil."

"What is it supposed to do?" asked Miss Swenson.

"It's used in reducing fever, fighting parasitic diseases, and relieving sore throat."

"Really?" Miss Swenson was surprised. She had fully expected a toxic elixir.

Deputy Blaine continued, "Yes, indeed. It's antibacterial, anti-infectious, anti-inflammatory, and anti-spasmodic. It's supposed to be uplifting, improve your digestion, and keep your bowels working tip top." He sat down with resignation and tipped back his chair.

Mrs. Blaine sputtered, "I certainly couldn't say about her bowels, but she's not showing signs of improved health in any other way. In fact, she looks to be getting worse."

Her husband looked sharply at her. "Mrs. Blaine, I do believe you are looking a little peaked, too. You haven't been eating anything at the boarding house, have you?"

Mrs. Blaine looked guilty but said, "No. I've been working hard, that's all."

Miss Swenson felt a little light-headed herself, but could honestly say she'd been eating lightly, much to Mrs. Milner's disapproval and curiosity.

Deputy Blaine sat forward. "Get me a sample of the boarding house food. Rudolph doesn't seem to have a motive or means. Maybe it's the landlady."

"What motive would she have?" asked Miss Swenson, although she had also turned her suspicions in that direction. "I'm sure she collects a tidy sum in boarding fees from Cordelia. Why kill the golden goose?"

"You never know about people," said the deputy. "They do things for the damnedest reasons." He shook his head. "I suppose I could have someone look into her background. Maybe there's a connection between her and Huntington that we aren't aware of. The actress could be the daughter of her estranged sister and she thinks she's being spied upon. Who knows with these people?"

"These people?" asked Miss Swenson.

"Yes. Criminals," said the deputy with authority.

"What about the other lady? Mrs. Williams?" asked Mrs. Blaine.

"Mrs. Williams?" asked the deputy.

"Oh, Mrs. Williams is a retired teacher. She's an avid fan of Cordelia's. Sort of a simple, fussy, gossipy creature, really."

"Where did she teach? What did she teach?" pressed the deputy.

"I don't think I know. I recall she taught English for a high school in a nearby town," said Miss Swenson. "I hardly think she is a suspect. What possible motive could she have?"

"I suppose you're right on that one," said the deputy. "Let's concentrate on the landlady. She's the one with control of the household."

***

Two weeks later, the three of them were back at the Blaines' kitchen table.

"Not a thing," said Deputy Blaine. "Just the four food groups."

"Really?" Mrs. Blaine was shocked.

Deputy Blaine asked, "Could it be coming from the theater? Someone is slipping something into food or drink there?"

"Now that you mention it, she hasn't gone to the theater in the last few weeks," said Miss Swenson. "She still takes tea with us, but I can't see her doing that much longer."

"I do believe they will be carrying that elegant bag of bones out on a stretcher any day now," said Mrs. Blaine, who had herself taken on a pallor, but still refused to admit she'd eaten anything at the boarding house.

"Could it be the air?" asked Deputy Blaine.

"I breathe the air, too," said Miss Swenson.

"So, do I, dear," said Mrs. Blaine.

"Has there been any construction? Painting? Caustic materials?" asked the deputy.

Both ladies shook their heads.

"If that doctor is paying any attention to her declining health, he'll get her out of there," said Mrs. Blaine.

"Don't forget, he's not a doctor," said the deputy. Then he snapped his fingers. "I have an idea." He scribbled a name on a scrap of paper and handed it to Miss Swenson. "You will have a guest for tea tomorrow. It will be this lady, who is also...a pathologist. She may be able to take one look at Cordelia and tell us what's going on."

***

The next morning, Miss Swenson told Mrs. Milner she would be having a guest for tea that afternoon.

Mrs. Milner grumbled, "Fine. I'll put it on your monthly bill, and don't let your friend bother her ladyship." Mrs. Milner was no fan of Cordelia's but she prided herself in upholding the reputation of her boarding house as a place of discretion.

At precisely three p.m. the doorbell rang and Mrs. Blaine escorted Miss Hart into the parlor, where Miss Swenson made a fuss over her and positioned her in a seat next to Cordelia. Miss Hart pretended not to recognize the star, which wasn't difficult given her deteriorated condition.

Mrs. Williams became extremely agitated. She snapped her "How do you do," and did not accompany it with a "How lovely to meet you." In fact, she looked so shocked by the visitor that she nearly dropped the plate of cookies she'd been arranging.

Miss Swenson started to apologize to Mrs. Williams but then changed her mind. The insufferable woman was probably worried she would get one less cookie or was simply being resentful about her time with Cordelia. In either case, she wasn't going to apologize for inconveniencing her.

As they sipped their tea, there was little conversation.

Miss Hart took sideways glances at Cordelia and appeared to be taking mental notes.

Mrs. Williams huffed, put three cookies in front of Cordelia, and urged her to eat them.

When Miss Swenson reached for the cookie plate to hand it to Miss Hart, Mrs. Williams glared at her and whispered, "These are for Cordelia."

Miss Swenson drew her hand back as if she'd been slapped and glared at Mrs. Williams.

Then something came over Miss Swenson. She simply wasn't going to stand for such rude behavior from Mrs. Williams. They may have been trying to solve an attempted murder case, but she wasn't going to allow her undercover pathologist to be treated rudely or deprived of a simple cookie. She grabbed the plate with its remaining cookies and walked to the kitchen.

"I'll get more cookies and be back in a minute," said Miss Swenson.

Mrs. Blaine was hovering in the hallway, watching this scene. When Miss Swenson came toward her with the plate, she reached for it and said, "I'll fill the plate for you."

As she turned toward the kitchen, she popped one of the cookies from the plate in her mouth.

Miss Swenson gasped, then laughed. "I hardly think your husband would be pleased with that!" Then she gasped and clutched Mrs. Blaine's arm. "Wait, have you been eating a cookie every day?"

Mrs. Blaine looked sheepish. "Yes. Just one or two that are left on the plate. Haven't you?"

"No. I don't care for sweets, I never eat them," said Miss Swenson. She looked at the plate and looked back in the parlor. "The only people who eat these are Mrs. Williams and Cordelia... and you. Hurry, hurry. Spit it out, chuck it up."

One lone cookie remained on the plate. Miss Swenson wrapped it in a napkin and slipped it into her pocket for evidence. Then Mrs. Blaine filled the plate with cookies in the kitchen and handed it to Miss Swenson.

"Here we are." Miss Swenson handed the plate of cookies to the anxious Mrs. Williams, who studied it.

When Miss Hart started to reach for one, Mrs. Williams said, "I really wouldn't if I were you. They have been known to give one intestinal distress...if you're not used to eating sweets, that is."

This sufficiently put Miss Hart off the cookies.

***

It took Dr. Hart only twenty-four hours to identify the poison on the cookies. It had been applied to the surface.

"Could the poison have been patted on?" asked Miss Swenson.

"Yes, exactly," said Dr. Hart. "That would work."

"Even with gloves on?"

"Well, yes. Especially with gloves on," said Dr. Hart. "Gloves would absorb the poison and be a transfer vehicle to the cookies."

"I'm beginning to think our Mrs. Williams is not much of a Cordelia fan," said Miss Swenson.

That afternoon, Miss Swenson advised Mrs. Milner that she would have two guests for tea.

"I see you are starting to make a habit of this, Miss Swenson," said Mrs. Milner. "Quite a few of my cookies are being consumed. I will be adding them to your bill."

"As you wish, Mrs. Milner," said Miss Swenson.

Dr. Hart and Deputy Blaine arrived at three p.m. Mrs. Blaine escorted them to the parlor. Mrs. Williams was busy fussing with the cookies when they walked in. She glared at Miss Swenson. Mrs. Blaine walked over to her and grabbed the plate away from her, using a napkin so she wouldn't leave her fingerprints.

"What are you doing?" cried Mrs. Williams. "Those are for Cordelia! Those are Cordelia's cookies!"

"Not anymore," said Deputy Blaine. "Do you want to tell us about the cookies?"

There must have been something about the authoritarian tone

of Deputy Blaine's voice, or perhaps it was the sight of him pulling handcuffs out of his pocket, but instantly Mrs. Williams' eyes filled with tears and she spilled her story without using her affected tea party voice.

"I should have played Aunt Martha eight times. I should have been the star. She ruined my career."

Cordelia raised her eyes to look at Mrs. Williams in a way she hadn't looked at her before.

Deputy Blaine slipped a paper from his breast pocket. "You mean before you were a drama teacher at Bolton High School? When you were an actress in the same company as Cordelia?"

"Mrs. Williams was an actress?" said Miss Swenson.

"Your maiden name is Jane Sherman, isn't it, Mrs. Williams?"

Mrs. Williams nodded in misery.

Cordelia spoke, "Jane? Is that you?"

"And you competed for roles against Cordelia but never got them? And you were forced to serve as understudy in several productions but never received a chance to step up?" pressed the deputy.

"She canoodled with the director!" cried Mrs. Williams, her eyes wild. "It wasn't fair. She knew she was stabbing me in the heart."

Cordelia pointed a shaky finger at Jane Sherman. "You talentless, hateful shrew."

Mrs. Williams cried out, "You conniving, overrated, heartless whore," and she lunged at Cordelia.

Deputy Blaine sprang to the ready and wrestled Jane Sherman to the ground. "Mrs. Jane Sherman Williams," said Deputy Blaine, "you are under arrest."

Mrs. Williams sobbed and pressed her gloved fingertips to her eyes to wipe her tears, then she looked at her hands. "Oh no!"

"Oh, yes," said Dr. Hart. "The poison will travel from your gloves to your eyes."

Mrs. Williams cried in anguish and gave the swooning performance of her life.

But then again, you know how actresses are.

FIVE WORDS
By Elaine Togneri

Sometimes improv performance can be more true-to-life than the audience realizes. It was Devyn Ross's first skit and Ed's last.

I sat onstage on a metal folding chair, my legs extended. To compensate for my lack of experience, I wore tight jean shorts and a pink halter top as Miriam, the stage manager, had directed. The audience tittered as I shifted slightly to the right, then left. When I couldn't hold my legs out straight anymore, I jumped up and pretended to dig around in the empty space that represented the bed. I pinched my fingers together and appeared to examine something gripped between them.

"What is it?" Ed, my partner in the skit and in life for the last month, asked. He sat in an adjoining folding chair, khaki-clad long legs still outstretched, showing off his superior muscular strength. A hunk of black hair hung on his forehead and accented his dark eyes, the pose a perfect ad for Five Word Theater.

"Bedbug," I said, flicking it at him to a smattering of applause. I, Devyn Ross, had managed to work the first of five words chosen by the audience into the improv. John, Roger, and Brenda, the experienced members of the troupe who had opened the show, watched from the cheap seats in the back of the theater. John nodded and I smiled. Not bad for my first time. Miriam, who stood off to the side of the open stage, crossed the word off the small white board she held.

Ed caught the imaginary insect. "It's a grain of rice." He glared at me. "You've never even seen a bedbug."

I didn't like his tone. He still seemed mad at me. But he was only acting, right? "They showed one on *Dr. Oz.*"

"All you do is sit around and watch TV." He shook his head and stood. "I've had it. I want a divorce." He walked to the edge of the stage, perusing the audience. Odds were he was looking for my replacement. He refused to meet my gaze.

I sighed and I wasn't pretending. It wasn't the first time he'd told me I was hooked on the tube. I had no clue what he intended here. The next word was "Nile." He could have said we were on a boat and looked out the window. Training from my improv classes said to agree with the direction chosen by your partner. "What about taking a vacation?" I asked, taking the high road and giving him a huge opening.

He didn't take it. "It wouldn't work." He strode across the stage, a large frown on his expressive lips. He spoke and stressed the second syllable of his last word. "You're in de-Nial." The audience laughed and his frown morphed into a smile. He shifted his gaze away as if he couldn't bear to see me.

Miriam looked around the crowd where several heads bobbed. She crossed off the second word. Roger and Brenda scowled as if Ed had cheated. Maybe he had. I didn't know enough to complain.

It was my turn and the next word was "xenograft." I didn't even know what it meant. I walked toward Ed. He had to have heard my footsteps behind him, but didn't face me. I stopped and threw up my hands. The audience laughed. I pivoted, folded one arm over my chest, and leaned my chin on my hand. I nodded as if considering options, feeling everyone's gaze settling on me. He would be no help. My spine stiffened and I bit my lip, fed up. "How much alimony are you willing to pay?" I asked.

"Alimony? Pay you to go away?" He shifted partially toward me.

I smiled. He had expected me to beg. "I keep your secrets and you go on with your life." I spoke truth because I was better at innuendo than improv. I had a second thought and added, "I won't tell anyone about your xenograft. That's got to be worth something."

The guy who had originally added the word to our list whistled. His partner laughed loudly. The people sitting near them joined in. A few whispered to their neighbors, and gradually the whole audience was roaring. Miriam had hesitated to cross it off initially, but relented.

Ed scowled and ran a hand through his hair to push it off his face. It was on him to make sense of the word in the scene. He clenched his hands. "You wouldn't dare." He tried to throw it back to me.

I held out a manicured hand. "Silence is worth quite a lot. But you won't pay because you're not really as rich as you pretend to be, are you?" I'd just stumbled onto that truth. He was staying at my place and we were working for whatever showed up in the hat we would pass at the end of the show. He called improv his hobby, but didn't know the tax rate on capital gains so I doubted his day-trading story. I, on the other hand, had a sizable portfolio from the insurance settlement paid on my parents' deaths.

Ed's lips twisted, transforming his handsome face into

something ugly, exposing his true character. "You don't know anything, honey. Your mind is like a swamp. Anything that goes in sinks to the bottom and clogs the pipes."

"Swamp" was the fourth word. One to go. I looked at the smiling audience. They thought we were acting, but this was a redefinition of our relationship. He was still mad at me and I wanted to hurt him back. "That's it. I want you out of my life. I'd rather have hepatitis than be with you. Matter of fact, maybe you gave me hepatitis. Which you caught when you got your xenograft."

The crowd erupted into applause and cheers. Miriam crossed off the final word. Our skit was over.

Ed grabbed my hand, yanked me forward, and forced a bow in concert with his own. John, Roger, and Brenda joined us onstage while Miriam passed the hat.

"That was great, Devyn. You're a natural," he whispered.

I released his hand. "I'll drop your stuff here tomorrow."

Roger smirked and strolled away. Brenda shook her head.

A couple of female fans rushed the stage.

"We'll talk later," Ed said to me and then flashed a wide smile toward his groupies. He probably hadn't taken me seriously, thinking he had the right to be the angry one. He stepped off the stage and still towered over the young women. They giggled. The blonde dressed in black leggings said, "I loved this. You're so creative. Do you give lessons?"

The opportunity to follow their conversation faded as I approached Miriam. "See you tomorrow," I said.

"I told you he'd be mad. He doesn't like people talking about him." Her brows furrowed as she glanced over at Ed. "Now I'm in trouble."

"No worries. I'll handle it."

I drove home, powered off my phone, and boxed up Ed's stuff while I had a good cry. What was I going to do? I liked improv. It felt a bit like therapy. I could see things so clearly. Could I continue my life on stage? Mom always said to sleep on things and look at them with a fresh eye in the morning, so I went to bed.

The next day I checked my phone. A couple of calls and messages from Ed. I carried a cardboard box with his things to my car and drove to Five Words Theater, wondering what I was going to say if he was there.

A large truck was parked near the stage door. Yellow streamers hung across the frame. I left the box in my car and headed to the entrance. Lettering on the truck read Weberton Forensics. I ran to the door. "Hello, hello, what's going on?"

A Weberton officer stopped me from scooting under the yellow tape that I now saw read *Crime Scene*. "Can I see your ID, miss?" he asked.

As I rummaged through my purse for my wallet, I asked, "What happened?"

"I'm not at liberty to say, miss."

I handed over my driver's license.

He stared at my name. "Stay here," he said, giving it back before calling someone on his radio. When he got off, he said, "They want to talk to you."

"They" turned out to be the detective on the case. A short, dumpy woman in her mid-forties. I followed her car to the local police station. Detective Shoemaker escorted me to an interrogation room. She still hadn't told me what was going on. I kind of hoped the skinny blonde who came on to Ed last night had had an unfortunate accident. I didn't know her and liked the idea of him in massive trouble. Did that mean I still had feelings for him? I didn't want to think about it.

"I understand you and Ed Wilson were seeing each other," Shoemaker said.

"Did something happen to Ed?" I asked, not sure how to play this.

"He was staying with you?"

"For the last month or so, but not last night."

"Did you have a fight?"

Did Miriam tell them that? "No, just time to move on."

"When did you leave the theater? And can anyone confirm your whereabouts?"

"I left right after the last improv sketch finished. I think Miriam saw me leave. But after that I was home alone. Can you please tell me what's going on?"

A knock on the door interrupted any explanation. Another detective entered, one I recognized immediately. Detective Lou Armon. I closed my eyes for a second as memories of my parents' deaths and the hours I spent with this guy badgering me came flooding back.

"So I hear you're doing quite well," he said. "But I knew we would meet again. Trouble always seems to find people like you."

I sat up straight and grabbed my purse. "Somebody tells me what happened now, or I'm out of here."

Lou took over the interview. "We've been told you seemed pretty angry at Mr. Wilson last night in your set."

"It's called acting." I pushed my chair back. "Nice seeing you again, Lou." I stood, waiting for someone to stop me. I headed for the door and actually had my hand on the handle.

Shoemaker gave in first. "Ed's dead. It appears someone spiked his liquor with some pills. We found a couple of Xanax on the floor," she said. "Miriam told us you were dumping him, so we've got a lot of questions for you."

I swung around and fixed them with an unflinching gaze. "I didn't kill him. We had a fling and it was over. End of story. I didn't see him last night after I left the theater. I packed his stuff and was bringing it back to the theater today so he could pick it up." *And move on to his next conquest*, I added to myself, conscious enough not to say that out loud and stir up Lou's interest.

He jumped in anyway. "People close to you seem to have a habit of dying."

Shoemaker stood. "I'll walk you to your car and pick up Ed's things. That would be a big help. Plus if you could forward any messages from him yesterday to my cell."

I nodded, knowing I had no choice unless I wanted to delay the investigation and look even more guilty. The sooner they found the killer, the sooner Lou would be off my back.

Shoemaker followed behind me with Lou bringing up the rear. The guy was relentless. I increased my pace until Shoemaker's breath came out in small puffs. At the car, I clicked my remote to swing the trunk open automatically, revealing the cardboard box that held two pairs of pants, four shirts, a pair of running shoes, and several *GQ* magazines.

Lou picked up the box and Shoemaker handed me a card with her cell number on it. "We'll be in touch," she said.

Lou added, "Count on it."

Despite my threat in the improv, I wasn't about to share Ed's secret with anyone. Maybe they'd get lucky when questioning the others.

I wanted more info to protect myself. I called Miriam and met her at Brews, the local coffeehouse that didn't serve alcohol in spite of its name. They had an open mike Thursday through Saturday evenings where I'd been considering reading some of my dreary poems now that I had gotten up the nerve to perform.

I found her at a table for two, drinking chamomile tea. After ordering an iced coffee, I dropped my purse on the floor, sat across from her, and noted her red-rimmed eyes.

"I found him," she said with a hiccup. "I thought he was sleeping in his dressing room because you threw him out."

"I didn't. But don't worry about that. Tell me."

She lifted the cup and took a sip. "He was still in the same clothes as last night, lying on the floor. There was an empty bottle of whiskey and a couple of pills. I thought he was drunk, but he didn't move and when I touched him..." She sobbed. Her hand shook.

I grasped it and helped her maneuver the cup to the table without a spill.

Miriam regained control. "What's going to happen to Five Words? How can we live this down? He was our draw. A handsome, single heartthrob. An artist, too."

Five Words was Miriam's sole source of income. She ran the whole place, advertising, selling tickets, hiring the actors. Even being closed for a short time would bring her to the financial edge. I realized why she put up with philandering Ed. "Why was he so angry when he overheard me asking if you'd dated him?"

"I don't know how you picked up on that."

"Just a talent I have." Or a curse. I didn't want to know everyone's business, but I picked up on things others didn't see. Just like when my dad called me for the last time.

"I'm older than him. He didn't like anyone knowing he always came to me when things went wrong. I waited up last night, but figured you two had worked things out. Instead, he drank himself to death."

"Not exactly. The police are calling it murder."

***

Working out always helped me think. I dressed in all black workout gear. Brenda had introduced me to her gym, saying we needed to stay in shape if we wanted to stay in the show. Today was our Zumba class and we usually warmed up on the treadmill half an hour before. I wasn't sure she'd be there, but she was, dressed in form-fitting navy active wear, not an ounce of fat on her. I dropped my purse, jumped on the machine next to hers, and started walking, which automatically activated the manual program.

"I didn't think you'd be here," she said, keeping up her pace.

Because she'd probably ratted me out to the cops. "You don't seem upset." I increased my speed.

"Ed wasn't my favorite person. When I joined the act, he was involved with someone else. He came on to me anyway. I don't date people I work with. Learned that lesson a long time ago. No offense." She glanced at me as if to gauge my reaction.

"My first and last time, I hope. The cops are all over me."

She grunted. "I had my turn early this morning. Luckily my mom is visiting from out of town and we did dinner and a movie. After the police spoke to her, she kept trying to talk me into coming home with her, away from my sordid acting life."

I glanced at my speed and returned my gaze to her. "Was Ed ever serious with anyone?"

She frowned and clicked up the incline. "Before my time, but supposedly he was gaga about Stephanie Jutter."

"The film actress?"

"Rumor has it she got a part and cut him loose. Off to Hollywood with barely a wave goodbye."

That explained a lot. Ed didn't want to get hurt again. Stephanie Jutter was a true star, a gorgeous and talented actress with a son who'd inherited her good looks. I jumped off the treadmill. It was worth looking into, but Hollywood was on the other side of the country. I didn't think it would lead anywhere. "I've got to run," I said. Brenda picked up the pace, going for a strong finale.

"Talk to John. He's been in the company forever."

I'd learned that John believed doing the same thing at the same time every day gave structure to life and kept problems away. The clock read noon on my way out of the gym so he would be at the diner around the corner from Five Words. I headed over, but when I glanced at his favorite table, no one was sitting there. Since his theory of life hadn't worked, I had no clue where he'd be. "Has John been in?" I asked the cashier.

Footsteps sounded behind me and I stepped into a large hand slapping me on the side of the head. Wow. Now I knew what they meant by "seeing stars." My neck achieved a new position with the force of the blow, one it never could have managed on its own. I ducked both from the pain and the sight of another hand ready to whack me. Still in my cross-trainers, I kicked the guy's knee hard with the chunky rubber and his hands dropped to clutch the spot.

"John! John! Stop it!" the cashier shouted, running around the counter.

"She killed Ed," he said. "He's dead. My best friend is dead." He crumpled into a sobbing mess.

"I didn't do it. I swear," I called, one hand on my neck, making sure everything was still connected. "I'm so sorry, John." Why was he accusing me? "I didn't even see Ed after the show last night."

"But all the detective's questions were about you." He stood. "I don't understand."

That would be my pal Lou. He thought I was holding something back about my parents' death and wouldn't let it go. Professional pride, no interest in my parents. Just a need to be right. I did have a secret, but I would take it to my own grave. The situation with Ed had given him a second shot at me. "That's got nothing to do with Ed. Lou's just out to get me."

The cashier walked John back to his favorite table. "Stay here," she said. "You can't attack people like that. I'm calling the police."

"Please don't," I said. "I need a chiropractor more than the cops." I slid into the booth opposite John and set my purse on the seat next to me. "We can talk this out."

"Are you sure, miss?" she asked.

I grabbed my neck again. "Yeah, sure. Can I get a diet cola and a BLT?"

She nodded and left.

"John, tell me about Ed and Stephanie Jutter."

"That's old news." He didn't even look at me.

"What about the baby?" I asked.

"I don't know anything—" he started, but broke off when I pursed my lips and nodded.

"Ed told me."

"Why should I believe you?"

"Think about it. How else would I know? He felt so guilty for abandoning his son that he got drunk and blabbed one night. No names. He didn't tell me about Stephanie, just that someone he was serious with got pregnant and he broke it off."

"Nobody knew about the baby. He told everyone she dumped him for a part. She did go to Hollywood, and had the baby while filming. They can do that with camera angles. Her broken heart made her a star. Ed always told me he did her a favor."

My diet soda arrived. True confession sessions made me thirsty, like I had to wash and rinse the insides of my mouth to clean out the dirty secrets I'd heard. I drank and swallowed until I'd finished half of the cola. By the time I left, John was back to crying. I'd drunk the rest and also got a to-go cup. I didn't think it would be enough. I was at a total dead end and still standing right in the center of the police's bullseye.

I walked to the theater. Forensics was gone. A CLOSED sign hung on the front door. Miriam, ever efficient. I wandered around to the side stage door and tried the handle. It was open. I knew it was hopeless, but maybe the security tape would reveal something. I checked. The system had been switched off. The police must have taken it. I set my purse on the desk and wended my way through the building, not sure what I was looking for. Ed's dressing room still had crime scene tape across the door. When I slipped under, small flags that marked where his body had been found confronted me. The tainted liquor bottle was gone, collected for evidence.

I had given him a bottle of Fireball for our one-month anniversary. What if that was what he'd been drinking? It would have my fingerprints on it. Lou had insisted on taking my prints while he investigated the fire at my parents' house. I don't know what purpose he thought they would serve. Their bedroom had burnt to a crisp. The house had been condemned. I had proof that I was Florida. He'd demanded records from my phone carrier because it was only a two-hour flight back to Jersey. They cleared me. But my prints could be used against me in a circumstantial case. The only saving grace was I didn't have access to Xanax. I shivered in the empty theater, retrieved my stuff, and left.

I drove home to find the detectives searching my apartment. The search warrant was signed off on by a judge and the police were allowed to look any place a pill bottle could be. Shoemaker was in the bathroom rummaging through the medicine chest and the cabinet under the sink. Lou focused on my bedroom and slid open each dresser drawer. My bras used to be folded neatly, but no more. He approached the nightstands with a flourish of his hand, and slid the first one open, revealing my face cream and body lotions. The other one had various earbuds, chargers, cords for my phone and tablet.

Shoemaker finished in the bathroom and approached me. "Your purse, please." She dumped the contents on the dining room table and there, inside a tissue, was the bottle I never had. Xanax. Someone had slipped it into my purse. I'd seen Miriam, Brenda, and John. They all had access to my purse. I'd even left it alone during my trip to the theater.

"Fingerprint that, please," I said. "It's not mine."

Lou ran to the table and bent over it. "No prescription label, so she bought it on the street."

"Or ripped off the label. I'll check it out," Shoemaker said. Her eyes looked dark and troubled. I know mine did when she slapped cuffs around my wrists.

Lou booked me at the station and took my prints again. It was so late in the day, I spent the night in jail. The next day, I called my lawyer and she arranged to bail me out despite Lou's protests. I returned home for a hot shower and a change of clothes. I'd barely finished when someone knocked on my door. Miriam. I let her in and offered her a seat on my sofa.

"Are you okay? Detective Shoemaker wants to see me again and mentioned you'd been arrested and released," she said. "I didn't want to go in without talking to you."

"I guess they're trying to line up witnesses. Do you remember what brand of whiskey you saw in Ed's dressing room?"

"Not sure, but it smelled like cinnamon in there."

Yep, that was Fireball. "How about Xanax? Does anyone of the improv company use that, you know, for stage fright or something?"

"I don't know. I shouldn't say anything, but John did have a breakdown a couple of years ago. He might take something."

That I could believe after him slugging me. He was definitely off his meds. "A couple of years ago? Around when Stephanie Jutter left the team?"

"How do you know about Stephanie? Boy that was tough. She left. Ed was off his game and then John was out for a bit. I had to close for a few weeks until I could find replacements. Luckily Brenda and Roger came along."

"At the same time?"

"I don't remember. Anyway, I came to ask you to stay with the company."

"I may be in prison if I can't prove my innocence."

"I think you owe me as long as you're able. I'll be looking for replacements in the meantime. Can you perform tonight?"

Boy was she financially strapped. But it might be my last chance to perform and I'd get to interact with my suspects. I still needed to talk to Roger. "Okay."

I showed up an hour early to find everyone huddled in the main dressing room. Miriam and Brenda sat facing John, who was crying. Roger stood off to the side. "What's going on?" I whispered to him.

"John's refusing to perform. He's been blubbering about Ed."

"It is kind of quick for a reopening." I stepped closer to Miriam, ready to advise her to call tonight off.

Miriam said, "John, you didn't have anything to do with Ed's dying."

My radar went off. Oh boy. I knew what was coming. I pulled out my phone and flicked on video record.

John whined, "But he called me. I could have stopped him."

"What are you saying, John?" I asked. I'd had one of those calls from my dad and felt so helpless. Mom not feeling good had worked out to be full-blown inoperable cancer, but that wasn't the worst of it.

"Ed thanked me for my Xanax. I didn't even know it was gone. Said it was going to make it all easier once he mixed it with the liquor."

"When did he call you?" I asked. Lou wouldn't be happy with this video.

"Late. He was depressed. Said he'd messed up another relationship. He was already drunk." Tears squeezed out of John's eyes and ran down his cheeks. "When he told me he was adding my pills to the booze, I begged him not to. He said not to worry, he got rid of the prescription bottle. It wouldn't come back at me. I ran out to my car and drove here."

"Did you find him?" Miriam's voice held a trace of accusation. I understood entirely.

"I should have called the police. I didn't want to get him in trouble. It took twenty minutes to get here. I sat in the car and realized I didn't have a key."

"Why didn't you call me?" Miriam asked.

"I kept dialing Ed, but he didn't answer." John looked at me. "Sorry, Devyn, I blamed you and slipped an empty Xanax bottle in your purse, but it really is all my fault." John sobbed again.

I knew it wasn't. I stopped recording, and forwarded the video to Shoemaker and Lou. They needed to know Ed's death was by his own doing.

The fault lay in Ed, just like the fault lay in my dad. I'd picked up on something in that last call from Dad and kept questioning him. He wasn't going to tell me he'd put Mom out of her misery and was going to do the same for himself, but then he did. He had the fan with the sparking plug ready to go. The fire would hide all the evidence. I guess Lou's sixth sense made him keep badgering me for the truth, but there was no way the tragic story of my parents' murder-suicide would come from my lips. I gave up only five words: "It was a terrible accident."

ASK FRED THE USHER
By Arthur Vidro

When trying to solve a murder that occurs during a performance, it often helps to know something about the show.

"Sir, may I see your ticket?" I purposely shone my metal flashlight at him, even though the house lights were still on full.

The man glanced at my uniform and pillbox hat and blushed as his date gave him a glare. "Er, sorry, kid, we were so eager to get good seats we must have forgotten about tickets. How much does Royal Clown charge?"

"Five dollars for adults." I didn't bother telling him the student price. He fumbled in his wallet and handed me a ten-spot. "Seems like a lot," he muttered out of the side of his mouth, making sure his date didn't hear.

"Tell President Carter," I whispered back.

I returned to the ticket table outside the high-school auditorium entrance. Vickie Fish was manning the table and cashbox by herself. She had sent me in after the non-paying couple. I waited until there was a lull in customers buying tickets.

"You were right," I reported. "That couple hadn't paid." As I turned the money over to Vickie, my flashlight dropped and bounced off my foot. I winced in pain. The darned thing was heavy. I stared at it curiously, then retrieved it and stuck it inside my inner jacket pocket.

"I'm just glad you were hanging around," Vickie said. "I can't leave my post, and your uniform lets them know you're connected to the show." She turned away as a short line of ticket-buyers formed.

I returned into the auditorium and glared at the man who had called me "kid." Heck, I'm a senior, albeit undersized. Oh, well. Nothing to be done about it. I politely helped an elderly couple find their seats, then glanced at my watch. Time for the backstage meeting.

The cast and crew crowded into the makeup room as the director, Nick Mandwacher, gave his final instructions and asked some last-minute questions.

Yes, the set was ready, the lights had been tested, the sound system was working just fine, and the special-effects machine was in place.

"How about the cast?" he asked.

"Everyone's here," stage manager Beth Peril reported, staring down for confirmation at the checkmarks she had made on the roster attached to her clipboard. Then she looked up impishly. "But a few of the actors aren't feeling well. Probably something they ate—"

A few of us chuckled, but Mandwacher shook his head in disapproval. He was a distinguished elderly gentleman with a white beard, like a thin Santa Claus without much mirth. It was about ten minutes before the opening curtain. Although some patrons were just now entering the building, most of the audience was comfortably ensconced in the auditorium. "Wait. What about the defective door hinge?"

"Just finished replacing it, sir," Brian Silver reported. "The set door is fine now." He placed a handful of tools, including a wrench, onto a small side table and wiped the sweat off his forehead. His genial face always made me think of leprechauns.

"Very good," said Mandwacher. "Now I'm off to my back-row seat. Any questions? Last chance to ask me, because you're all stuck backstage now." There were no questions. "Remember, no matter what size your role, whether you perform onstage or help out offstage, you are all Royal Clown Players. I know you'll make me proud."

He strode off.

There was small talk and costume adjustments. Andrew Ordiv, president of the Royal Clown Players, whipped out his aviation-style eyeglasses and consulted a scribbled welcoming speech he would make to the audience. Andrew always exuded calm intelligence leavened with wit.

Eddy Wisser, the lead actor, vainly announced he needed help to perfect his makeup and thick curly hair. The makeup girls squealed in delight and jumped at the chance. Eddy and I had been the two final candidates for the lead role. Mandwacher had stunned me by giving it to Eddy, even though I was able to act circles around him and display the compassionate family-man persona needed (and which Eddy lacked).

"You gave a much better audition," Jodi Tassel, a highly talented junior, had told me. "But Eddy is much bigger and looks a lot older. That's why he got the part." She was right. Eddy, though a sophomore, had a full mustache while I, two years older, still awaited my first shave.

I walked over to Eddy and told him to break a leg. I meant it.

"Aw, go seat some senior citizens," he snarled, and returned his attention to the fourteen-year-olds puffing up his hair.

Nothing I could say to Eddy would do any good so I headed out. If I hustled, I'd have time for a quick chat with Vickie before closing the auditorium doors.

As I looked back at the last of the cast and crew dispersing, I saw the pile of tools on the table. One tool was no longer there....

***

"We welcome you to our opening performance," Andrew Ordiv told the audience. He had changed into a suit and tie. "Tonight's drama earned playwright Thornton Wilder his third and final Pulitzer Prize, and after tonight we hope you'll understand why. If you enjoy the show, then be sure to return for our next production, which will be the Gershwin musical *Girl Crazy*."

Polite applause. I stood silent and motionless in the darkened rear of the auditorium. I had closed the huge, slow-moving auditorium doors behind me, shutting out the light from the lobby where Vickie remained to greet and collect money from tardy patrons.

The curtain opened and the show began.

Vickie and I closed the doors together when act two began. And again for act three. All that time, the cast and crew were backstage or in the wings or dressing rooms or makeup room or the backstage rest rooms, away from the audience. And each time we closed the auditorium doors, I noticed Nick Mandwacher in his seat, scribbling notes. Unlike some other directors, he never went backstage during intermissions. To him, audience and participants should be kept separated until the show was over.

But when the show was over, Nick Mandwacher was no longer in his seat. He was sprawled awkwardly face down on the carpeted floor. Blood trickled from the back of his head. He was dead.

***

Much, much later, after the crowd had gone home and the body carted away, a ruddy homicide lieutenant was interrogating all us Royal Clown Players while a plainclothes officer took notes. To our dismay, we hadn't been allowed to change out of our costumes. We sat or loitered onstage while Lieutenant Florin paced the apron. He was quite tall, a head taller than our tallest member, Eddy Wisser.

"Who found the body?" Florin demanded.

Vickie raised her hand. "I guess that was me. As the show was ending, I inched back to the auditorium doors so I could open them as soon as the house lights came on. That's when I saw him. Some people in the audience must have seen him then, too."

"You were in the audience, not in the lobby?"

"That's right. When act three was ready to start, the usher and I closed the auditorium doors but remained on the inside. Then we found seats for ourselves and watched the show."

"Were you and this usher sitting next to each other?"

"No. I was in the middle section, he was along one of the sides. That was easier for him because when the announcement was made about actors getting food—"

"Never mind that. Just answer the questions." He glared at her, then glared at all of us. He seemed quite fond of glaring.

He asked a few specific questions that elicited from Vickie and me that we closed the doors before the start of each act.

"How many acts in this kiddie show?"

Andrew Ordiv answered. "This is a three-act show, sir. Thornton Wilder tended to write—"

"Stop telling me more than I asked." He glared again. "I don't know anything about theater, but I don't need to know. Now, let's focus on the weapon. A bloodstained wrench was found on the floor in a backstage corner. It's too soon to know for certain, but it could be the murder weapon. It's been removed for analysis." He paused for dramatic effect, then sprang as if to catch us by surprise. "Whose wrench was it?"

Brian Silver explained that the theater troupe owned several tools, including a wrench, which he had used shortly before act one to replace a door hinge onstage. "But I never saw the wrench again since our pre-curtain meeting with Mr. Mandwacher. There was no blood on it at the time."

"Did anyone else here see that wrench?"

A few of us confirmed Brian's having placed the wrench down while talking to Mandwacher, and the absence then of blood on the tool, and of Brian's not having picked it up again. But no one reported having noticed the presence or absence of the wrench after that point.

Florin sprang at Brian Silver. "Where were you during act three?"

Brian shrank back. "In the makeup room. For the entire act and beyond. Since I'm not in the cast, I wasn't in the curtain call, so I stayed backstage."

"Makeup room? Do you wear makeup?" he asked with a sneer.

"No. But it's a comfortable room and reasonably large."

"Can anyone vouch for your being in the makeup room for the entire third act?"

"Sure. Evan Katt can vouch for me."

Evan stepped forward. "That's true. Brian and I were playing chess. We're teammates. We've got a great shot at the county championship this year. So we practice whenever we can. Right before act three began, we broke out the chessboard. I had white. I opened with a Ruy Lopez and Brian countered with—"

"Stop answering beyond my questions!" screamed Florin. He glared again at all of us. One by one he questioned the members of the crew, and they all corroborated that everyone not in the cast had been watching the riveting chess match, which had been interrupted only by the hoopla following the discovery of Mandwacher's body.

Florin shifted his attention to us cast members. "Where were each of you during the third act?"

Jodi Tassel responded first. She had enough talent to make it in Hollywood, we all thought. A year earlier, she and I had played a married couple in *The Male Animal*. She had stage presence but also excelled at subtly enhancing the performances of others, sometimes without their knowing it. Offstage, however, she could be flippant.

"I have an alibi," she said.

The lieutenant rubbed his hands eagerly. "Such as?"

"I was kidnapped by gypsies."

Eddy Wisser guffawed like a hyena.

"You kids may find this amusing, but this is a homicide, and when I find out who's guilty, that person will be in a heap of trouble. I realize most and possibly all of you are innocent of homicide. But anyone who hinders my investigation will be arrested pronto. Clear?"

Jodi rolled her eyes. "*Capiche.*"

"But, Lieutenant," said Andrew Ordiv, "you're approaching this problem the wrong way."

"Oh, I am, am I? And how would you approach it, wise-guy?"

"This is clearly a case of opportunity."

"Meaning?"

"Think about it. Until I stepped out in front of the curtain, the house lights were on. Only then were they turned off. Naturally, if Mr. Mandwacher had been attacked before I gave my talk, the attack would have been witnessed by a couple hundred people who came to see the show."

The lieutenant nodded. "Makes sense so far. Keep going."

"You're saying somebody took a weapon from backstage and assaulted Mr. Mandwacher. But if that's true, then when did the assault take place?"

"After your speech and before the play ended."

"The house lights are always on for the intermissions. During both intermissions, if Mr. Mandwacher was on the floor of the auditorium, he would have been noticed—especially since he was sitting near the exit door."

Florin nodded. "That means he must have been alive as the house lights, as you call them, were turned off at the end of the final intermission. For confirmation, there was a writing tablet found by his body. It contains notes, apparently in the victim's own handwriting, covering the first two acts and the start of act three. That suggests the assault must have occurred during the final act. But his notes were scribbled so sloppily, it makes me wonder if he was already ailing or wounded."

"If I could see the notes," piped up Beth Peril, "I could tell you if they're in Mr. Mandwacher's handwriting."

Florin focused on her. "And who are you, little girl?" Beth was a good deal short of five feet tall and could still pass for a preteen.

"I'm the stage manager."

"If it becomes necessary, little girl, we'll have you identify the victim's notes. But they were so sloppy—"

"Probably," said Andrew politely, "the notes were sloppy because Mandwacher was scribbling in the dark. The house is dark while the play is being performed."

"Oh." Florin cleared his throat. "Of course."

"Right," said Andrew. "So we know Mandwacher was alive and unharmed at the start of every act. And all the actors and actresses were onstage, or backstage waiting to go on, or had finished with their roles and were waiting for the curtain call. There is no way for us to get to the back of the auditorium without walking down either of the two aisles leading from the base of the stage to the main exit. And if anyone in the cast did that, they would have been seen by everyone in the audience."

"But couldn't someone in the cast have snuck down that way before the show started? And then after it began, made the attack?"

"But then they'd be out of place. You can't make an entrance onto the stage except from either of the two wings or from the curtain behind the stage. And once you're down in the audience you can't get to the wings, or anywhere backstage, or onstage here, without being seen by everyone in the audience."

Florin smiled slowly. "That's true for the cast. But what about all the backstage workers?"

Beth Peril spoke up. "The crew stays backstage or off in the wings the entire time."

"But can't they head into the audience? After all, they're not in costume."

"Physically, they can descend the one set of stairs leading from the stage to the two aisles in the audience, but they would have been seen by everyone in the auditorium."

"True enough. We've released the audience, because they didn't see anybody walking down those steps...or anything else of importance. But wait! Couldn't someone have gone down those steps during intermission—"

Beth held up her clipboard. "I'm sitting backstage where I can see the stairs leading off. Nobody went down them. Nobody went up them."

The lieutenant shook his head. "Doesn't add up. Not if the weapon came from back here."

Andrew nodded in agreement. "You're right that it doesn't add up, sir. For the weapon to have reached the scene of the crime prior to the crime is impossible."

"And yet it happened. Wait! Could the victim himself have brought the wrench from backstage into the auditorium?"

"Doubtful. All eyes were on Mandwacher while he spoke to us and then left. And you said the bloody wrench was found backstage. Mandwacher certainly didn't put it there. Looks like what we have here is an impossible crime."

Florin shook his head. "Nothing's impossible here. We just have to find the answer." He looked around at us and pointed at Beth. "Little girl, was the staircase under your observation the entire time?"

"Well," she hedged, "for the intermissions, yes."

Florin seized on her hesitancy. "And the rest of the time?"

"I wasn't watching the steps when I went onstage during act three."

Florin did a double-take. "*During* act three? But you're the stage manager, not an actress. Or am I missing something here?"

Beth blushed. "At one point I go onstage and tell George Antrobus about the poisonings—"

"Whoa! You're going too fast for me. Who's this George guy?"

Eddy Wisser strutted forward. "He's the lead character. I, of course, perform that role."

"And what's this about poisonings? More crimes during the show?"

Despite the gravity of the situation, a few of us chuckled.

"No, no," said Beth. "It's make-believe poisonings."

Florin extended his arms and gazed heavenward. "Isn't there anything normal about this case?" He turned back to little Beth. "Tell me about the make-believe poisonings."

"It's food poison. Could be ptomaine, we're not one hundred percent sure. Anyway, I go onstage and tell George Antrobus—the character played by Eddy there—that the four actors he's expecting to appear can't appear, because they all ate something that disagreed with them. Food poisoning. That's why we have substitutes fill in for the sick actors—"

"Enough!" Florin lowered his head. "This is getting wackier and wackier. Let me make sure I understand. The actors were poisoned, except you're not sure what the poison was, but it doesn't matter, because it's make-believe poison; and it's not the real actors who were poisoned but make-believe actors that nobody ever sees, and now they had to be replaced?"

Beth beamed. "That's it exactly, sir. A seamstress from the wardrobe department goes onstage as a substitute actress, and also two other folks from backstage, plus the ush—"

"Wait!" Another plainclothes officer had entered the room and whispered something to Florin, who frowned. Then he sighed, adjusted his necktie, and paused, thinking. Finally, he looked around at us.

"We're going to let you go home now. It's probably past some of your bedtimes anyway. On the way out, you will each give your name, address, and telephone number to one of the officers standing at the door. If you can think of anything else that happened tonight, please get in touch with us."

Most of the crew headed for the exit. Most of the cast went backstage to the dressing rooms to remove their costumes. Andrew, Beth, and I remained onstage.

"Lieutenant," asked Andrew, "are you allowed to tell us why you're suddenly letting us go?"

Florin hung his head. "We've heard back from a police technician. The bloody wrench we confiscated was not the murder weapon. Although the blood on it matches the victim's type, the weapon itself doesn't fit any of the wounds. Going to have to rethink this case entirely before proceeding." He summoned the officer who had been taking notes. "Let's go, Ralph. We've learned all we can for now."

They walked out.

Beth headed for the pay phone to call her mom. Andrew and I went into the boys' dressing room. He changed into jeans and a polo shirt. I changed out of my uniform pants, put on my sneakers, hung up my pillbox hat, but left on my ushering shirt and jacket.

As usual, Andrew turned out the backstage and auditorium lights and locked all the doors behind us. A member of the custodial staff was still cleaning up in the main hall and could unlock any doors if the remaining police requested it.

The few students who had cars drove home. Brian and Evan hopped on their bicycles and pedaled away, calling chess moves to each other in the dark as they played a mental game without a board. Mr. Wisser picked up Eddy and his neighbor Vickie in his Trans Am. All the others had already gone.

When four of us remained, I asked, "So, do you think the police will solve this soon?"

"I don't think they'll solve it at all," said Jodi Tassel. "At least not with that Florin guy on the case. He's not bright enough." Her mother arrived in a station wagon and Jodi clambered in, waving good night.

Andrew and I waited with Beth for her mom to pick her up. After all, it was late at night, and we felt it only proper.

"Who do you think could have killed Mr. Mandwacher?" Beth asked. "I liked him."

"Guess somebody else didn't," said Andrew, eying the bulge in my jacket pocket.

I nodded my agreement. "An auditorium full of people, an unknown murder weapon…it might be asking too much to expect the police to solve it."

"Oh, darn," said Beth. "I just lost an earring. Help me find it, guys."

We got on our knees and patted the ground in the dark.

"Maybe," said Andrew to me, "if you turned on your flashlight—"

I cleared my throat. "Sorry. The, er, batteries died."

A minute later Joan Peril had pulled into the car circle. In the beam of the headlights from her AMC Gremlin flashed a little sparkle.

"My earring!" squealed Beth with delight, hastily retrieving it.

We bade her good night and waved to Mrs. Peril, who offered us rides home, too, but Andrew and I lived in the other direction and turned her down.

During the walk home, Andrew stopped and stared at me curiously. "Why?" he asked.

"Why what?"

"Why did you kill Mandwacher?"

"What the…me? You must…" I didn't want to tell Andrew a lie, but I wasn't ready to confess. "What gives you the idea that I did it?"

"It had to be you. Any member of the cast or crew could have taken the wrench—"

"Which wasn't the murder weapon," I interrupted.

"—but if the blood on it was Mandwacher's type—well, let's suppose it was his blood. Although anyone in the show could have taken the wrench, only one person could have brought the wrench backstage after it had gotten Mandwacher's blood on it. In your usher costume, you—and only you—could go from backstage to the audience and vice versa, without calling attention to yourself. But you didn't even have to resort to subterfuge. When the lights went out to start act three, Mandwacher was alive. You were in the audience. You must have dealt with Mandwacher before you climbed onstage to take the place of one of the stricken actors. You brought that wrench onstage with you, in that pocket where your flashlight is now. Then after your scene you exited backstage along with the other substitute actors. You started the act in the audience but ended the act backstage. No one else could have brought that bloody wrench backstage. It had to be you."

We had paused at the corner where our residential area began. I was silent.

"It's not proof that you killed Mandwacher, but it is proof that you brought the wrench that had his blood type on it backstage. No one else could have done that. But why did you take the wrench at all? You already had your murder weapon on you."

I stared at him. "You know?"

"I've figured it out."

I leaned against a mailbox. I was exhausted. Too exhausted to lie. "I took the wrench to produce the effect it caused—to get the victim's blood on it and, no pun intended, throw a monkey wrench into the investigation. I brought it backstage after the deed—and after I dipped it into the little puddle of blood next to Mandwacher—to allow everyone backstage to be considered a suspect. Maybe it was a mistake. But I figured if the police concentrated on the wrench, they wouldn't be looking around for the real weapon, which I had decided on earlier, when it bashed my foot. The real weapon would have pointed straight at me."

"The flashlight, which is still in your pocket," said Andrew.

"Still in my pocket," I agreed.

"I bet the batteries didn't die. You were just afraid someone might spot blood on it, so you've kept the flashlight in your inner pocket all along. The bulge is obvious."

"And it's uncomfortable," I said with a nod. I took it out and showed it to him. "And you're right. The batteries still work. I'll turn it on so we can see better." I did so. "What else did you figure?"

"You left the top part of your costume on because you couldn't change back into your normal shirt without the rest of us in the dressing room seeing the bloodstained flashlight. Even if you wiped or washed most of the blood away, you couldn't risk anyone—either the police or us—noticing even a single drop of blood on you or the flashlight. But why did you do it?"

"Isn't it obvious? Mandwacher should have cast me as George Antrobus. Instead he went with Eddy Wisser, who's no actor."

"That much is true," nodded Andrew. "Wisser's a wuss."

He walked on ahead, slightly uphill, deep in thought. I followed. We soon reached the intersection where normally Andrew turned left and I continued straight. I was huffing and sweating, which had never happened on our walks home before.

"So," I said.

"So," he replied.

"So what are you going to do about it?"

"Nothing."

My eyes widened. "Why not?"

"Three reasons. One, we have another show tomorrow night, and then the following weekend, too. It's too late to recast your role. Besides, the costume fits you and not anyone else; it would take too long to alter it. The show must go on."

"And the other reasons?"

"You're my friend. I don't condone what you did, but I don't want anything to happen to you. Though as president of Royal Clown, I'm going to suspend you from our next production."

"And that's it?" I asked, incredulous.

"That's it. Make the punishment fit the crime."

"You said three reasons—you've only given two."

"Ah, yes. The third reason might be the biggest. Because you were right—Mandwacher should have cast you in the lead. That makes it quasi-justifiable homicide. Just don't ever do it—or anything like it—again. Good night, Art. See you tomorrow." He extended a hand.

I raised my right hand, which still wielded the flashlight. Then I transferred it to my left and shook Andrew's hand.

He walked his way, I walked mine.

A block from home I dropped the still-good flashlight into a curbside garbage can, just in case.

I could deal with being left out of the next show. At least I was still Fred the usher in *The Skin of Our Teeth*.

DEATH TAKES A BOW
By Mo Walsh

When Burt Beulow's wife, ex-wife, and new girlfriend are all cast in the production of Julia Caesaria, *an all-female version of Shakespeare's famous tragedy, not all of the backstabbing is in the script.*

If only one of the prop knives secreted in the robes of the eight senators onstage were capable of killing, Penelope Veesey vowed she would plunge it—not into the breast of Traci Freeman, playing Julia Caesaria—but into the back of the actor kneeling at the dictator's feet.

"'Most *puissant* Caesaria!' Not pissant! *Pwee-sent,* rhymes with 'recent,' remember?" Penelope smacked the script in her lap. "If you can't, I'll replace you, final rehearsal or not!" It was a bluff, but Penelope was certain the "pissant" had been a deliberate bid for a laugh—a problem in community theater. "Take it from 'Most high, most mighty, and most *puissant* Caesaria.' Now!"

The cast of *Julia Caesaria*, an all-female production of the Shakespearean tragedy, made it through the rest of Act III. Penelope congratulated herself on the effect of red lighting during the assassination scene, and the inspired casting of the former and the current wives of Burt Beulow as Bruta and Antonia. Their barely suppressed hostility offstage infused their onstage speeches with extra passion. On the other hand, Penelope made a note *never* again to cast either woman with Traci Freeman. The intense young realtor, turning in a stellar performance as Caesaria, was rumored to be auditioning for the part of Burt Beulow's wife number three.

Act IV proceeded smoothly between Cassia and Bruta, with the blue lighting lending the desired effect to the appearance of Caesaria's ghost near the end of Scene III. Act V opened in the same tent on the plains of Philippi, now illuminated with the soft rose of early dawn. Penelope made a note to compliment the lighting technician and stage crew on a job well done. One after another—and blessedly offstage—the bodies fell: Cassia, Titinia, Catia, Statilia, Bruta.

Onstage, Octavia proclaimed: "'Within my tent her bones tonight shall lie, most like a soldier, order'd honourably. So call the field to rest; and let's away, to part the glories of this happy day.'"

Exeunt.

"Go to black," Penelope muttered from her director's seat in the middle row, center. "Curtain." She released the stranglehold she'd held on the script ever since Messalia missed her cue in Act V, Scene III, leaving Titinia alone onstage declaiming over the dead body of Cassia. All that was left of the dress rehearsal was for the cast of the Williston Queen's Players to take their bows. Then Penelope would go through her extensive notes in the hope that tomorrow's opening would, by some miracle, go smoothly.

The curtain swept open. The stage lights came up on cue to the recorded track of "Pomp and Circumstance," the unsatisfactory, but still grandest, music Penelope had found for the *finale.* The cast members tripped out from the wings, in reverse order of importance, to take their bows. The scattering of close relatives and support crew in the audience applauded the company of nameless Roman soldiers and citizens, then the minor senators who had stabbed Caesaria with the dramatic relish of characters who had few lines to speak. As they cleared center stage to either side, the next group entered—those senators, soldiers, and servants with dialogue. Octavia shared center stage with Bruta's friend Portia and Caesaria's friend Calpurnia—the two wives of the original adapted for this all-female production. Next to take their solo bows came Cassia, then Marcia Antonia, then Bruta, and finally, as subject of the play though not the actual lead...

A pox upon it! Penelope swore. Caesaria had missed her cue. The tired smiles on the faces of the cast turned to confusion, irritation, then resignation to repeating the curtain call from the beginning. Just as Penelope rose from her seat, Caesaria stumbled onstage in the bloodstained robes of a Roman tribune, laurel wreath askew on her head. Then, despite Penelope's rule against pranks or hijinks at rehearsal, Caesaria crumpled at center stage—much better than she had in Act III, Scene 1—and fell prone, as if dead.

***

"There's an extra 'stab wound' in the costume," the medical examiner told Sheriff Annie Keeley. "The others were made by the costume designer, and the 'bloodstains' were stamped on by the fake knives when the silicone blades retracted. Pretty clever, actually." The body of Traci Freeman in the slashed and red-stained robe had been jostled and turned by panicked members of the Queen's Players cast and crew, who'd also trampled the crime scene in their efforts to help or to escape. Annie stuck to procedure, anyway, holding back while the M.E. and crime scene technicians did their jobs.

"So, there's only one actual wound?"

"Eight fakes and just one entering at about the left kidney." The M.E. smacked a hand on his lower back, above the left hip. "Not much blood really."

The body had been removed to the morgue, and the autopsy would have to confirm cause of death, but Annie didn't expect any surprises. It was not uncommon, she knew, for stab wounds to produce little external bleeding while causing massive internal loss of blood. Obviously, the victim had lived long enough to stagger onstage, but no one could report any coherent dying words, their testimony ranging from "My Guy" to "Olga" to "By Gah."

The probable murder weapon, a common camping knife showing years of wear, was found discarded far backstage right, where Traci Freeman awaited her cue for the final bow. Fingerprints seemed unlikely from a cursory inspection, but Annie hoped for some trace evidence under the microscope. The county crime scene team continued to record and search the stage and backstage areas. Annie kept out of the way, but her gaze followed the series of evidence markers that indicated blood drops and other marks or objects of potential interest. Now that the body had been removed, she would interview her witnesses in the theater to get their most accurate recollections of who had been where and the sequence of events.

She exited through the backstage left door leading to a narrow, slanted corridor. To the right, the passage ran uphill parallel to the theater's side aisle, past a fire exit at audience level, to the lobby exit. That door could not be opened from the lobby side, nor could the door from a similar passage on the other side of the theater. No one could have entered from the lobby through either door to gain access to the backstage area and Traci Freeman. Annie turned left to the dressing rooms.

"Any problems, Fergus?" she asked the deputy stationed there, a recent criminal justice graduate whose uncle had been her predecessor. Yes, connections did count.

"No, Sheriff. It's *too* quiet in there, if you ask me." He flushed pink, a habit whenever *he* thought that *she* thought he had overstepped his bounds.

"Quiet's good," she reassured him. "We don't want our witnesses mixing up their stories, right? I'll talk to the director first, if you'd send her out, please." None of the minor players already onstage nor any of the characters waiting backstage left could have struck the fatal blow. Their costumes had been bagged and tagged, just in case, and they'd been questioned early and released. Others vouched for by performers nearby had been handled next, so only three witnesses remained: the director and the final two characters to take their solo bows.

Fortunately or not, Annie was acquainted with most of the women in the Queen's Players, a fixture of the community since World War II had deprived Williston of most of its male thespians. As a teen she had been cast as a delinquent girl turned to a donkey in *Pinocchia*, and in her twenties—about fifteen near-anorexic pounds lighter—she'd played a junkie street walker in *The Ice Woman Cometh*. She had long since left the onstage dramatics to others, finding plenty of overwrought emotion in the reality of law enforcement. Nor did she need to imagine herself as anyone other than a sturdy, mid-size woman with pleasantly average looks and a sharper than average intellect.

"Penelope!" Annie called to the director (who had starred as bar owner Harriet Hope in *Ice Woman* fifteen years earlier). "You were seated center row, center seat, right? Let's talk there." Leaving the seat next to Penelope empty, so the director wouldn't feel pressured, Annie asked, "Are the lighting and curtain positions the same as they were when Traci appeared onstage?"

"The house lights weren't on." Penelope gestured to the wall sconces that illuminated the theater for the audience before and after the play and during intermission. "The onstage lighting is the same, no spots, just full-stage. We never closed the curtain after the…after, so it's the same."

"Where was it at the end of the play, before it closed and opened again?"

"In the same position. It sticks, so we just use it at the start and finish and otherwise forget about it."

"You don't close it during scene changes?"

"No. The stage crew wear all-black, so they're more or less invisible, and they only need a dim light backstage to move the flats and props."

"Good. Thanks." From her seat, Annie could see only a foot or so behind the side curtains. "How do we turn off the house lights?"

Penelope turned to the back of the theater and called, "Delia! Are you there?"

"Where else?" a voice floated in reply.

"Kill the house lights, please!"

"You got it."

A few minutes later, with the sconces extinguished, the stage area came into sharper focus. "That sure doesn't help. Now I can't see behind the side curtains at all," said Annie. "What about you, Penelope? Did you notice anything off at the end or during the curtain call?"

"I was so busy with the choreography—making sure the right

groups were coming onstage in the right order and hitting their marks—I just didn't notice anything else," the director said, her voice rising with each word. "Everything was going perfectly until Traci didn't make her cue, and then... Do I have to go through it again, Annie—I mean, Sheriff?" The director's long, sensitive face twitched with tension, her thin hands wringing like Lady Macbeth's.

"It's okay, Penelope," Annie soothed her. "Let's just sit while you tell me how the show's been going, how the cast and crew members have been getting along."

"Oh, I couldn't *accuse* anyone of such a thing! This just doesn't happen, not really! People don't—" Penelope sagged in her director's seat.

"Tell me what you know about Traci Freeman. I've seen her photo in the real estate section, but never met her. Was she new to the Queen's Players?"

"This was her first starring role, but she's been with us about three months. You know my policy—you have to work on the crew for at least one show before you audition for a lead. Traci worked publicity and house for *Molls and Dolls.* I had a feeling she was going to be good, and she nailed the part of Caesaria." Penelope pressed the palms of her hands to her eyes. "She said she acted in plays all through high school in...Scranton? She definitely knew her way around a theater."

"How did she get along with the other players? Anyone have a grudge over her getting a major part? Did she upstage or pull any *prima donna* crap?" Annie drew spirals in her notebook as she drew closer to the questions she really needed to ask. "Did she fit in?"

"Well...she was younger than our core members, and not as reserved as our generation is about her private life." Penelope had gone back to twisting her hands together, with particular attention to slight chips in her manicure. "Naturally, she had a more active social life, and—not knowing the local dynamics and relationships—she may have made a—a *faux pas.*"

"Such as?" Annie tapped her pen on the arm of the director's seat. "Come on, Penelope. You know at least one of those folks backstage is bursting to tell me."

"Burt Beulow!" Penelope hissed the name. "She met him doing publicity. He always takes a full-page ad on the inside front cover. Naturally, I told Traci to call on him, but I never thought...no one did, but then Traci told someone who told someone in the show that Burt invited her—Traci, that is—to spend the Thanksgiving week with him in the Poconos."

Annie straightened in her seat. "Didn't Traci know Burt's married to Christy? Did she know he's married, period?"

"Well, as to that, Christy never did change her name, you know, and she and Burt have been—not precisely estranged, but she's turned a blind eye to several of his *petites liaisons.* I got the impression she and Burt just couldn't be bothered to file for divorce."

"At least until Traci Freeman came along."

"I wouldn't say that." Penelope looked about the theater, as if expecting to be accused of treason. "In fact, I've said too much. I didn't mean anything by it."

"Just answer this, Penelope: The last three actors backstage for the curtain call were Emma, Christy, and Traci—three women all involved with Burt Beulow?"

The director nodded.

***

Annie directed Fergus to escort Penelope out of the theater. Before questioning the two remaining women, she decided to check the view of the stage from the lighting booth. This was accessible from a passage stage right, similar to the one on the left, with a short stairway up to the booth before the lobby exit. She found the technician who had cut the house lights half-asleep at the lighting board.

"I didn't know anyone was still up here." Annie peered at the woman, face and hair pale against her black crew clothes, except for black eyebrows defiantly thick and unshaped over pale, sleepy eyes. "You're Delia?"

"You got me, Sheriff." The technician uncoiled from her swivel seat and extended her hand. "Delia Chirko. What can I do for you?"

"I came up to check the view of the stage and backstage areas, but first, can you show me the lighting from Traci Freeman's last appearance onstage to the end of the curtain call?"

"Sure."

Annie called down to tell the crime scene team they'd be experimenting with the lighting for a few minutes. Delia produced a ring-binder holding an annotated copy of the script for *Julia Caesaria.* She flipped back from the last page to an earlier section blocked in blue marker. "That's my reminder to cue the spotlight with the blue gel for the ghost sequence," she said. "Caesaria exits, there's about a minute of dialogue, then fade to black for the end of Act IV." The blue marker bled into a pink box. "Act V opens at dawn, low light with a rose gel." She put down the binder and held up two squares of colored transparent film, showing Annie how they slotted onto a spotlight accessible from the booth. "We aren't fancy enough to have more than two spots, so I made these fit our old lights and I change the gels manually. The next scene is daylight, no gels." Delia continued through the pages of the script till the final fade to black. "The stage lights are down for about thirty seconds, just long enough for the cast to sort themselves out, then fast fade up to full light onstage."

"Just what I'm seeing now," said Annie, scanning the stage below, with the same limited view to either side of the curtain. The quick lesson in lighting had been interesting, but unhelpful as far as the case was concerned. Without much hope, she asked, "Did you notice anything from up here?"

"No, my attention was on the script, the board, and making sure what should be on was on, and off was off."

"Okay, thanks, Delia. You can bring up the house lights again."

***

Christy Germaine, the current wife of Burt Beulow, was a small woman. Annie was nonetheless surprised at the deliberately childlike figure clinging to Fergus as if he were the nice policeman helping to find her lost kitty. She turned large brown eyes, unconvincingly red-rimmed, to the spot on the stage where Traci Freeman had died. She seemed to shudder and suppress a sob, then crossed herself—with her left hand, Annie noted, her right hand still clutching the deputy's sleeve.

Annie ignored the dark-haired little doll's performance and addressed Fergus. "Thank you, Deputy. Please check with the crime scene team for any developments." Fergus backed away toward the passageway. Annie studied the allegedly wronged wife in silence until she sank into a nearby seat.

"Tears for Traci? Come on, Ms. Germaine!" Annie waited.

"You don't have to...be close to a person to cry when they're *murdered*!" Christy's look of reproach said *Where are your tears?* "You didn't work with her day after day. You didn't see her bleeding to death before your eyes!"

"I didn't have a husband who was whisking her off to the Poconos either," said Annie. "That may not move a person to tears, but I can see how it could move her to murder."

"That's ridiculous!" Christy snapped. "Burt and I have an understanding."

"But did Traci share that understanding? I've heard she, at least, was serious."

"Yeah, yeah, well, it takes two to tango and all that," said Christy, dropping her display of grief. "Burt's not made for monogamy, and I understand *that*."

"She was a young woman. Even without marriage, she might have gotten pregnant, produced more Beulow boys and girls to cut into the family fortune," Annie suggested.

Christy waved the thought away. "Check the prenup. What's gonna be mine is gonna be mine, as long as I don't divorce him. The kids split most of the rest, as many ways as there are of them when he dies. I don't care."

An interesting detail to check out. Annie would have to consider the ramifications for all parties, if true. She wrapped up the interview with Christy Germaine and turned her back over to Fergus for escort to her car.

Emma Beulow was even more blunt about her ex-husband's affair. "Up yours, Christy! What goes around comes around. That's all I have to say. I just wish she cared, but they've pretty much been going their separate ways." Emma was one of those unfortunate blondes whose hair turns dingy yellow with age. She'd chosen to go red instead with a deep maroon shade and black eyebrows plucked to high, thin arches, rather like two halves of the McDonald's sign.

"If Burt had divorced Christy to marry Traci, that would have affected you and your three children, wouldn't it, if Burt ended up supporting a wife and *two* exes?"

Emma shrugged. "It wasn't going to happen. Trust Christy to see to that."

"Are you saying she killed Traci?"

Emma's eyebrows arched higher. "She wouldn't need to. That baby doll's sunk her claws so deep in Burt he'll never squirm free."

"Not even if Traci got pregnant?" Annie posed the same situation she had before. "Even if they didn't marry, any child Traci had would cut into your kids' inheritance. You don't have to worry about that with Christy, right?"

"No way. She got her tubes tied with her premarital tummy tuck... And she finds somewhere else, anywhere else, to be on my kids' weekends." Emma smirked. "Anyway, I found out Burt got snipped before the divorce. He paid me big bucks to keep his reputation as a stud, so you're the only other one who knows he shoots blanks."

"So, no more kids for Burt." Annie suppressed a scowl at another motive gone.

"The kids are the only reason I kept the name," Emma confided. "Delia wanted us all to take my maiden name or, since I couldn't legally do that, at least hyphenate it, but can you imagine being named Chirko-Beulow? Please!"

"Delia?" repeated Annie.

"My sister, who is even now waiting to drive me home, where a chilled bottle of Conundrum is waiting for us." The arched eyebrows climbed to the middle of Emma's forehead. "Look, Sheriff, I was nowhere near Traci before she was stabbed, and I was onstage when it must have happened. So why am I still here?"

"No reason," said Annie, quickly losing interest in Emma Beulow. "You won't be able to leave just yet, though. I need to talk to your sister."

***

It was just possible that Emma Beulow had slipped across the backstage area amidst the commotion of the curtain call, stabbed Traci, and slipped back again, Annie figured. It all depended on the M.E.'s opinion of how long the victim would have been able to move about before collapsing. For Christy Germaine, positioned backstage right, it would have been easier to strike the blow, but more time would have elapsed as she got rid of the knife and made it onstage for her bow, followed by Emma's bow, and then the delayed appearance of the victim. Maybe this last witness of the night would yield some answers.

Annie chose to interview Delia Chirko in the lighting booth. "You didn't tell me you were Emma Beulow's sister," she said without a greeting. "I'm surprised I didn't know that."

"I was too old to cross your path when we were kids." The lighting technician relaxed in her swivel chair.

Another piece slotted into place. "The eyebrows! I see the resemblance now." Annie turned her back on the theater below. "Did you know about Traci and your brother-in-law?"

The abrupt question didn't faze Delia at all. "I'll admit to ex-brother-in-law, if I have to," she said, "and everyone in the theater knew Traci-with-an-I was Burt's new bimbo. Although maybe that's not fair to her. He's a good-looking jerk, he can be charming, and he's rich. I think she was serious and wanted him to be serious, too."

"Did that bother you?"

Delia barked with what was probably meant to be laughter. "She was welcome to him! Nothing to do with me, or Emma either. In fact, we kind of liked seeing Wife Number Two get the same treatment she gave Wife Number One. Just what she deserved."

"What about Emma's kids—your two nieces and your nephew? What do they deserve?"

"A better dad than Burt Beulow, but there's no changing that. A better stepmother than Christy. Even Traci would have been an improvement."

"Even if she had her own little Beulow baby to love—and share in their inheritance?"

Delia snapped control knobs on her lighting board and cut the house lights in the theater. "It's late, Sheriff, and I've been at this board nonstop since dinner. I'm going home."

"But you haven't been here nonstop, have you, Delia?"

"Right. I left to pee about an hour ago. Sorry, I forgot." She flipped a switch and the passage lights at the base of the stairs went dark.

"And you took a break right after you brought up the lights for the curtain call. Exit Traci and any Freeman kids cutting into the Chirko-Beulow heirs' fortune." Annie edged away from the stairs. "It was easy for you to scoot down the passage and through the door in the wings. If anyone did see you backstage, all in black, they'd take you for one of the stage crew, and I bet we find a black ski mask or something like it hidden up here or in your bag."

"You're crazy, and I'm tired. Good night, Sheriff." Delia started down the stairs.

"Fergus!" Annie called to the deputy waiting in the passage. "Take Ms. Chirko to the costume racks, then send her home—after the crime scene techs bag her clothes."

***

"We got her, Fergus!" Annie ended the call from the lab three days later. "We've got a sliver of that blue gel material between the knife blade and the hilt. And we've got blood on Delia's pants."

"We got blood on some of the cast members' costumes, too," Fergus noted. "Won't the defense bring that up?"

"The thing about blood," Annie said, shaking her head, "is it drips. Even small amounts. She'll say she got blood on her clothes from handling the body, even though no one remembers her being on stage. But under the microscope, the blood on her pants is a drop, not a smear. And another thing about blood, Fergus, is it never drips up."

DEAL WITH THE DEVIL
By James Lincoln Warren

Welcome to a production of Doctor Faustus that shouldn't be magical—except as approved by the faculty of St. Cyprian's Academy of the Thaumaturgical Arts and Sciences...

The first sabotage to the Thaumaturgical Thespians' production of *Doctor Faustus* came during a blocking rehearsal.

"You're doing it all wrong!" my stepsister Kelly blared, so loud she almost blew out my eardrums. She was standing right next to me and Monsieur Justus, our club's faculty sponsor and director, just off stage right.

The target of yon broadside was Callista Fairchild. The reason for yon broadside wasn't that Callista was doing anything "all wrong"—I mean, all she was doing was walking down the center stage ramp like she was supposed to—but because Kelly was jealous.

Callista was cast in the role that Kelly thought only she deserved: Helen of Troy.

Kelly has been known to describe herself as "the hottest girl at school" (meaning St. Cyprian's Academy of the Thaumaturgical Arts and Sciences for Young Ladies and Gentlemen)—but then Callista transferred in and effortlessly pried every boy in the senior class from Kelly's talons.

Callista looked and moved like an exotic supermodel on a runway in a Paris boutique. Kelly looked and moved like an exotic dancer on a runway in a strip club. (Not that I've ever been to a strip club, but the image is inescapable.)

"Queens don't answer to serving wenches," Callista quipped, full of snide and pride. To Kelly, this was like waving a red flag in front of a cow. (I could've said *bull*, but you know.)

She'd been cast as a barmaid and was still steaming over it. True, it was the only speaking role for a female character—all one line of it—but still, a barmaid.

"*Assez! Moi, I* am directing this play," M. Justus bellowed. "Miss Kelly Mercury, *tu vas te taire*, shut up!"

M. Justus spoke to me very softly so no one would hear: "Miss Dee, of all my students, you are *la plus intelligente*. With all my heart, I wish *you* had auditioned. This unpleasantness, it could have been avoided."

"I appreciate your confidence, sir, but no, thanks," I replied, "I'd much rather remain behind the scenes."

Mistake. Kelly overheard me.

She hated that M. Justus was paying more attention to me than to her. Almost every girl in school—Kelly and I were both juniors, but I skipped a grade so she's a year older than me—considered him to be about as sexy as a fifty-year-old tortoise in a tuxedo. Kelly, though, considers all male teachers her natural prey, so for her, annihilating any competition against any other potential seductress, even skinny me, is a matter of principle. Her only principle, she being generally free of *any* principles.

"I think you should remain behind the scenes, too," she muttered, "'cause you have all the stage presence of a bad smell."

She added a moo, pursing her lips. (She'd spell it *moue* if she could spell, but my version is more in character.)

"I think you're confused," I said. "I work outside the limelight. On the other hand, every time you speak your lines you prove how much you stink."

Kelly may be *so stupid* that she thinks that a chiromancer is a masseur with a doctorate, but I have to admit that she has a royal gift for drama—being *such* a drama queen.

Yes, Kelly's the Mercury family actress, if you can call what she does acting, but I'm the family stagehand. Full disclosure: stage *manager*. To me, that's a lot more fun, because technical theatre is much more interesting than exaggerated posing and melodramatic declaiming and tragic eye-rolling.

And even *more* interesting, stagecraft at St. Cyprian's Academy of Thaumaturgical Arts and Sciences for Young Ladies and Gentlemen is different than at other schools.

Because—*ta da!*—we get to use *magic*.

Nothing risky, of course. Mostly, it's applied for benign special effects. Pyrotechnics, for example, magical or otherwise, are forbidden, because they're way too dangerous and against the fire code. Our auditorium, which doubles as the school's theatre, is a decrepit rat trap, like the entire school—so even thinking about using fire there is dumber than asking a guy wearing a hockey mask and toting a chainsaw if he'd like to go camping at the lake.

Safety is paramount.

Which is why we were all stunned when Callista screamed as the ramp collapsed.

***

As Callista writhed in pain on the stage, fussed over by M.

Justus and everybody else, I ran to the ramp to see why it had fallen apart.

Stage platforms are bolted together instead of being nailed or glued, so they can be disassembled and stored for future use. The stainless steel bolts holding it together, which were brand new, were now nothing but flaky rust, and had sheared. I *knew* that they'd been perfectly fine just before the rehearsal, because as stage manager, the first thing I do is check *everything*. No wonder the ramp had caved—there had been nothing holding it together.

Sabotage.

Worse, *sorcerous* sabotage. How else do you corrupt steel in a couple hours?

Callista's right ankle was horribly swollen, turning purple and red. Monsieur Justus wasn't big enough to lift her by himself, so Diego Rincón Guerra, the handsome senior who had the lead role, helped him. She was obviously in terrific pain, tears streaming down her crumpled visage. She stared at Kelly with sheer hatred.

"This is *your* fault!" she bawled. "I'll pay you back, I swear it, if it's the last thing I ever do!"

I looked at Kelly. There was a veneer of concern on her face, but beneath it, I could see she was gloating.

***

Real sorcery isn't like in books or in the movies. Even the simplest spell will take hours, if not weeks or even years, to set up and execute.

Callista had fractured her ankle, and there are no spells that can heal broken bones faster than modern medicine.

She was out of the show. If we even had a show.

***

Dr. van Doorn, our despotic and dyspeptic she-wolverine of a vice principal, isn't exactly a fan of the Mercury sisters. Not to put too strong a spin on it, but she regards both of us as Satan's spawn, tolerable only so long as our dad, Dr. Merlyn Mercury, Th.D., continues to cut big checks for the school.

I was the stage manager, responsible for safety on the set. Kelly was suspected because of her rivalry with Callista.

If it hadn't been for M. Justus's advocacy, whose idea it was to perform it in the first place, the play would have been canceled, even though the investigation into the magical decay of the bolts yielded nothing.

Nevertheless, Dr. van Doorn called me into her office.

"I think I need hardly remind you of last year's imbroglio," she began.

Not hardly.

The Thaumaturgical Thespians had performed Shakespeare's *The Tempest*. The big senior prank that year was to curse everybody in the cast with flatulence and magically amplify the resulting cacophony. Courtesy of the senior *boys*, of course, because girls are never that puerile. Anyway, the flatuses were so loud that they drowned out the dialogue. All the 12th grade guys found it knee-slapping hilarious.

Not me. Stage manager was a plum assignment for a sophomore, responsible for *everything* on stage except the actors—props, lights, changing sets, and so on. So for me, it was just as humiliating as for the cast.

The jaded Kelly, miscast as the naïve Miranda, blamed *me* instead of the male morons of the senior class, put out because her big chance to shine was spoiled. I told her she should be grateful that nobody could hear her muff all her lines.

***

"I understand that you have taken measures to prevent a reprise," Dr. van Doorn said.

"That's true. Yes."

I had sworn it would never happen again, and had already spent a lot of time on stage setting up counter-spells and wards to prevent it. But forestalling a fabulous fart fest and preventing powerful dark magic intended to inflict bodily harm are tasks of different magnitudes.

She droned on, telling me more or less what an arrogant little snot I was, meaning she knows I'm smarter than she is but can't admit it, and blah blah blah, and finally closed with:

"I fully expect you to do everything possible to deflect any such future incidents as the one we have recently endured."

"I will," I said. And I meant it.

***

St. Cyprian's does not teach drama as a course of study, so M. Justus was not a drama teacher. He taught Advance Placement Conjuration, my most difficult subject.

After my lovely interview with Dr. van Doorn, I was not surprised when he asked me to linger after class for a few seconds.

"Did you know that it was the theatre that inspired me to study *la magique*?"

"No, I didn't," I replied.

"*Oui, c'est vrai.* The sawdust, I have it in my veins! My mother even named me 'Euphorion' for the son of Eschyle, or as you would say, Aeschylus."

"Oh."

"But I have asked you to stay because I have an idea to solve the Helen of Troy problem," he said.

There was a problem?

"It will require the administration's consent," he said, "but it may set some minds at rest concerning risk. I ask your help."

I had no idea what he was on about. "Help with what?"

"I have always wanted to apply some special conjurations to a theatre production, ever since the years, long gone, when I worked in the Théâtre du Grand Guignol in Paris."

"I don't really—"

"Have you read Stesichorus?"

The gong (which in any normal school would be a bell) sounded. I was already late to my next class.

"Sorry!" I cried, rushing off.

***

The next day was Saturday, and I decided to spend the morning riding my bike. The neighborhood is old and quaint, and along Maple Street, there are a lot of old-growth trees, none of them maples.

One yard, in front of a red brick house, was alive with yellow flowers, dominated by a huge, verdant mimosa tree. When it blooms, the flowers look like yellow and white puffballs, very pretty. A bed of graceful yellow-topped clubmoss grew below the living room's picture window.

The tree wasn't then in bloom, though, and I watched an elderly man standing on a long ladder, wearing gardening gloves to pick bean pods off the branches and dropping them in a plastic bucket. He looked down and waved.

I stopped.

"M. Justus?"

"*Bonjour*, Miss Mercury," he said, climbing down. "I had hoped to see you. I have several times noticed you ride by, on weekends."

He put down the bucket and removed his gloves.

"You looked *un peu* uncertain when I suggested you help me," he said. "I shall explain. I want you to help convince Dr. van Doorn of my plan."

"She doesn't really like me, you know," I said. "She thinks I'm stuck up."

"Yes, because you are bright and she, *hélas*, is not. But if you can bring credit to the school, she will *change de refrain*—'change her tune,' you know."

"I don't see how."

He smiled. "*Doctor Faustus* provides opportunity to perform impressive magical special effects. There is one in particular, a conjuration, that could be what I believe is known as a 'real showstopper.' It is perfectly safe, but *très compliqué*, and as you are my best student, I think you are the one to succeed."

"Really?" I felt an embarrassing surge of pride. "What spell?"

"*Une phantasmagorie.* Will you consider it?"

"Uh…sure!"

He waved his hand and smiled, picking up the bucket.

"Then I will see you in school Monday. *Au revoir.*"

"Bye."

I remounted my bike and pedaled home.

***

After dinner, I sought Dad's advice, because M. Justus lying in wait for me was so unexpected.

"Am I right in thinking that all the magical stage effects have to be performed by students?" Dad asked.

"Yes, under supervision," I replied.

"That's why he needs the administration's approval." He got up from his desk and pulled an ancient leather-bound book from his shelf, and opened it to a page about two thirds of the way through.

"Read this. This book is *Histrio-Mastix*, 1632, by William Prynne. The entire book is a screed against the theatre."

I looked at the yellowed page and read.

> Not to relate the various tragicall ends of many, who in my remembrance at London, have been ſlaine in Play-houſes or upon quarrels there commenced ; Nor yet to recite the ſudden fearefull burning even to the ground, both of the *Globe* and *Fortune* Play-houſes, no man perceiving how theſe fires came : together with the *viſible apparition of the Devill on the ſtage at the Belſavage Play-houſe, in Queene* Elizabeths *days, (to the great amazement both of the Actors and ſpectators), whiles they were there profanely playing the Hiſtory of* Fauſtus (the truth of which I have heard from many now alive, who well remember it,) *there being ſome diſtracted by that fearefull ſight…*

At first I couldn't tell the difference between the old-fashioned long "s" and "f," so in my mind, it read like it was written by Daffy Duck: "fome diftracted by that fearefull fight"—which reminded me of, "I thuppothe your realithe that thith meanth war!"

"Uh-oh. This play can summon Satan?" My feelings of pride promptly went cold.

"Not only that," Dad said. "In the seventeenth century, to be 'distracted' didn't mean what it means now. It meant being driven insane."

"He can't want me to summon the Devil!"

"I believe he has something much less threatening in mind. Hence Stesichorus."

"Who was he? A necromancer?"

"Not at all. He was an ancient Greek poet. According to legend, he was struck blind by the gods for treating Helen of Troy with disrespect. The curse was lifted only after he claimed that the Helen at Troy was an eidolon, an imitation. The real Helen, according to his account, actually dwelt in Egypt during the war, and was faithful to her husband Menelaus the whole time, thus rehabilitating her reputation.

"I suspect M. Justus wants you to conjure that same ancient eidolon as a special effect. Because all the magic has to be done by students, that would, too. By you."

"Stesichorus was struck blind?"

"I wouldn't worry too much about that. The Greek gods were famous for punishing blasphemy by causing blindness—it's practically a trope."

"Okay, I get it. But it sounds dangerous. So I can promise that it absolutely won't happen, not if I have anything to say about it. Teacher or not, he can't make me."

I don't usually fidget, but right then I was having a little trouble sitting still. It felt like I didn't know enough.

"Dad, do you know where Christopher Marlowe got his idea for the play?"

He laughed. "As it happens, I do. It's called *The History of the Damnable Life and Deserved Death of Doctor John Faustus*, 1592, translated from a 1587 German original."

"Where can I find a copy?"

***

At a magnet school for sorcerers like St. Cyprian's, demonic apparitions are taken seriously. Somehow a rumor had started and spread throughout the school that our play was going to summon one.

Dr. van Doorn did her level best to brutally suppress any such speculation—brutal suppression being one of her purposes in life.

And then in the hallway, I heard two teachers, Mr. Rasselbock and Mrs. Widdershins, talking.

"Summoning the image of Helen of Troy is beyond foolish," he said.

"I agree," she replied. "Men who see her become obsessed—she caused ten years of brutal war just for running away from them."

Next, something else caused a brief kerfuffle. I already mentioned that there is only one speaking role for a female, but there are a few more nonspeaking roles for women. Of those, the most important is Helen.

You're probably way ahead of me here, but it struck me that getting between Kelly and a role as the Most Beautiful Woman in the World is like getting between an enraged mother manticore and her young.

After my last class, I went to find Kelly so we could go home together. Her sixth period class is Scrying, and I found her in the classroom talking with Miss Brazil, an upstanding feminist and her favorite teacher.

"Miss Brazil?" I heard her ask. "Have you ever done any acting?"

I didn't listen to the rest—I'm not a spy—but I soon found out what it was about.

Miss Brazil took up Kelly's cause and made a *cause célèbre* out of it, objecting to the paucity of female roles. M. Justus pointed out that in Marlowe's day, there weren't any female actors at all, but eventually he had to capitulate to Miss Brazil's formidable opposition. He agreed to reassign half the roles to girls—the Good and Bad Angels, for example.

But that didn't satisfy Miss Brazil—she particularly wanted to include Helen, the most prominent feminine presence in the entire play.

She got Dr. van Doorn to agree with her, and that was that. Nix one eidolon.

M. Justus, clearly disappointed, switched from sweet old man to grumpy old man.

And we only had a month to pull everything together.

***

The principal roles were unchanged. Diego was still Faustus with his trumpet-like voice. Mephistopheles was still Damian Shapiro, another senior, whose gorgeous clear baritone was a good contrast with Diego. Likewise some others.

And Kelly, flush with victory, finally landed Helen of Troy.

Set design and carpentry were done, so we plunged into lighting design, stretched muslin over frames for our flats and painted them, conducted read-throughs, learned blocking, held regular rehearsals, arranged costumes, makeup design, and props: everything that makes the theatre magic, even without magic. Last, we added the *authentic* magic.

I might be off the hook for the eidolon, but Dr. van Doorn's warning loomed. I spent hours preparing the stage with every ward and counter-spell I could think of against magical mischief, including a few new ones, aided by M. Justus. That took over two weeks, and wasn't at all easy, what with all the pressure and actors running all over the place while I was drawing chalk seals and arranging charms. Before it was all done, I was completely fried.

The dress rehearsal was lousy. Believe it or not, that's a really good sign.

My protections were all intact and working.

And finally, inexorably—it was opening night.

***

The cast all had the pre-curtain jitters as M. Justus delivered his pep talk.

I hate to admit it, but Kelly looked breathtaking. She wore a plaited *peplos*, an ancient Greek ankle-length dress, embroidered with a golden Greek key, with a gilded belt around her thin waist, and flat sandals on her dainty feet. Her hair, always dyed a pale blonde, had been given an undulating wave cascading down her back. For once, it didn't look artificial at all.

M. Justus ended his speech with, "*Allons-y!* Everybody—break the leg!"

Showtime.

***

Four acts down, and everything, *everything,* had been perfect. It was exhilarating. My wards, charms, and counter-spells had all worked. Act V, the one featuring Helen of Troy, began without a hitch.

Diego delivered the cue for Kelly's entrance: "Be silent, for danger is in words."

We'd worked really hard to make her appearance as wondrous as we could. I'd picked a special spell that gave her a translucent ethereal glow.

Kelly glided forward, graceful as a swan, from the high center stage platform down the ramp—the bolts now completely invulnerable to interfering magic—to greet her lover. I held my breath.

Suddenly the stage in front of her erupted in fire! I lifted my right arm to cover my eyes against the glare. Billowing smoke arose from nowhere, and the stink of sulfur was everywhere.

A brilliant flash blinded almost everyone, but not me. I'd

blocked it just in time.

Kelly's costume was aflame!

I grabbed the fire extinguisher, always kept handy in the wings, and ran onstage.

But then I saw—and was terrified. The very image of the Prince of Darkness, limned in the billowing white smoke, reached out to me, his goat horns scintillating, his maw open, prepared to devour the world.

I heard his awful commands.

"Look upon my works, ye mighty," a thundering voice announced, "and despair!"

I knew I didn't have time for fear. I sprayed Kelly with a fog of CO_2 as she screamed and fell to the floor. Then I froze in total panic, completely bewildered. *My brain wasn't working.*

The crowd went crazy. People in the aisles stared blindly around, scattering in all directions like sightless pigeons, falling over each other trying to escape.

And suddenly I thought: Wait a minute. *I know those words.*

Shelley. "Ozymandias."

Why would the Devil quote Percy Bysshe Shelley?

None of this was in the script. Not in *our* script. But it was obviously in somebody else's.

That pissed me off.

***

Dad and Vivian, my stepmother, clambered onstage, although they were almost knocked down by all the teenagers jumping off.

I didn't even notice them.

Kelly was hysterical, her hair singed and stinking, her lovely Greek dress charred.

My brain still wasn't working the way it should. I snarled at both of my parents like some wild animal, standing protectively over her—because *I* was the protective manticore mommy now.

But somehow I understood they were trying to help.

It was almost a quarter of an hour before my brain came back. When it did, I suddenly knew exactly what had happened, and how it had happened. And then I fainted.

***

When I came to, I lay on the couch in our principal Dr. Strabismus's office. He was leaning over me, taking my pulse, with his shock of wild white hair and the perpetual expression of surprise on his thin, lined face.

Behind him, I saw a scarlet-faced Dr. van Doorn, a grey-faced M. Justus, and a white-with-worry-faced Dr. Mercury. A green-faced Callista Fairchild was there, too, crutches and all, the cast on her leg scrawled with boys' signatures. She looked scared.

"How are you feeling, Miss Mercury?" Dr. Strabismus asked.

"I—I'm fine," I said, sitting up. "Is Kelly okay?"

"Your sister is in the infirmary with your mother," Dad said. "She has some first-degree burns, but thank God, your quick actions saved her from far worse."

Dr. van Doorn frowned.

"I warned you, but here we are," she declared. "There were injuries, and I hold *you* responsible."

"For what?" I said, filled with anger. "Do you really think I would hurt my own sister? With *fire*? She could have been killed!"

"The two of you are perpetually at each other's throats," she said. "Perhaps you took it too far."

"That's quite enough, Dr. van Doorn," Dad said. He'd never sounded that stern with me. Or even Kelly.

Dr. van Doorn then turned her basilisk stare on Callista.

"Then there's you," she said. "The one with a motive."

"It wasn't me, I swear!" Callista's voice was pleading.

"You also swore revenge," Dr. van Doorn said. "Why should I believe you now?"

"Dr. van Doorn," M. Justus said, "we deal with very advanced magic here, far beyond the skills of young girls. The wards, they were all working. I assisted Miss Mercury in placing them myself. Yet somehow, they were defeated."

I exploded. "Liar! It was only a few weeks ago you wanted me to conjure an eidolon of Helen of Troy. *That's* very advanced magic, too."

"Dee, calm down," Dad said. "There's no reason to be angry with M. Justus."

"Isn't there?" I asked. "He's lying. None of the wards seemed to work because they're designed to protect against magic, but there wasn't any."

"What do you mean?" Dr. Strabismus asked.

"When M. Justus asked me to conjure an eidolon, he called it 'une phantasmagorie,' an image—but phantasmagoria is *also* a genre of theatre," I said. "What we saw was *stage magic*—pure showmanship using deception and misdirection. The whole thing was intended to deceive the audience, the actors, and especially me. *You tried to murder my sister, M. Justus!*"

He turned red. "*Incroyable! C'est outrageant!*"

"Stage magic?" Dr. van Doorn snorted. "Right under our noses?"

"Stage magic is meant to be hidden," I said, "and this kind of stage magic isn't as complicated as you might think. Search the stage. I bet you'll find a projector hidden somewhere."

"Brunhilde," Dr. Strabismus said to Dr. van Doorn. The command was clear in his voice.

"At once, Dr. Strabismus," she replied, and out she marched.

"I will assist," M. Justus said, turning to leave.

"You will remain here, Euphorion," the principal said.

"I have the right to demonstrate my innocence," M. Justus said with great indignation.

"I believe we may put our entire confidence in the vice principal," Dr. Strabismus said. "In the meantime, please explain, Miss Mercury."

I nodded. "We were all fooled because as sorcerers we *expect* to see magic.

"The flash flames, the image of demons projected on smoke from hidden lanterns, the stench of brimstone, scary voices and sound effects—these were all used in late eighteenth century Europe in entertainments called phantasmagorias. Anybody who has studied the history of theatre will have heard of them. Some of them also employed drugs to induce fear, and I think that happened to us, too.

"I once saw Justus removing bean pods from a mimosa tree in his front yard and putting them in a bucket. Later, it occurred to me that the mimosa was probably a cojóbana tree. South American Indians used such beans to make cohoba, a hallucinogenic powder they inhaled to produce visions. If cohoba was refined to great purity and dispersed in an explosion, everybody in range would start tripping in seconds.

"He also grew a kind of clubmoss in his yard—it's called lycopodium, and is used to create sudden explosive flares for pyrotechnic effects."

"Preposterous," M. Justus said.

"You yourself told me you had once worked at the Grand Guignol Theatre in Paris, which specialized in gory special effects. You know how to stage things *without magic*. You planned the whole thing."

"But why?" Mr. Carroll asked.

"Because of who he is, and what he wanted and didn't get. Look at his name."

"What about his name?"

"*Euphorion Justus*. Do you know who else was named Euphorion? And who was named Justus?"

"Aeschylus's son was named Euphorion," Dad said. "It was also the name of Antiochus the Great's librarian in the third century BCE. Where's the connection?"

"Neither of them is the right one," I said. "According to some dude named Ptolemy Hephaestion, Euphorion was the name of a son that Helen of Troy had with Achilles—Goethe even included him in his version of the Faust legend. In mythology, he was her only male child."

"*Absurdité*. The girl is mad. Do I look three thousand years old?" M. Justus asked, sneering.

"I didn't say you were him," I replied. "You only adopted his name. But your other name, now—!'"

"Justus?" asked Dr. Strabismus. "I recall that name being mentioned by St. Paul, in Colossians. There was also a seventh century Archbishop of Canterbury so called."

"Neither of those guys," I said. "Dad, remember when I asked you about Marlowe's source for the play?"

"Yes, and I told you about the 1592 book."

"I bet you've never read it, or you'd know that it claims Faustus *also* had a son with Helen of Troy. And guess what *his* name was?"

"*Fantastique*! From having three *thousand* years, I am now down to a mere *four hundred. Quelle folle!*"

"I don't know how old you are, but you've got to be a lot older than you look. The Grand Guignol folded in 1962."

"The sixteenth century was the golden age of alchemy," said Dr. Strabismus. "It is possible."

"Why do you think he chose this play to begin with? Helen's beauty was enough to cause bloody war and murder. Can you imagine her effect on her own son? He wanted her back. First step, eliminate Callista—"

"*You* did this to me?" she cried. "What if I'd died?"

"—and then he could proceed. I don't think he wanted an eidolon at all, even though he said he did. Helen's son would never be satisfied with a mere image. He wanted the real thing. Faustus was a necromancer, a sorcerer who raised the spirits of the dead— and so are you, M. Justus.

"You couldn't risk doing it without exposing yourself, so you attempted to get me to do it. We don't study necromancy at St. Cyprian's. You thought I wouldn't be able to tell the difference.

"How bitter you must have felt when your plan fell through. That's when you decided on exacting revenge instead."

Dr. van Doorn returned, carrying a black wooden box. It stank of sulfur.

"It was hidden beneath the platforms on stage," she said. "It contains a spent smoke bomb, a fan, and a magic lantern with a very realistic portrait of Lucifer painted on its concave mirror.

There was also a WiFi loudspeaker."

Justus raised his eyebrows. Then he smiled and shrugged.

"I did not try to murder your idiot sister, *chérie*, nor you, vain Fairchild, although I would not care if either of you had died. Did the idiot Kelly think I did not know who defeated my purpose? I simply punished her for daring to compare herself to my beloved mother."

"Dee," Dad said, "why don't you step out for a minute?"

***

I visited Kelly and Viv in the infirmary. Kelly looked awful. But right then, stupid as she is, she was the most beautiful thing I'd ever seen.

"Mom says you saved my life," she said.

"Yeah, that was hard," I said. "You know that I'd much rather remain behind the scenes."

METHOD FOR MURDER
By Carol L. Wright

*There's such a thing as taking Method Acting just a
little bit too far.*

"You know, I really never could stand the woman," she said,
fumbling to pull a cigarette out of the pack I'd brought her and
lighting up. "It's been that way since college. Me versus Ivy
Mason, as she was known then. She only became 'Kara Alexander'
after graduation." She waved her arm in grandiose fashion. Then
she shook her head. "She and I were always up for the same parts
in the school's theater productions, and she nearly always got the
lead." She took a drag and exhaled smoke, creating a cloud
between us.

I coughed, but she didn't seem to notice. I was just there to tell
the client what to expect during arraignment—a quick in-and-out—
but she clearly wanted to make her moments out of the cell last as
long as possible.

"I'm sure she was sleeping with the director, even back then,"
she said, locking her eyes on mine. I looked away first, as she
continued. "But she always pretended this…" She shook her head,
waving her cigarette in a circle, searching for the right word. "This
doe-eyed innocence and mock surprise when the casting lists were
posted." She flung her hand, spraying ashes into the air.
"Ridiculous. No one bought it. We all knew the fix was in. That *I*
was the more talented of the two." A bit of an accent had crept into
her speech and I wondered if she was channeling a character she'd
once played.

"Well, nonetheless—" I began, but she cut me off.

"I was always prettier, too. Okay—not beautiful, but better
looking than she was even then. I should have had the starring
roles." She shivered. "I mean, with that horse-face of hers. No
wonder she did all her work on Broadway."

I must have looked confused because she clarified.

"No close ups."

I couldn't stop my eye-roll in time, but fortunately she wasn't
looking at me. I leaned back in the hard chair. It was nice to get
away from the stress of the office for a change, even if the change
of scenery was a consultation room at the local jail. I thought I

might as well let her talk.

She gazed off into the distance and continued her monologue. "I always should have been the star, but I ended up playing her mother or her best friend. That was no way to showcase my talent."

I shifted my position and pretended to take notes. Who knew? Maybe some of this would be interesting to my boss.

As an associate at my law firm, I would normally never have a chance to talk to a high-profile client, but my supervising partner, "Iron Lady," had even bigger fish to fry that day, and Glinda, her other senior associate, was tied up in court. So here I was, across the table from a delusional, washed-up, second-banana actress.

"So anyway," I began, "Judge James is on arraignments tomorrow, and…" I could see she wasn't listening. When your client is a "creative," you can't always be sure you're getting through to them, but I was supposed to try.

"It's not my fault, you know," she said as if I hadn't spoken. "I just finally had enough." It sounded like she was quoting from a play. "Enough of getting the scraps from her table. Enough of playing second fiddle. I knew this play was my ticket. Two leading female roles. Finally, it would be clear to everyone that she and I were at least equals, right?"

She expected me to fuel her delusion, but that wasn't my job. "I'm afraid I don't know much about the play."

"Then how can you possibly defend me?" She squinted at me, appraising me. I could tell I didn't come out well.

I didn't dodge her stare this time, nor did I think I needed to go into the office politics that put me in this seat today instead of the high-priced counsel she expected. Actors are so self-centered. They think the whole world pays attention only to them. Who had time for Broadway shows when trying to make partner, anyway?

Still, helping to get a famous actress off a murder charge should help my chances for advancement—but Glinda and I were both up this year, and the firm had said they'd only elevate one of us. I closed my eyes. I knew I was the better lawyer, but Glinda was better at office politics. Still, I had more billable hours, and a law firm runs on its billables. Maybe spending a little more time listening to a well-heeled client couldn't hurt.

"Why don't you tell me about the play. I'd like to learn about it from your point of view," I said in my practiced "I'm in control here, not you" voice.

"Well then," she began, leaning forward. "The director contacted my agent about it. Said they really wanted me to star in this new play, *Jackie and Jill*, by that wonderful young playwright, Sarah Townsend. You know her?"

I looked up from my legal pad and shook my head. I got another disdainful look that said, "plebeian."

"Well, she's wonderful. Writes women particularly well. Great, meaty roles that get to the heart of a woman's passions. Obviously, I was very interested."

"Of course," I said, trying to be encouraging, but I got another look from her that told me I had best not interrupt again. "Go on," I urged.

She flicked cigarette ash across the gray, metal table that separated us and looked out the barred window.

"Anyway, they had me read both parts, Jackie and Jill. They were fairly equal in importance, so I didn't much care which one I played." She looked at me through narrowed eyes. "I really didn't care."

By then, I knew better than to respond, so I simply nodded.

"Then they brought us both in to see us together." She paused, apparently to let me know that this was when the trouble started. "As I said, I didn't care which part I played, but *Ivy* had set her heart on the Jill role." An arched eyebrow said this was all part of an evil plot.

"But if you didn't care…"

"Well, I didn't want *her* to get first choice and leave me with her leftovers again, so I said I preferred to play Jackie." She stubbed out her cigarette and folded her hands, staring at them. "Top billing," she said, *sotto voce*. "That means I'm the star."

"So, you read both parts together?" I asked, trying to draw her back to her narrative.

"Yes. It went perfectly well no matter which part either of us played. You see, Jackie and Jill are supposed to be best friends, but they secretly hate each other. It's a very complex play."

"I see," I said, hoping I hadn't said too much.

"Yes, so our natural antagonism toward each other really worked in those scenes. I could say things to her that I had wanted to say for years, but of course could not. I wouldn't want to appear petty. It wouldn't look good, and I wouldn't do anything to damage my career."

I took in the stale room, the bars, the gray furniture, the locked door with a reinforced window, and wondered how much good *this* would do for her career.

"Anyway," she continued, "I got the part of Jackie, and she got Jill. We pretended to be happy to be working together, but I knew it bothered her as much as it did me." She pulled out another cigarette but didn't light it. "But before all the world, it would finally be clear that I was the better actress."

She opened her arms as if embracing the globe—or perhaps "her public." Wasn't that what actors called it?

"Together we made great box office. Tickets were snapped up as soon as they were made available." She tapped the end of the unlit cigarette on the tabletop. "In fact, if you want to know the truth, Jackie really was the better part. It demanded that I plumb the depths of human angst in a way that the Jill part just didn't allow."

"Good for you then," I said. She looked at me quizzically, so I added, "That they trusted you with the tougher role."

"Yes, you're right," she said. "It was a tougher role. All through rehearsal, the director kept giving me lots of notes. Of course, the great Ivy hardly got anything but praise. But her role was easier. Anyone could have played Jill."

"So, what turned things nasty?"

She lit the cigarette and took a drag. Smoke puffed out as she spoke. "Well, clearly the actor playing Jackie should have gotten top billing, but when the marquee went up, *her* name was first."

"Well, her name comes first alphabetically—"

"That's not the point!"

I tried to keep my look steady and again pretended to take notes.

"So, in the play, Jackie stabs Jill, you know?"

I couldn't help arching my brow, but I looked down so she might not notice.

"It actually helped to unleash some of those feelings that one tries to suppress. And I was magnificent." She took another drag and let out a long stream of smoke. "You see, I'm a method actor."

I looked up, afraid to ask for an explanation of what that meant. She must have understood my expression as confusion.

"Stanislavski? Strasberg? Meisner? Adler? Haven't you ever heard of The Method?"

I shrugged. I'd heard the term, but if pressed, I couldn't define it.

"It's about experiencing your character's life by re-experiencing things from your past, immersing yourself in your emotional memory. Some of the best actors use it: Olivier, Brando, De Niro, Pacino, Day-Lewis, Jack Freakin' Nicholson?"

I nodded to indicate I got it. I *sort of* did. I had heard about actors starving themselves, breaking their bones, or pulling their own teeth without anesthesia so they could appreciate what their characters were going through. Some, I'd heard, stayed in character the whole time they were filming, refusing to talk to their coworkers except as their character while involved in a project.

"Those are mostly movie actors," I ventured. I couldn't

imagine an actor staying in character for months on end in a successful Broadway show.

"Good acting is good acting, whether on stage or screen," she said. A self-satisfied smile curled her lips.

"You mean your character plotted to kill Jill, so you started to plot to kill the actress who played her?"

She looked at me as if I were insane. "Of course not. That would be crazy. Without her, the show might close, and I would be out of a job." She shook her head as if she doubted my intelligence. "I won't do *anything* to hurt my career, remember?"

"Sorry," I said. "Go on."

"Well, the set was being built in the theater, so we had to rehearse in a different space. All perfectly normal." She stubbed out her cigarette, then reached for another. "Rehearsals went well. The playwright tweaked the story, gave us new lines, cut others. The director played with the blocking. We were getting some really good stuff to work with. It was, you know, therapeutic I think, to finally get out some of those long-held emotions. I could tell her what I thought of her without anyone knowing it was the real me talking to the real her. I was having a pretty good time of it, actually."

"So, what changed?"

She shifted in her chair, turning away from me to look toward the window. I waited.

"It came time for tech rehearsals—you know—when the set is ready, and we move into the theater to work on all the sound and lighting cues. Tech is a long, laborious process. You say a line and wait while the crew figures out how to light you and checks your mic balance."

"Sounds like a drag," I said, more to have something to say than because I cared. I didn't. This little break from the office was getting old. I wished for a more comfortable chair, better smelling air, a fresh cup of coffee, and gentle music in the background. Here, the chairs were straight and hard, the air reeked of smoke and sweat, and the background music was muted voices, shuffling feet, and the occasional clanging of cell doors.

"These are the longest rehearsal days. Tiring—no, exhausting. The only bright side is that we get to go to our dressing rooms when there's a break."

I put my pen down. I was ready to leave.

"But what should happen when we went for our first break?" she asked rhetorically.

Okay—she had my interest. "What?"

"I found out that Ivy's dresser had moved her into the largest dressing room."

I knew the client well enough by now to realize this must be a big deal. "What do you mean her 'dresser'?" I asked. Wasn't that a piece of furniture?

She gave me another impatient look. "In a play, we need to make quick costume changes, and our dressers help us do it. I always get one assigned to me for each play—not that they're ever any good. I've had to fire so many of them, I can't even..." She drifted off for a moment, as if lost in the memory of dressers she had fired.

"But Ivy is such a diva," she continued. "She insists on having the same dresser for every show she's in. They've been together for years and, they say, the two were as close as sisters. I never much liked my sister, so I was never sure whether that was a good thing or bad." She snickered, then continued. "But in this case, her dresser just wedged her into *my* dressing room, and had it all set up just the way she likes it before Ivy ever set eyes on it. Soft chairs, a thick carpet, a Tiffany lamp, roses on the makeup counter, a box of imported chocolates, a mini-fridge, and a coffee bar. It was..." She spat out the last word. "Elegant."

"What did your dresser say about that?"

"*My* dresser was the usual incompetent staffer provided by the theater. She hadn't done a thing to protect my rightful territory. Not a single thing. She'd let Ivy's dresser steal the bigger room without so much as an argument. Here I was, the star, and my room was at least a foot narrower than Ivy's. Unacceptable."

"Had she at least gotten it set up nicely?"

She stood and loomed over me. "Of course not. The idiot." She threw down the cigarette and started pacing. "She hadn't put anything more in my room than a single, rolling clothes rack. That was it. One metal chair, a wall mirror surrounded by bare bulbs, and an empty clothes rack."

She was shrieking, and I noticed a guard peer in through the meshed window in the door. I nodded to indicate I was okay, and he disappeared again despite the continuing rant.

"Not even a pitcher of ice water was there when I went in during the break. It was intolerable, and I told her so. 'I didn't know how you'd like it,' she said in a whiny voice. 'Well not like this,' I told her. But at least this one was smart enough to quit that day before I had a chance to fire her. I told her she would never work in this town again."

I was beginning to wonder about an insanity defense when she took her seat and continued.

"But I am a pro," she said in a manufactured calm. "I don't let such things get in the way of an excellent performance. Previews were only a few days away. Reviewers would start coming so they could write their reviews and release them on our official opening night. And, after all, the show must go on despite such hardships."

"So, you'd had a couple of weeks of shows before the incident, right?"

"Yes, and I knew I was wonderful in the part. 'Magic! Yes, yes, magic! I try to give that to people.'"

The way she said it, I was pretty sure *that* was a quote from a play—or maybe a film. With my job, I didn't get to watch any movies either.

"It's from *Streetcar*," she said with a dismissive wave.

"So that's when you decided to kill Miss Alexan…er, Ivy?"

"No. You haven't been listening. If I killed her, the show could close, and what good would that do? I would be out of work, and…" She waggled an eyebrow. "I wouldn't do *anything* to hurt my career."

"But, you…"

"I didn't want her *dead*. I just wanted her to *look* bad. More to the point, I wanted her *reviews* to be bad. That way, everyone would have to acknowledge that without *me*, the show would fold. *I* am the *star*."

"Okay, but you substituted a real knife for the prop knife in the scene where your character tries to kill hers."

"Ah yes, but I didn't use it in the scene, did I?"

"But, you…"

"I threw it off stage where I knew her dresser always stood. I have great aim. I once played a knife thrower, you know. Got her right in the heart." Her smirk was a mix of evil and bloodlust. "I knew without her precious dresser, Ivy would be too distraught to go on. Either her understudy would have to take her place, or she'd go on and give a bad performance. Either way, the reviewers would crucify her." She laughed deep in her throat. "A perfect crime." She laughed again.

"But it wasn't perfect," I said. "You didn't get away with it. You're going to be arraigned for murder tomorrow."

"So what?" she said with a flip of her hand. "It was an accident as anyone could plainly see. You will make sure they know that, won't you?"

I winced. At least I wouldn't be the one standing up in court trying to make that argument. Iron Lady would—if it ever got to court.

"And, best of all, Ivy will never be the same. Jackie killed Jill after all." The smirk returned—more smug than evil this time.

I'd had enough and stood to go. After getting the guard's attention, I gave her one last bit of advice. "Remember not to talk to anyone. Not the guards, not your cellmate, no one. No matter how proud you are of what you've done, just act like a nun. You ever play a nun?"

"Oh sure," she said. "Mother Superior in *Sound of Music*. Wise, strict, compassionate. I can do that."

"Great, but this nun has taken a vow of silence."

She flashed an "okay" sign, and silently left with the guard, her cuffed hands pressed together as if in prayer. I hoped she was as good an actor as she thought she was.

As I left the jail and descended the concrete stairs, I had to shake my head. I couldn't believe how deeply into her delusion she had sunk. The lady was batshit crazy, that was certain, but not in a legal sense. She was lucky New York no longer had the death penalty.

On one level, though, I could understand her desire to promote her career. Don't we all want to do that? But all she had accomplished was to make her play notorious and to give her understudy her big break—to co-star with Kara Alexander. As Iron Lady says, they're not in jail because they're smart. Nope. Not smart at all.

Now if she were *really* smart, I thought, as I took the subway back to the office, she would have gotten rid of the competition. She could have arranged an "accident." Like maybe a piece of scenery falling at the right time. Or maybe an assisted stumble in front of a bus. After all, accidents happen every day.

I turned it over in my head as I reached the crosswalk near our Midtown office building. Looking up at our windows, I couldn't help but worry about the partners' promotion vote next week.

With a glance at my phone, I realized that Glinda should be by any minute. Maybe I could wait in the corner Starbucks and help her across the street. Her balance is bound to be compromised by the five-inch heels she wears to court.

Like I said, you have to be smart if you want to promote your career.

**AUTHOR
BIOGRAPHIES**

AUTHORS

FRANCES AYLOR won the IngramSpark Rising Star Award for her first novel, financial thriller *Money Grab*. She holds the Chartered Financial Analyst (CFA) designation, is a past president of CFA Society of Virginia, and gives presentations on money management. President of Sisters in Crime–Central Virginia and a member of International Thriller Writers, she has participated in several panel discussions on writing. An avid traveler, she has paraglided in Switzerland, gone white-water rafting in Costa Rica, and fished for piranha in the Amazon. Her short stories appear in *Deadly Southern Charm* and other anthologies. She lives in Virginia and is currently at work on her second novel.
Visit her website at www.francesaylor.com.

ANNE LOUISE BANNON is an author and journalist who wrote her first novel at age 15. Her journalistic work has appeared in newspapers across the country. She was a TV critic for over 15 years, founded the YourFamilyViewer blog, and created the OddBallGrape.com wine education blog with her husband, Michael Holland. She is the co-author of *Howdunit: Book of Poisons*, with Serita Stevens, as well as author of the Freddie and Kathy mystery series, set in the 1920s, the Operation Quickline Series, and the Old Los Angeles series, set in the 1870s. Her most recent title is *Death of the City Marshal*. She and her husband live in Southern California with an assortment of critters.
Visit her website at AnneLouiseBannon.com.

MICHELE BAZAN REED's Jazz Age private detective, Harry Jerome, debuted in "The Lady in Black," in Flame Tree Publishing's *Detective Mysteries* anthology (2019). Harry's adventure of "The Canine Caper" will appear in *The Fish That Got Away,* Sisters in Crime's Guppy chapter anthology (2021). Michele's recent stories also appeared in the *Wrong Turn* and *Mid-Century Murder* anthologies, and *Woman's World* magazine. A member of Sisters in Crime and SinC's Guppy Chapter, she is the 2017 Daphne award winner in the Unpublished Mainstream Mystery/Suspense category. Michele and her husband split their time between Harry Jerome's Central New York stomping grounds and a tiny wine-making village in France.

CINDY BROWN has been a theater geek (actor, director, playwright, etc.) since her first professional gig at age 14. Now a full-time writer, she's the author of the Agatha-nominated Ivy Meadows series, madcap mysteries set in the off, off, OFF Broadway world of theater. Cindy lives in Portland, Oregon, though she made her home in Phoenix, Arizona, for more than 25 years and knows all the good places to hide dead bodies in both cities. She'd love to connect with readers at cindybrownwriter.com where they can sign up for her Slightly Silly Newsletter or on Facebook or Twitter.

M. E. BROWNING served twenty-two years in law enforcement and retired as a captain before turning to a life of crime fiction. Writing as Micki Browning, she penned the Agatha-nominated and award-winning Mer Cavallo mysteries, and her short stories and nonfiction have appeared in anthologies, mystery and diving magazines, and textbooks. As M. E. Browning, she recently began a new series of Jo Wyatt mysteries with *Shadow Ridge* (October 2020). Micki is a member of Sisters in Crime, International Thriller Writers, and Mystery Writers of America. She proudly served as a former president of the Guppy Chapter of SinC. A professional divemaster, she resides in Florida with her partner in crime and a vast array of scuba equipment she uses for "research."

KAREN CANTWELL writes short stories and novels. Her mystery short stories have appeared in e-zines, anthologies, and *Woman's World Magazine*. In the world of novels, Karen loves to make people laugh with her *USA Today* best-selling Barbara Marr Murder Mystery series. You can learn more about Karen and her works at www.KarenCantwell.com.

Ever since she could read, **R. M. CHASTLETON** has been intrigued by stories of mystery and suspense but didn't start seriously writing until recently. She is elated that her debut short story "The Ghost of Hamnet" was chosen for Malice Domestic's *Mystery Most Theatrical* Anthology and is completing a follow-up novel involving amateur detective Ham Laurence. Although she has led a nomadic life, currently she is raising her family in the New York City area. When not writing in the wee hours of the morning, she can be found skulking around the city seeking inspiration, at the bookstore buying yet another mystery novel, or blogging on her website, *www.mysteriousnook.com*. She is a member of the Mystery Writers of America, Sisters in Crime, and SCBWI.

LEONE CIPORIN's short stories have been published in *Flash Bang Mysteries, Woman's World,* and several anthologies, with more stories slated to appear in *Mystery Weekly* and *Black Cat Mystery Magazine*. She's a member of Sisters in Crime and Mystery Writers of America. When she's not writing mysteries, Leone works as a manager in an insurance company's law department, which is more interesting than it sounds. Leone lives in Charlottesville, Virginia.
Read more about her stories at leoneciporin.com.

CARLA COUPE's short stories have appeared in several of the *Chesapeake Crimes* series, as well as Malice Domestic's *Mystery Most Geographical* and *Mystery Most Historical*. Two of her short stories were nominated for Agatha Awards. She has also written many Sherlock Holmes pastiches, which have appeared in *Sherlock Holmes Mystery Magazine, Sherlock's Home: The Empty House, The MX Book of New Sherlock Holmes Stories, Part VI, Irene's Cabinet*, and *The Newspapers*. Her story "The Book of Tobit" was included in *The Best American Mystery Stories of 2012*.

SUSAN DALY finds joy in writing short crime fiction, since it lets her crusade for social justice and punish the guilty. Her stories have appeared in a surprising number of anthologies, most recently *Heartbreaks & Half-truths*. "A Death at the Parsonage" won the 2017 Arthur Ellis Award for best short story from the Crime Writers of Canada. She lives in Toronto, a short social distance from her excellent grandkids, and can be found at her website: www.susandaly.com.

PHILLIP DEPOY is the Edgar® Award-winning author of 20 novels and 43 plays. An internationally reviewed performance artist, he was writer in residence for the Georgia Council for the Arts in the 1980s. In the 1990s he was the Artistic Director of a professional, Equity theatre. Since then he has served as director of several university theatre programs. He was Georgia Author of the Year in 2015. Publications include the Shamus finalist Flap Tucker mysteries (Dell), Fever Devilin novels and Christopher Marlowe mysteries (St. Martins), and the Foggy Moscowitz series from Severn House of London. Nonfiction publications include *The Tao and The Bard* and *Messages from Beyond*. Phillip DePoy also holds degrees in English literature and folklore, and performance art.

MARGARET DUMAS writes books about smart, funny women who are searching for adventure, love, and the occasional murderer in the San Francisco Bay area. Her Movie Palace Mysteries are set in a classic movie theater that she really wishes was real. The series brings together Margaret's love of traditional mysteries with her lifelong passion for classic movies. The first three books in the series, *Murder at the Palace*, *Murder in the Balcony*, and *Murder on the Silver Screen*, are available now. When not writing, Margaret spends most of her time reading mysteries and watching old movies. See what she's up to at www.margaretdumas.com.

ELIZABETH ELWOOD spent many years performing with Vancouver Lower Mainland music and theatre groups and singing in the Vancouver Opera chorus. Having turned her talents to writing and design, she created 20 marionette musicals for Elwoodettes Marionettes and has written four plays that have entertained audiences in both Canada and the United States. She is the author of six books in the Beary Mystery Series and her short stories have been featured in *Ellery Queen's Mystery Magazine*. Visit her website at www.elihuentertainment.com.

Agatha Award-winning author **DARYL WOOD GERBER** writes the nationally best-selling Cookbook Nook Mysteries, the Fairy Garden Mysteries, and the French Bistro Mysteries. As Avery Aames, she pens the popular Cheese Shop Mysteries. In addition, Daryl writes the Aspen Adams novels of suspense as well as stand-alone suspense. Daryl loves to cook, fairy garden, and read, and she has a frisky Goldendoodle who keeps her in line!

B. J. GRAF lives in Los Angeles with her family and a menagerie of four-footers. "Deus ex Machina" is her fourth published short story, following in the wake of "Sandman, Blood Shadows" and "Shikata Ga Nai." Her near-future-mystery-novel, *Genesys X*, also featuring Detectives Piedmont & Miyaguchi, will be published November 2020 by Fairwood Press. In her alternate identity, Dr. Graf is an Adjunct Professor who teaches Film Studies and Classical Mythology at Pepperdine, UCLA, and CSUN. Previously, she worked as V.P. of Development for Abilene Pictures where they produced several features and television projects including *Primal Fear*, *Frequency*, *Fallen*, *Fracture,* and *NYPD 2069*.

ELLEN HART is the author of thirty-five crime novels in two series. She is a six-time winner of the Lambda Literary Award for Best Lesbian Mystery and a four-time winner of the Minnesota Book Award for Best Popular Fiction. In 2010, Ellen received the GCLS Trailblazer Award for lifetime achievement in the field of lesbian literature. In 2017, she became the first openly LGBT author to be named a Grand Master by Mystery Writers of America, an award that represents the pinnacle of achievement in mystery writing, one that was established to acknowledge important contributions to the genre as well as for a body of work that is both significant and of consistent high quality. She lives in Minnesota with her partner of forty years.

A. P. JAMISON is a former investment banker who received her MFA from Columbia University in 2013. Her short story "Death of the Hollywood Sign Girl" appeared in the Sisters in Crime/LA's 2019 Anthology, *Fatally Haunted*. In December of 2018, she won the Sisters in Crime–LA/Mystery Writers of America 12-word short, short story contest. She is currently completing her first two novels (a Wall Street thriller and the debut "Gus" murder mystery, respectively). "The Nine Deaths in Hamlet?" is dedicated to the magic memory of her darling Texan dad and her neighbor's dog who were the inspiration for this short story. She can be reached at APJamison1025@gmail.com.

MAUREEN JENNINGS was born in UK but is now a Canadian citizen living in Toronto. She is the author of the *Murdoch Mysteries*, now a popular TV show which is going into its fourteenth season. She has also written a series set in WW2 featuring DCI Tom Tyler. These were the inspiration for another TV series called *Bomb Girls*. Her latest series is set in 1936 Toronto and features a PI named Charlotte Frayne. She is married to photographer Iden Ford, and they have a docile labradoodle name Murdoch.

MARGARET LUCKE flings words around as a writer and editor in the San Francisco Bay Area. She writes tales of love, ghosts, and murder, sometimes all three in one book. Two of her novels *(Snow Angel* and *A Relative Stranger,* an Anthony Award finalist) feature artist/private eye Jess Randolph, and two others (*House of Whispers* and *House of Desire)* star Claire Scanlan, a real estate agent who specializes in haunted houses. Margaret edited Sister in Crime NorCal's anthology, *Fault Lines,* and has published more than 60 short stories and feature articles. A teacher of fiction writing classes, she has authored several how-to books on writing. She takes great pleasure in sharing her love of writing with others. Visit her at www.margaretlucke.com.

JAQUELYN LYMAN-THOMAS is a college professor, specializing in creative writing and early British literature. In addition to her degrees in English, she has most of a bachelor's degree in music composition and over thirty hours of art and architecture courses. While her ADHD drives myriad creative interests, her main passion has always been writing fiction. She is currently working on a mystery novel set near Chestertown on Maryland's eastern shore.

SHARON LYNN's mystery short story "Carne Diem" (2019) is published in the Anthony Award-nominated *Malice Domestic 14: Mystery Most Edible*. Her story "Death on Tap" (2017) is published in Sisters in Crime's Desert Sleuths anthology *SoWest: Killer Nights*. Sharon also has recipes and writing tips included in *Recipes to Kill For* (2019). The scandalous crimes and vibrant cultures of the Southwest are her inspirations. Her husband, daughter, and a Maine coon cat keep her on track.

CHERYL MARCEAU's short story "The Mask" is her second to be included in a Malice Domestic anthology. Previous stories have been published in a number of anthologies including *Malice Domestic 13: Mystery Most Geographical*, five of the Level Best Books collections including *Thin Ice*, and in the Guppy anthology, *Fish or Cut Bait*. Her short story *Stress Kills* will appear in the upcoming Guppy anthology, *The Fish That Got Away*. Cheryl loves traveling to mysterious or ancient places, some of them with dark stories of their own. She and her husband live in the Boston area.

DEBORAH MAXEY, PhD, winner of numerous writing awards, has several short stories soon to be released in devotions and anthologies. Her first novel, *The Endling*, is scheduled to be published by Firefly Southern Fiction, Iron Stream Media. Along with a love for storytelling, Deborah is worship leader at her church, devoted wife, mother, grandmother, fine artist, and a licensed professional therapist in Lynchburg, Virginia.

ADAM MEYER is the author of the upcoming novel *Missing Rachel*, the young adult novel *The Last Domino*, and more than two dozen short stories. His short fiction has been nominated for the Shamus Award and has recently appeared in *Crime Travel*, *Chesapeake Crimes: Invitation to Murder*, *The Beat of Black Wings,* and *Seascape: Best New England Crime Stories 2019*. He's also written many TV movies and true-crime series for Lifetime, Discovery, National Geographic, and other networks. After several years as a television writer in Los Angeles, he now lives with his family in northern Virginia. You can learn more at his website, adammeyerwriter.com.

SHAWN REILLY SIMMONS is the author of The Red Carpet Catering Mysteries and of over a dozen short stories appearing in various anthologies including Malice Domestic, Best New England Crime Stories, Bouchercon, the Crime Writers' Association, and the Writers' Police Academy. Shawn's short story "The Last Word" won the Agatha in 2019, and she was nominated for an Anthony Award as co-editor of the anthology in which it appeared, *Malice Domestic 14: Mystery Most Edible*. Shawn serves on the Board of Malice Domestic, is an editor at Level Best Books, and is a member of Sisters in Crime, Mystery Writers of America, the International Thriller Writers, and the Crime Writers' Association. She lives in historic Frederick, Maryland, with her husband and ten-year-old son.

RAQUEL V. REYES writes stories with sabor y sazón featuring Latina main characters. Her Cuban-American heritage, Miami, and the Caribbean feature prominently in her work. Raquel is a co-chair for SleuthFest and a board member of the Florida Chapter of Mystery Writers of America. She is a member of both Sisters in Crime and Crime Writers of Color. Her blog Cozy in Miami features Interviews and reviews. Find her on Twitter @writerRVR and on Instagram @LatinaSleuths.

A servant to two cats, **MERRILEE ROBSON** uses the time when the cats are sleeping to write mysteries. Fortunately, cats sleep a lot. Her first novel, *Murder is Uncooperative*, is a traditional mystery set in a Vancouver housing co-op. Recent short stories have been published in *Ellery Queen's Mystery Magazine, Mystery Weekly, The People's Friend, Over My Dead Body, Mysteryrat's Maze* podcast, and other magazines and anthologies. She lives in Vancouver, with her husband and the cats, in a house that is 110 years old and was first owned by a policeman.
Website: merrileerobson.ca.

LEE SAUER read his first mystery at age eight, and began attending Malice Domestic in 2008. He's been hooked on both ever since. In his "real" life, Lee has been a software developer for almost 50 years. As a child actor, he was an adorable Winnie the Pooh in Sacramento where he still lives. Alas, he is no longer adorable. At age 70, this is his first published work of fiction, but he's hard at work on a cozy mystery series.

LYNN SLAUGHTER is addicted to the arts, chocolate, and her husband's cooking. Following a long career as a professional dancer and dance educator, she earned her MFA in Writing Popular Fiction from Seton Hill University. She's the author of three young adult novels: *It Should Have Been You,* a Silver Falchion finalist; *While I Danced,* an EPIC finalist; and *Leisha's Song* (forthcoming from Fire and Ice/Melange Books, 2021). The mother of two grown sons, she lives in Louisville, Kentucky, where she is at work on her next young adult novel, *Deadly Setup.*

C. M. SURRISI is the author of the Agatha-nominated middle grade mystery series The Quinnie Boyd Mysteries: *The Maypop Kidnapping, Vampires On the Run*, and *A Side of Sabotage*; and adult short stories: "The Bequest" in Sisters in Crime's anthology *Crimes of the Heartland* and "Know Nothing" in Guppy Anthology *The Fish That Got Away.* Not only does she write for middle grade and adult readers, she's the author of *The Best Mother*, a Junior Library Guild Gold Standard picture book selection. She is a member of the Author's Guild, Mystery Writers of America, The National League of American Pen Women, and is the current president of the Minnesota chapter of Sisters in Crime.

ELAINE TOGNERI's short fiction has appeared in several anthologies, including *Blood on Their Hands, The Rich and the Dead*, and *Noir at the Salad Bar.* She has sold both romance and mysteries to *Woman's World.* Elaine holds an MA in English from Rutgers University. She is founder and a past president of the Sisters in Crime–Central New Jersey chapter. Look for her story "Genius" in MWA's 2021 anthology, *A Stranger Comes to Town.*

ARTHUR VIDRO has sold stories to *Ellery Queen's Mystery Magazine* and *Mystery Weekly Magazine*; he has sold nonfiction to *Mystery Scene* magazine. He has served three times as an Edgars® judge. He earns his living editing and proofreading, and by writing a weekly column for his hometown newspaper. He writes an editing column for the quarterly journal *Calliope on the Web.* He publishes *Old-Time Detection*, a journal that explores mystery fiction of the past. Theater has been one of his long-time hobbies. He acted in a professional production of *The Bad Seed*. In high school, he appeared in a production of the show being staged in "Ask Fred the Usher."

MAUREEN "MO" WALSH's first published crime story, "Roadside Roulette," won the 1995 Mary Higgins Clark Short Mystery/Suspense Contest. Her stories have appeared in the new *Super Puzzletastic Mysteries* middle-grade anthology from MWA, *Mary Higgins Clark Mystery Magazine*, *Woman's World*, the *Fish Out of Water* Guppy anthology, five issues of *Best New England Crime Stories*, and other publications. Mo is a Derringer Award finalist, coauthor of the "killer trivia" book *A Miscellany of Murder*, and a five-time NaNoWriMo "winner." A member of Sisters in Crime and Mystery Writers of America, Mo is chapter president of MWA-New England. She is a recovering advertising copywriter and journalist who lives near Boston with her husband and two of their three sons.
Visit her website at www.mowalshwriter.com.

JAMES LINCOLN WARREN is a frequent contributor to *Alfred Hitchcock's Mystery Magazine* and *Ellery Queen's Mystery Magazine*, and the winner of the Wolfe Pack's 2011 Black Orchid Novella Ward for a story written in the tradition of Rex Stout. His fiction runs the gamut from historical to contemporary, and from humor to hard-boiled. He is a past President of Mystery Writers of America's Southern California Chapter. He received his B.A. in the Humanities from the University of Texas San Antonio and resides in Los Angeles.

CAROL L. WRIGHT escaped a career in law and academia for one in writing. She loves creating her Gracie McIntyre Mysteries where, unlike in life, justice always prevails. The first in the series, *Death in Glenville Falls,* was a finalist for the 2018 Killer Nashville Silver Falchion Award and the Next Generation Indie Book Award. She writes short stories in many genres that have been published in award-winning journals and anthologies. Some of her favorites appear in her recent collection, *A Christmas on Nantucket and Other Stories.* She is a founder of the award-winning Bethlehem Writers Group, LLC. She is married to her college sweetheart and they live in eastern Pennsylvania with their rescue dog and clowder of cats.
Learn more on her website: CarolLWright.com.